KATHL

HARDWIRED

MOTH

First published in 2016 by Moth, an imprint of Mayfly Press, a partnership between New Writing North and Business Education Publishers Limited, Chase House, Rainton Bridge, Tyne and Wear, DH4 5RA

Cover design by Courage, UK

A CIP catalogue record for this book is available from the British Library

Paperback ISBN 978 1911356011
Ebook ISBN 978 1911356042

Printed and bound by Martins the Printers Ltd, UK

www.mayfly.press

For Conchita Hernandez-Sierra Varnes,
1956-2016

HARD WIRED

1

Orchard House probation and bail hostel, Newcastle upon Tyne

CHARLIE GLANCED AT the wall clock. 10.30pm. Time for room checks. She closed the file she was reading and forced herself up from the desk, feeling slightly sick, as always after these sessions. You read one murderer or abuser's file, you'd read them all. Deprived childhood, mother in prison, father an alcoholic, little education and undiagnosed dyslexia. Your heart bleeds. She locked her desk and turned to Martin, on the other side of the office. Six months into the job and Charlie had lost sympathy with most residents. She could tolerate arsonists like Eddie. Martin, on the other hand, three years at Orchard House, had no time for anyone.

Her mouth tasted of sleep, and too many cups of strong tea. 'Are you ready?'

Martin grunted. He'd been playing some stupid fantasy game, Charlie knew. He was an elf in an online fantasy, and spent all his spare time dialling up the internet. When she asked him once what was the attraction he said, 'It's immersive. Takes me away from here. Everybody'll be doing it soon.'

She couldn't see it herself. She took in Martin's stomach, hanging out like a shelf over his belt. He was fat; there was no other way to say it. You could perch a cup of tea on his stomach. It seemed to have its own topography of ripples and dents, like a mountain range. You could get lost in his stomach. Every day it grew bigger.

He shuffled along behind her. Martin never wanted to do room checks. Said he didn't care whether the bastards died or not.

'If they want to string themselves up, then let them,' was his philosophy.

Charlie didn't want any of them to die on her. She needed this job. With overtime, she could just about break even, every penny accounted for.

There was the usual stale smell of too many male bodies stacked in close, the occasional whiff of deodorant. And something worse: hopelessness. Charlie breathed in, but not too deep. There was not enough air in the place.

He was a lazy sod, Martin. Rounds had to be done; they needed to tick forms for the records. Every now and again, someone from Orchard Services would drop in and check the paperwork. Besides, occasionally they saved people. That young lad who tried to hang himself: Charlie was the one who cut him down. Good job she'd been on the First Aid refresher. His parents came to thank her afterwards. She couldn't look them in the eye: she'd read his file. Just one of a stream of ex-soldiers passing through, after ending up in prison. Yet somebody's son, and all that.

The ex-soldiers weren't all like him, thank God. Most had just fallen through the cracks, and were neat and tidy: polishing shoes; laying out clothes; setting alarms; arranging their breakfast cereal just so, as they'd been taught, as if order could keep chaos at bay. But you could feel the tension off them, volcanoes ready to pop.

She and Martin took it in turns to knock at each door and lift up the spyhole cover. Most men were lying on their beds, sitting up reading, or listening to music.

One guy, Donny, had his head down on the table, law books spread out in front of him. Donny was studying for a law degree, and was always quoting case precedents. 'Did you know?' he would begin his sentences.

'I want to turn my life around,' he'd told her once. 'Make something of myself.'

'Lights out soon,' she told him.

Donny gave a thumbs up. She knew he'd read under the bedclothes with a torch, like she did as a kid. And come down to breakfast white-faced and trembly.

AFTER THE ROOM check, they wrote up reports, sitting in the kitchen. Or at least Charlie did. Warmer in there, although the fluorescent lights made everything look harsh and one-dimensional. After a while, Martin disappeared back to the office, probably elfing. She read up notes, the words growing fuzzy. Sometimes Charlie thought they should just file according to offences: A for Arson, or Abuse, B for Burglary. And buggery, and battery and lots more, C for Criminal Damage, and Child Molesting, K for Kidnap, R for Rape. She closed the files: too depressing. Sometimes she didn't want to know.

Back in the office, she handed Martin a pile of reports for signature. Now he was feeding paper into the shredder.

'What are you doing?'

'Thought I'd get rid of stuff. It's always the same old crap.'

'We're supposed to read them.'

'No one will notice. It's all getting computerised eventually anyway.'

He was right. But Charlie didn't like him being right. As often, there was an atmosphere between them. She stood by his desk, tired of his skiving.

'What?' he growled at last, putting the papers down. 'OK, I'll make the coffee.'

So he did. Real coffee that brought a taste of richness to the dump. He put more effort into making coffee than he did his job. It was the one luxury they allowed themselves. Both shifts had chipped in for a proper coffee maker, and Martin bought the beans from an Italian place he knew, and ground them fresh. It always took him a while, but the wait was worth it.

He brought Charlie a steaming cup. She inhaled the aroma, and then sipped, and smiled at him. At least he was good at something. She savoured the taste, making it last, pacing herself. Too much coffee and she'd be rattling as bad as the men waiting for their pills.

At 1am, with her stomach churning away, Charlie ate three onion bhajis. It was the shift changes that got you in the stomach. Just as you settled into one pattern, management would demand back-to-back shifts, and your insides never got a chance to adjust. Mostly she tried to work nights. OK when your body grew used to it.

At 3am, the police returned Dave, who had broken his curfew. Out on the town; he'd got drunk, and was arrested and sent to a special night court. Now he was back, looking the worse for wear, unlikely to make it to his café job in the morning. He had already been late several times. Charlie's shift finished at seven, and she knew the day staff wouldn't bother waking him. If he lost the job, the cycle would start again.

They let him into his room, and within minutes, he was snoring. Dave was on his way down again. On a yellow warning; if he broke curfew again he'd be back in prison. His girlfriend would leave him for good this time, he'd had so many second chances. They'd often spoken about Dave. His girlfriend couldn't understand his self-destructive streak. Everything Dave touched he messed up eventually. But care, prison, then this hostel: Dave didn't know anything else.

At 4am, just before the next room check, they saw on camera that Carl was sitting on the bed in Nick's room. It was curfew until six.

Charlie stood with Martin at the door to Nick's room.

'You're not allowed in each other's rooms at this time. You know that.'

Carl and Nick, hard-faced and smoking, stared Charlie out.

'Come on then, lads,' said Martin, jingling his keys and doing the jolly mates routine. Neither of them moved. 'No messing about, now.'

The men turned to each other, weighing up their chances: Charlie at five feet nothing, soft muscled, carrying a few extra pounds, Martin with his belly and the red face of a drinker. Carl and Nick were 20 years younger, and wiry-looking.

Charlie kept her finger on the bell for Security. And then with a shrug and a sly look on his face, Carl slid from the edge of the bed, came close enough for her to smell his tobacco breath, and sauntered back to his room. The encounter had lasted two minutes. Charlie sniffed and rubbed her eyes. Another crisis over. Don't let the bastards see any hint of tears.

On their return, they passed Michael's door, and he started up, complaining loudly that his heating wasn't working properly.

'Tough,' Charlie wanted to say. 'You can freeze for all I care.' But 'I'll see what we can do,' she promised, as they both entered, and Martin fiddled round with the controls.

'Prick,' was Martin's verdict, back in the kitchen. He held his head in his hands. 'I'm knackered.'

Soon he was asleep, head on the table. Both staff were supposed to stay awake. If there were three staff members on, you could take it in turns to sleep. There were never three staff members on.

On camera, Charlie watched Graham tossing and turning. Graham always slept badly, poor man. You couldn't force people to sleep. You could get them in their rooms, you could control the TV, but you couldn't make them sleep.

Graham was someone she did have sympathy for. One of the saddest cases. Never in trouble before, Graham came home

11

one day, found his wife in bed with a neighbour, and stabbed the man with a kitchen knife. Pierced an artery and the man died. Five minutes and everything changed. He'd done his jail time, and he now had to live with the consequences for the rest of his life: not allowed to visit the family home, could only see his children under supervision. Counselling, probation, weekly meetings.

His wife had stood next to Charlie in the supermarket once. Dead eyes and a premature stoop.

Five minutes.

Now he'd started a window cleaning business, and an old woman let him leave his ladders at her house, so he did her windows for free. He was reliable and hard-working, but you couldn't change what had happened. He'd taken a life. How did you go on? Charlie watched him wriggle and turn, mouth open. If Graham didn't live in the hostel, she'd get him to do her windows.

Five minutes, that's all it took for your life to change. Charlie shivered.

Twenty minutes later Michael's buzzer went again. Martin was snoring, slumped towards the one spider plant that was still alive, just, with its browning ashy leaves.

She waited outside Michael's room.

'Why are you awake?'

'I woke up cold. Can't sleep. Too cold. My heating's still not working.'

'I'll contact maintenance tomorrow.'

'I'm freezing now.'

Charlie slowed her breath. The summer heat had disappeared, bringing a sudden cold snap. She told herself that Michael hadn't reoffended, he'd been on good behaviour, and he had the right to heat. She wasn't convinced.

'I've got democratic rights. I'm fucking freezing here.'

'No need to swear. It's nearly time to get up anyway. You've only got a couple of hours. What about a hot water bottle?'

'Or you could warm me up yourself.'

'I'll get you the spare heater.'

'And I'm running out of toilet roll,' he shouted over.

Charlie ignored him. He could wait. One of the recent management cuts included cheaper toilet paper. It fell apart, so you used twice as much. False economy.

She checked the cameras as she made her way to the store cupboard in the office. Most men asleep: Dave talking to himself, Donny showing a faint torch light under the bedclothes as he pored over his books. Eddie lay with his eyes open, staring at the ceiling, holding his hand to his mouth as he coughed. His asthma was giving him trouble again. Charlie had a soft spot for Eddie. He loved music, knew a lot about it, and collected vinyl. Yes, he set fires. But he only damaged things, not people. Everyone in his work liked him.

Whereas Michael, the bastard, had put families through hell, following young girls, charming them and then terrorising them. Most were too scared to press charges, and there'd been no evidence that he'd ever touched them. With him, it was all mind games. But Charlie had read the reports. 'Sociopathic tendencies', said one, and 'a worrying escalation in his behaviour' said another. She didn't trust him. Nobody really had any idea what he was capable of.

And Michael had a grievance, which was always threatening to erupt. Although he'd been done for several instances of threatening behaviour, he ended up inside because of a conviction for GBH, and possession of cocaine. He claimed the fight was a fit-up and the cocaine was planted. Even Charlie thought that might be true. He was the 'My body is a temple' type, always going on about eating good food. He was also a keen gardener. Somebody might have decided to get him out of the way, as he was unlikely to get done for the young girls. Charlie never felt easy with him.

The office was cold now, with Martin's chocolate wrappers strewn on the floor. Martin was a slob, still asleep in the kitchen. He would be impossible to wake up. They weren't supposed to approach the men alone, but what choice did she have? When she heard the scurry of mice in a far corner, Charlie left quickly with the heater.

She kept her finger on her alarm as she knocked at the door of Michael's room. She had read somewhere that if a boa constrictor wound itself around your neck, you should make your breathing shallow, to confuse it. She made her breathing shallow. Michael was a snake; he squeezed the breath out of you.

'You're sweating.' He smirked.

'Heater.'

Charlie pushed it towards him and quickly shut the door. The animal smell of him lingered as she walked away.

It was 5am before she had a chance to look at the magazine she'd bundled into her bag. Some do-gooders dropped off a new pile every week. This one was *True Crime*. She laughed, but the picture of a man on the front with an axe in his hand did nothing for her peace of mind. And the headline made her turn away: 'I killed my wife, and then my three-year-old.'

Charlie stashed the magazine, and made tea. Ate three chocolate chip cookies. Martin was still snoring.

She was skimming through a leaflet about language courses, when on camera she saw a white-coated figure heading straight for the hostel. Fast. He had a hood over his head, and you couldn't see his face. Rain was lashing down.

She put her hand over her mouth to stop herself screaming, and pressed the emergency buzzer that connected them to the police. A few weeks before the local rag had published a grainy photo of the hostel headlined: 'Do we want this centre in our area?' They didn't give the address, but it wasn't hard to work out. A menacing group had congregated outside until the police moved them on. For a few weeks they'd been nervous, and paid more attention to security, but then they got lax again. She prodded Martin. Dead to the world. Useless. She needed to lock the kitchen door, keep them safe. The police would take ages, they always did. And they would send the older, knackered officers who wouldn't be able to chase after anyone. She might be murdered before they arrived.

Then Charlie heard the clink of milk bottles as their milkman took off his hood, grinned at the camera and delivered 12 pints of semi-skimmed, three full fats, one blue top, and two cartons of orange juice. Bastard.

She collected the crate from the front door, and stacked milk in the fridge.

There was quiet for a time. Then doors opened and with it came the sound of running water as early risers went to bathrooms, played radios, made breakfast.

Orchard House was domestic and ordinary in daylight, with cleaners wiping surfaces and mopping out bathrooms, and a phone-in on the radio, with someone rabbiting on about low tax economies. She caught the tail end of a local programme debating whether Alan Shearer was worth all the money paid for him. 'Why-aye, man,' one local was shouting. 'That penalty against Blackburn on Saturday was pure belta.'

A fresh-faced probation officer buzzed in for a pre-work appointment with Graham.

Michael was one of the first up, his hair wet, and his clothes smelling freshly dried.

'I used the utility room.'

'Why?'

Michael knew the rules. Residents were only supposed to use the machines on Wednesdays and Saturdays, and they had to ask permission first. The door must have been left open.

'Needed to wash my clothes, didn't I?' He was daring her to challenge him.

'And dry 'em.'

'Naturally.'

Charlie let it go. She didn't care. For all she knew he could have wet his pants, or shat himself after all that roughage he insisted on eating. If he wanted to wash and dry his clothes, let him.

He looked almost disappointed that she hadn't risen to the bait, but started preparing his breakfast, arranging cutlery and crockery with precision. Charlie sneaked a glance. Michael could have been a good-looking man, but she had the strangest feeling that her hand would go through him if she touched him. He was missing something. A soul. The man had no interest in anyone except himself.

He filled a bowl with unsugared organic muesli, poured on blue top milk, and arranged a plate of top of the range whole-wheat bread with seeds and nuts, a yellow pat of butter, and organic honey. His breakfast each day. He was different to many of the other men, who were rattling with e numbers and had stubby, misshapen brown teeth. His teeth were white and small, pointy, rat-like. Twice a week he had eggs. She knew this because he'd told her, and she'd watched him prepare them.

'It's not good to eat too many eggs. Need to keep an eye on my cholesterol.'

Charlie had already disagreed with him over this: 'I bet at some point in the future they'll find out that eggs are good for you.' She loved eggs – silken, scrambled, omelettes, boiled or fried. He'd looked at her with pity. It wasn't an egg day today.

On Sundays, he ate organic sausages, tomatoes and mushrooms, baked beans, his only concession to junk food, and perfectly poached eggs, arranging them on his plate like an art installation. He was as neat as an army person in his appearance, and contained in the way he moved, giving an impression of wiry strength. He did Thai boxing, and often came back drenched in sweat, carrying a smelly sports bag full of equally drenched gym clothes. Twice a week he went to the local Buddhist Centre. He said he did yoga and Tai Chi and practised meditation. She didn't know if it was true. Really she had no idea what he did. Could someone who practised meditation have treated those girls like he did? But it had all been approved.

Exact and precise in his movements, Michael cut his bread into halves and ate. Afterwards, he cleared up his mess and dried his crockery. He made real coffee with decent beans he had ground himself earlier in the week, and offered Charlie a cup. She loved the smell, but she'd rather poke her eye out than accept anything from him.

'No thanks.' It came out primly.

'Coffee make you nervous?'

He was close enough for her to smell a slight tinge of fresh sweat on him, overlain by pine deodorant. The kitchen was too warm, now that a few of the other men had made toast and fried bacon. His deodorant smelt too close to toilet cleaner.

'Sure I can't tempt you?' The smug smile round his mouth widened. She recoiled and turned away. Eventually he left the kitchen, off to his restaurant job. Afterwards, it was as if the air had come back into the room.

And then sun flooded the kitchen, turning the surfaces golden. Eddie walked in to a haze of burnt orange light, clutching Pop-Tarts.

'Morning, Eddie.'

'Morning.'

'How's your asthma?'

'Better now, thanks.'

He grinned, his teeth brown and stained and crowded into a too small mouth. Charlie classed Eddie as an Ordinary Decent Criminal, or an 'ODC', compared to Michael. Eddie ate cornflakes with semi-skimmed milk, his concession to health, a Pop Tart, and white sliced toast with butter and Marmite.

And a big mug of tea. Most others had cereals or a fry-up.

Eddie went for a top-up, and as he idled by the kettle, absent-mindedly fiddled with a box of matches left near the cooker. She held out her hand, and he passed them over. Soon he too was off, to his job in a Chinese supermarket, stacking and moving boxes. All the other staff were ex-cons, and everyone there loved Eddie. 'No trouble,' the owner had said. 'Very nice man.'

AFTER THE NEW shift drifted in, Charlie signed out and walked along Shields Road, past the closed charity shops and furniture shops, past the butchers with its models of pigs and its plastic parsley, past the old cinema, and the baths on their last legs. Before she reached her door, she saw the police car parked outside Di's. A parked police car brought a little blip to her heart, and she was back to the day ten years ago, the police coming to tell her of Sean's accident. When she went to see him there wasn't a mark round the front of his body. They didn't turn him over.

'Probably Darren,' she told herself. 'In trouble again. It'll all blow over.' Darren was Di's son. Charlie and Di had been good friends once. Maybe she'd call round, make sure Di was OK. It wouldn't be anything serious, it never was. Charlie hadn't seen Di for ages. But as she rummaged in her bag for keys, she remembered that Casey had asked her to catch a programme that night.

'Changing Rooms, Mum, it's funny. These people swap houses and decorate each other's.' It wasn't what she'd choose, but it was good to be mindless and it was rare nowadays that Casey wanted to spend time with her. Charlie put the key in the door, and glanced back down the road.

2

TUESDAY 17 SEPTEMBER

7.45AM, AND CASEY needed to leave for school by 8.30. The house was silent except for the cat mewing pathetically at the back door. Charlie let it in. It looked at her reproachfully, and bit her ankle. Little bastard, it always got grumpy when it was hungry. After a few episodes of it bringing in mice, and once a rat, large and furry, and a terrible time with a squealing baby bird between its teeth and the hallway covered in feathers, she'd taken to locking the cat out at night. She spooned out jellied meat, and poured brewed tea from the old misshapen teapot that Casey hated. The cat ate, and curled up on a kitchen chair.

She knocked at Casey's door, bringing a cup of tea.

'Come on, girl.'

Casey's face was flushed, and the bedclothes scrunched up in her usual messy fashion, a pillow on the floor. Mouth open, she sounded phlegmy, with the beginning of a cold.

'What?' One eye opened. 'I'm tired.' She seemed sleepier than usual.

'Aren't we all? I'll make you toast.'

Twenty minutes later Casey was washed and dressed, face plastered in foundation, with panda eyes, eating toast and slurping down tea.

'Got your PE kit?'

Casey nodded.

'And your trainers?'

'I'm 15.'

And then there was a knock on the door and three doe-eyed girls with long shiny hair. 'Areet there, Casey's mam?' said the tallest, Emma. It was a standing joke between them.

Charlie waved goodbye.

'Mum,' Casey squealed, embarrassed, flapping her hands for Charlie to go back inside. 'Eeh, did ya see me sister?' one of the girls said to Casey, and then they giggled and shrieked their way down the road. Charlie knew that Casey's voice would change, so that by the end of the road she'd be as Geordie as the other girls. She often moaned that being brought up by a mother from Liverpool meant she had to be bilingual.

The police car was still by Di's house. She hoped Darren hadn't done anything serious. He'd been picked up lots of times by the police for minor things: riding without lights, stealing a packet of crisps, smashing a street lamp. That's how it went with lads; eventually most of them grew bored with getting into trouble. But there'd also been a few more serious things, and then a rash of burglaries. He was caught for one burglary, and cautioned, and now people looked at him suspiciously. That was a while ago. As far as she knew, he hadn't been in trouble for months. Come to think of it, she hadn't seen him for weeks. She huddled into her dressing gown. Maybe Di had sent him to his dad in Gateshead. Nice man, John, but a waste of space. *Not my business,* she told herself. She and Di didn't have much to say to each other anymore. Sure, they'd been close once, and Di had been great when Sean died. Even though it was ten years, Charlie could remember like yesterday those nights when Di would turn up at the door with a tuna casserole, and sit with her. Charlie didn't even like tuna casserole, but she was grateful for the company. After the funeral, the majority of people disappeared, as if the funeral marked the end of things, rather than the beginning. But Di kept coming, and held Charlie when she cried, without telling her to 'move on', or 'think positive', or all that garbage that people spoke about around death. Sometimes they sat in silence, or watched comedy programmes. You didn't forget a friend who did that for you.

But Di had changed over the years, and Charlie didn't like the way she shouted at Darren and James in the street. Embarrassing, no shame. And that deadbeat Suzy who was always at her house: dyed blonde hair and a full glass of vodka, on a permanent diet. You couldn't hold a conversation with Suzy. She'd had her stomach stapled, and Charlie suspected they'd stapled her brain at the same time.

Charlie closed the door, her insides churning away. If Darren was in trouble, Di would make excuses for him. She always did, even though his petty thieving got up people's noses, as he stole off people who didn't have much. Charlie had gradually tried to edge Casey out of his orbit. But for Di, the sun shone out of his arse. Maybe it was guilt because John, his dad, had never been around much, sodding off back to Gateshead years before. Charlie pulled her dressing gown cord tighter. Still, James was a nice lad, close to Casey, and treated her like a younger sister. James had it harder than Darren in some ways. His dad worked on the oil rigs off Aberdeen, the only contact an occasional birthday cheque.

As Charlie scrubbed pans and wiped surfaces, and sorted clothes for washing, feeling that deep tiredness that threatened to make you fall over, she was hit by a pang of regret. She missed her friendship with Di. They used to have such a laugh. Other friends had moved away, and it was no use looking to work for friendship – Martin was weird, and the people on the other shifts were all men, and married, and only interested in talking about football. Her football days were over. A sudden image surfaced of being on the Kop with an equally football-mad mate from her Saturday job at the burger bar, cheering and screaming for Liverpool. She could feel bodies packed around her, smell that faint smell of piss, the tang of fried onions and hot dogs. They had such passion then. Now everything seemed grey and ordinary.

She showered, letting the trickle of hot water flow over her, and lay down in bed. It was still hard getting to sleep in the day. Once she was off she slept deeply enough, unless the newly retired guy next door decided to do DIY. But his wife, a witty woman from Cumbria, had banned him from home improvements, saying he was 'bloody useless at it anyway, all his shelves fell down.'

Charlie wriggled and pulled the duvet over her, and automatically turned on her right side. She always slept this side of the bed. Sean had slept on the left, on his back. She still missed him, the feel of him, the give of him: the bed too big, too empty without him. Usually she piled up books and clothes on his side, filling up the space, but today she left his side empty. His laughing blue eyes still seemed to dance with life from the photograph on a corner shelf. How would he think she was doing? She got by. The house wasn't a dump; Casey was all right. But Charlie knew she was dead really. Tears started, as they always did when she was tired. And then the doorbell rang. She wiped her face.

The policewoman was young and fresh-faced, swamped by her bulky hi-vis uniform and the truncheon and radio hanging from her jacket.

Her accent was local.

'Sorry, pet, really sorry to have disturbed you, are you just up, like?'

Charlie smoothed her hair.

'Just in bed actually.'

The woman raised her eyebrows.

'Night shift,' Charlie supplied.

'Oh. Sorry.'

When she smiled, she had large even straight white teeth.

Two years at the orthodontist, Charlie figured.

'Do you mind if I have a word, pet?'

She nodded. What was going on?

'Do you need to come in?' She held the door open. The place was as neat as it ever would be.

'No, it's OK, pet. I only need to ask you something.'

'OK.'

Charlie's mind raced on. What had Darren done now? She hoped he hadn't burgled the neighbours. Eejit. He'd end up inside if he wasn't careful. She should take him to work and show him what the prison system turned out. That might shock him. If they were going to ask her anything about him, she couldn't lie.

Or maybe it wasn't Darren. The neighbourhood went up and down. At times there were spates of burglaries. A few months ago an elderly neighbour had the police in her living room all night, doing a stakeout, *Hill Street Blues*-style, to try and catch a local drug dealer who was preying on elderly women. The neighbour had lived off the excitement for weeks, accosting anyone she met in the post office, hooking them with the word 'stakeout.' Or maybe that old bat two doors along had complained. She moaned if there was a sound a decibel above a whisper, even though she was probably deaf.

'The only time I play music loud is when I'm cleaning,' Charlie was about to defend herself. *'Helps get me through it. Doesn't happen that often.'*

'What's it about?'

'It's just your friend up the road, she's not too good like, and I'd really like somebody to go up and sit with her. You'd not mind going up? It would be a real help. So she's not on her own, like.'

The policewoman pointed towards Di's house.

'Friend?'

'Yes, Dinah. She said you were close.'

'We were. I mean we are. What's happened?'

'Well, it may turn out to be nothing. These things often do. You know lads; you know what they're like. They forget to phone home, tell their mam what they're doing.'

'What do you mean?'

The policewoman looked surprised. You could see she was thinking: *What kind of a friend are you? Do you not know what's going on with your mate?*

But how could she? They didn't really talk anymore. Besides, she'd been working all the hours God gave her; most of the time she was like a zombie and not fit for anything except watching TV.

'Her son Darren has been missing for over 24 hours.'

'What do you mean, missing?'

'He's not come home, like.'

The policewoman was speaking to her very slowly, as if she was simple.

'Have you tried his dad's?'

The policewoman's tone was even and calm: 'We've tried his father. He's not been seen or heard of for over 24 hours. He was supposed to be home yesterday morning, after saying he was going out with a friend.'

'Which friend?'

'He didn't say, and no one knows. We've checked all his contacts, of course. Do you have any idea where he could be, pet?'

'Me? No.'

'Di said he and your daughter know each other, like.'

'Well, yes, but she can't know anything, or she would have said. Has he done this before?'

'Not come back for this long? His mam said he tried to run away once when he was ten. But he came back for his tea.'

They both smiled. And then Charlie shivered.

'I'll get my coat.'

The policewoman's eyes glided over Charlie's leopard spot pyjama bottoms. Charlie stood up straight. So what? People went to the shops in their pyjamas.

'And put on some trousers,' she added wearily, running upstairs to change.

3

TUESDAY 17 SEPTEMBER

JAMES OPENED THE door, his face white, his long skinny body drooping. Last time she'd seen him he was a 17-year-old becoming a man. Now he gave the impression of being a little boy. Behind him, angry hip-hop blasted out.

Automatically, Charlie hugged him. He fell into her hug. She stroked his head and he offered no resistance. Then he broke away and threw his hands out in a helpless gesture. His eyes were tear-stained. She kept her voice calm, and spoke slowly, as if talking to someone who didn't understand the language.

'Darling, do you think you could go and put the kettle on for us all? Can you do that?'

'Areet, Auntie Charlie.'

'Great. Now you make us all a cup of tea, strong. And see if you can find some biscuits.'

He looked as if this might be beyond him, but nodded.

'Where's your mum?'

He pointed over to the living room.

'And shouldn't you be at college?'

He shrugged, helpless. He was doing A levels at the local FE College: Art and Design: Photography; Biology and Sociology.

'Mam said it'd be OK. In the circumstances,' he added, wrapping his tongue round the phrase.

'All right. Never mind for now, but you were doing so well, remember, we should phone your college. We'll sort it out later. You get on with that tea, darling.'

In the back room, Di sat slumped in front of the TV. On the screen was a quiz show where everybody had to buzz in with three missing letters in a word.

She looked up briefly, and her mouth hung open. Her eyes were dead, but she shouted 'R' as a letter was filled in. Then it was 'S', and Charlie watched as the letters on the screen pixelated, exposing the word 'Sacrifice'.

'I didn't know you liked game shows.'

'I don't.'

Di switched off the TV, and rummaged in her pocket.

On the wall behind her was a large photograph of a tree in full leaf. A mountain ash. Charlie knew this because James had pointed out such a tree once and told her he'd taken a photograph.

'Is that one of James's?'

'That?' Di swivelled round, and with no interest, inclined her head. 'I think so… Make us both a cuppa, love,' she shouted through to James.

Sometimes Di sounded East Yorkshire, where she originated from, sometimes Newcastle. She'd lived in the North East for years, but now the Yorkshire was coming through stronger.

'He already is.'

'Good.'

Di lit up a Benson and Hedges and blew out smoke.

'Aye, and before you say anything, I'm back on the tabs.'

They sat in silence until James brought the tea in, and then they busied themselves with sipping, and dunking stale digestive biscuits. Thoughts whizzed through Charlie's head. Darren would turn up. Wouldn't he? Crumbs caught in her throat and it closed up as she spluttered and coughed.

'You don't have to be so dramatic. I'll put it out.'

The ashtray said 'Welcome to Scarborough'. The clock on the mantelpiece ticked on. A few cars passed in the street; two women walking by were talking animatedly about someone called Kate, 'who was a bit of a cow, like.' The sound of their voices faded as they drew further away.

Charlie broke the silence.

'Can someone tell me what's going on? The policewoman said Darren hadn't come home. They're not really worried, are they?'

James stuttered 'W... w... w... we've not seen him since the night before last, Auntie Charlie. He di... di... He's not come back, like.'

Charlie couldn't look at James; it was heart-breaking to hear him now. He'd worked so hard as a kid to curb his stutter, and still did breathing exercises. The stutter only resurfaced when he was nervous.

Di slumped further back in her chair, and opening the window as a concession to Charlie, lit another cigarette.

'He didn't come home?'

'He said that,' rasped Di.

'Won't he be at a mate's somewhere?'

The words sounded hollow in her ears. Di didn't grace her with a reply.

'The police have checked, Auntie Charlie,' said James earnestly.

'You know what kids are like.' Charlie addressed Di.

'We've tried his mates an all.' James' face was pale and strained. 'They've not seen him. We're scared, Auntie Charlie, scared that something's happened to our Darren.'

'His dad's?'

The policewoman had already told her they'd checked.

'That waste of space,' Di spat out. 'He can't even be a proper criminal.'

James shook his head. Charlie could guess what he was thinking. At least Darren's dad wasn't hundreds of miles away.

'I'm sure he'll turn up soon,' Charlie said, faux cheerful,

like an upbeat American TV presenter, a cold feeling in her stomach. She kept talking.

'Maybe he had a drink with his mates, and he's sleeping it off. He'll wake up late tonight and slink home, tail between his legs. You know what he can be like.'

She trailed off as Di's eyes flashed.

'What can he be like? How do you know? You haven't seen us for ages.'

True. Charlie laboured on.

'Forgetful, like all teenagers.'

Inconsiderate, selfish, she wanted to say.

Di looked at her with scorn.

'What, forget where he lived?'

'The police said that he might have lost track of time, forgot how long he'd been gone. Mebbies he'd had a drink...' James's voice rose, hopeful, as he glanced over at his mother.

'Yeah, exactly.' Charlie averted her eyes. 'And when he comes back we'll have a word with him, tell him what he's put you all through.'

The false words hung in the air, as Di smoked and James fidgeted. Charlie jumped up. She had to do something. If Casey was missing, she'd be out scouring the streets. This cowed Di scared her; it was as if she'd given up.

'Has he taken anything with him, from his room?'

'Ye cannat tell,' said James. 'The police went through it, and asked us things. Maybe a sweatshirt and a jacket? And his scarf. He always wore his scarf.'

'Can I have a look?'

It came out of nowhere. They both gave her a curious glance, but Di shrugged her shoulders, so Charlie took that as a yes.

His room was as you'd expect. A mussed-up bed, clothes on the floor, dirty plates, an empty pizza box, and a not very well hidden can of lager. Charlie opened his wardrobe and sniffed the T-shirts and tracksuits piled on the floor. There was a musty, feral smell. From a pile of art postcards scattered on the floor, curious, she picked one up. Who was Darren sending postcards to? But there was nothing written on the back. She placed them back down, set her jaw, and shut the bedroom door. In the kitchen she embarked on a mad blitz of clearing up: emptying bins, washing dishes, putting them away. Then she made them an omelette and salad for lunch.

James shovelled it in.

'Thanks, Auntie Charlie.'

Charlie's legs buckled, and her hands shook. She needed sleep.

'How about you going back into college this afternoon, James? We forgot to phone, but you could explain, it'll be OK. Take your mind off things. I'm sure the police are doing everything they can, and they'll let us know if…'

She stopped. If what? 'If there's any news.'

He stayed put, reluctant to move.

'Didn't Casey say you've got a photography project?'

His eyes lit up.

'Yeah, Auntie Charlie. They gave us a theme: "Impressions". That tree's one of mine.'

'It's great. Listen, James, you go in. We'll be OK. And we'll phone up and get you if we need to.'

His eyes were moist. He looked over at his mother.

'I'll make sure your mum's OK. I won't leave her.'

Di blinked her eyes in assent.

With quick movements, James gathered up a few papers and an art folder, and left.

Charlie scraped the leftovers into the bin. Di had only picked at her lunch, and soon she was back on the sofa, a throw wrapped tightly round her, losing herself in its fabric. She systematically made her way through a big box of chocolates.

It was quiet with James gone, and the house felt in limbo, waiting. When Charlie woke from a nap she hadn't intended to take, she was in the armchair, covered by a blanket. For a minute she didn't know where she was, and then gradually took in her surroundings, adjusting herself. Di was in the same position as before, snoring; an empty can of lager at her feet. She looked wrinkled, old and tired, flecks of grey showing in her hair. Outside it was already growing dark, one of those autumn days that were more like winter, short and damp. Charlie sat up. The house was too quiet. Normally with Darren around, there would be music blasting out, or he'd be darting around, practising his dance moves. Darren was a nifty street dancer. Where the bloody hell was he? She could kill him.

'Christ, what time is it?' she asked aloud. 'I'm on shift tonight, and Casey will be home from school.'

She prodded Di: 'Can I use your phone?'

Di stirred, and waved her hand.

When Casey answered, the music from *Neighbours* floated down the phone.

'Mum, where are you? There was no one here when I got home. You know I don't like coming in by myself. And there was no food. I'm starving.'

'There is food. Look in the fridge. There are oven chips, and fish fingers and ice cream.'

'I'm not ten. I want something proper. I want spaghetti.'

'You'll have to make do.'

There was silence the other end of the line. Casey hated that phrase. 'Making do' was what they did whenever Charlie didn't have work. The last time was a couple of years ago. 'Making do' meant eating soup, and lentils and the cheapest bread, or worse, from Casey's point of view, Charlie making homemade bread. Casey hated making do.

'Where are you anyway? What's so important that you can't even come home to your daughter? And you'll be at work all

31

night.'

Charlie was swiftly calculating. Just time to nip home and have something to eat and a shower. Two bloody hours sleep in an armchair. It wasn't enough. She had to face the men tonight. If they detected any weakness, they'd go for you. You had to have chutzpah, be bigger than them.

'I'm at Di's.'

'What are you doing there? You can come home, it's only up the road, and you could make something proper before you go to work. I'm starving, Mum, I'm starving.'

'Darren's gone missing.'

'What do you mean, missing?'

'What I said, missing. Nobody's seen him for two nights.'

'He'll turn up, you know him. Why do you need to be there? Just come home. He's probably at a mate's. Or up to something.'

'Don't say that.'

Charlie checked to see if Di was listening, but she had the TV on again, watching a local news programme.

'You'd say it. You've changed your tune. And you're not even really friends with Di. Me and James were talking about how you used to see each other all the time. You never go over there now. So just come home.'

'I can't. Di needs me.'

'I need you. And you're never here.'

'I work,' Charlie said. 'I have to.'

'You're always at work. How come we never have any money? Why can't I go on skiing holidays like my mates?'

Because they have fathers, Charlie wanted to say. She bit her tongue. 'Di's in a state. I'm sorry, love, I'm sorry. I'll be coming back for a shower. We could have a cup of tea together.'

'Don't bother,' Casey said, and put the phone down. 'It doesn't matter.'

CHARLIE WAS GATHERING up her things, about to write a note that she'd nip over in the morning after her shift, when Di opened one eye.

'Pass me my tabs.'

She opened a new can of extra strength lager and grimaced as the first gulp went down.

'I've got to go home now, see Casey. Get a shower, go to work. But I'll come back tomorrow morning after I finish.'

'Right.'

'Will you be all right?'

'I've got James; he's upstairs working on his project. And his granda Frank is coming over. I have to stay here. In case Darren phones.'

'Right. OK then, I'm off. Try and sleep. We've got to stay positive.'

The words sounded hollow and melodramatic. She was almost out the door when Di called her back.

'But I'm scared, Charlie. What if something has happened to our Darren?'

'Don't think like that. Kids don't just disappear. He'll be back.'

'Charlie?'

'Yes, Di.'

She wouldn't even have time for that cup of tea with Casey, poor kid. She'd have to make sure she had breakfast with her tomorrow before nipping back to Di's.

'Do you remember when he was born?'

And then they had their arms wrapped round each other, recalling that autumn night in the hospital, and Darren screaming until the morning. She could still hear the faint sound of his cries.

It was dark when she left. She ran in the house, changed her clothes, and ordered a cab to work, skipping the shower.

'I'll phone you,' she shouted to Casey. 'Remember to bolt

33

and lock the door.'

'Yeah, right,' said Casey, gazing after her with big reproachful eyes from the stairs. Charlie wondered about pulling a sicky. Stay with Casey, spend a whole evening in front of the TV, not just a rushed hour before work. Then she tightened her hood, and headed out into a cold blast of wind, keeping her head down.

4

SATURDAY 21 SEPTEMBER

IN THE PARK, with Di and James beside her, Charlie scanned the motley collection of people and waited for the police signal. An impressive turnout considering it was a Saturday and lots of people had gone to Leeds to watch the match. The neighbourhood had felt tense all week, everyone on edge, keeping their children close. Now that they had been given the go-ahead to search, there was almost a carnival atmosphere as they lined up, ready to drop to their hands and knees. Early afternoon. Policemen in bobby hats every few yards, an inspector with a megaphone yelling out instructions, emphasising the importance of staying together and not disturbing anything that might be evidence.

'How are you supposed to know what might be evidence?' someone asked.

'Anything that makes you suspicious,' said a police officer. 'Items of clothing for instance.'

They pulled on disposable gloves and kneeled. It was a higgledy-piggledy sort of group. Di and assorted friends, women she used to work with at the call centre, women from the Community Café, people from the surrounding streets, dressed drably and looking solemn, Darren's dad John, and Frank, his dad, next to James. The Community Café, popular for Saturday lunches and snacks, was closed today so that everyone could help. Suzy had turned up in a tight skirt and tottery high heels, even though the police had said to dress in appropriate clothes. Charlie caught James's eye as he suppressed a smile.

The arty lot, with coloured hair, bright scarves and tights, milled around. More theatrical-looking than those who had always lived in the area, most were former students who had settled locally and produced kids and were now fixing up terraced houses and becoming involved in the community. Some volunteered at the café, and Charlie often saw them taking their kids to the local primary school.

The current crop of students had also turned up. Many had stayed on during the summer; others had drifted back for the start of term. Mostly they were slim and tall, casually dressed, with good teeth. In contrast, Donny and Graham and Eddie looked rough, battered by life. Only Michael appeared well-fed and healthy. Charlie was surprised he was bothering to help. The police had emphasised that the men should be under 'strict supervision'. Today that meant they were the responsibility of Martin and a tough-looking young guy with a kerchief from the day shift. Called himself Art, but Charlie had discovered his full name was Arthur. Didn't have the same edge somehow. Charlie was glad she wasn't on duty today. It was enough keeping an eye on Di and James.

She glanced over at the men from St Jude's Catholic Social Club. They'd probably been on the ale already, but were hiding it well. Good men, kind men. And Stella, chair of the Community Association, now with a crowd of earnest, serious-looking thirtysomethings, most with dirt on their trousers, as if they'd just come from the allotment. And a few older men and women from the area who always smiled at Charlie in the street.

Everyone knew Di, and patted her on the shoulder or had a quiet word. Good people, all giving up their time. Darren had burgled a few of their houses. But still they turned up.

And you couldn't really fault the police. They'd questioned people house to house, interrogated Darren's friends, trawled through clubs in town known to admit under-age lads and lasses, examined his school work, his room, Di's house, and been over his dad's house. Result: nada, zilch, nothing.

Charlie waited with Di and James. Darren had been gone for almost a week. The police had caved in on the search because they knew that otherwise people would take the law into their own hands. John, suddenly waking to his duties as a father, had pestered them day and night, and threatened to organise his own. Frank backed him up in his own quiet way. The police knew feelings were running high. Charlie reckoned they had a theory about what had happened to Darren. They'd seen these cases before. A young lad didn't just disappear into thin air. And why were they searching the park? A potential dumping ground? Had someone or something alerted them? Or was it just the nearest open space?

There were posters of Darren on bus stops and trees, and outside his school: 'Missing. Have you seen this boy?'

Di had been interviewed on local TV news, a tired-looking detective beside her, saying they were 'increasingly concerned' the longer they heard nothing from Darren.

'He's my boy,' Di had cried on TV, her rat's tail hair sticking up. Red eyes, blotchy skin, sweat patches on her shirt, her body bent as if she'd been punched, Di had aged ten years. 'We've got to find him.'

Charlie looked across at Stella, the chair of the Community Association, and involved in most things in the area. Stella would be a good person to find out things from. Stella was a bossy cow, but she got things done. She was rumoured to know the Chief Constable, and the police had dropped objections to the search after she'd got involved.

Charlie handed Di a piece of chocolate. 'What happened to that officer?'

For the past week, a policeman had been glued to Di's side, keeping guard outside her house, calling in on her, answering their questions. For the first two days he insisted that Darren would be at a mate's. By Thursday he was more evasive. Now he was nowhere to be seen.

'Reassigned,' said Di simply. 'He phoned up yesterday.'

'Aren't they offering you anything else?'

'Gave me a number for Victim Support.'

'Aren't you going to phone them?'

'Don't know if I'm a victim yet.' And Di laughed a hollow, weird laugh, worry and grief sunk into her death's head skull.

'We do appreciate your help.' Through the megaphone, the police inspector's voice sounded out. And then they were off, for the slowest, most painstaking afternoon. It had been raining, and their disposable gloves quickly muddied. The grass was damp and cold on their knees. They shifted towards woodland near the park wall. Dog walkers stayed higher up. This area was overgrown, with thick, spiky bushes. The path down to the road had been cordoned off. Charlie shivered. This part of the park had always given Charlie the creeps. At times she'd walked the neighbour's Belgian shepherd, and when it ran off into the bushes Charlie hated it, as no one could hear you if anything happened here. Further down, and over the wall you came out on traffic, noise, a pavement. To the right were houses, to the left the children's playground: normality. Today the cries and shouts of children, muffled by the wood, seemed other-worldly. There were shoes in the trees, thrown up by departing students. They creaked and swung in the slight breeze. Charlie closed her eyes and saw an image of a hanged man swinging and creaking. She opened them, and there were only shoes.

It was boring searching on your hands and knees, when you didn't even know what you were looking for. Snails, stones, grass, glass, crisp packets, lemonade bottles. What might they find that would be useful? A sock? A shoe? Her eyes were drawn upwards. Mostly trainers, the occasional high heel or flat shoe. Darren always wore trainers, if he wasn't wearing football boots. She forced her eyes back to the earth, as the line of searchers inched forward.

In the distance, curious dog walkers stared over. A terrier barked excitedly and tried to rush the police dogs, but was shooed away by handlers. Music started up from a group of students, but a man from St Jude's put his hand on a young man's shoulder and soon there was quiet.

They searched all afternoon, going higher and higher up near the ridge, only stopping for drinks of water and biscuits that a WRVS person brought round. On one such break, Di gave up the hands and knees search and police brought her a striped camping chair. She lit up. Charlie nibbled broken biscuits.

They neared the top of the park just as it was getting dark. You could see over the city from here. Lights came on in high rises, planes winked overhead as they dropped height for landing. There was an ache in her gut. The land undulated. Somewhere below the river gouged out a valley, the two cities spilling out either side. A great city needed a river: Liverpool, London, Newcastle, and Hull. All those Midlands cities with their canals and their piddling little rivers, they did nothing for her. A great river gave a pulse to a city, a beat. Elsewhere, it promised. Had Darren responded to its pulse, taken off? Where was he?

Lights went on in rows of terraces; the air shimmered with an autumn haze. Her nostrils quickened at the faint smell of wood smoke. Soon the world would close up for winter, everyone would stay indoors and eat roasts and snuggle down in duvets until spring. In the near distance were tower blocks and cranes and scaffolding. Beyond, houses were getting ripped up, warehouses demolished, roads tarmacked. Everyone going about their lives. Out there was Darren. Someone knew where he was. Charlie saw Di shift along her chair, chain-smoking, while James doggedly felt the ground, grim-faced. Not much of a Saturday for a 17-year-old.

'Could Casey not have come with us, like?' James's question was sudden.

Charlie's stomach lurched as if she'd been hit. The previous night's argument with Casey had been running for three days: 'You're always at work, or Di's. You care more about her than you do me. You could spend some time with your own daughter. It's your day off tomorrow. I thought we could do something together.'

Charlie was so surprised she'd said nothing. Casey had taken this as disagreement, and then went off on one.

'And you're a hypocrite – you didn't even like Darren, you said he'd turned bad. He's probably just gone off to London or somewhere with a mate, he'll come crawling back soon enough, you'll see. Go on the search. Of course you will. I'm only your daughter.'

Charlie tried to meet James's eyes.

'She isn't feeling well.'

To her surprise, James said, 'Oh sorry, poor Casey. Give her my love.'

Somewhere in the back of Charlie's brain an alarm went off.

Charlie tried to focus on the ground in front of her. This place gave her the shivers. It had a terrible lonely atmosphere, and after just two hours sleep the night before, she was practically hallucinating. The ground danced. Out of the corner of her eye, there were darting creatures, unknown shapes, wriggling worms. For three days she had been calling in at Di's every day, sometimes staying for hours, and tending to her and James. Usually followed by a quick rush home to Casey, another round of cooking, and then work each night. Even Martin, never the most observant, had asked whether she was OK. Of course she wasn't OK.

And then it was dark, spotlights came on, small animals

scurried across the grass, crows gathered to roost and bats zig-zagged between trees.

The Inspector's voice surprised them, a soft Scottish lilt, the consonants carefully pronounced.

'We thank you all for coming. We do appreciate your efforts and co-operation and we ask that you disperse swiftly and safely. And you must appreciate that at this time of heightened caution you should ensure that you're not walking home alone. Our officers will take over now, and rest assured that we will continue the search for as long as possible. If we need your assistance again, we will be in touch.'

Charlie slipped her arm through Di's to hold her up, and they walked back past the shoes in the trees, past the ghostly, empty children's playground, past the final dog walkers and the keen runners and the pizza place. Di was nervous and excited now, buoyed up by the fact that they'd found nothing.

'See, Darren's not here. He's OK, I know he is; a mother knows these things.'

Charlie grunted. Di may as well hope. Charlie couldn't shake off a heaviness in her bones. She hoped she wasn't getting the flu.

'He could have got a train somewhere, like people said. He liked trains, and he had a bit of money left that his dad had given him for his birthday coming up… He always wanted to go to London, you know. I promised him I'd take him for his birthday, maybe he thought it would never happen and decided to take himself down there. We never made it to Disneyland, remember, and I'd promised him that for years. He'll phone up when he's run out of money and say, "Mam, what were you worrying about?" I think there's a lad from his school who is from London, maybe he's gone down with him.'

Charlie knew the police had already checked this lad. Di was grasping at straws. Yet she'd be the same if it was Casey. A sudden stab of guilt pinched her. Casey. She hoped Casey would still be awake: she was always so tired lately, and slept so much.

But then they neared Di's house, and Charlie soothed and helped her into the bath, throwing in some pink powder that promised Dead Sea relaxation. And Di emerged pink-faced and healthier-looking, and Charlie cooked the three of them silky scrambled eggs, keeping the tea coming, and then it was nine o'clock. She phoned Casey to tell her to come round, have something to eat, but there was no answer. She promised herself she'd leave soon if Casey didn't arrive.

James said, 'One nil at Elland Road.' Then he went back to his food, and washed up without a word. Next they heard him pacing round his room. When Di nodded off in her chair, Charlie gathered her things. Time to go. But Di started up, instantly awake.

'You need to help us, Charlie. The police aren't doing enough. It'd be different if Darren was a pretty little girl. Or rich. They'd be pulling out all the stops then.'

Charlie didn't know what to think.

'Promise me you'll help us, Charlie.'

'Help you?'

'Find out what's happened to Darren. My Darren. My baby Darren.'

Then she cried, big plops of tears mixing with the snot pouring out of her nose, the hair falling across her face, one sticky mass. Charlie recoiled, disgusted. Darren would come back and all this would blow over. She had enough to do. Her bones felt heavy, weighed down. And then she saw the date on the calendar. Of course. Next week it would be ten years since Sean died. The body knew, the body remembered. They usually made a nice meal on the Sunday of the anniversary, and even though Casey could hardly remember him, Charlie would tell her stories about her dad, and the funny tricks he played, and the phrases he used, so that there was something of her dad that came alive for her. Casey probably thought she had forgotten. She had to go home, get back to her daughter.

So when Di asked her again, 'Will you help us, Charlie, will you?' she answered, 'Of course I will,' as much to get rid of her as anything else, but instantly she felt bonds tighten around her, the call of Di's plea.

'Even if it's bad?' Di entreated with her eyes.

'Even if it's bad,' she agreed, not really paying attention.

When Charlie tried her home number, this time Casey answered after an age. She greeted her with, 'I'm going to sleep at Emma's tonight. So you may as well stay at Di's. You like it better there anyway. And I'm staying tomorrow night as well. We've got a history project due in next week.'

'Are you sure? What about the anniversary?'

'Whatever. You're never here, and we haven't arranged anything.'

'We'll do something later in the week, darling. I promise.'

'Sure,' Casey said coldly. 'Sure. Bye.'

After the phone call Charlie helped Di up the stairs, extinguished the cigarette in her hand on the bedside ashtray, and covered her with the duvet, then lay down on the sofa herself.

Above her head, James paced. Such a mournful sound, back and forth, back and forth. Charlie pulled a blanket over her head and the house closed around them.

5

SUNDAY 22 SEPTEMBER

CHARLIE WOKE UP after nine, sweating, her neck sore from
lying on Di's couch. She was working tonight. Sundays she
usually lazed around with Casey, and they ate a full cooked
breakfast and had pasta or something easy for tea. With the
anniversary coming up she would have made something
better. But that plan was out the window. Casey wouldn't
be home today. Was the history project with Emma just an
excuse? Casey, angry at her for some reason, was avoiding her.
'Must go home,' Charlie thought. Even if Casey wasn't there,
she could clean up, make the house nice. Charlie pulled on the
previous day's jeans and top. She'd leave before Di woke.

Outside it was sleeting, miserable, cold for this time of
year. She folded up the blanket, and turned down the central
heating, which had been on all night. Di liked it tropical. Her
bills would be enormous.

In the kitchen, she was on automatic: kettle on, bread
in the toaster. Keep busy, let everything go back to normal.
Darren would turn up. She heard Frank's heavy tread. It
had slipped her mind he was staying. Last night she'd hardly
noticed him: he had gone straight to bed after the search. A
good man, Frank, he'd worked steadily at the Nissan factory
in Sunderland for years, until he retired. Di said that now
he busied himself with his allotment, and 'fixing things'.
Completely different to John, who couldn't seem to keep a job.
Frank was usually sprightly and energetic, but now his walk
sounded laboured and old, and when he reached the kitchen,

he was grey-faced and stricken-eyed.

'Areet, hinny? Anything?' He lifted his face, expectant.

She shook her head, and handed him tea and toast. Carefully he spread a thin layer of Marmite on one buttered slice and a thick layer of strawberry jam on the other, and cut them into triangles. Charlie nibbled at a corner of buttered toast. They munched and sipped in silence. Di's snores rattled above them, and there was the occasional squeak of bedsprings from James's room.

'They was gannin carry on until the light faded,' Frank offered. More of a question than a statement.

'They were.'

'Do you not think they'll call us all back, pet?'

'Maybe.'

Outside, the sleet slowed down and a weak sun angled triangles of light into the room. Charlie took this as hopeful. Darren had gone off with a friend, or had some work and no time to contact anyone. Or he was with a girl and didn't want to tell his girlfriend. He'd been in bed all week with this girl, in that mad phase when you first got together and time fell away. Teenagers never understood the worry they caused you. But a week was a long time. Unless he couldn't phone, unless someone was holding him. Charlie shivered, and picked up a breakfast plate.

SHE WAS STILL clearing the table when the phone call came.

'Yes. OK. She's in bed. He's up, with me here. Now? I'll tell him. Thank you.'

Frank's expression was fearful.

'They want someone to go the station.'

He nodded, as if this was expected.

'I'll get my coat then. Mebbies the poliss found something.' His voice had a tinge of hope in it.

'Maybe.'

Neither of them believed that.

'I'll stay here, shall I?'

'Aye, pet, best to let them sleep. Although wor James said he'd to catch up with college work.'

'I'll make sure he's awake.'

'Nee, hinny, let them sleep.'

'OK. In case it's nothing,' Charlie added.

'Aye.'

It wouldn't be nothing. Charlie squashed down an image of Darren as a small child, crying his eyes out after he cut his finger. Darren was no good with pain.

'You know the way?'

'I do.'

Of course he did. Frank had been up the station many a time with Darren. Shoplifting, theft of a bike ('it was just lying there, honest'), running off from the cinema without paying for popcorn. All this before he graduated to burglary.

'I'll take the car, pet. I can park near that waste ground they're keeping for the student flats.'

The plans for the flats were plastered on lampposts, and there was a leaflet on the kitchen table. Wasteland would be dug up, built on. Luxury student accommodation. En suite bathrooms and communal kitchens, designer gardens. There were rumours that the rents would be three times higher than usual. What type of students could afford that? No one from round here.

'OK.'

Frank shuffled out. He had aged in the night, grown smaller and thinner and there was a white streak in his hair she hadn't noticed before. They were all exhausted. She wanted to lie down in her own bed and curl up her toes and Darren to be back and everything to be normal again.

Something must have happened.

Frank's exhaust stuttered out of the road with an irregular

rattle. For somebody who'd worked in a car factory he had a crap car.

She flicked the kettle on again. Peeked in at Di. Downstairs, James was at the kitchen window.

'Where's granda away to?'

'The police called.'

'Is my mam awake?'

'Not just yet. Here.'

He devoured the toast and jam as if he hadn't eaten for a long time, slushed down the tea she offered, poured one for his mother and went upstairs.

He returned with the tea untouched, and shook his head.

Then he banged plates around the sink, ran water over them, and left, slamming the back door.

Charlie was mopping the kitchen floor when she heard the phut phut of Frank's car.

His tight face and the set of his shoulders as he walked up the path told her. As he came in, he buckled, as if he'd been punched. She placed a hand on his shoulder and guided him into a chair in the kitchen. They were in a film she didn't want to be in. Frank put his head in his hands, and ignored the tea she offered. Di and James materialised, James red-faced as if he'd been running, Di with puffy, sleep-encrusted eyes.

'What's happened?' Di's voice was small and weak.

There were tears in Frank's eyes, and the face that looked back was lined and shadowed, pain etched into his hollow eyes and cheeks.

'It's Darren.'

'What? Have they found him?'

'They found him.'

There was a spark of hope in Di's eyes, her hand went to her mouth and she gave a strange high laugh.

Frank spoke slowly and deliberately.

'His body, hinny, they found his body. Darren's dead, pet.

Our Darren's dede.'

Di reeled back.

'No.'

James held her arm and pulled her down.

'Aye, pet, I'm sorry, I'm so sorry.'

'No. It can't be Darren. It can't be. It's a mistake, Frank, it's a mistake. Isn't it, James?'

'Is it not a mistake, granda, is it not?'

Frank crumpled, and held his arms out to James, who stayed rigid next to Di.

'It's nae mistake, son. It's Darren, son, our Darren. Wor Darren's dede, they found his body.'

Di's left hand went to her mouth again, and her right hand twitched towards a packet of cigarettes. James automatically handed her the packet, and then keeled over. She extracted a cigarette with shaking hands, lit it quickly, and puffed in and out. Then she ran to the sink, fell forward and vomited. James shot upstairs to his room. There was the sound of low sobbing.

'Sorry,' Charlie found herself saying. 'Sorry, sorry.'

It was late afternoon when Di came to, and the sun was round the back of the house, so that the living room was cold, and the light muted, everything stained a sorrowful red or purple. The room was gloomy and shadowy, even with the lights on. Di had cried so much she'd fallen asleep on the sofa, face sticky and puffy, arms and legs flung out. Frank stayed upstairs. Charlie wanted to go home, get Casey from Emma's, tell her before she found out, but she couldn't leave. Instead she busied herself brewing tea and making sandwiches that nobody touched.

As Di stirred, her eyes were hopeful for a few seconds, and then they dulled as she remembered. Charlie doused her in sweet tea. James glided silently into the kitchen, and held his mum's hand.

'The poliss on the phone.' Frank reappeared, cradling a

mug. 'They're coming round.'

'Why?' Something went off in Charlie's head. Why did the police need to come round? Frank had identified Darren. What more was there to do?

'He looked so young.' Frank gripped the handle of the mug, and blew the hot tea. 'Remember like what our Darren used to look like when he was about 12? Before…'

Before he started acting like a little bastard, Charlie thought. *Before he began robbing money out of our purses, and progressed to burglary? Before he got an attitude problem, and thought the world owed him a living. When he was still beautiful, and cheeky, and smart.*

Her eyes filled with tears. 15.

Di gave a low moan.

'Kind of flat, you know, surprised, an' all, as if it was a joke. Remember how he was always playing jokes? That time he dressed as a ghost and jumped out to scare us? Remember, James, remember?'

James nodded, whimpering.

'They done their best. Tidied him up, you know, but you could see the marks on his face, bruises and scratches.'

'What do you mean, bruises and scratches?' Charlie snapped. 'Why did he have bruises and scratches?'

'What happened, Granda? What happened to our Darren?' James said sharply, alerted by Charlie.

'He would have fought, our Darren, wouldn't he? He would have put up a fight?'

'What do you mean, a fight?' Charlie made Frank face her. 'Are the police saying there was a fight? That it wasn't an accident?'

James's face was pinched as he tried to control his upset.

'They just said it was a suspicious death. He had a head injury. Somebody might have hit him.'

Di gave another strangled cry, and her body concertinaed.

'Some gadgie's confessed,' said Frank.

'Someone's confessed?' Charlie's voice rose. Everything was happening too quickly.

James put his hands on his grandfather's heaving shoulders. 'Who, Granda, who?'

Frank lowered his head again.

'What happened, Granda? Was there a fight? Did our Darren get in a fight?'

'I dinna knaa, son. But someone confessed.'

'Who?' Di rallied, furious now. 'What bastard hurt my Darren? Tell me.'

'Have they arrested someone?' Charlie asked. She was trying to process what had happened. Her brain felt foggy.

'Not yet. Apparently this gadgie is not all there, and is always confessing to things. He told them he'd assassinated John Major. They said not to get your hopes up.'

And then they all dissolved into silence, the news too much to take in.

An hour went past. The sun went down and streetlamps came on. Up the street you could hear children playing. An ice cream van played *Greensleeves*, and a woman shouted at a kid she was dragging along, 'Walk, you little bugger, walk.'

Charlie switched on lights, and kept the tea flowing. James seemed fired with renewed energy.

'We need to get him. Whoever did it. If it wasn't that nutter.'

'We don't really know what happened yet.' Charlie patted his arm.

'It divvent matter anyway,' said Frank.

'But it does, Granda, it does.'

'It won't bring our Darren back.' Frank threw up his arms. The wrinkles on his face had deepened, his hair had whitened, his cheeks sunk.

Di reached for a can of lager. There were already three crumpled by her chair. Her eyes grew glazed.

James's face was red and blotchy, and he held his fists tight against his body, about to lash out. 'The poliss won't bother much about Darren. They'll think he was some proper charver like.'

'Nae lad, we divvent know that. Stay strong.'

'What for? Darren's dead, Granda, dead.'

The bare words made everybody flinch. *Darren was dead.*

'I bet we'll have to find out for ourselves who did it, won't we, Mam?'

Di blinked with wide-pupiled eyes, as if she had just woken up from a dream.

'Charlie here will help us, won't you, Charlie; you're good at things like that.'

Good at things like what? Reading detective novels from the library, figuring out whodunit?

Three faces turned to her. Charlie threw her arms out and shrugged.

Frank produced a bottle of brandy, sticky round the opening, and poured a generous measure for them all.

Di downed hers, reached for the bottle, and poured a second measure. Soon she was snoring on the couch. Charlie put a blanket over her. Poor Di. The news hadn't sunk in yet.

'Let her sleep, poor pet. Shock, it can take you sudden, like.'

Frank's face was impassive. Frank had been a boxer. He'd knocked people out. Frank knew about shock.

'What about Casey? James whispered.

'She needs to know.'

'Christ, I'll get hold of Emma's parents.'

'Bring her here.'

''I will.'

'They're finishing off a project. She was telling me about it.'

Charlie felt a stab of envy. James knew more about Casey's life than she did. Her own daughter didn't talk to her anymore.

'We should all stay together, Auntie Charlie, shouldn't we?'

'Yes, darling.' She held him while he sobbed, then got on the phone to Emma's. Her dad was puzzled at her cryptic message, but recognising Charlie's serious tone promised to drop Casey first thing in the morning. The girls were asleep already. She thanked him.

It was going to be a long night. Di was asleep, but James kept on at Frank.

'Where was our Darren found? What happened? When did it happen?'

'Heaton Park, up near the railings. Not far from where they had us searching. Whoever did it didn't really try to hide him. The police reckon he'd only been there since last night. Otherwise the dogs would have found him.'

'You mean it didn't happen till yesterday?'

'They don't know yet. They have to do all that forensics.'

'So where was Darren earlier in the week, before…?' Charlie, taking her cue from James, couldn't bring herself to say the word 'killed'.

'They don't know. They think that he did go off somewhere for a few days, and was gannin home when something happened. He was under some bushes. A lass out walking her dog early morning found him. Poor lass, she must have got a shock. So still when I saw him. And you know our Darren, he was never still. I kept thinking he would wake up, and say with that cheeky grin of his: "Gotcha, Granda, gotcha."'

They sat in silence, emptied out, shadows lengthening outside, the world carrying on. So Darren was still alive until yesterday. Di had been right. He had gone off somewhere for a few days. Where? And then came back, met up with someone, and bam, he was dead. Someone knew where he'd been. Someone would come forward. They would piece it together. The person he'd gone off with maybe had nothing to do with his murder. They might be totally innocent. They might not know what had happened.

52

Charlie phoned work and without going into details, said she wasn't coming in. 'Emergency at Di's,' she said. Martin said 'no problem', they had enough staff.

'And I don't want to worry you at this time,' he added, 'but there's been a few bricks over the gate. They missed the windows, but I think somebody's got it in for us.'

Charlie said nothing. She couldn't concentrate. Nobody could have found out already, but when the news did come out about Darren, locals would automatically blame the hostel residents. There'd be more bricks over the gate, more protests.

'Anyway, you look after yourself. Sounds like you need some sleep.'

She put the phone down and sat doing nothing, overcome with tiredness. She knew there was a plethora of phone calls to make: Di had given her a list. Frank had already phoned John, and Darren's other grandparents in Spain. But she held the list in her hand and sat staring into space

On Monday morning at seven, Emma's dad brought Casey. When Casey heard the news she folded into James's arms, and the pair spent the morning lying on the sofa, blankets over them, watching video after video. Charlie made the phone calls: Casey's school, James's college, and Di's relatives. The news soon spread, and the day passed with knocks at the door and neighbours arriving with tuna casseroles and pies. What was it about tuna casseroles? One brought a bottle of cava, others brought flowers. A pile of bouquets grew opposite, tied to the lamppost. Wind whipped at the plastic wrapping and the unnaturally bright flowers, the cards with their 'Always in our hearts'; 'we luv u Darren.'

That night Charlie sent out for pizzas, and they all huddled together watching a film about men stuck on a boat somewhere in the Atlantic. Rain lashed the boat, sharks circled, and sailors hallucinated, thinking they saw mermaids. For an hour or so the five of them immersed themselves in the watery world. When Charlie took the pizza boxes into the kitchen, she was struck by the first of two photos of Darren from when he'd played for the school, proud in his school football kit.

'Tea?' she shouted.

'Ask Darren if he wants one,' Di called back, and next thing she was in the kitchen and they were both staring at the two photos – Darren in his school football kit, holding up the Inter-Schools trophy, and Darren in his Newcastle kit. They held each other, crying, Di sobbing, 'My baby, my baby' until the early hours of the morning. She smoked and drank and dozed off, woke up, and continued the cycle.

James, his back bent and hunched as he went up to bed, heard his mother's words, and turned, his eyes beseeching.

It was dawn when Charlie finally slept. Casey was lying at the other end of the sofa. Charlie didn't have the heart to wake her for school.

6

TUESDAY 24 SEPTEMBER

THEY WERE IN a strange limbo of a time. The man picked up for questioning was arrested, and after a couple of days they charged him and remanded him in custody. Frank went along to the preliminary hearing, telling Di to wait until later.

'All legal mumbo jumbo at this stage,' he said. 'No point upsetting yourself further.'

Everything was on hold. They couldn't even arrange a funeral yet, as they waited for the results of a second post-mortem the man's lawyers had requested. The first one had found a massive haematoma, the result of a blow to the head.

'Bruise,' Charlie explained to Di, who flinched at the word.

Casey was alternately angry and tearful with Charlie, pushing her away and then leaning into her for hugs. For the first time, she was fearful about Charlie leaving her alone at night.

'What if someone breaks in?'

'We've never had a break in before.'

But Darren's never died before was the unspoken reply.

'Do you want me to get a babysitter again?'

'I'm not a baby.'

Up until the previous year, whenever Charlie was on night shift, an older teenage girl had always stayed the night. It was Casey herself who said she didn't need them anymore.

But now a killer was at large.

'You know to go next door if you're worried about anything?'

'Of course.'

The woman next door, hands full with five kids, had agreed to keep an eye on Casey. The yard gate was locked, the kitchen had a double lock. If anyone came down the alley, there were eyes on the street, and the council had just installed new lights at the front. 'Like Colditz', everyone said. It was hard to slip into their street now without being seen. But still Charlie worried, and each morning she was relieved to find Casey safe.

The neighbour solved the problem, offering her Belgian shepherd to stay with Casey whenever Charlie was on nights, 'In return for her walking him on those days. It would help me out.'

Casey was delighted. She loved that dog, with its intelligent eyes and watchful gaze, and the dog was enthusiastic about her, bounding up to lick her each time, as if it had been months since she'd seen her. Charlie felt reassured. If anyone came near the house, the dog's size and fierce bark would scare them off. Only the cat was unhappy, and disappeared to the top of the house.

After finishing each night shift, Charlie saw Casey off to school, grabbed a couple of hours' sleep and headed over to Di's house, where she cleaned and cooked, fussing round so that she didn't have to think. If she stopped, she saw an image of Darren lying on the path, a massive bruise on his head, and she couldn't get up again.

Each afternoon she left Di's house tidy. Each morning when she arrived it was a tip: ashtrays full, the bins spilling over with takeaway containers, the air a hovering grey haze of cigarette smoke. James always helped tidy up, but Di never moved, creating a circle of ash and cigarette stubs and rubbish. Frank, back in his own flat, appeared each morning, happy to give a hand: the type of man who could fix a dripping tap, put mastic on a leak, and fill in a hole in plaster. Charlie suspected he did all this to stop himself thinking as well. Anything to stop dwelling on that muddy path, the undergrowth, Darren's body lying in the cold and wet.

The weather forecast showed a cold front descending on their region: frozen clouds, mist, daylight struggling through. The heating was on full. You could hardly breathe.

A new policeman began to call in. A short-haired, pimply-faced, awkward man, each day he drank tea with them and kept them up to date. There were no more leads, and it looked like the evidence was slack against the man who had been charged. His lawyers were calling for mental health reports. Frank and John went to the inquest, opened and adjourned pending the court case, and returned with an interim death certificate and the news that they could start arranging the funeral even though Darren's body hadn't been released.

'So that we're ready when they let Darren go,' said Frank. 'It'll all take a while more.'

'I'll wait until they release Darren,' Di said.

It felt as if they were all underwater.

On the Thursday morning Charlie was frying eggs and Di piling hot chilli sauce on her plate.

Charlie had read somewhere that grief dulled your taste buds. It made sense, but she kept it to herself. She'd already eaten porridge at home with Casey. Having the dog forced Casey to get up earlier. The 'walk' consisted of putting her coat over her pyjamas and letting the dog out onto the patch of waste ground.

Di added clouds of pepper and salt, and bit in. She discarded the egg sandwich after one bite, and lit another cigarette. Wearily, Charlie scraped the plate into the bin. She couldn't keep up helping Di. Di had other friends. She would withdraw a little, do it gradually, so that Di didn't notice.

By the end of the week a friend of Darren's came forward and the police pieced together Darren's movements in his last week. This friend lived in Darlington now and nobody had realized Darren kept in touch. The lad was supposed to have gone down south to stay with his brother, but instead he and Darren had gone to Brighton to try to get jobs. With no success – they'd ended up sleeping on benches, and used the last of their money to get a coach back to Newcastle on the Saturday, the night of the search. The lad's mother had confirmed she met them, and had taken her son home, leaving Darren heading for a bus. She'd assumed he was going home.

'He did say he was meeting someone first before he went home, the dopey cow told us,' the police officer informed them in Di's living room. 'So that narrows it down.'

'How come she never spoke up before?'

Charlie couldn't understand how somebody could have missed the TV coverage and the articles in the local paper.

'Said she never read newspapers, and had no time for TV, what with her three cleaning jobs. She'd been up the coast in a caravan, mind, said she just switched off. Most of her family don't even talk to her. Something about her son, petty thefts and all that. And the son's been in bed with flu ever since he got back. That's why, pet. She came forward as soon as she saw a paper in the doctor's.'

So Darren had met someone on the Saturday. Who? And the killer must have thought that the park was a good place to go to after the search was over. There were bound to be clues.

Charlie felt a prickle of excitement. She tried to suppress it, but it kept bubbling up. She channelled it into comforting James, who acted fuzzy and dazed by the new information, and lowered his shoulders despondently, as if to say, 'How much worse could things get?'

In a sudden burst of energy, Charlie blitzed the dishes at Di's house, emptied bins and wiped kitchen surfaces until they sparkled. But when she got home she fizzled out, and stared into space. The mess in her own house had piled up – toppling piles of unsorted washing, a layer of dust, unwashed dishes in the sink, the cat bowl encrusted with dried food. She had no energy to tackle it. She puzzled over what had happened. Who had Darren met? Whoever he met had killed him. Blood or money, that's what most murder came down to. Blood or money.

That week the GP prescribed Di tablets, so that her face became wide-eyed and her pupils grew even larger. Charlie kept Suzy away, Suzy whose specialist subject was her own gastric band. Charlie knew exactly how many pounds Suzy had lost since getting her gastric band fitted. Was aware how the gastric band had changed her life. That she'd be living on soup and squashed up baby food for the rest of her life didn't seem to bother her.

'Do you think I look attractive?' she'd ask, mid-conversation, chin tilted, hand on hip. Stupid cow, with her face like a heifer's. Meantime her husband was working all hours God gave him, and looking after the kids. Earlier in the year she'd managed to swing a grant to go on a business course for older women, and had used the money on a boob job. Charlie had a good mind to report her.

Friday morning Suzy was at the door again. She must have been watching with binoculars to see when the coast was clear. Emotional leech.

'Di needs to rest,' Charlie said.

And this time, Di agreed.

'I am a bit tired, Suzy.'

'The doctor has given instructions she's not to see anyone,' Charlie added. 'She's in shock.'

'Oh, doctors,' Suzy smiled in a knowing manner, with her whitened teeth. She respected people like doctors; she wouldn't have her gastric band without them. 'Well, pet, I'm away home, divvent forget to tell us if you need us.'

Charlie could tell from her expression that she was relieved. Now she could get back to thinking about herself.

Charlie left early that day when the next door neighbour, a grey-haired thin string of a woman, promised to look in. The neighbour and Di had their differences, but she was a kind woman, and her son and Darren had been at primary school together.

'Poor woman,' she kept saying to Charlie at the door. 'Poor poor woman.'

At home, Casey was short with her: 'You're back early.'

'I thought I'd spend some time with you.'

'I'm busy. Got so much coursework, I'm really stressed. I'll come down for tea.'

'And I'm running a hotel as well.'

Later, over burnt macaroni cheese, Casey answered in monosyllables, cleared her plate and went back upstairs.

'Shout me when you're going.'

The dog's bark reassured Charlie as she switched into work mode, and left the house.

At work she was impatient with the men, who were subdued. They knew they'd be the first people under suspicion if the case collapsed against the fantasist. Everything annoyed her.

The next morning revolved round burnt toast and rubbish. Why were they alive and Darren dead at 15? She didn't care about them. They'd stay here a few weeks or months. Some would get jobs, most would reoffend. Not much point trying.

She attempted to catch up on admin, but it was useless.

'Do you think you should take some time off?' Martin asked, surprising her once again. 'Have a holiday?'

'I can't afford a holiday.'

'At least go and have a sit down. I can do the rounds myself. Go on. You've been through a lot. You can have my chair.'

That clinched it. She dozed in Martin's armchair while he did the rounds. When she woke there were only two hours of shift to go. Martin brought her fresh coffee.

On Saturday morning there were newspaper reporters at Di's door, and a different officer stood awkwardly outside. Di appeared to be enjoying the buzz. She also had a new hairdo, courtesy of Suzy, and had discarded her nightie for a smart dress, and wore lipstick and mascara. The lipstick was too pink and showed the cracks round her puckered lips.

Suzy had sneaked in, and was wafting cigarette smoke. There was a tang of alcohol in the air. It was 11 in the morning.

'Hello, Charlie.' She flashed a smile. 'I came round to cheer poor Di up. She needed a little pick me up,' she said, glass in hand

Yeah, 40% proof...

Di had an air of excitement about her, as if what had happened had made her interesting. She flirted with the reporters at the door, and told them the police investigation was 'ongoing'. They called her by her first name, as if they knew her. 'Di! Di!' they called.

That afternoon Charlie fielded phone calls. The police had said there were always 'weirdos' after a death, and Di's name was in the paper, so it was easy enough to look up her number. Charlie was prepared for people who promised they could contact the 'loved one' or put you in touch with the 'other side'. Di had her share of those, leaving cards at the door, phoning at odd times. A couple of the religious lunatics knocked in person, sniffing out misfortune. Men in smart suits, or women in shapeless knee-length skirts, claiming 'Darren is in a better place.'

'Where? Jesmond?' Charlie shouted. 'Has he got an en suite?'

She wanted to yell at those idiots that Darren was in the General Hospital mortuary, just by the incinerator where they burnt the body parts, near the bins where the staff smoked, and that he had been cut up twice and examined and that he was never going to wear his Newcastle United kit again. That he was 15 years old. *15.*

But she didn't yell, and kept her voice low, suppressing her rage, and went home saddened. Casey was pale and tired.

'You all right, love?'

Casey grunted.

Charlie made them hot chocolate and they sat in front of the box watching a game show the point of which she had no idea of. Casey's cup was hardly touched.

'Don't you want your drink?'

'Aren't you going to work?'

'I'm off this weekend, remember? We redid the rota: I'm doing a day shift Monday, and then two till ten Wednesday and Thursday.'

'What about Di?'

'Been there. She's all right, the neighbour's calling in. And Gastric Band Suzy's round.'

Casey laughed.

'I'm here tonight.'

'Makes a change.'

'I know, love, I know. It's been hard.'

'How is Di?'

'Not good.'

'And James?'

'Quiet.'

'I didn't even really like Darren, you know.'

'I know, love; he wasn't the easiest to like. He just went a bit off the rails.'

'I'm not saying I wanted anything to happen to him.'

'I know you're not, darling, I know.'

'It's awful, Mum, it's all awful. Everything.'

Charlie held her while she cried.

They sat like that for a few minutes. Then Casey pulled away.

'I need to talk to you about something, Mum.'

'Of course, darling. Is it something at school?'

Casey grunted, and jumped up.

'But I'm starving. I'll make some toast first. Do you want some?'

'That would be nice. I'll wait here.'

Charlie closed her eyes. 'For a minute,' she thought. She heard the toaster popping, the kettle boiling, Casey scraping butter onto the toast. Then Casey flushed the toilet, stepped back into the room, bounced on to the settee, and sat down. Then there were the sounds of her disappointed voice: 'Mum, Mum', and her angry stomp up the stairs as Charlie gave in to sleep and darkness. Mentally she made a list of suspects. She would start with the family. Blood or money. And poke around, see who Darren had been meeting. Everyone had secrets. Her last thought was: *Must buy a notebook.*

7

TUESDAY 1 OCTOBER

CHARLIE WAS SURPRISED by the doorbell going so early in the morning. For once she felt well rested, and in the mirror, she saw that her cheeks had colour. On day shift the day before, she'd had a proper sleep. She'd give Di's a miss this morning. Casey still wasn't talking to her properly after Charlie fell asleep on her, and they still hadn't done anything to mark Sean's death. And now there was a new death to mourn.

There was a small figure visible through the glass panel.

She held the door open, and Frank stepped hesitantly into the hall. Red-eyed, as if he'd been crying. Of course he'd been crying. Everybody had.

Autumn light streaked through and she saw cobwebs hanging from the ceiling, a spider scuttle across. The place needed a proper clean. But it wasn't going to happen. How did people manage? Cleaning and washing and cooking and tidying and putting things away, and cleaning and... it took forever. When Sean was alive the small patch of garden at the front was always neat and tidy, plants growing. Not now.

'Thought I'd tell ye the news,' Frank said. 'Divvent knaa if Di would a bothered. She's not up to much.'

'Oh. Cuppa?' asked Charlie, easing Frank in. She rattled through the cupboards for biscuits and teabags, sniffed at a carton of milk, and opened the curtains to let the weak sun dance over the dust and the saggy cushions on the sofa and the photo album she'd been examining. Frank clocked the photo album, opened at a picture of Darren and James and Casey as youngsters, all grinning, their faces smeared with ice cream as they sat on a bench in the park.

'That's a nice one of wor Darren,' he said softly.

'Aye,' she agreed.

'What was it you wanted to tell me, Frank? Any more news?' Have they found anything out?'

'The bloke they arrested has been released. Said there was no case to answer. None of us ever thought it was him.'

'I'm not surprised. It was a bit too cut and dried.'

'Aye, poor bugger, he's not right in the heed, hissel, is ee, man? They've detained him under the Mental Health Act.'

'So we're back to square one?'

'Aye. They said the inquest will resume, they'll let us know when, but it'll be adjourned again. It means they'll release wor Darren's body. We could start planning the funeral. Thought you might have a word with Di.'

'OK, I will. How is she?'

'Shopping. With that Suzy.' They caught each other's eye, and both laughed.

'Now there's a lass who blathers on. And I divvent see the point of shopping.'

'I'm with you there, Frank. Not my thing,' Charlie said.

'The allotment's more for us. Aye. Wor Darren used to gan doon there with us.'

Charlie nodded.

'A miss wor lad like.'

'I know you do, Frank. We all do.'

'As a bairn, he was a bonny laddie.'

She passed him the photograph album and he ran his fingers over the photo, as if conjuring Darren up. They drank their tea silently, Charlie suddenly shy in her own house. She didn't really know Frank. Darren had adored him when he was younger, and Di said he'd loved going up the allotment with him, or fishing, had loved listening to all his tales of 'the olden days'. Frank seemed like a kind man, old school type, not speaking much.

A streak of sun made its way through the thin curtains. Trees swayed in the breeze, but the day was dry and bright.

'Not a bad day there, like.' Frank shook himself, like a dog waking up.

'A must admit, mind, there's another reason I called in. I wondered if…'

'Yes, Frank?'

She waited. He wouldn't be hurried.

'Do ye fancy keeping us company in the allotment?'

Charlie hesitated. Poor Frank, he was lonely without Darren. But she wasn't really a plants person. All her house plants shrivelled up and died. The only one left was a spider plant in the bathroom. Like the one at work, that seemed indestructible.

'Divvent feel ye have to say aye.'

And suddenly, getting out in the fresh air, away from the tension in her own house, away from mess, from dishes, from piles of washing, seemed the best idea ever. Move before they all hunkered down for the winter, before the central heating was on full all the time, before they piled on jumpers and tights and boots and scarves.

'Thought you'd never ask.'

'Well, I bought a couple of stotties and a flask of tea. It's hard work, and we'll get hungry. Darren was always starving, bless him.'

'I bet he was.'

Frank seemed like a proud man. Maybe he didn't have many friends. He wasn't going to sit round feeling sorry for himself. Important to keep talking about Darren, keep his memory alive. This was how you went on. This was how you faced each morning.

'I'm sure I could find something to take,' Charlie added, rifling through, piling crisps and biscuits into a bag, and filling a bottle with diluted squash. Frank perked up.

'What else have you got in your bag?' she asked. 'You came prepared, didn't you? How did you know I'd say yes?'

He smiled, and when he smiled, the hollows in his cheeks filled out and you could see the handsome man he'd once been.

'Di can be hard to be around. Understandable, like,' he added quickly, as if he was being unfair. 'I just reckoned you might need a break, like.'

And he showed Charlie his kneeling pad and gardening gloves.

'I haven't gardened for ages,' she told him as she closed the door.

'Have ye not? Nee bother, lass. It doesn't matter; we'll just get back to it today, catch up with things. Ah haven't been since...'

The words hung in the air.

But as she looked up, their mood lightened. The day was clear. Bright leaves coated the trees and formed a mushy carpet on the pavements, hurting your eyes with their orange and red and yellow. In a few weeks the trees would be bare, stick outlines. Charlie let their colours sink in.

They walked down her front path. Hardly a garden. Frank, politely, made no comment. The space was a mess. Room for only the bin and a climber in a large pot that someone had given her years before. She didn't even know the name of the plant and was surprised it had survived. Every May large purple flowers spread over her front wall. The back yard was just as basic, stacked with white plastic chairs and a table and umbrella still in its package. She had visions of putting it out the front, her and Casey sipping drinks in the sunshine. It had probably rusted and rotted by now. At the back the yard walls were bare, the few plants in pots withered and brown.

She needed to empty the pots, scrub them out, and refill them with flowering autumn bulbs for colour. Yet another thing that would fill up her time. Sean had always had hanging baskets and pots filled with colourful flowers all year round. He'd been about to whitewash the backyard walls, 'make them look Mediterranean, you know'. Charlie sighed. Her garden was more Baltic than Mediterranean. Maybe Frank could give her a hand.

The allotment was up a slope, and on the way, Charlie had to adjust her pace to Frank's. He'd slowed since Darren's death, his shoulders hunched, as if he was carrying a great burden. You could hear his lungs wheezing, although she knew from Di he'd never smoked. From being spry and fit he seemed to have shrunk and lost muscle tone. But he was a still a wiry, spare figure. When they reached the top, he stopped, ostensibly to admire the view, but his breathing was rapid, and only gradually slowed down. The city spread before them, caught in autumn sunlight. Rows of red brick terraces with slate roofs climbing slopes, streets of semi-detacheds with lighter coloured roofs, new builds surrounded by bags of cement and sand, concrete mixers and men in hard hats, white vans parked nearby. Handsome larger houses further out were framed by mature trees, interspersed with blocks of green like in a child's drawing. The motorway snaked past. People were on their way to work or back from work after hard nights tending, bathing, fixing broken bodies, cleaning and mopping so that the whole cycle could begin again. The endless wheel.

Frank fiddled round with the allotment padlock. Through the gate they arrived in a secret green world she'd only ever walked past. The sound of traffic grew distant as trees and bushes bent and whispered in the soft wind. Charlie took in a great long breath. Her fingers touched on the notebook in her pocket. From the corner shop, it was old fashioned, like ones they used to have in primary school: red, A5 size, with wide lines. In the back was a list of weights and measures with the title *Avoirdupois Weight*. She knew the lines off by heart.

16 ounces = 1 pound
14 pounds = 1 stone
28 pounds = 1 quarter
4 quarters = 1 hundredweight
20 hundredweights = 1 ton

FURTHER DOWN THE page were poles and roods and acres and chains and bushels and gills and pecks. Charlie had no idea what the words meant, but she liked the sound of them.

She pulled the notebook out. It was pretty impractical. The paper was porous, as if it was turning back into wool or rags, so the gel pen she'd tested on it went through, making puddled words, and really it was too big for her pocket. She needed a smaller one, waterproof, like a proper detective. Her fingers closed on the pen she'd taken from the office: 'Orchard Services – Protect and Support.' Must pick up a better pen: good worker, good tools and all that.

It wasn't as if she had made up her mind to help Di, not yet. She'd just not said no, and Di had assumed she would. But now, with no one in the frame for Darren's killing, Di would need her. A good start would be asking Frank some questions. It didn't mean she was committed. It wouldn't hurt.

Frank glanced over kindly at her gripping the notebook.

'A spade'll be more use to you up here.'

Charlie laughed.

'I just thought I'd ask you a few things about Darren. If you don't mind?'

He stared at her.

'Sorry, it's just Di asked me to help, see if I could find anything out that might be useful. Background stuff, like. She doesn't think the police'll do enough. So anything we can add…'

His face softened.

'Of course, lass, of course, you just want to help, like. Shall we get stuck in here first? You can ask away when we're having some scran. Fair enough?'

He looked more animated than she had seen him for weeks.

She nodded, and slipped the notebook back in her pocket.

Frank handed her a hoe and trowel from a shed at the end of the allotment and set her to work clearing dead foliage and lifting dying plants to put on the compost. Meanwhile he was piling earth round leeks. 'To keep the stems white,' he told her. It was pleasant, mindless work. Trowel out the dead plant, throw it on a pile, and take it to the compost bin. It was good not to think, to concentrate on what was in front of you. Frank was running his fingers over a raised bed of orangey red tomatoes. He looked up at the sky, then down at their skins, examining them as closely as a surgeon would assess an organ for surgery.

'No frost yet,' he said. 'Aye and it's not teeming doon. I'll leave them another week. Give them a good water an' all.'

'I'll do it.'

Charlie was eager to move, to tire herself out. She strode to the tap with the two watering cans, filled them and carried them, poured water at the base of the tomato plants. Repeated the action again and again.

Some plots were neat and ordered, with raised beds and few weeds, plants labelled and tied, netting over them. There were wooden sheds with creosoted roofs. Some plots seemed more anarchic, everything on them looking filched or fossicked. A tyre framed a bed of green; pallets were arranged as display tables, and cups without handles sprouted cabbages. There seemed many small cabbages, covered by netting.

Frank lifted carrots and beetroot, amassing a pile. He

showed her a gnarled apple tree, laden with fruit, surrounded by apples.

'Pick the ones on the ground first, but check they haven't got slugs in them.'

The apples were odd sizes, and mottled, some bruised, but Charlie gathered them anyway, Frank telling her to keep the bruised ones separate: 'We'll eat those first.' Then she started on the ones on the tree. Her bags filled. What on earth was he going to do with so many apples?

'I'll store them,' he said, reading her thoughts.

She moved onto helping him clear away bean poles. Frank tied them up neatly and arranged them in his shed. Then they forked over the compost, putting their backs into it. The sun came out and the morning grew warm. Charlie was enjoying her first fresh air for weeks, concentrating on the moment, forgetting everything that had happened.

An hour went by. The chatter and laughter of children along the green passageway behind the allotment alerted them to the time. A procession of men hurried to the mosque. Must get home.

Frank had other ideas. He offered her his flask, and a ham and pease pudding stotty, and squatted down. Charlie took out the crisps and biscuits and spread them on a blanket. They sat on a plank balanced on two bricks. The tea was strong and hot, and the bread tasted delicious.

'There's a fox sometimes,' Frank said when they'd sated the worst of their hunger. He gestured towards a thicket of brambles where wizened blackberries were covered in fur.

'Rats, of course. Lang tails.'

Charlie shivered.

'Grass snakes sometimes.'

'You kidding?'

'Only occasionally. Harmless. Mostly slow worms. I come here sometimes really early in the morning, when the birds have the place to themselves.'

'That must be nice.'

Keep him talking. If she kept him talking they wouldn't have to think, and Darren would not be dead. But the small prickle of excitement nagged at her, like toothache. She needed to know things.

'How was he lately, Frank?'

'Our Darren? Oh, you know, just the same an' all.'

'There was nothing different about him? He hadn't changed?'

'Everything changes.'

'Alles wandelt sich,' she said automatically. Somewhere at the back of her brain a memory kicked in of scribing the Brecht poem for a student of German who had difficulty writing because of arthritis.

'Was geschehen,' said Frank, looking at her in surprise.

'Has happened,' she finished. 'What's happened has happened.'

Charlie recited the poem, the German words trotting out, as Frank gazed at her, a dreamy, faraway expression in his eyes.

'Alles wandelt sich,' he repeated , and they started again, sounding out the poem together this time, both word perfect . 'Neu beginnen' and 'was geschehen' echoed as they continued. Afterwards they turned, and said to each other in surprise: 'I didn't know you could speak German.'

'I didn't know you could.'

'I can't.'

She explained about the student support job she'd had, and scribing for the student of German, and learning the poem by heart.

'What about you?'

'We had a German kid in our class at school. His dad was an engineer who worked for Parsons. He got some stick in school. It wasn't that long after the war, and kids used to stand outside the classroom and call him Hitler. But once in class the teacher asked him to read a poem out in German. I was bowled over. We became friends after that, and I learnt the poem. Didn't really know what it meant before. I just loved the sound of the words.'

They were silent, still eating, both aware that something had shifted between them. Frank, his grief an open wound, had let down his guard.

And then, as if grief hung heavy in the bushes, he pointed to a thorny, spindly bush.

'Five and a half years since my Abigail went. Planted it for her.'

'I bet it's lovely when it flowers.'

'Canny bush that, like. Doesn't look much now, but there's a mass of yellow flowers in the summer, an' all.'

There were a few brown leaves on the ground.

'I'll tidy it up a bit. Youse have to hold off pruning proper like until early spring.'

He raked up fading petals with his large capable hands, adding them to a cage of rotting leaf mould. And as if now that he'd started talking, he couldn't stop, he spoke about compost. And Charlie, who had never been remotely interested in such things, listened, entranced as he came alive.

'Amazing stuff, compost. All that lot'll break down. Become black and peaty, go back into the earth, and nourish it.' She saw worms wriggling in the compost bin, churning up vegetable cuttings and banana skins.

'In the spring we'll spread it on the soil. It'll be all crumbly and friable like, lovely.'

While everything looked dead, there would be work going on.

'I'll have to get a rose bush for Darren now.'

'Yes.'

Charlie held her jacket close, feeling useless.

Unlike Frank, she couldn't really do anything practical.

'Everyone underestimated our Darren. He was clever.'

'Nobody's saying he wasn't.'

'It's just school didn't suit him. Think he had a touch of that AD...'

'ADHD?'

'You know about that?'

'I know a bit. A student I used to support. Couldn't sit still, and would go from one task to another dead quick, he found it hard to concentrate.'

'Sounds like wor Darren. He often stayed up all night and then he'd be proper paggered next day. We tried talking to the teachers, but there were too many kids in that school with too many problems. There was only one teacher who liked him – the art teacher. He said she was mint and she called him really talented. And when he drew or painted he wasn't restless, he didn't fidget. It was like it calmed him. And films of course. He liked watching films. He always had since he was a bairn. When he was three I sat him doon and we watched *Dial M for Murder*. We used to discuss Hitchcock. He loved all the old films, bless him.'

Frank wiped his arm on his sleeve and pocketed his secateurs in an economical movement.

'He was my marra,' he added. 'I was the first one who held him.' He crossed his fingers. 'We were like that. When he was a bairn I was always the one who could calm him doon.'

'"Granda," he'd say. "I love you, Granda." And then the last words we had were an argument.'

Charlie snapped to.

'What? You never told us about that.'

'It would have blown over, like all these things. He was a hothead at times, too much temper for his own good, and I can be stubborn, my Abigail used to say.'

'What happened?'

74

Frank stared into space.

'He wanted me to lend him money. He wanted to leave school and as soon as he could, go down south, get a job. Said he wanted to be an artist. I said he had to stay at school, like, that his mum wanted him to. He knew I had some money put away. I'm on the pension, like, but I don't need much, he knew I'd cave in. I always gave in to Darren, he knew how to twist me round his little finger. But when I said I wouldn't, he stormed off, told me I was nothing but a radgie gadgie. And them words were the last we spoke.'

Frank turned away and brought his hand up to his eyes. She shifted round so that she couldn't see him. Let him have his privacy. He would hate her to see him crying.

And then he snapped to, as if nothing had been said. But something had. They'd argued. Could Frank have lost his temper completely with Darren? Frank was strong. She filed the question away and stood up.

'Aye, let's get on then. Do a bit more.'

He packed up the sandwich container and the flask. And then sat down again, seemingly exhausted. The grief was taking them like that, stopping and starting.

'A miss wor lad. I miss him.'

There was nothing to say. Then, as much to distract Frank as anything, she pointed at a shed on the other side of the allotment that caught her eye. Big and wooden, with Unit 14 painted on it, and a proper double-glazed window, as if it was a suburban house.

'You could practically live there. Who built it?'

Fred laughed, glad to take his mind off the previous conversation.

'Some Kosovan guy. Asylum seeker. Had to flee. I reckon he stays here some nights. You're not supposed to, but good on him, like. He's been here when I arrive really early sometimes. He likes growing pumpkins.'

Charlie took in his plot. Pumpkins, giant, like something out of a science-fiction film, plucked and laid on the ground, their skins hardening.

'He'll be popular at Halloween.'

She bit into the last chocolate biscuit, warmed her mouth with the last of her tea, and handed the cup to Frank. Simple pleasures.

She wondered if Di knew about the argument.

'She's not right,' Frank whispered, tuning into her thoughts. Charlie strained to hear. 'Don't think she'll ever be right again.' And then, 'Darren planted that plum tree.'

There was a bare stick of a bush to their right. Yellowed leaves, gnarled branches. 'Late summer it's laden with fruit. It's like the tree is drunk with them. They're the sweetest plums.'

'I like plums.' Charlie wanted to keep him talking. 'I tried to get Di to make jam,' she added, and they both laughed. The idea of Di making jam was ridiculous. The closest she got to jam was opening a jar.

Charlie put her hand on his taut strong arm and imagined sweetness taking away pain.

Frank raised his eyes.

'If I could get the bastard that did this.'

Charlie kept her hand on his arm, and squeezed it.

'We need to find out what happened. We need to tell the police everything.'

She bet he hadn't told them about the argument. But then Darren argued with everyone.

'We know what happened. Someone hit him on the head, and we can't rest until we find out who it was. You've got to help us, Charlie. You've got to. Di's no good on her own.'

'It's the police's job, not mine.'

'But you knew him. The police don't know him. And why did you buy a notebook if you're not going to use it, like?'

Charlie blushed. He was right.

'A young lad, that's all he was. Our lad. Yersel has gorra help us, Charlie.'

That prickle of excitement started up again. She wanted to do this. She wanted to find out what happened to Darren. She wanted to be good at something, finish it. In that moment Charlie made up her mind.

'OK,' she said. Then Frank did cry, and she patted his back, and soon they were packing up and he was telling her again about all the times Darren had visited the allotment.

'How am I going to do this?' Charlie wondered on the way to the gate. Frank hadn't told her everything yet. She'd question all the relatives. Murder was usually done by somebody close. Who would kill Darren?

But then, as they approached the gate, two things happened. Firstly, she saw a sign on the notice board which said 'Allotment under threat. Fight the redevelopment. Write to the Secretary of State.' She skimmed the leaflet next to it, which detailed plans for buying up the allotments and redeveloping the land for retail and residential use.

'Did you know about this, Frank?' she asked, noting down the date and time of the next allotment meeting.

He looked confused, like Di did nowadays if you presented her with new information.

'You have to get involved. Otherwise you could lose the allotment.'

Frank's face was blank. His concentration had gone. She'd remind him again later. People needed their allotments. Frank would collapse without his.

And the second thing that happened was that she saw a couple of young people up the far end of the allotment, where the couch grass was worst and blackberry bushes were thick and impenetrable. A boy and a girl, laughing, and the noise of the gate opening must have alerted them, because they looked over. The girl raised her hand in a friendly wave, and Charlie automatically waved back, following Frank's lead. The boy had his head turned away.

'Students,' said Frank. 'Nice kids. Some of the students used to have a kick-about with Darren, and they've got involved in the plans for the new community garden that Stella is organising. Good people, those kids.'

Right, thought Charlie. They would be first on her list. The police probably hadn't bothered with them. That's what detectives did – asked questions. She'd arrange to go and see them. Even the smallest bit of information could be useful. You had to start somewhere. *Neu beginnen.*

'Hang on,' she told Frank.

And that's how, a few minutes later, she had an appointment to see the pair of them the next day. She made a resolution to get a decent pen. For the first time since Darren's death, she felt hope stir. Yes, she thought, yes she would help Di and her family, do the last thing for Darren.

As the gate closed behind them, a mournful jangling reverberated through the allotment. The sun went in and the day turned cold. Charlie shivered. As if, like her granny used to say, someone had walked over her grave.

8

CHARLIE STOOD OUTSIDE the student house. Ivy over the windows, bins spilling out pizza boxes, a collection of beer bottles next to the bin, rubbish in the garden. Dead plants. Weak October sun filtered through thick but tatty charity shop curtains. Charlie sneezed. She always sneezed this time of year, as well as spring. A test had once confirmed what she suspected, and she was given a list of allergens to avoid. Life. In her bag were anti-histamines she took a few months every year.

Charlie remembered these types of houses; she'd lived in them herself. Whatever you did, you could never get the place clean enough. There was always dust in corners, spiders' webs, black mould behind the sink, and no matter how you scrubbed, the toilet still kept that brown stain. The communal areas had strange dust balls in them, scraps of paper. Water gurgled into a drain: someone was running a shower or the washing machine. So they were up. She needed to see them early before her two till ten this afternoon. She knocked firmly.

The girl was taller close up, pale skin, a few freckles, but good bones and teeth. Even dressed in an orange T-shirt with the name of a band Charlie had never heard of, and baggy jogging bottoms, she looked young and vital. She peered at Charlie, not unfriendly, just curious. Recognition dawned.

'From the allotment,' Charlie reminded her.

'I was with Frank.'

'Of course, I remembered you were coming.' The girl had a

good smile, guileless and trusting. 'How is Frank?'

Charlie shrugged her shoulders.

'You kind of took me by surprise yesterday. I didn't really get a chance to say, we were really sorry about what happened.'

'Thanks. As you can imagine, his mum's in a state. She's desperate to find out anything. Piece it all together, you know.'

'Of course, anything to help, but I don't know if we would be much use... Oh, sorry, do you want to come in? Where are my manners? My mother is always going on at me about not leaving people on the step. Come in, come in, excuse the mess. I'll just be a minute. I was taking Pete a cup of tea.'

'Pete?'

The girl smiled.

'From the allotment. We take it in turns to make tea. His chance for a lie-in. My seminar's not till twelve, and Pete's got afternoon classes. And facing the kitchen first thing in the morning can be a bit much. You never know what you might find.'

The kitchen was a spectacular mess, with food-encrusted dishes piled up in the sink, an overflowing bin, a dirty mop, dishcloths that gave off a musty odour even from a distance, a layer of crumbs on the floor, open cans of discarded beans and tuna, packets of cereal and used teabags.

'Are there just the two of you? I didn't catch your name.'

Charlie tried to gauge the relationship. The girl seemed protective, maybe even besotted with Pete.

'Lara. Sorry, I should have introduced myself. Pleased to meet you. Oh, and we're not a couple.' There was a wistful look on her face. Then she became business-like. 'We share with two medics. But they're hardly ever here. They often have to sleep over at the hospital Mind you, it can be handy having medics around.'

'Yes,' Charlie agreed, imagining free painkillers and plasters.

'Party animals, you know, and they always have plenty of cheap booze.'

Charlie smiled.

She sat down on the chair offered, and Lara presented her with tea in a stained mug, after shifting magazines and papers off the seat.

'I'll make myself respectable.'

When she returned her hair was dragged back in a bobble, and the shapeless sweater she'd pulled on matched the grey-blue of her eyes.

'Pete'll be here in a minute. You'll want to speak to him as well.'

'Sure.'

How to start? Charlie didn't really have anything prepared. The night before, she'd meant to sort a list of questions, but then she'd fallen asleep and there was no time.

Lara helped her out.

'Are you doing some kind of amateur detective thing? You don't trust the police to do their job properly? Checking up on what they might miss after all the miscarriages of justice in recent years?'

The girl was quick.

Charlie mumbled.

'How exciting. Sorry, I didn't mean it like that, the circumstances are awful. Of course we'll help. Don't tell Pete too much though, he thinks all that amateur stuff is rubbish. Says leave it to the experts. He's training to be a lawyer. And he'll point out that the police have been round already, asking us about Darren.'

'Did you know Darren?'

'I'd seen him with Frank a few times, but I didn't know his name. And then of course, there was the football.'

'Football?'

'Some students have a kick-about with local kids in the

park every Sunday during term. It's starting up again now.'

'Oh, yes, Frank mentioned it. Did either of you two ever join in that?'

'Me? No, my thing's running. And my family were rugby union.'

'What about Pete?'

'What about Pete?' and the lad was there himself, smaller than Lara, dark hair, skinny, neat, and smartly dressed.

'Remember, Pete's doing law,' Lara said, catching Charlie's glance. She was sharp. 'They all dress like that. Lawyers in waiting.'

There was affection in her voice, and the glance she gave Pete.

He was clutching a big cup of Earl Grey.

Charlie introduced herself as Lara refilled her mug. It was now or never. She plunged straight in: 'Were you ever involved in the kick-abouts last year?'

Puzzled, he turned to Lara.

'It's all right, Charlie's a friend of Di, who lost her son. Remember, she said yesterday. She's just poking around a bit for Di.'

'Oh, I wasn't really listening yesterday,' he said. 'I was thinking about my first essay. Have to do the reading, and the books in the library get taken out unless you order them. Anyway, aren't the police investigating?'

His mouth tightened in disapproval.

'Of course, I'm not stepping on their toes. It's just – you know how it is.'

His eyes darkened. Maybe he didn't.

'Di thought maybe the police had missed something,' Lara supplied.

He relaxed a little, running his eyes over Charlie and deciding she was harmless. She repeated her question.

'So were you involved in the kick-abouts?'

He held her gaze.

'I went once,' he said. 'But I've got too much work on with my course, and Thursdays weren't a particularly good day for me. Why are you asking these questions? The police have already been around.'

'Typical lawyer,' said Lara. 'Darren's mother needs to know as much as possible. There's no harm in asking questions. She's not going to get in the way of the police.' She smiled conspiratorially at Charlie.

'Of course not. And it was terrible what happened to Darren. Terrible.'

The way he said 'terrible'… Charlie, ever alert to accents, detected the North of Ireland.

'Are you from the North?'

He looked wary.

'I've got relatives over there.'

'Aye. Grew up on the Ards Peninsula, County Down.'

'Oh, whereabouts?'

As soon as he named the village she saw Union Jacks painted on the paving stones, 'The End is Nigh' daubed on planks of wood nailed to trees, alongside 'Prepare to meet thy doom,' and 'God is a jealous god' in the peaceful, fuchsia-hedged lanes.

'Pretty round there,' was all she managed. He grunted.

'What about Darren? Did you meet him at football?'

'I might have done.' He paused to consider. 'Quite a big lad, so he was?'

She let it go. By no stretch of the imagination could Darren have been called a big lad.

'And how about at the allotment?'

When he smiled, he looked much younger, and his colour was good.

'The allotment's more Lara's thing.'

'I've managed to drag you along a few times, and sure,

83

we saw Darren there, with his granddad. They gave us a few seedlings.' She punched him affectionately in the ribs. The way she'd said 'sure' was how people from the North said it. Lara had taken on some of his speech patterns, the way people grew into one another. Charlie heard her aunt's voice, and felt her own accent edging closer to his. Every summer when she went over to the North as a child, she became more Irish, every autumn returned to being English.

'I didn't really notice him, sure,' said Pete. 'Lara's the one with the green fingers. I was probably too busy trying to make sure my seedlings didn't shrivel up and die, so I was.'

'I'm the same, so I am,' said Charlie, the idiom slipping out before she could stop it. He'd probably close up on her, think she was taking the piss. They were all smiling, but the word 'die' resonated rounded the kitchen.

Charlie kept on.

'Were you two on the search?'

'I was,' said Lara. 'Anything to help.'

'I wasn't able to,' said Pete. 'As I said, I have this essay coming up. I heard there were a lot of people.'

Lara was wriggling around in her chair. She seemed antsy.

'Yeah, this young policeman knocked at the door and asked did we want to help out: "Young eyes, and all that." He was quite dishy really, only a few years older than us. Could have almost fancied him. I blanked him of course. I'd never be able to go out with a policeman, not the way my parents brought me up. I wanted to question him, ask him what he felt like being an arm of the capitalist war machine, but Pete here just said, "Of course, officer, certainly, officer, we'll come along if we can." Turned out he couldn't, he had to go the library. My knees are still sore from all that crawling. And my shoulders. I came back and fell into bed. Sorry, I really need a fag. Do you mind?'

Charlie shook her head, and watched as Lara expertly

rolled a thin cigarette.

'Want one?'

'No, thanks.' Years since she'd smoked, and she had no desire now.

'Pass me one over,' said Pete.

'Are you sure?' Lara seemed surprised, but rolled one. He took the spindly tube eagerly, inhaled too deeply, coughed, and left it burning between his fingers.

'I've never seen you smoke.'

'Well, there you go then. I did once.'

He inhaled more steadily.

'When?'

'While I was away.'

'When?'

'It doesn't matter when, sure.'

'You told me they disapproved of smoking where you came from, especially for women.'

'I said it came with the territory. It was just the way I was brought up. Women were frowned on if they smoked in public. Although my mother indulges at times. Not sure if my da knows or not.'

He stopped talking suddenly, as if he had said too much. Charlie stayed quiet. Wasn't that how you found out about things? People letting out information they didn't think was important? She'd write it all down later. She was too embarrassed to get her amateur notebook out now. They probably had proper student notebooks, and neat handwriting. When she'd scribed for students, some had complicated colour-coded filing systems. She always had to type up her incoherent scrawls.

They continued talking as if Charlie wasn't there. She got the feeling that Lara was using Charlie's presence as a chance to ask questions of Pete she wouldn't normally ask.

'You hardly ever talk about your family,' the girl said.

'Not much to say.'

'And I'm sure your accent's toned down since you came here.'

'It happens. Had no choice. No one could understand me.'

Lara shrugged, and began talking to herself more than anyone, dragging on her cigarette. 'Sorry about the smoking. Disgusting habit, really. My parents are always going on about it. And I'm going on, aren't I? My mother said I should have been born on a soapbox.'

'I'm sure your parents are very proud of you. Remind me what you are studying.'

'History.'

'Must be fun.'

Lara looked grateful for her intervention.

'Yes, but of course I had to do the opposite of what they suggested. Plants are more my thing, and they encouraged me to apply for horticulture. But I went for history. And they were right; it's mostly about those in power. But you have to learn about those in power if you want to change things. Don't you think?'

Charlie didn't have an answer ready.

'Oh, sorry, I'm going on again,' said Lara, laughing. 'My mother says I have to stop ramming my views down people's throats. Let people make their own minds up.'

Charlie cleared her throat. The interview was running away from her. She'd found out nothing.

'So coming back to Darren. Is there anything else either of you could tell me? Anything at all? You never know when something might be useful.'

Pete suddenly came alive, drumming his fingers together and leaning forward in his chair: 'I did see Darren with someone once. A man.'

'I thought you didn't know who Darren was?' Lara's tone was surprised.

'I presume it was him, up near his granda's allotment. And his granda was there. I didn't really know it was Darren at the time.'

Charlie sat up straight, alert. Lara got in first.

'I never saw him with anyone,' she said, sharply.

'It was that time in spring when you nipped back home to pick up some seeds.'

'Did you tell the police?' asked Charlie.

'They didn't ask.'

'You should. What did he look like, this man?'

He turned face on.

'Quite a big man, I'd say. Dark hair, curly. Kind of intense-looking.'

Michael was tall, with dark curly hair and was kind of intense looking.

'Would you be able to identify him?' Charlie could tell the police to follow this up; she could phone up anonymously, she could...

'I wouldn't have thought so,' he said, as if he was reconsidering what he'd said. 'It was far away, you know.'

'So how could you tell that he was intense looking?' Nothing escaped Lara.

'It was just an impression, sure.'

Charlie made a mental note: *Ask around, see if anyone else saw Darren with a man.*

Pete took another drag of his cigarette, and coughed, his face flushing as he caught his breath.

'That'll teach you,' said Lara, laughing.

'Well, I'm away off then,' he said, recovering himself, and stubbing the cigarette out on a saucer. 'Sorry I couldn't be any more help, but I've got to keep on with the reading for this essay: *At what point do public and private ethics coincide?*

'Jesus,' said Lara. She blew smoke from the side of her mouth. 'Charlie, I don't mean to rush you, but is there anything else? It's just we've both got things on, and I must have a shower.'

Charlie gave them her phone number, and Lara pinned it on an ancient noticeboard on the kitchen wall, full of takeaway cards and the programme for the local cinema.

Charlie shook hands with each of them. Make physical contact, establish a bond. Lara's grip was light and cool, but Pete's hands were clammy.

Cold hands, warm heart.

'Thanks, you've been really helpful. And for the tea.'

'No problem.'

Lara bounded up.

'I've got to get ready now.'

She lifted jeans from the back of a chair and plucked socks off a radiator.

'OK if I use the loo?' Charlie asked.

Lara nodded.

'First on the left upstairs.' She was distracted now, piling papers and pens into a bag.

Detectives always snooped in bathrooms. See if she could salvage something from the trip. There was a door open next to the bathroom. She glanced in. Comfy but tatty. Obviously Lara's room. Posters, plants, clothes on the floor. The door next to it was shut. She pushed it open. In this room the duvet was neatly arranged, books carefully positioned. Tidy as a monk's cell. *Or a prison cell,* the thought came. There was a photograph in a frame of a good-looking woman, dark hair and a heart-shaped face, together with a younger version of Pete. You could see the likeness between them. Taken about four years ago, she reckoned. They were perched on a garden wall.

Suddenly she felt an arm on her shoulder, and smelt tobacco breath. Pete, close to her face. Fine-featured, like his mother, dark hair.

'Can I help you?'

'Oh, sorry, I was looking for the bathroom.'

He pointed across. Sheepishly she started for it.

'Is that your mum?'

'Aye,' he said, his voice cold.

'She looks lovely,' Charlie said foolishly, as he waited for her to close the bathroom door.

Back downstairs, the door banged as Pete left.

Lara, who seemed to have forgotten about the shower, had her shoes on, but no longer seemed in a hurry. She relaxed against a kitchen chair.

'That was a terrible day that, the day of the search,' she said, picking up the conversation. 'Sorry, what am I saying; of course it was a terrible day, especially for your friend. What am I thinking of?'

Charlie warmed to Lara. She was rather refreshing. It was a relief to be around someone who wasn't po-faced, pussyfooting around death. Everyone was tip-toeing round Di. This young woman seemed to say the first thing that came into her head. Charlie wanted to sit for a while, be young again, fancy free. But she dragged herself up.

She was heading for the door when she remembered about the development plans. Probably nothing to do with anything. But you never knew when the smallest clue might turn out to be significant.

'What about the plans to build on the allotments?'

'Oh, you've heard about them?'

'I saw the notice pinned up there.'

'Well, we've just got to stop them, haven't we? It's going to be a long hard fight. It has to go to the Secretary of State. More and more allotments are getting threatened. They just have to offer you somewhere else, or show that there isn't much of a need. They can't just fob us off with a community garden, which is what they're doing. A community garden will be nice, but it's not the same, there's not enough space. And you know allotments have a lot of legal protection behind them, Pete says. Although he did say we shouldn't stand in the way of progress, whatever that means. It's not progress, taking something away. A community garden, if they wanted to change it into a car park, there would be nothing to stop them in the future. Anyway, for people like Frank, the allotments are a lifeline.'

'And for you?'

Lara smiled a proper smile.

'I've faced up to the fact that plants are my thing. I'm doing a part-time horticulture course. And I was planning on planting an apple tree, and a gooseberry bush. Fruit bushes look after themselves. And last forever. Although nothing lasts forever, does it?'

There was a moment of silence between them. Then Lara good-naturedly bundled Charlie out the door, and waved her off. Charlie clutched her notebook, ready to write down her observations before they floated off, forgotten.

9

BACK IN WORK everything seemed pointless. It was early evening and she was on two till ten, as was Martin. Unusual. Charlie liked Martin better at night: he was less in your face, less intrusive somehow, as if the night diluted him. And the men were all getting on her nerves. She should be following things up, finding things out. On the allotment she'd been filled with new energy, but now she felt drained, sapped of initiative. She did her job, dealing with the men's complaints about the lack of hot water, and dirty dishes in the sink; she drank the coffee that Martin made.

Late afternoon Eddie came out of his room and into the lounge. He had a cold and had spent the day in bed, and sat with her in silence, doing a jigsaw puzzle of Tottenham Court Road, with the stereotypical London bus and the policeman in a bobby hat and the Post Office Tower in the background, the streets full of tourists and bookshops and cafes, stalls with clothes and cheap jewellery displays. Eddie loved jigsaws. He had one of the Eiffel Tower. That was difficult. And the Leaning Tower of Pisa. What was it with towers? And jigsaws? On his room wall he had a photograph of a completed jigsaw of the statue of Christ the Redeemer in Rio de Janeiro. Jigsaws bored Charlie silly. Fit one bit of cardboard to another. When the scene was completed, throw all the pieces in the box and start again. But it was soothing to sit with Eddie as he scanned pieces, closed his eyes, and visualised the whole scene. She'd fit the occasional piece in – a corner or a top or bottom edge, or an especially brightly coloured piece that was obvious, like the red and green of the traffic lights.

'You only see parts,' said Eddie. 'I can see the whole image in my head. Ever since I were a kid, I've been able to do that.'

She let him talk, even though she'd heard it all before.

'My step-mother would send me upstairs to be quiet while she poured her first gin. And I'd work on my jigsaws. Hours would go by. I heard my stepmother once telling my father that there was something wrong with me, that I was simple. But she didn't understand.'

'Your grandmother liked jigsaws, didn't she Eddie?'

'Aye, she did.'

Eddie always said that with no mother around, his grandmother was the only one who understood him. She'd died in a fire in mysterious circumstances, and shortly afterwards his father had remarried. And then the fires became regular, with Eddie stealing his stepmother's matches. Small fires at first, out in the yard; progressing to more serious ones that damaged property, until eventually he was caught.

Charlie watched Eddie, as, quiet and patient, he gazed at the board, holding a corner piece in his hand. Nothing made any sense. Most of these men were bastards. But Eddie wasn't a bastard; he was a likeable guy with an unfortunate habit of setting fire to things.

'You're quiet today, Eddie. Anything wrong?'

He rolled his eyes.

'Anyone bothering you?' There'd been periods when Eddie was bullied. There was something about Eddie that was ripe for bullying, as if he had a sign painted in the middle of his forehead: 'Kick me now.' More than once they'd had words with the other men over Eddie.

He shrugged.

'Was it Carl or Nick? They'll be leaving soon, you know.'

Both were getting transferred to a hostel nearer their home

towns, down south.

He shook his head.

'Dave?'

He snorted. 'Dave wouldn't hurt anyone.'

'Except himself,' Charlie thought. And she couldn't tell Eddie, but Dave was almost certainly getting recalled to prison. 'Someone else?'

He mumbled.

After a cup of tea, she wangled it out of him. Michael had been saying things.

'What things?'

He wouldn't tell her any more, and concentrated on the pieces. She made a mental note to keep an eye on Michael. Michael was tall, with dark curly hair. Could he be the one Pete had seen Darren with? How was she going to follow up what Pete had said? But it was irrational to go round accusing Michael of things because she didn't like him.

She was refilling her cup in the kitchen when she smelt Michael. He had a distinctive, almost chemical aroma, overlaid with pine deodorant. And then he was in front of her, and spoke before she could make a comment.

'They let us go early.'

It was 4.30. Was that true? She could phone up to check. But she was too tired to go through the rigmarole. The hostel debilitated you.

Others trickled in as the afternoon wore on. Donny took his law books into the lounge after a bowl of soup; Graham demolished fish and chips and turned on a quiz show. The smell of grease lingered. Michael made his healthy eating 'my body is a temple' concoction, and went on about 'that Marco Pierre White. Uses a bit too much cream for my liking.' Charlie didn't know what he was talking about. She zoned out.

At nine she was on duty in the common room and there were still a few men with the TV on, Michael amongst them. The nine o'clock news came on, followed by a local bulletin. The news wasn't popular, but Donny always caught it, and Graham, who would sit mesmerised in front of any programme.

Suddenly her attention was fixed on Di on screen, standing next to a policeman reading out a statement.

'Police are still pursuing a number of leads in the tragic case of Darren Pearson, the 15-year-old boy who lost his life in Heaton Park, and are appealing to any member of the public with further information to please come forward.'

Di was made up to the nines. You could see wrinkles round her eyes through the make-up. Her hair was swept back in a way Charlie had never seen before and she wore an unfortunately short skirt which exposed her substantial thighs. She kept hitching it up. Her skin looked an unhealthy yellow.

'Look at that fat cow flirting with the presenter. Slag.' Michael almost spat the words out.

'Easy,' said Charlie. The last thing she wanted was a run-in with him tonight.

'Well, see her now, fat cow, her son got bloody murdered and she doesn't seem bothered. He's hardly dead in the ground and see the state of her, bloody eyelashes and lipstick and everything. Fuckin' slag.'

Who did he think he was? 'Just keep your mouth shut, Michael. Don't talk about women like that.'

'Why, what's it to you? She a friend of yours or something?'

Charlie felt herself colouring.

'She is. Well, well. You could have done better there. She looks like a right loser.'

Charlie said nothing.

They watched Di mouth words that somebody else seemed to have written, about the police needing to 'step up to the mark'. Under questioning from the bald-headed reporter, who thrust a microphone under her chin, she said that she wasn't sure the police were doing enough.

'Are you confident that the police will catch the right person?'

Di faltered, but was whisked away before she could answer, and the camera moved back to the reporter.

'Bloody rubbish.'

'What do you mean?' Charlie turned to Michael.

'It was obvious that guy had nothing to do with it. I don't know why they arrested him in the first place. And now that they've let him go the case is wide open again. They haven't got any more leads. For God's sake, that guy confesses to anything. He confessed to robbing that horse and riding it into the supermarket last year. Thinks he's bloody Robin Hood.'

Charlie forced a smile back, but said, 'Don't you think the police might know what they're doing?'

The face he pulled gave her the answer. 'No. And neither do you.'

She blushed again, annoyed at her face betraying her. Graham and Donny had gone to bed. There was only an hour left of her shift. She needed to sleep. She could lie in tomorrow, before she started a run of night shifts.

'Besides, I might know something about it.'

'Might?'

'I might have seen something. I see things, you know.'

'Don't we all?'

'But I saw something'.

'What?'

'What would you give me for it?'

Charlie drew herself up, and tried to assert herself. Be professional. It was probably bravado on his part, but still, she needed to find out if he did know anything.

'Michael John Faseby. If you know anything that will help solve the murder of Darren, you have to go the police.'

'No, I don't.'

'You do. It's your duty.'

'My duty? Since when have I had a duty to the police? All they've ever done is lock me up and harass me. They wouldn't believe me. An ex-con, with my record? I'm saying nothing. I'm off to read a recipe book.'

Later, as she packed her bag, Charlie heard whimpering, and found Eddie in the common room crying over the scattered pieces of his jigsaw. When she asked who had done it, he kept repeating,

'Hate that bastard. Wanna kill him.'

The look on his face was awful. For the first time she wondered: was even Eddie capable of murder?

10

FRIDAY 4 OCTOBER

AN OPPORTUNITY TO find out more came the next day when she was called in at the last minute to do an 8-4 shift before starting nights. Charlie had slept, so she didn't feel too bad, and she could nip home to change and shower and eat with Casey before the night shift. Martin was called in as well. The arrangement suited Charlie. She needed the money, and besides, she didn't really want to go to Di's today. It was wearing her out. And Casey was like a ghost, they might as well not be living in the same house.

She phoned Di's and told an outright lie that she was 'following something up.' Di sounded pleased, or drunk.

'I'm going to start arranging the funeral. Suzy said she'll give me a hand. I'll let you know when I'm sorted.' That cow Suzy, mooning round, putting her oar in. This made Charlie more determined to continue investigating. She checked her notebook. Still no decent pen.

It was quiet in the day with most of the men in work. Really there wasn't much to do. Martin was off in the common room: a couple of the men were in bed with flu. They didn't need her. But regulations said two staff had to be on duty at all times, in case of emergencies. She was looking through the rotas and the day books, and then, without really thinking about it, started tracing back through the weeks. The day Darren was found, the 22nd, Michael was in the hostel with everyone else. She went further back. 15 September, the day Darren went off to Brighton. She checked it against the men's records. Michael was signed out for work as usual, and returned on time. *But that didn't mean anything*, a small voice in her head said. Working in a kitchen they had split shifts. He could have left work and gone back without anybody noticing. Had anybody gone over his breaks? There were a few hours missing. Maybe he had seen something before Darren left. And because of her promise to Di and because she needed to do something, it seemed as good an idea as any to go and see Michael's employers. Start somewhere. What did Sherlock Holmes say? Eliminate the impossible? What's left, however improbable, must be the truth? She knew Michael was at college today. Great. He wouldn't be around.

'I've got to go out.'

Martin didn't even raise his head. He never asked questions. 'It's a quiet day, but don't be too long. Back by 1.30. I'll need a hand.'

The restaurant was a bus ride across town, in an old cobbled street near the quayside, surrounded by clubs and bars. Quiet now, but at the weekend this place would be heaving.

There was no answer at the restaurant side door, but a light was on, so she kept on knocking until a sleepy-looking guy in a chef's hat came outside, rolling a cigarette.

'Yes?' His tone was curt, the door open only a crack.

'Friendly, aren't you? Can I come in?'

'We're closed.'

'I can see that.'

'There's no jobs. I've got my full quota.' He looked her up and down. Obvious from his expression she didn't seem high end enough to be a chef, and she was too old to be a minion.

'I don't want a job.'

'What do you want?'

'I just want to ask a few questions.'

'What about? Who are you? The police? They've gone

downhill.'

She let that go. No point antagonising him straight away.

'Immigration? Everyone I've taken on is legit, they've got papers.'

'No, not immigration. I work at Orchard House.'

His face lightened.

'Oh, Michael? No trouble, I hope? He's a good worker, that lad, I'm pleased with him. Glad I decided to give him a chance.'

'Nothing to worry about. I just need to make sure our paperwork's in order.'

He sized her up again, and opened the door wider.

'Come in then, pet,' he said in a friendlier tone. 'Coffee?'

She nodded.

He checked the cobbled street as if someone else might be lurking, and closed the door.

The kitchen was clean and scrubbed. An evil looking collection of knives on a knife block was the first thing that hit you. He saw her glance.

'They're always supervised, the trainees. So what do you need to know? The police have already been round. It's about that lad, is it not, the one that was killed?'

She ignored his question.

'I want to make sure of something.'

'Michael's a grafter, a good worker. Proper interested in food. He suggested doing the herbs.'

She followed the direction of his eyes to a neat row of herbs in pots catching the light from the window.

There was a faint tinge of Yorkshire in the man's voice, although he had the sing-song Geordie cadence.

The kitchen was bright with fluorescent lights. A multi-coloured collection of chopping boards was lined up on the counter, pots and pans hung from hooks, a massive mixing bowl, a collection of small bowls, and a giant jar of green olives occupied the table. Different oils and vinegars were arranged neatly near the catering size cooker, and garlic hung in a rope.

'I know he's good with food.'

'I don't see you making any notes.'

She rummaged in her bag and took out the notebook. He smirked, saw that her pen wasn't working properly, and handed over one which said 'Phoenix Services.' They could have been a laundry company. She wrote the date neatly at the top of the page, Michael's full name and work address and his occupation. The restaurant was called 'Phoenix.' The man's name badge said Stuart Jones. She wrote that. She wondered what services they offered. Maybe outside catering. She tried to look intelligent, pen poised.

'Nobody told me you were coming.'

'Last minute.'

'You're supposed to warn us. You canna just turn up.'

'Thanks for letting me in.'

'We might be in the middle of something.'

'I know.'

'And have these men not served their time? What's with harassing them, like?'

'I'm not harassing. I need to check a few things.'

'I would have thought you of all people believed in second chances.'

Charlie blushed. Truth was, she wasn't sure anymore. Were the men in the hostel worth saving? Donny, and Dave, and Graham? Eddie? Michael? Would they change?

'How long have you been in the job?' There was a touch of sympathy in his voice now, professional to professional.

'Too long,' she grinned. 'About that coffee?'

And then he poured two cups of wonderful smelling coffee from an espresso maker, and expertly pushed one along to her without spilling a drop, together with milk, sugar, a spoon and a wrapped café au lait biscuit.

She spooned two sugars in. The coffee was divine.

'Delicious, isn't it?'

'Mmm.'

'I keep the good stuff for first thing in the morning before the others arrive, and last thing at night. In the day we drink instant shit.'

The coffee seemed to loosen his tongue.

'So you want to know about Michael?'

'That's what I said. Just a routine check to make sure he's doing OK, that we made the right decision sending him here. Paperwork, evaluations, you know.'

The man looked sceptical, but shrugged his shoulders, his mind on other things.

'You don't mind if I smoke?'

'Go ahead.'

'We'll have to open the door. Health and safety and all that. Smoke alarms.'

'Of course.'

She suspected he would have smoked in the kitchen after disconnecting the smoke alarm if she hadn't arrived. That was why he'd been so sharp with her at first, looking forward to his first fag of the day before the trainees turned up.

He stood against the door, blowing smoke into the street. There was the loud chatter of schoolkids near the bus stop. Wasn't it late to be going to school? Up the street was the drone and whistle of a bin lorry, and the sound of a digger in the distance. A man ran past, holding on to a Rottweiler on a lead. It was cold with the door open, a wind funnelling up from the river. She shivered.

'You know he's on day release at college today?'

'Of course.'

'That's why you came. You don't want him to know you're here.'

She sipped her coffee and gestured for a refill.

As he made another cup, he confessed, 'Well, I must admit I wasn't sure about him at first. He's a bit of a smug bastard.'

She smiled.

'Thinks he's better than everybody else. That he's the only one who does everything right.'

She nodded. The placement had been arranged by a worker who'd since left. Martin was his key worker, but as Martin never did anything if he could help it, she didn't know if all the checks were up to date. Michael could have been roaming free for months. Martin was not above fiddling the notes.

The guy blew out a long stream of smoke, finished his cigarette, stamped it into the ground and shut the door. Instant quiet.

'I've taken quite a few ex-cons.'

'That's good.' She stopped herself adding 'Stuart'.

'They're always good workers. Want to prove they've changed, like.'

She nodded, encouraging him.

'And the way I look at it; you can't give up on people, can you? I mean, what are we supposed to do with people? Lock them up and throw away the key?'

Charlie said nothing.

'Have you ever been in trouble?'

She shook her head, remembering the one time her punk friend had stolen a car and they'd roared through the night streets. The power they felt. Lucky they hadn't killed anyone. Or themselves.

'It's easy to fall through the net. I was in trouble mesel when I was younger.'

She wasn't surprised. He had the wariness of someone who had been inside. You could never allow yourself to totally relax inside; you always had to be looking over your shoulder.

'Most people have something in their past,' she said.

It sounded patronising. He ignored it.

'Nothing major, you know, just a bit of breaking and entering, burglary.'

She muttered.

'I was lucky. I wasn't a very good criminal. I got caught. Best thing that happened to me. And a probation officer who gave a shit. Do they still have them jobs?'

'Some.'

She looked closely at his face . There were fine lines round his eyes, and his lips were puckered. Mid to late forties.

'Signed me up for this scheme. A police guy ran it, getting the kids involved in football and youth clubs. Cooking and stuff. Give us badges.'

She laughed.

'It worked. I decided I was better at cooking than burglary. I remember that policeman sitting me down. He says, "Lad, you're never going make a master criminal. How about going after a chef job?" So I did my City and Guilds, and here I am.'

'I'm glad it worked out for you. What about Michael? Do you think he's doing OK?'

'He's doing champion at the cooking, if that's what you mean. A quick learner, an' all, tidy, organised and neat.'

What wasn't he saying? She'd have to get back soon. The lunch rota would be underway.

'But?'

He smiled.

'He's not the most likeable.'

You can say that again.

'A good worker. Learnt all kinds. Never lets us down. Well, mebbe hardly ever.'

'What do you mean, hardly ever?'

'There was the one time he turned up late.'

She paused, her pen over her notebook.

'When?'

'I don't know. Not long ago. I wasn't checking the rota that week.'

'Who was?'

'A temporary. They just told me he was a bit late. Said he was in a traffic jam.'

'He gets a bus.'

'Well, the bus was in a traffic jam. I don't know. The police came and went through the records.'

'So you don't mind if I look?'

'Not at all. The police already did.'

The rota and log book – hand-written, scratty affairs – didn't tell them much. Sunday 15 September: Michael was a few minutes late. Darren's mate said they hadn't left for Brighton until the afternoon. Where had Darren been before that? 'Traffic jam due to road works' was written in neat handwriting under 'Reason for lateness.' What could that prove? Nothing. It would be easy enough for the police to check if any buses were involved in a traffic jam that morning, easy enough to see if there were road works. The police would have done that. Wouldn't they?

So what was Michael on about? He'd said he knew something, that he'd seen something.

'And since then?'

'No trouble at all. All he's really interested in is food and getting on. I'm very pleased with him. I would say he's a pleasure to work with.'

'Except he's not.'

'As I said, not the most likeable.'

Slimy bastard, more like, she kept to herself.

'Has he ever said anything about…?'

She tailed off. They weren't supposed to talk about their crimes.

'About what he did?'

'Do you know what he did?'

The man looked away.

'I made it my business to find out. I know what he actually got done for, but I also know what he's supposed to have done. I've got a daughter out there somewhere. Haven't seen her for years. Still. I told Michael.' He drew himself up to his full height, exposing his sallow skin and spots. 'I said if there was ever anything. I mean anything…' And the way he emphasised 'anything' gave her a glimpse of the man he could be, not to be messed with. 'That he was out. "Understand," I said to him? "Out."'

And she believed him. An ex-con had too much at stake. He needed to keep himself squeaky clean.

'Did you ever talk about what happened to Darren?'

'What do you think ex-cons talk about? Crime, of course. Of course we did. We all thought it terrible, him only 15 and all. Poor lad.'

Her coffee was finished. She put the cup down; he swept it up and into the dishwasher, and gave the counter a quick wipe.

'Did Michael say anything?'

'Not much. But I do remember him saying that they hadn't got the right person when they first arrested that man. And he said it right forcefully, as if he knew what he were talking about.'

The man's voice was pure Yorkshire now.

'What do you mean?'

'I asked him how he knew, and he just said, "Obvious. It's always someone what knows them." And he were right, weren't he? They let him go, no case to answer. It's usually the step-father or someone. Remember that case up in Sunderland where the step-father looked heartbroken at the press conference, and then they found out later that he had chopped the girl up and hidden her body?'

Charlie was pondering his words. It usually was someone close to home. She'd have to methodically go through all the family.

The man spied the time on the wall clock, and stood up.

'I've got to get on; the trainees arrive at ten, must set up their stations.'

She thanked him for his time, and excused herself. He waved her away.

All the way back she thought about Michael. Did he know something? And was he the person Pete had seen all those months ago?

On the bus she made herself a list, with columns. On one side she put Family, on the other Friends. Divided it up further. Mother. Brother. Girlfriend. Grandfather. Friends from school.

Back at the centre, the few men in were eating lunch, and those who worked locally had returned for a sandwich.

A phone call came from Di.

'Can you come round when you finish work?'

'What's wrong?'

'Nothing. Got fed up of Suzy helping. She was useless. That guy she found us, I didn't like him. All lanky and miserable-looking. Kept talking about the 'remains' and the 'arrangements' and the 'deceased', as if he couldn't say Darren's name. Too serious for me.'

'I'm a bit busy.'

Di never did understand that other people had things to do.

'Well, this is it, my neighbour she suggested someone else. It would be great if you could come over. Said when her auntie died, this funeral guy was brilliant. He's coming round at five. Can you make it? Local firm, you know, the neighbour said he couldn't do enough for them.'

Charlie agreed. She'd have time to go to Di's before nipping home and returning for the night shift. Anything for a quiet life.

'See you.'

She shared a salmon roll with Martin, and while they were eating the kitchen filled with acrid smoke and the smell of burning. One of the men came rushing in, to scrape burnt toast and throw the rest in the bin. Long after they'd opened the windows and put the fan on high the smell of burning lingered.

11

THE FUNERAL GUY, who introduced himself as Richard, was smiley, with wild grey curls and a suit the right side of crumpled, a slight paunch, and wide hands with clean short nails. She and Di perched near him, and James ensconced himself in a corner, with his arms wrapped round himself.

Richard sat wriggling in Di's living room on one of the so-called comfy chairs, looking too big for it. He listened. He nodded along, mirroring body movements: leaned forward, and held his hands together, as if in prayer, expressing sympathy with his eyes. Like a sponge, he absorbed their pain.

He was brilliant with Di.

'Have you thought about what Darren will wear? If you're not ready, no problem yet, there's plenty of time.'

And the way he said 'Darren' as if he were still a person, still present and alive, brought a catch to their throats.

In that room, caught in the limbo between death and the funeral, with the heating turned up full, they had nothing but time. Time stretched out in front of them, to be got through. How did people go on? Charlie wondered. If it had been Casey… She turned away from the thought.

His psychology was great. Get Di to concentrate on the specific. For a second there was panic in Di's eyes, but Richard's presence soothed her, and her breathing slowed.

'I haven't had a chance to go through his things. I need to sort them out.' She threw her arms out, appealing to Charlie.

Charlie's chin slumped into her chest. Yes, she owed Di. But how long did she have to go on paying her friend back?

Richard smiled.

'There's always a lot for your friends and family to do. It's hard for them as well.'

Di sat up, alert now, taking this in, as if she'd never thought that other people might be affected.

'He was always wearing his Newcastle kit, but it needs a wash.'

Richard cupped his tea.

'There's a stain round the back: grass, I think. He used to tackle hard, James said. I haven't got any stain remover.'

Richard held his expression, seeming to understand that finding stain remover was beyond her.

'I want Darren to look his best.'

'Of course,' he agreed: the most natural and important thing in the world.

'Bring it to us,' he said, 'we'll launder Darren's kit. No problem.' There was something soothing about the word 'launder'. Clever, this man. He could have said 'wash'. But no, 'launder' was the word he'd chosen. Charlie wondered about his home life. Did he go home and shout at a partner, yell at his kids? Or was he kind to them, knowing that things could change in an instant, that you could be dead?

'I'm here to do whatever you want,' this Richard said. He looked like a Richard. Richard, Richard, she repeated to herself, trying to imprint his name. Nothing stuck anymore. Facts floated across her mind, and were lost. There was silence as they contemplated what he'd said. He couldn't do whatever they wanted. He couldn't bring Darren back. He couldn't make everything normal again.

'Within reason, of course,' he said, picking up on the mood. 'Maybe not a roller disco.'

And then they were all laughing, as if it was the funniest joke in the world, and natural to laugh. Darren would have been laughing, and taking the piss, telling them to stop being so po-faced and serious. Darren would have been the first one cracking jokes.

And then they were on to cremation or burial and Di said straight away she didn't want Darren lying in a hole in the ground with worms and insects. He nodded, asking if they wanted a double spot in the crematorium: 'Forty minutes instead of twenty? And will you be hiring a church as well as the crem? You have to give them notice. Do you want a priest or a minister delivering the eulogy?'

Di turned to Charlie: 'What about you, Charlie? You're his godmother, you could say something. Didn't you used to be good at public speaking; you won that prize once at school when you were a teenager.'

Charlie was sorry she had ever mentioned that to Di. A public speaking contest against a Welsh comprehensive: 'This house thinks that all children should learn a second language at primary school.'

Charlie, always envious of friends with parents from somewhere else, and the ability to speak another language, argued passionately for it.

The Welsh kid, with Liverpudlian parents who had forced her to go to a Welsh-speaking school, was against the motion: 'I've had bloody Welsh rammed down my throat since I was knee high. What good's that gonna do in the wider world? The only place they speak Welsh outside Wales is some small place in Patagonia. Who wants to go to Patagonia? I would rather have waited until later and learnt French and Spanish and German and Italian, languages that don't sound like you are clearing your throat.'

Charlie won, and had a gold plated trophy somewhere in a suitcase. She'd made the mistake of showing it to Di once.

'Best public speaker' and 'Siaradwr cyhoeddus Gorau' were written side by side.

She'd rarely spoken in public since.

'That was ages ago,' she said feebly.

'But me and James will be no good, will we? We won't be able to speak. We might not even be able to stand.'

'And what makes you think I'll be able to do it?' Even as Charlie said it, she knew she'd agree. There was no one else. Sean's funeral had passed in a blur, and she'd always wished she'd done something more personal. Some priest she didn't even know, who had got Sean's middle name – Aloysius – wrong, mouthed sanctimonious pieties, and then to crown it most of their friends didn't know the words to the hymns. Embarrassing.

'I would be there to support you.' Richard again. And suddenly, she wanted to fold into this guy's arms, and have him support her. She'd been responsible for herself for so long.

She grunted, and they took this as a yes, and before she had a chance to back down they were on to how many cars and did they want to see Darren in the Chapel of Rest. Yes, said Di.

An hour had gone by when Charlie went to refill the kettle. Di followed her into the kitchen, and perched on a stool.

'I like this guy,' Di said. 'He's all right. I didn't like that last one.'

Charlie hadn't liked the sound of him either.

Charlie brought in another tray of tea and biscuits. She'd eaten so many biscuits lately; she'd be the size of a house soon.

'Do you have any more questions?' Richard asked, taking a hearty slug of his tea. For a man who worked around death, Charlie thought, he was in the world.

'My head's all over the place, but we'll probably think of something after you go,' Charlie answered for both.

'Not to worry, you can phone me. I'll leave my card. Contact me any time, day or night.'

'I'm not sure about this speaking.'

He sized her up frankly, the way a baby takes in the essence of you.

'You'll be fine. People often find it helps, the more actively they participate.'

'What about you? What will you be doing?'

He smiled kindly, keeping a steady gaze. She wondered for a minute if he could see a person's character when they were dead. Did you get a sense of who they were?

His eyes were a lovely dancing blue. He was quite fanciable. The thought surprised Charlie. She hadn't allowed herself to fancy anyone for ages.

'My job would be to look after Darren, and to take some of the weight off the family and friends, supporting you in any way I can.'

Charlie had the physical sensation of her shoulders unknotting, and behind her, Di let out a long breath.

They ate more chocolate chip cookies. He had two. And more tea, in mugs this time, as if Richard was becoming a member of the family, and gradually they made a plan.

'He can definitely wear his Newcastle kit?'

James spoke up at last. She'd forgotten he was there. And so had Di it seemed, registering him with surprise. She'd always favoured Darren; the way people did have a favourite child, but pretended not to. James was easily overlooked. He wasn't loud and forever making a fuss like Darren.

'Of course, lad, even though I'm a Mackem.'

Then followed a lively discussion about the current team line-ups, and Shearer's goal scoring, and the merits of Kevin Keegan versus Peter Reid.

'Howay the lads. So Darren's Newcastle kit?' Richard said, skilfully leading the conversation back. 'And his tracksuit bottoms. If you bring the clothes in, we'll get them ready.'

'Thanks,' said Di.

'And what type of coffin did you have in mind?'

That sobered them. He showed them a selection, all pretty

similar, with names like Harmony and Repose.

'Something plain,' Di said. He could interpret that, guiding her to the less expensive ones. She picked the second cheapest, a plain light wood.

'Can we put photos on the coffin?' asked James, blushing. 'A girl at school, her family decorated the coffin when her auntie died. Said it was lovely.'

'You can do whatever makes you happy. But make sure you keep copies. Sometimes people make the mistake of including a favourite photo, and then they're upset because they haven't got one to remember their loved one by.'

'I can do it as an art project,' said James.

Di raised her eyebrows.

'Sounds like a good idea,' said Richard. 'It can really help, the more personal you make it. I can talk to you more later, when you decide exactly what you want to do.'

James beamed.

They moved on to the order of service.

'Did you want a priest or a minister at all?'

Di looked confused again. Charlie knew she was having trouble remembering things nowadays. Probably the pills.

'Do we have to? I thought Charlie here was going to do it. Didn't I say that before?'

'The whole thing? You already asked me to do the eulogy,' Charlie snapped.

'I know, but we don't really want a priest or a vicar or anything. Remember what it was like at Sean's? The priest didn't even know him. Remember afterwards you said you'd rather have done it yourself? You're the one who knows Darren.'

Knew, Charlie wanted to say. *Knew.* She felt her shoulders tighten up. Why did Di always rely on her?

'Well, I suppose I could ask Suzy.'

Enough. If Suzy did it would be all about her. Sentimental

shite and masses of showy wreaths and a low-cut dress and sending Darren off in a leopard skin coffin, and her crying harder than anyone. Useless. There'd be no room for anyone else's grief.

Richard held her gaze.

'Again, I'd be there to support you. It would entail giving a short introduction and making sure everyone speaks in order.'

Easier said than done. It would be like herding cats. But she nodded, already having an idea. Keep it simple – photos. James liked taking photos. They could show them. It didn't all have to be words. What could you say about a 15-year-old?

'Maybe.'

She turned to Richard. She had an urge to touch his grey curls. He was probably used to people acting strange.

'Would it be OK?'

She was desperately hoping he would say no, of course it wasn't allowed, what did she know about conducting a funeral service, who did she think she was? She couldn't speak in front of all those people, she wasn't a professional.

Instead he smiled and said, 'Champion idea. As I said, always good to have something more personal.' He caught her expression, and put his hand on her shoulder. 'No need to be frightened. I'll be there.'

'Christ,' she thought, as he got a diary out to sort out a date. 'As if I haven't got enough to do. Solve Darren's murder, deliver a eulogy, sort out and preside over the service, figure out what's going on with Casey.'

'I'm a bit backed up,' he was saying to Di. 'I know now you've decided you want to go ahead as soon as possible, but the earliest possible date is…'

And the funeral was decided.

As Charlie was packing up to go home for a nap before work, her hands rested on her notebook. She looked at her list. Who to question next? She needed to keep up the momentum.

Start with the nearest and dearest. Darren's girlfriend. His dad. Then move on to the Community Association. Stella would certainly talk. There was something circling in the back of Charlie's mind; she'd missed a connection, something obvious. What had she overlooked? Go back to the beginning. Comb through everything.

She thanked Richard, and said goodbye to James and Di. James muttered something about running, but she couldn't take any more in.

'Tell me tomorrow.'

Home, bed for a couple of hours, then back on the wheel.

12

THAT WEEK CHARLIE had worked four nights on the run, and when she arrived home on the Wednesday morning it was to a new sound. Retching, upstairs. At first she thought it was the dog, but the dog's lead was gone. Casey in the bathroom, heaved over the toilet. In-between retches she said she'd picked up a bug.

'That prawn and cream cheese sandwich I had yesterday. I thought it had been sitting round.'

'So why did you eat it?'

'I was hungry.'

She held her stomach again, and bent over the toilet. A thin dribble of bile trickled down the toilet pan.

'Mum, I need the morning off.'

Charlie didn't argue. They slept most of the day and by early evening Casey was eating normally again, and said she would be fine with the dog.

Charlie didn't want to leave her, but it was true, if anyone did come near their place, the dog's bark would frighten them off. No one was to know that it was soft as anything: it looked and sounded fierce.

Casey had that closed look about her again, that blankness that teenagers get, the way they hate everything you do, from the way you dress to the way you breathe. *Your breasts are too small and flat, why don't you wear a proper bra, don't you ever smarten yourself up?* was her usual type of communication, as sulky, she stamped out of rooms. It was all starting again, like when she was a new teenager.

But tonight, before Charlie left, her daughter surprised her by holding Charlie's hair between her fingers.

'You've got really nice hair,' she said. 'One of your best assets.'

The moment passed and Casey pulled away.

'Go to work,' she snapped, waving her off.

It had been raining for days, the sky permanently dark. The TV weather map showed rain all over Europe: Cologne, Rotterdam, and Copenhagen. Charlie had an urge to take off somewhere, but there was still the funeral to get through, booked for the following week. Di was happy about the delay: 'Gives me more time to contact people. And get in more money.' Funerals cost. Charlie was shocked at the prices of the coffin, the cars, the crematorium and the flowers, and you had to stand people a drink, and feed them afterwards: people were always starving at funerals. It wasn't even as if Di was being extravagant. There were only two cars for the immediate family. Everyone else was making their own way.

Charlie knew there was another reason Di was glad to wait. A funeral was so final. After the funeral, Darren would definitely be dead, for ever and ever.

Next morning Casey was bright as a pin in her school clothes, her hair tied back in a ponytail, looking impossibly young.

'Feeling OK?' Charlie asked. 'Want some toast?' It had been an easy night at work for once. No one had kicked off.

'I'm not hungry.'

'I hope you're not getting anorexic.'

It slipped out without thinking. You heard terrible tales of girls and their eating problems. Casey had a healthy appetite. Except for that minor blip when she was 13, she'd always eaten well.

Casey gave Charlie a withering look, and rolled her eyes.

Then it was 8.25, with the school bus leaving shortly, and Casey had been late three times that week already. Mornings were not the best time, but Charlie wanted to keep a connection.

'How about fish and chips before I leave tonight?'

Casey's face brightened.

'I get to pick the film, right?'

The rom-com with loads of squealing girls gave them a laugh, until Charlie reluctantly had to drag herself away from the screen and pack her bag for work. She enjoyed these rare evenings with Casey; she wished she didn't have to go to work. Maybe there was a chance of becoming close again, like when Casey was young. Darren's death had hit them all hard.

She made her sandwiches. Casey watched her, sitting on the kitchen table.

'Tell me about my dad.' This blindsided Charlie. Where had this come from?

Not many people asked about Sean anymore, and she liked to talk about him. So she did, as she packed a packet of crisps and an apple and magazine. She said how funny he was, and how talkative, and how he loved to dance.

'I remember that, how he used to dance me round the kitchen.'

'You were only three.'

'I've told you; I remember my dad's smell, and being on his shoulders when he carried me to nursery. Tell me about how he died.'

Charlie looked at the clock. There was enough time. What had come over Casey? She was regressing. The story was familiar; she'd heard it so many times. But Charlie told it again. One of those stupid accidents that shouldn't have happened. Up a ladder, fixing the gutter.

'Your father was always so sensible about risk.' He would have weighted the ladder, and usually not shimmied up until his mate held it steady. That mate only skipped off for a minute, he didn't think Sean would go up again. And you don't think a couple of kids will come along and rock the ladder. They had to live with the consequences.

When Charlie saw him, there was no visible bruising.

'Your dad loved you very much. Why are you asking about him now?'

'Fathers are important.'

Charlie was about to ask more, when the phone rang. Di, asking her to drop by again on her way home in the morning.

'What's up?'

'Richard said we needed to get the clothes ready for Darren. I thought we could sort them out. Could you give us a hand?'

Charlie grunted.

'I need to catch up on a few things tomorrow. Yeah, like sleep. Can't be Saturday. The community fair. How about Sunday? I'm on shift in half an hour. I've got to go.'

Di carried on talking.

'He's got a nice voice, that Richard, he's much nicer than that other one Suzy found.'

Charlie hopped from foot to foot, and put her arms in her jacket. Not having worked for so long herself, Di never understood that Charlie was busy. She kept on.

'It's for James really. He keeps going into Darren's room and fingering his clothes. It's driving me crazy.'

Poor James. Of course she'd have to help.

'We need to sort them out anyway. I thought I may as well have a clear out. Darren's stuff needs washing. You know what he was like.'

Yes, a slob. *Too quick,* Charlie wanted to say. *He's not even in the ground.*

As if reading her thoughts, Di went on: 'We've got to get on. It needs doing at some point, it won't get any easier. You said you'd help.'

'I know I did. And I will. Have you heard anything from the police?'

'Just the usual: "We are continuing our lines of investigation." Nothing. What about you? Found anything out?'

'Once the funeral's out the way, I'll be able to concentrate more.'

'Yeah.' Di's voice was dead.

'Got a few ideas though.' Did she? 'Be round first thing Sunday morning. Night.'

The news was on in the living room when she went to say goodbye to Casey. A government minister said that most handguns would be banned, after 'lessons have been learned' from the Dunblane massacre. Casey had her head in a book, the dog curled at her feet. Distant again, she waved. Charlie closed the door, and headed out.

13

SATURDAY 12 OCTOBER

SATURDAY DAWNED TO bright autumn sunshine. After the continuous rain, it was one of those beautiful October days – burnished leaves and all that – a day that made you glad to be alive and living in a country with grass that stayed green, and seasons. Charlie liked the sun as much as the next person. But she liked seasons, and change. And those parks in Spain with their dry, dusty paths? She'd take green any day.

The community fair was to be held on a patch of waste ground with a hall attached. You could walk there easily. Its prime position also meant that it was a valuable piece of real estate, its worth not lost on the council. They were fielding offers.

Even walking the short distance from the hostel to deposit boxes full of plants and cakes on the stalls, Charlie saw how the year had moved on. They were deep into autumn. Leaves on the pavement were massed solid, trees turned skeletal, Darren further and further away.

The hostel was full of boxes, trays of plants and bags of produce. A buzz in the air, as glad of a change from everyday routine, the men threw themselves into tasks. The community fair was one of the few ways their centre was accepted in the area. After Darren's death the workers had discussed pulling out.

'Why?' Art, who with his earring and kerchief was modelling himself on a hardcore gangster, asked, 'Someone got murdered? People get murdered all the time.'

The look Martin gave him had shut him up, and in the end they decided to carry on as normal. Put on the back burner that a murder had taken place nearby, that they were under suspicion, and that the centre could be closed down. Forget that people hated them, and were looking to blame someone. *Including me*, Charlie thought. She never told anyone where she worked. But some people had found out.

Charlie arranged boxes, helped stack winter seedlings, sand smooth the corner of a handmade bookshelf, and put the sleeves on vinyl records.

It was easier to be in work rather than round at Di's or at home. The weight of the anniversary of Sean's death had passed; her shoulders were looser, even though all they'd done in the end was raise a glass and eat a bag of chips on the previous Saturday, before work. What had Michael's boss said? You couldn't just throw away the key. Could you? Did Michael know something about Darren's death? Or was he just playing with them? She couldn't take him at face value, even when he was being nice, like now, before he left for a breakfast shift, smiling away at everyone, handling plants with his well-groomed hands; soft palms and perfect nails. She looked at her own hands. Unevenly cut nails, lined, dry hands, blue veins standing out, brown spots. She was getting old. She turned her attention back to Michael. He was hiding something. Creep. She needed to dig deeper.

Then Eddie was at her side.

'All right, Eddie?' Eddie had got over his upset over the jigsaw. In the past, something like that would have kept him moping for weeks. Yet even a nice guy had secrets. He needed to be questioned. *Assume nothing. Believe no one. Check everything*, she'd read once. Fires. Eddie liked lighting fires, that's why he'd ended up inside. They all had a laugh about Eddie and his fires; there were always jokes about matches. But he'd damaged buildings and premises. Fires killed. His grandmother had died in a fire. Had that ever really been investigated, or did they just put it down to an old woman being forgetful?

Check Eddie's story.

Eddie jigged about happily as he sorted through records. Eddie specialised in blues and soul. He handled each record as if it was bone china, holding it by the edges, giving it a quick wipe, and placing it carefully in its sleeve.

'Fancy some music while we're getting ready?' They were in the wide front hall of the hostel. She smiled. He had brought his turntable down to carry over to the community hall, and provide the 'ambience', as he said. He selected a record and put it on. He grinned: 'The Great Bessie Smith.' Her ears filled with that extraordinary voice: 'If I should take a notion,' Eddie sang along with her. 'To jump into the ocean. Ain't nobody's business if I do. What do you think?'

Charlie gave a thumbs up.

Eddie's eyes gleamed. Jigsaws were his bubble gum, something to keep him calm, but music was his passion. He was always listening to music, and the only writing he did was of lyrics.

He'd told her once that he spent his formative years at Wigan Casino. With his mates from Leeds, on nothing more than bottles of coke, they'd get the train to Huddersfield, and then a coach, pitching up outside Wigan Casino at 12, waiting for it to open.

'We'd dance from two till eight, and then get the coach and train home, high on the dancing. That's when I got interested in collecting records. We'd take along a few records after rooting round in shops. Girls would ask what we had. Understand there were no tapes or anything in those days. "Sing it for me," they'd ask. So we did. What we made on the records paid for our fare home.'

Today he wore his Wigan Casino All-Nighter jacket, the

sewn-on badge big and loud.

Charlie welled up at the music. Music was something lost to her lately, pushed out. She listened to Radio 1 and a local rock station, and Casey's music, all trolling girl singers and plaintive strings mixed with something she called psy trance, with repetitive beats and trippy, floaty music. All that was like wallpaper to her, and didn't really affect her emotionally. 'Nobody knows you when you're down and out,' came on, and something shifted inside her.

Eddie changed the mood by putting on one of his Northern Soul specials: 'Do I love you? (Indeed I do)'. Charlie's feet twitched. For the first time it struck her that Eddie had a life before the hostel. All the men did. Remember that. Dig out clues hidden in the past.

After his Northern Soul, Eddie played a poppy, light record. The centre felt domestic, almost pleasant. Then she remembered. Darren was still dead. They had to get through the funeral. There was someone out there who attacked people. Most of the men were still bastards. The world wasn't nice and sugar-coated; the world was full of crap.

Eddie hummed as he worked: happy in his world of records. They stacked neatly one on top of another, fitting together, like his jigsaws.

'Had any more letters, Eddie?'

He nodded. Eddie advertised in a magazine, and got a continuous stream of letters from vinyl fans.

'Vinyl's not going away, you know.'

'I know.'

She didn't, but she humoured him. She hadn't even got on properly to CDs yet and they would probably be gone soon. Casey had saved up for a MiniDisc Walkman and Charlie couldn't understand how to work it. 'Mum!' Casey would shout. 'You're so *old*!'

Eddie wasn't allowed to run a business, but he had a mate

keeping it ticking over for when he was off licence, and he had a box number. His plan was to open a record shop when he was finally free. Charlie wondered how that would work. You got £46 when you left prison, and working in the supermarket he didn't earn much. And weren't record shops on the way out? But Eddie was determined.

'There's always room for specialisms,' he said, breaking into her thoughts. 'No matter about tapes and CDs, people will always like the sound of vinyl. It's the purity. Vinyl won't die, you'll see.'

Eddie was relaxed. As good a time as any to question him.

'How's work going, Eddie?'

'Fine.'

In the Chinese supermarket, where he helped pack cakes into boxes, and shifted and loaded rice, noodles and flour, they employed quite a few ex-cons. Charlie suspected they paid them less than the regular workers, but still, Eddie was happy to have a job. Eddie had a side of him that was funny and smart, that he hardly ever showed in the hostel, and he was a good worker. Occasionally the workers were given a cake past its sell-by date, and Eddie brought back the spongy concoction, and shared it. People liked Eddie, felt affection for him, and appreciated his generosity. Michael probably could have brought stuff back from the restaurant, better stuff. But he never did.

'Any problems?'

'No, I'm fine.'

'You haven't been upset again?'

'Me, no, what about?'

His eyes glistened. Then he unplugged the record player, put the lid on and carried it to the van ready to transport the heavier items. He came back for his records, carrying them carefully as you would a baby.

'Suit yourself,' Charlie thought. She'd try another time.

She turned to another lad, who had made small bird boxes.

'How much?' They proceeded to put price labels on. Darren would be in a small wooden box. She clenched her fists in tension.

The morning wore on with such tasks, as they set up stalls. The fair was to open at 1.30. Around lunchtime, Michael arrived back in from his shift, and a whiff of grease and meat hit her. For all his clean appearance and filed nails and well-cut hair, the animal was just below the skin. The arrogance steamed off him. He thought he was better than them. Yet he was just meat and flesh. And maybe knew something. What?

Next thing he was back with them, flushed, with wet hair after a shower, smelling of pine aftershave. A wave of mint hit her.

'I'm making *puttanesca*. Do you know what it means?'

She wasn't going to give him the satisfaction.

'Whore's pasta,' he shouted, daring her to challenge him, and flounced off to the kitchen.

Charlie stared after him. They did take food to sell at the stalls. Usually cakes or biscuits. They hadn't agreed that he was making pasta. Would it sell? And how would you transport it? You'd need plates and forks and spoons. She raised her eyebrows at Martin, but he looked away. His attitude towards Michael was always: 'Let him get on with it. If it keeps him out of trouble, and off our backs, fine.'

She followed Michael into the kitchen, and got in quick.

'You didn't have anything to do with Eddie's jigsaw the other night?'

'*Moi*?' He went back to chopping anchovies.

'He was upset.'

'I heard.' And as if he was speaking to himself, he went on: 'The secret with this sauce is to have no onion. People make that mistake; they think that everything has to have onion. But a lot of Italian food doesn't use onion.'

'Fascinating.'

He ignored her sarcasm.

'You only use garlic.'

'Is that so?'

'And the thing about garlic is that it goes sweet when you cook it, loses its bitterness.'

'Glad to hear that.'

Michael glared as the garlic in the pan sizzled.

'No need to be sarcastic. Try cooking something decent instead of that crap you eat. You're getting porky.'

Automatically, Charlie pulled in her stomach. Cheeky sod.

'Like your daughter.'

She glared back. What did he know about Casey? When had he ever seen her?

'Nice looking girl that. Good figure.'

Charlie held her breath, and then exhaled. Bastard, trying to rile her.

'You said you knew something about Darren.'

He added chopped tomatoes, black olives, capers, chopped anchovies, dried chillies. On the stove pasta bubbled away, next to a saucerful of chopped fresh herbs. He filled his hands with them, and sprinkled them on the sauce. There was a deep tomato smell.

'Did I?'

Innocent eyes.

'Yes, remember, you implied you knew something.'

'Oh, "implied". One of those lawyer words.'

'You've got to go the police.'

'Have I?'

'You know you have. His poor mother's going berserk.'

'That fat ugly cow. Don't know why you're friends with her.'

I'm not sure that I am, Charlie wanted to say. *But I know I'm useful to her and once when I most needed it she helped me.* And then his face turned cold and expressionless. Had he ever been close to anyone? Did his mother love him?

'She didn't deserve her son. Other people paid him more attention than she did. And if you say anything, I'll make out that you're mistaken. Lack of sleep, stressful job and home life. And you're friends with the victim's mother. You want to find someone responsible.'

At his words, Charlie bit her lip. She was tired of working crazy hours with these men who got money and help pumped into them for their problems, probation officers who visited several times a month, attention. What did she get? Nothing. When Sean died she had to get up in the morning and go to work and arrange the funeral, and look after Casey, and explain again and again, that no, Daddy wasn't coming back tonight, Daddy wasn't coming back tomorrow, Daddy wasn't coming back ever ever again. And the bed would always be empty and cold, and she'd always turn her head to the left and he'd be gone. Always it would be that time of coming home and turning into the street and seeing a police car parked, and thinking everything was OK, because it didn't have its flashing lights on. Not knowing that the emergency had already passed, when she put her key in the door and Di wrapped her arms around her and held her for hours. Everything so cold.

She wanted to spit at Michael. But she stood her ground as he picked up his fork and ate.

'I thought you were making pasta for the community fair.'

'This, no, too good to waste on that lot. I'll just help pack up those crap sponge cakes you try and palm off on the poor buggers. Want some?' He held the fork out. Pasta in rich dark sauce glistened. The smell enticed her and her stomach rumbled. All she'd eaten for breakfast was a piece of toast.

'It's delicious,' he said, smiling.

She turned away.

There was movement behind her. When she looked up, Eddie was standing in the doorway, his face white. How much had he heard? Did he think Michael knew something? She wrenched herself away from the smell, put her hand on Eddie's arm and walked back with him to the body of men. They made their way over to the stalls. A while later Michael joined them, licking his lips like a well-fed cat. He helped load and unload sponge cakes. Then Stella, sitting at a table at the entrance to the fair, welcomed the first of the public in. *Talk* to *her*, Charlie reminded herself. Stella might know things.

14

SATURDAY 12 OCTOBER

CHARLIE KEPT HER eyes open as they arrived at the fair. The police had got nowhere with the investigation.

The killer could be anyone. A stranger, any of the men in the centre, one of the family. Michael was still top of her list. *No evidence, no evidence,* a little voice said. She'd keep watch on him today. And now he was in front of her, unloading plants.

The day was clear. Charlie prayed the rain wouldn't start up again. These events were miserable if it rained, even though they could decamp to the hall. The hostel's contribution – a couple of plant stalls, cakes, and second-hand books and records – never seemed to do as well inside the hall. Michael was looking after the plants, but after the conversation in the kitchen Charlie thought it might go either way. He was a bastard, but a green-fingered one. All week the kitchen had been full of seedlings of different sizes that he'd nurtured in the hostel greenhouse, a musty place with dirty, mould-encrusted panes of glass that sat at the bottom of the garden.

He also had trays of winter pansies and violas, ready to be planted out, and boxes of bulbs. He'd got them cheap, said he could make the hostel some money. And he'd grafted an apple tree himself, ready for planting, and a few bushes and climbers in pots. Michael got on better with plants and food than he did with people. Martin said that when Michael was first at the centre they'd tried to get him a job in a park. Nothing doing, with his record. But any time he wasn't in the kitchen cooking up concoctions, he was out in the greenhouse. He grew a row of herbs and salad greens on the kitchen window ledge, like in his work, and was forever sprinkling herbs on his meals. Charlie had to admit the bright row of greens made the place look less institutional. She knew nothing about plants, and the few times she'd tried to tend the kitchen geraniums, Michael sought her out and hovered, disapproving.

'Overwatering,' he'd rasp, his too sweet breath on her.

Eddie lugged a box of records from the van. He'd been humping boxes about for weeks, and had parcels covered in exotic stamps arriving every day.

Casey came running up behind, her face flushed.

'You made it. Are you OK?'

Casey was wearing some ridiculous hippy top from two summers back, but she still looked overheated. Her breasts had grown; she was bursting out of it. Not a little girl anymore.

'I'm fine. I said I'd help, didn't I?'

'Well, just be careful.'

Casey laughed. Her face looked fuller, older.

Charlie glanced over her shoulder.

'I mean it, Case; some of these men are nasty.'

'Who, those?' There was a cluster of laughing and relaxed men round the van, parked near the stalls.

'They're not as innocent as they seem.'

'Who is?' said Casey, laughing.

'They've done things.'

'What things?'

'Not nice things. I can't say any more.'

'Him?' and Casey pointed to Eddie, who'd broken away from Charlie to check that his records were being unpacked properly. He was the picture of innocence.

'Not…' She stopped herself.

'Who then?' Casey's eyes lit on Michael.

He felt her gaze, and smiled. Casey returned the smile.

'Who then?'

'Never mind.' Charlie took hold of Casey's arm.

'Be careful. Don't be alone with any of them.'

Red rag to a bull, she realised. Any teenager worth their salt would defy that order.

Stella, the chair of the community organisation, directed traffic through to parking. People always melted away before her, and did her bidding. She was different to the others on the committee, with 'lady of the manor' type ways about her. She wore a sleeveless jerkin and wellies, as if she'd just stepped off the farm. Underneath her jerkin was a worn and comfortable jumper in an unflattering brown. Through its threadbare elbows, you could see the whites of her arms. The rest of the committee seemed fond of her, and in awe. Stella had pushed for the hostel to stay involved. Charlie was grateful for her trust.

They helped Eddie unload records. Di arrived with James. 'I wanted to get out of the house for a while,' she said. 'Before next week.'

Charlie nodded. The funeral would be tough.

'I got some money through,' Di added.

'One of the policies?'

'Yeah, we took a taxi here,' James laughed.

It was no distance from Di's. Di could spend her money how she liked, but all the takeaways and smoking were having an effect. She was flabby and puffed up. Charlie felt a sudden anger at her friend. If Di got ill, what would happen to James? She suppressed an urge to shake her, and turned away.

Di breathed heavily from the slight exertion of walking from one stall to another.

'And she got me this,' James laughed, awkwardly clutching a games console. James would probably have preferred drawing pens. Games consoles were more Darren's thing.

Let it go, Charlie warned herself.

On the book and record stall there was an excess of detective novels, and true crime books. A couple of dozen shifted in the first hour. Some of the men had made wooden toys: caterpillars and toy cars and trains, and soon there was a small crowd of potential buyers. Eddie's first customers were teenage goths and retro punks he joked with. Later on, a succession of middle-aged men in leather jackets turned up, fingering the records as if they were sacred relics, deliberating before finally handing over money.

Charlie stood next to Michael as he charmed women with his seedlings. He held up thriving plants, his long delicate fingers waving in the air, his perfect teeth flashing. He gave a good impression of caring, making eye contact, paying attention. She wanted to warn the women. Weren't they suspicious of too white teeth? His attentive grooming? Apparently not. Charlie rattled money in the till, and slammed down empty boxes. He smiled tolerantly over at her, infuriating her even more. Women rolled their eyes, commiserating with him over the bad-tempered old cow.

Then she relaxed as Eddie flogged his records. He soon built up a crowd, who clustered round as he told tales about the music and its provenance. The eyes of his audience lit up. A fellow fan. Men as well as women, Eddie got on with them all. The thing about Eddie was that he genuinely loved the records, and he liked people. Just because he had a minor problem of setting fire to things. 'Nobody's perfect,' he'd started saying after *Some Like It Hot* was on TV one rainy weekend afternoon.

He'd put together a really good selection. Blues, rock, soul, punk. She watched him perform, coming alive under the attention, his face animated, instead of the dull flat plate he often presented to the world. There was more to Eddie than met the eye. Charlie was enjoying watching him so much it took her a while to realise that Michael was gone. And Casey.

Michael was her responsibility. She hopped from one foot to another, and scoured the surroundings. He was nowhere to be seen.

'Go, I'll mind the stall. Find them,' Martin said tersely. Eddie, in full flow, seemed unaware, and mouthed, 'OK,' when she said she had to check something. Eddie would be fine on the stall. Even if he got the urge to start a fire, they were in the open.

Charlie raced past curry stalls, and stalls selling veggie burgers and candyfloss. Di had her face in a burger, while James took pot shots at a row of revolving yellow ducks.

'Have you seen Casey?'

Panic hit Di's face. Then she retreated into her own grief.

'She'll be around. She's a big girl.' She turned to James, now cradling a giant teddy bear.

Charlie was standing outside the communal unisex portaloos, wondering what to do, when Michael emerged from one, his face flushed. Charlie turned away. She hated looking at him. When she refocused Casey was emerging from a cubicle. Had she come out of the same one? Was something going on between them?

Close to Michael, there was a slight musky smell. Charlie's stomach somersaulted. Had Casey been in the same cubicle as that bastard? What had he done to her?

'Where the fuck have you been?' Charlie pushed him roughly.

He held his hands up.

'Whoa there, I don't think you're allowed to do that to me. Inappropriate physical contact.'

'And you?' she yelled at Casey. 'What were you doing in there?'

Casey blushed, but her voice was sarcastic.

'Mum, what do you think? It's a toilet. I'm 15. I can go to the toilet by myself.'

'But why were you near…?' Charlie couldn't say his name.

'Oh, you mean Michael?'

A smug smile played round Michael's lips.

'Yeah, him.'

Charlie put her hand on Casey's shoulder, but Casey shrugged her off. They headed towards the stalls.

'I was just talking to him.'

'What about?' *Why was she talking to that bastard? Why doesn't she talk to me?*

'It's private.'

What on earth could she have to say to Michael that was private?

Beside them, Michael smirked, enjoying Charlie's discomfort. Charlie wanted to hit him. If she did she would lose her job. If she lost her job she wouldn't be able to pay the rent. If she couldn't pay the rent…

'You don't know what he's like.'

'I do know he's a good listener. Unlike some. And you're the one who always used to say that everyone deserves a second chance.'

Michael threw Casey a dazzling smile. Charlie felt sick. She'd read his file.

'You don't know what he's done.'

Even as she said the words she knew she shouldn't have. He'd have grounds for a complaint. She was past caring.

But Michael fixed his now cold eyes on Charlie, and in a monotone that made her shiver, said: 'Need to keep an eye on her, do you? Daughter like that?'

'Hey,' Casey yelled, 'what do you mean? I thought we were friends. And don't talk to my mother like that.'

'Should pay attention to your daughter instead of running round after your slag of a mate, shouldn't you? That fat cow deserved all she got.'

And then his face was close, and he was laughing at her,

and she pummelled him, her fists battering into his chest, harder and harder. And he kept the smirk on his face, and whispered into her ear, 'So you've done it now, you've really stepped over the line, you'll never know what happened to that kid.' Fury in her, she hit him more, to shut him up, get rid of the sound of his voice. And even when his smirk was gone, and there were only low moans, she carried on punching. She wanted to kill him, quiet him, but the strength in her arms had gone, and her fists stung, and that's what saved him, for he offered no resistance. That, and Martin shouting, which brought her to. Martin ripped her away: 'My God, Charlie, look what you've done. I'll have to put in a report.'

Michael was quiet and subdued, but surfaced, waving away Martin's first aid offers.

'At least let me look,' said Martin, and pulled up Michael's T-shirt, revealing red marks from her punches all over his muscled stomach and chest. 'You'll probably bruise. I'll take you to the first aid tent.'

'I'll be all right,' said Michael, the smirk back in Charlie's direction. 'She can only do girl punches. I just tensed my muscles.'

'But still,' Martin said, loyalties obviously torn. 'If you want to…'

'Put in a complaint?' asked Michael. 'I'll think about it.' He smiled, showing his good teeth. 'I'll see.'

'And you, go home!' Martin ordered, turning to Charlie.

'You're in no state to be here. We know you're upset, Charlie, but really! 'You've gone too far this time.'

By this time a curious crowd of people were milling around them, drawn by the noise. Charlie was suddenly scared. Had anyone seen anything? How many witnesses were there to what she had done? She'd wanted to kill him. Martin shooed the onlookers away: 'Nothing to see here.' If Michael put in a complaint…

The scariest thing was that nothing separated her from the men she was looking after. She'd lost it, big time. Charlie knew she was no better than them.

LATER AT HOME Casey cuddled into her, and they stuffed themselves on a takeaway curry in front of a canine karaoke competition on *Pets Win Prizes*. The National Lottery, which followed, bored Charlie silly, but seemed to intrigue Casey. Charlie drank beer, Casey was on lemonade. Casey had seen the whole incident.

'You could have really hurt him, you know, Mum.'

'I know.'

'You were scary, Mum, that was frightening. You're always telling me that people who use violence are the lowest of the low.'

'I know. I don't know what came over me.'

She did know what came over her. She had wanted him to shut up, stop talking. Was that what the killer had done to Darren? Charlie shivered. How close the animal was in all of us? Five minutes, that's all it took. Your whole life changed forever. She pulled Casey towards her. Casey shook herself away, obviously worried at this new she-devil of a mother.

'And what would have happened to me if they arrested you?'

'I know, love, it was stupid. I didn't think.' That's what lots of the men said. 'I didn't think.' She'd always pooh-poohed it as an excuse. How easy it was to cross a line. Scary.

'I was only talking to him, you know. I thought he was OK.'

'He's a dangerous man, I'm telling you. And I don't want anything happening to you. You're all I've got.'

'What did he do?'

'You know I can't tell you that.'

'But I thought he was nice. He listened, and when I spoke, he took me seriously, listened to me like an adult. I'm nearly grown-up, Mum, nearly an adult.'

'I know, darling, but I'm still your mum. And that man's not safe.'

'And neither are you' was the unvoiced response.

And then the atmosphere changed as they both giggled, agreeing the funniest act was a Jack Russell crooning *Let it Be*.

Casey yawned.

'You seem tired, darling. Why don't you go to bed?'

'Soon. But… Mum, there's something I want to tell you.'

'OK, love, but it's late. Is it about school? I'll just put the kettle on. I think I've had enough beer.'

'Don't put the kettle on, Mum, sit here with me.'

'I'll just be a minute.'

'But…'

In the kitchen, Charlie shook uncontrollably, and stifled her sobs. What would happen now? If he put in a complaint, she'd lose her job. They'd be back to making do. Casey would hate her again, just as they had a chance of getting close again. She kicked her foot against a kitchen cabinet. Stupid woman! Putting them at risk like that. Couldn't she have controlled herself? Everyone knew what Michael was like. An arch manipulator. No excuse. She poured the water into two cups. What did Casey want to tell her?

When she got back in the living room, Casey was gone, and a TV announcer was solemn in front of the monitor: 'A 17-year-old girl has been found injured in bushes behind temporary toilets where a community fair was held in Heaton in Newcastle earlier today. The girl, whose identity is not being revealed until all members of her family are informed, has suffered serious injuries. Police cannot yet reveal whether this is also being viewed as an attack of a sexual nature.'

A reporter stood in front of the same toilet cubicles Casey had emerged from. Charlie sat down, winded. This was getting close. Had Casey seen this before she left the room?

'The girl was found behind bushes by a dog walker. Police have no further details at present, although concerns have been raised locally about the participation of a local bail hostel in the community fair. We will carry a further update on our late local news in an hour. This is…'

The camera cut to a local resident, who mouthed good wishes for the girl's recovery, after her 'traumatic ordeal' and expressed the shock of local residents. 'However, we in the Bridge Road Residents Association have not been happy at the involvement of the bail hostel in the community fair. We were expecting something like this to happen. These men are dangerous.'

When Charlie phoned Martin at the hostel, he answered sleepily. Yes, the police had taken all the men to the station, questioned them and let them go.

"Preliminary investigations," they said. They'll be back tomorrow morning. I'll stay on a couple of hours.'

Charlie promised to be at the hostel. She was due on two day shifts.

'I'll see you before you leave.'

'OK. And Charlie?'

'What?' No time for niceties.

'There'll be a bit of a mess when you come.'

'What do you mean?'

'Another brick through the side window. Probably some of the locals hearing what happened. And there was a group of men hanging round. I might not have time to clean it up before you arrive, there's only that divvo on with me, and he's a waste of space. Just be careful when you come in. You've not to use the side door, OK?'

She wasn't surprised: they'd been expecting something.

She looked in on Casey, sleeping with her mouth open, and shuddered. Nowhere was safe. If anything happened to Casey… Well, at least the police would have Michael on their radar again. She hoped that they did their job properly this time. She'd tell them what Michael had said about Darren, about seeing something. Or maybe not. He'd deny it, of course. And now he had her attack on him hanging over her. If he put in a complaint about her, they wouldn't take her accusations seriously. Had she messed up any chance of the police finding out if Michael did know something? Stupid, stupid woman! And suddenly she wanted Sean back. If Sean was here, none of this would have happened. Casey wouldn't be so angry at her; they wouldn't have to be facing making do again. It was all a mess. Wearily she took herself to bed.

15

SUNDAY 13 OCTOBER

THE FOLLOWING MORNING, Charlie had to phone Di to say she couldn't do the clothes: 'Something's come up,' she said.

'Is it about that girl?' Di said. She would have seen the news.

Charlie didn't give Di a chance to say anymore: 'Have to go.'

Charlie was at the centre early, spied a mass of broken glass and a brick on the floor by the side entrance, and took the front door. Already waiting in the office were two police officers. She offered to make them tea and caught up with Martin in the kitchen. He looked terrible.

'You can get off. I'll finish here,' she said.

'I'll go soon; I'll just hang round for a bit. They were real hot shots the coppers last night down at the station, the way they went through the men. And forensics came out – them guys in white suits an' all. They looked at the brick and the door, and lifted a few prints.'

'So what do these two want?'

'Dunno. All the men were accounted for; our lot are off the hook. Besides, they announced that they were looking for someone tall with bright ginger hair. We've got no one of that description here. Looks like there's no connection.'

'Maybe they're just fishing?'

'Or maybe they've got a new lead? Or they're worried about the local residents taking things into their own hands and lashing out? We're the obvious target. And you don't know some of the nutters who live round here.'

Charlie scrutinised Martin's face. He'd lived round this area as a teenager before his family moved to Wallsend, and could put on the Geordie with the best of them. She'd heard him talking to mates on the phone a few times and could hardly understand a word of what he said. He'd let slip once that he'd flirted with some dicey groups in his youth. 'Young and daft,' he'd dismissed himself.

What groups?

The BNP occasionally tried stirring things up, but this area wasn't their natural territory. Too mixed, too many people moving through.

'Could you blame locals for wanting a shot at our lot? They don't really want us round here.'

'Course not. But these two police say they're only making general enquiries. They're hardly professors. If they want to interview any of the men properly they have to take them down the station, and get them lawyered up.' Martin had been watching cop shows again: he liked to show he was on the ball.

But he was right, Charlie thought as she loaded the tea tray. The two police officers had probably been sent to reassure local residents that something was being done. The real work was going on elsewhere. Of course the police would try and connect Darren's murder with this attack. Obvious the police were frustrated. Maybe there was a memo out to keep an eye on the hostel. Put the brains on the latest case, send the plods out. With no suspect in sight for Darren's murder, they must be seen to be doing something.

'There's rumours going round of a serial killer,' said Martin. 'That the attack on the girl was meant to be another murder, but that somebody disturbed them before they could carry it out. Nobody knows if they're connected.'

'I know... You better take that tea in.'

Charlie gathered up the full tray and took it through, offering the two drinks and digestive biscuits just on the verge of going stale. She never felt at ease with the police. When she'd worked in Student Support, she'd met students who automatically thought the police were heroes, on the side of good. It wasn't in her DNA. Too many stories from relatives in the North. And then there were the Birmingham Six and the Maguire cases and the Miners' Strikes and Hillsborough. She was always surprised when individual police were decent. This pair enthusiastically dunked biscuits in their tea, as if they hadn't eaten for days. The younger one wolfed his down.

The police spoke to Eddie first.

'Not a formal interview,' they said. 'Just a chat.'

Charlie sat in. She wanted to warn Eddie about 'informal chats'. The police found out things through 'informal chats'. She wasn't even sure if it was legal questioning him like this, but Eddie was happy enough to co-operate.

'Now, Eddie,' said the older one.

Eddie shifted in his seat. He looked guilty of something. What?

'I'll come straight to the point. A phone call recently to the station said someone had information on Darren Pearson's murder. The caller rang off before they left their name. It wasn't you by any chance?'

Eddie blushed, but denied anything to do with the phone call.

'You can appreciate our problem; we're trying to see if there are any links between poor Darren's murder, and the attack on this lass. Understand?' Eddie nodded. 'So you definitely had nothing to do with that phone call?'

His denial came out in a whisper. They grew bored, their hearts not in the questioning, and didn't push. Eddie was definitely nervous. Was it him who phoned? Charlie wondered. He'd overheard Michael. Then again, she wouldn't put it past Michael himself phoning, to taunt them all.

The police knew Eddie's record.

'Not been near any matches lately?' said the younger one, and Eddie's voice faltered.

'I'm a reformed character, I am.' He used his steaming cup of tea as a prop.

'They all say that.' The young one suppressed a yawn.

Charlie watched him tick a box on a form. So much now was about ticking boxes. He glanced up, caught her eye, and smiled. He had a good smile. Charlie lowered her head. Casey would say she was flirting.

'Top up?'

They emptied the big teapot. The tea always tasted metallic. Martin hadn't graced them with his coffee. Charlie wondered what the insides of the policemen's stomachs were like. Irregular shifts, like her job, and terrible food eaten on the run did nothing for your digestion. A grabbed sausage roll, a doughnut. She smelt the harshness of their uniform, the old damp of clothes dried in unheated rooms, a whiff of tobacco. Institutional and not quite clean. Depressing.

When they let Eddie go he had to take his asthma inhaler, he was in such a state. Charlie could hear his wheezing lungs as she followed him downstairs. He made a jam sandwich, using his right hand to butter the bread. Eddie was left-handed. His left hand was bandaged up.

'What have you done?'

'Burnt myself.'

He offered no other explanation. They were supposed to list any accidents in the book.

'At the community fair,' he supplied.

This puzzled her.

'But you weren't anywhere near the cooking.'

'Well, I was.'

Had Michael done something to him? Had Michael hurt him? She was about to ask, when Eddie scooted off to his room.

The police took longer with Michael, who said he was due to have lunch.

'Well, you're going to have to wait for your lunch a bit longer,' said the older policeman with distaste. He sounded a peculiar mixture of London overlaid with a tinge of the North East. 'A young girl was attacked yesterday. She's in a bad state.'

'Yes, and I am sorry about that,' said Michael formally. 'Do I need my lawyer?'

'Only a friendly chat. We'll tell you if you need your lawyer. Do you know anything about the attack yesterday?'

'No, officer. As your colleagues last night found out, it was nothing to do with us in the hostel. We all came back together. They keep quite a tight rein here.'

The younger one changed tack: 'What do you like for lunch?'

The question wasn't innocent. Get the suspect relaxed, attack.

'Sunday roast?'

Michael snorted: 'Organic humus, tomatoes, olives, crusty bread, tuna, Parma ham, green beans, cheese.'

'Parma ham, eh? Expensive that stuff.'

'Yeah, but you only need a small amount.'

'Italian, isn't it?'

'Yes,' said Michael in an amused tone. A look which could only be described as orgasmic crossed his face. 'I love it. Special offer in Sainsbury's, so I bought two packets.'

Sainsbury's was up near the dual carriageway; Sainsbury's was nowhere near.

'Do you go up that way often, like?'

The young cop's question sounded friendly.

'Well, yes as a matter of fact. Their delicatessen counter is one of the best in the North. *Fine Food* magazine said that their pigeon breasts are to die for.' Michael was talking like some 1950s aristocrat.

'Oh, is that right there then?'

The tone of the older cop was harsher, less friendly. He tapped Michael on the shoulder.

'Listen, son, a lass was attacked, a lad killed not too long ago, and we need to know what happened, and whether there is any connection. Right? Stop faffing on about your bloody cordon blue, and give us what you know. Have you seen or heard anything which might shed light on events yesterday? Or have you any more to add to what you already told us about Darren, the young lad who was killed? Do you frequent that area of the park? Were you in that area of the park at all on the day the young lad was last seen, or the Saturday night when he must have been killed?'

Michael turned his head towards Charlie. She was pretty sure they weren't allowed to ask him such questions. He was as well.

'I have already informed the other officer who interviewed me properly that I was nowhere in the vicinity. And no, I have not heard or seen anything which might have any bearing on the case. I don't know anything about the attack on the girl. As I said, I was under watch the whole time yesterday evening.'

Not the whole time, Charlie wanted to say. *Not the whole time. And not the whole time when Darren first disappeared. Maybe you did see something.*

'Because if you do know anything, mate, we're going to find out. Right?'

'Of course, Officer,' said Michael. Then he turned towards Charlie and narrowed his eyebrows, as if in warning, daring her to say anything. The older policeman caught the look between them, and made a note in his book. When he looked up, Michael's face was blank.

'If there is anything, better for you if we find out now rather than later.'

Charlie took a deep breath. So what if he complained?

What was the worst that could happen?

'You said you knew something about Darren. You said you'd seen something,' she challenged him. The two policemen looked at her in surprise. Michael seemed highly amused, and smiled at the police, polite and civil, and denied everything. As he said he would.

'"People get things wrong," is what I said. Not everyone's as innocent as they seem. People do see things.'

'What's that supposed to mean?' said the older cop, annoyed. 'Don't waste our time, mate.'

They tried coming down hard on Michael, and then cajoling him, appealing to his better nature, but he didn't budge, and denied everything, so that eventually they gave up and let him go. Charlie's ears burnt. She felt a fool. Why had she even spoken up? She should have kept back her suspicions to herself until she was more sure. She couldn't push it.

The other men were routine. Donny asked questions about due procedures, and when he told them he was studying law they humoured him and let him talk about his studies. Carl and Nick were monosyllabic, but both had cast iron alibis, in the centre all afternoon and evening under the eyes of staff, after not being allowed to go to the community fair because of violating their privileges. And no, they hadn't known Darren so had never seen him with anyone, and no, they hadn't made a phone call.

Graham was nervous, and kept a cigarette burning all through his interview. Graham had a lot to lose. If he breached the terms of his licence, he'd be back inside. But no, he hadn't gone to the fair yesterday; he'd been working for an elderly client. Of course she would vouch for him. He supplied an address. And no, he didn't know anything about Darren.

After the men left, Martin sloped off, muttering something about paperwork. Charlie followed him out of the room in the guise of refilling the kettle.

'Paperwork, my arse. Go home. You need to sleep.' She knew he wanted to go on the computer to do online elfing. He could only do it at work. His wife refused to have the net at home. For a few seconds he debated between his fixation, and the need for rest, then picked up his coat and left.

Charlie made the police hot strong tea. The older cop sipped it gratefully. They seemed in no hurry to get back. Probably stringing out their day until their shift was over. Or maybe they'd been told to check her out. Charlie was itching for them to go. She was getting nowhere with her probing, and the police didn't seem any further on.

'How can you stand working here, pet?' asked the older one, sucking down his tea.

'Scumbags like that Michael?' He shot her a sympathetic glance.

'They're not all scumbags,' she said, surprising herself. 'How can you stand your job?'

'Fair enough,' he said. 'Sometimes it does get to you. Especially if it involves kids.'

He closed his eyes and ran his fingers over his thinning hair.

'Come on, Grandad. Let's leave this lady to get on with her work.'

The young cop put their cups in the sink.

'Thanks, pet,' said the older one. 'If you hear anything more, or have any suspicions at all, then don't hesitate to get in touch.'

He sounded like a train guard reading an announcement. He handed her a card. O'Reilly. With his battered face and his name, there was something familiar and comforting about this man.

'We're all keeping in mind that she is only a young lass, and he was only a young lad.'

As if I could forget.

He wasn't a cop for nothing. He caught her expression.

'You knew him, the lad that got murdered, didn't you? I'm sorry, pet, I didn't make the connection. You know his mother. I know she lives round here.'

Charlie nodded. These two weren't as green as they made out. They'd done their homework.

'Sorry, I'm always putting my foot in it.'

'Yeah, his ex-wife said he was like a bull in a china shop.'

At the words 'ex-wife' Charlie perked up, and registered the older cop more fully. He had a certain worn out charm if you took away the uniform and the general aura of tiredness and grime. *Don't go there.*

'You mind your words, you cheeky bugger. But she was right. Open my mouth before my brain is in gear. Anyway, pet, all I'm saying is, please do get in touch if anything – I mean, anything – bothers you.'

He put his hand on her arm. Charlie was very conscious of his touch. So long since she'd had physical contact.

'Of course I'll keep an eye out,' she assured them. 'How's the girl?' Is she going to be OK?'

'She's got a good family,' O'Reilly said. 'They picked up someone. They might have him. Forget I told you that.'

'It was on the local news tonight anyway,' the younger cop said.

Of course, that's why they weren't going so hard on the men. They thought they had the right one already. But the same thing had happened with Darren, and that fell to nothing.

'I don't suppose you can tell me anything about the investigation into my friend's lad's death? How's it going? Are you getting anywhere?'

The older cop shrugged. 'You know I can't say anything, pet, it's all confidential.'

The younger cop wouldn't meet her eye. The older one

sighed: 'There are some nasty pieces of work walking round out, free as anything. They could do it again. We need to get that one.' He shuddered. 'And make sure you get that window fixed.'

She nodded, and rose to shake their hands. His grip was dry and steady; the younger guy's hand was already in his glove, so all she felt was leather.

When they left, she cleared up the glass and mess by the side door with Art. The centre felt unsafe, vulnerable. She taped up the hole as best she could, and the emergency glazier, quoting a price that could have kept her and Casey for three weeks, said he would be two hours.

In a quiet time that afternoon, she phoned Di, who said the police had called. 'As far as they can tell there's no connection between this attack and Darren's murder. They said this latest attack wouldn't overshadow what had happened to Darren, and that they would still be pulling out all the stops to catch his killer.'

'But they won't, will they, Charlie? They won't be pulling out all the stops. That poor girl, of course I feel sorry for her and her family. But I want them to get the bastards who killed Darren. I need them to, Charlie. We won't be able to rest otherwise. I'm relying on you.'

After arranging to sort out the clothes the following Wednesday, Charlie replaced the phone. This latest attack had put the shivers up them all. Thank God Casey had the dog at night. Still, she might try and put in for more regular day shifts, be around more. Or give up the job altogether, she thought, suddenly weary. Do more of this detecting lark. That was a laugh. She'd got nowhere so far. Di had more faith in her than she had in herself. She was stumbling round in the dark. Time to get more organised.

16

WEDNESDAY 16 OCTOBER

FIFTEEN-YEAR-OLD BOYS DON'T have that much stuff.
They'd already postponed this twice, with everything that had
happened, and Charlie was dreading it. Charlie had come
straight to Di's after seeing Casey off to school. They were
in Darren's bedroom. There were medals for swimming and
basketball and cricket, and a certificate for 'Best all-round
athlete'. All that life of the body, all those push-ups and toning
exercises, all those muscles, gone.

They made four piles: *For James, The charity shop, To keep*,
and *Rags/bin*. Darren's clothes consisted of tracksuits and
T-shirts, jeans and hoodies. Most trousers were threadbare
and stained round the bottom where he'd trailed them in mud,
so went in Rags. The T-shirts were in better condition, ending
up in Charity. And the hoodies were better still: good quality
and thick. Charlie put a couple in James's pile, and passed
a blue one over to Di. The room was cold, even though the
heating was on full.

'Maybe you want to keep one?'

The hoody was oversize, as Darren always wore it baggy. Di
sniffed the hoody all over, like a dog, pulled off her sweatshirt
and angled it over her head. A tight fit, with her breasts.
She looked ridiculous, but seemed comforted somehow,
putting her hands deep in the pockets of the hoody as if she
was pulling Darren to her. A piece of paper fell to the floor.
Absent-mindedly Charlie picked it up and put it in her pocket.
Di's breath lengthened, and she grew quiet, soothed by the

monotony of sorting and piling. But when they found Darren's primary school certificate for 'Sitting nicely on the carpet', that's when she cried.

Charlie held her, stroked her hair, and let her cry. When she dozed off, lying on Darren's bed, Charlie covered her with his quilt, took the certificate out of her hand, placed it in the Keep pile and carried on: his Newcastle United Supporters' Club card, a bike bell, a pack of Embassy (which Charlie binned before Di could see), size 10 trainers, photos.

Di surfaced, lighting a cigarette, as Charlie was going through the photos. One set of photos were from the basketball team's summer visit to Copenhagen, the boys grinning outside the sex museum, the Danes looking bemused. Darren didn't even play basketball, it was James, but they'd allowed him to tag along, and a photo showed the brothers with their arms around each other, grinning. Other photos showed Darren with Melody, his girlfriend, and Darren posing with his friends. There were also a few art postcards. Some of the images Charlie recognised, but she couldn't name the artists.

'I didn't know Darren was into art.'

'Well, he was doing Art GCSE. They were probably for his projects.'

Charlie examined the back of the postcards. Degas. A leaflet advertised a travelling exhibition. And there was something from the Laing: *Serious Games. Interactive Art*, and another, *Priory and Castle, above Priors Haven Bay, Tynemouth*, by James Wilson Carmichael. And a leaflet: 'Thank you for your contribution to the Art Fund. We have now purchased the above.' So he'd been donating to buying art? How? Where did he get the money from? She filed the fact away in the back of her mind. Did you ever really know anyone?

There were a few history books from school, and a

biography of Michael Jordan.

Probably James's. Sure enough, when she opened the book, his name was written on the fly leaf. She put it aside. Shorts and socks and weights and resistance bands and dumbbells and all the paraphernalia a teenage boy has to build themself up. A photograph of Darren and his grandad. Deodorants and hair gel and a sports towel. Not much.

Charlie picked up his last school report, from the summer, and passed half to Di. Charlie read the teacher summary first.

'Darren has settled down well to some hard work after a disrupted start to the year. He is putting more effort in, especially in Art, and off his own back has visited a number of galleries. This will bring benefits. He is adopting a more independent attitude towards study. We wish him well, and we believe that with the right attitude he can achieve even more.'

'Read this,' Di said, thrusting his self-assessment over. 'Sounds like he was trying at last. I'd been going on at him for ages how he needed to work at school. Sounds like he listened.'

Charlie read the small, neat handwriting: 'I think that I have had a difficult start to the year, but now I have matured enough to get my head down and concentrate on the work. I hope I can learn to be more disciplined and keep focused. My best subjects this year have been English, Geography and Art. I have grown more interested in English and Art, and I have attended art exhibitions, and gone to see films I might not normally see. I need to work harder at Science and Maths as they are my weakest subjects.'

For a minute they both stayed quiet. This Darren sounded like a different lad to the one most people knew. It was true about the 'difficult start'. The start of his last year at school the police regularly picked Darren up. He was lucky not to have ended up in a Young Offenders' Institution. But there'd been no trouble for a while. This Darren was growing up, making plans.

Not anymore.

Lunchtime, and James arrived. When he picked up the report, his eyes filled with tears. Then he put all the saved papers together in a big file, and wrote in a surprisingly neat and legible hand that looked remarkably like Darren's, the word 'Darren'.

'Come on.'

James led them on now. Seeing the school report spurred him. Charlie's limbs felt leaden. If she found it hard to continue, what was it like for Di?

'I can only stay an hour,' said James. 'Got to get back to school. We still need to sort out his clothes.'

For the funeral, they didn't say.

They found his Newcastle top easy enough, under the bed, dirty and stained as Di had said, and a pair of his favourite tracksuit bottoms. Charlie put them in a plastic bag ready to take it to Richard.

'He'll need socks and trainers,' James said, and he rifled through Darren's drawers and pulled out a pair of black football socks.

'Trainers or football boots?' Di asked

'He always wore trainers in the park,' James said with authority. He picked up a pair, battered and muddied. Charlie forgot the brand as soon as she saw it. James would know what his favourites were.

'They're not his favourites,' James said, as if reading her thoughts.

'Why not his favourites?' asked Di. 'Where are they?'

'The police have got them,' Charlie reminded her. This sobered them.

Of course. That's what he was found in.

'What about his footy boots then?' said Di.

'Better than those manky trainers.'

The football boots were neat and newly cleaned in the

bottom of his wardrobe. Personally Charlie thought it was a waste, but it was Di's call. They hadn't had much wear. Of course, the football season had only been going for a few weeks when Darren went missing.

'He kept them for matches,' James explained. 'I suppose they'll look smarter.'

'Yeah, that's better,' said Di, shaking herself. 'We're getting somewhere.'

She seemed more composed with James about.

'And he needs his scarf,' she shouted through from the bathroom.

'Aye, he always wore that scarf,' James smiled. 'Even though he was embarrassed 'cos it wasn't a proper Newcastle one.'

'The hell he gave me when I knitted it for him,' Di returned. 'I couldn't afford a proper one when he first went the match, so I knitted him one. First and last time I've knitted anything. "Mum," he said. "Don't give up the day job." Cheeky bugger. Where is it? It must be round here somewhere.'

They scoured the room, tearing open drawers, peering under the bed, the pillows, the wardrobe, in his sports bag, damp and sweaty smelling, with mildewed kit. Nothing. They poked about in the washing machine, and behind the washing machine, even though Di said she always hand-washed it, it being wool; they examined all the coats and jackets and hoodies hanging on the clothes hooks. They even dug in the bin, full to overflowing, and they went back through the four lots of bags again in case one of them had thrown it away by mistake. Nothing. By this time, it was getting on for one o'clock. James, who'd been eating a pungent cheese and onion sandwich, said he had to go. Charlie's stomach was rumbling. She needed to get home, sleep, and then shop for something for tea. Casey had declared she was sick of fish fingers, she wanted some home cooking: 'Why don't you make something proper?'

Di had the hoodie pulled tight, and was crying.

It could be significant, the scarf missing.

'I'll phone the police,' Charlie said.

'Over a missing scarf?' James was scornful. 'They're not going to be bothered by that.'

'But don't you see? His scarf wasn't on him when he was found; they gave us a list of what he was wearing. If his scarf's missing, that might mean that whoever...'

She looked around to see whether Di was listening. 'You know, whoever did it might have it.' She finished the sentence quietly. Di was crying too much to make out what they were saying anyway.

'Phone them,' said James fiercely. 'Phone them now. I've got to go.'

'I'll phone them from home,' she said, glancing over at Di. 'I'll settle your mum first.'

Two cups of tea later and re-reading Darren's school reports, as if that would bring him closer, Di grew calmer, pulling out old bundles of wool, saying she was going to knit Darren a new scarf, if it was the last thing she did for her son. Charlie dumped the black bags outside in the alley. A strong wind buffeted plastic bags and empty crisp packets round the streets. Winter was coming.

17

MONDAY 21 OCTOBER

CHARLIE WAS ON a roll. She'd phoned O'Reilly, who promised to pass the detail on, and a posh English guy phoned back who listened carefully, took down all the facts and thanked her for the information. They said they would put out an alert, in case anyone saw a scarf of that description. Charlie decided to keep going. Do as much investigating as possible before the funeral, that was her plan.

So from work she phoned no nonsense, born to be involved Stella at the community centre.

'Can I ask a few questions?'

'Who's this? What about?'

When she explained, Stella barked a brusque, 'Of course, anything to help. I remember Darren. He was at a couple of meetings with his girlfriend.'

Charlie zoned out for a minute. Darren's girlfriend, of course. She made a mental note to ensure she saw her too. She zoned back in. Stella was still talking '… meeting tonight. We'll be discussing the idea of the Community Garden. There may well be others who remember him. I can see you after that.'

Another surprise. Darren at community meetings? He'd never expressed any interest in community anything. As well as sport, Darren was into drinking, smoking, enjoying himself. He'd gone fishing with his grandad; he'd tagged along to the allotment. The old Darren. The new Darren emerging was into art and films. A different Darren to the one they thought they knew.

Questioning Stella would take up time; stop her thinking about the funeral the following day. Charlie knew it was yet another diversionary activity. She had gone over her eulogy again and again, arranged copies of the service, with a lovely laughing photo of Darren. Checked who was speaking, what they were saying and how long it would take, asked all the speakers for what they were planning to say, sent Richard the programme so that he could order the music, and now had a pile of photocopied, badly spelled sheets of paper, mostly talking sentimental, clichéd rubbish. The hardest thing would be controlling people, and hoping no speakers turned up drunk or out of it. Di had insisted on some hymns, and James had inserted another couple, even though Di hadn't been in a church for years, and said herself she couldn't stick all the crap they spouted. Charlie, knowing no one would remember the words, had photocopied the words to *Amazing Grace* and *Abide with Me*, and hoped they could fudge their way through *Swing Low, Sweet Chariot*.

Richard warned her that speakers might dry up on the day. 'You always need a Plan B,' he said. Plan B was to keep on projecting photographs on repeat. She didn't want to think about it. Her throat was closing up already.

After a few hours' sleep, and tea and toast with Casey, she made her way to the meeting, promising to stop back and eat with Casey on her way to work. The meeting, held in the Community Hall, was set for 6.30. She wasn't on until nine. She'd arranged her shifts especially so that she could have tomorrow off. The hall was packed with rows of people, mostly middle-aged or elderly, dressed fairly smartly, with a handful of younger parents with children and a couple of crying babies. Stella, sitting behind a table at the front, nodded. Charlie was late, and had missed the first part of business.

'And now that you have heard the plans, are there any more questions?' Effortlessly, Stella's voice projected to the back of the hall.

'Is the idea to make it a sustainable garden?'

Charlie swivelled in the direction of the speaker, Lara, who made quite a startling sight, with her red hairband, puffy jacket and long skirt and muddy boots.

Stella smiled and turned to the room. 'Well, that's a very interesting question, and it's good to have input from younger members of the audience.'

She beamed at Lara, who grinned back. All eyes turned to Lara. Pete, next to her, blushed and squirmed in his seat. He obviously didn't like attention.

'So, is it?'

Stella scoured the rows for a response.

'Could you explain a wee bit what you mean by sustainable?' The question sounded aggressive, even though the speaker, a small guy with a beard, looked like he wouldn't hurt anyone.

'Yeah, sure,' said Lara, and then she was off on what sounded like a favourite topic. Words and phrases flew out of her mouth, as she talked about butterflies and bees and salvaging wood and making your own compost and mushroom manure and planting with the seasons.

'And the moon. Only joking,' she added, hearing giggles. 'Although biodynamic gardening – gardening taking into account the cycles of the moon – has had some scientific attention paid to it.'

There was a mild guffaw from the small guy.

'All opinions are welcome here,' said Stella, fixing the man with a steely glare. 'That's the nature of democracy.'

Charlie couldn't help but admire her. Stella knew how to handle this lot. Then talk turned to the council committee meetings and drawing up a proposal and planning the campaign for the community garden. There was consensus that it was a disgrace that there were so many neglected sites in the area. The proposed site was at the end of a row of houses, the last few of which had been knocked down years before. For a while it had been a children's playground, then the equipment became rusted and dangerous, and one day the council removed it all, and it had stayed overgrown with weeds and a dumping ground for rubbish ever since. They agreed that the area needed somewhere for people to relax.

An hour later the meeting dissolved into excited chatter, chocolate biscuits and terrible instant coffee. A group of men were deep in discussion about United's 5-0 defeat of Man United, and the news that Shearer would be off for a hernia operation. She heard snatches: 'Greatest performance of all time, man' and 'Seventy year we've waited for this.' She moved out of their range. Several people clustered round Lara as she explained her ideas. Pete was left standing on his own. May as well do something useful, thought Charlie. He might remember something more. She went over, tapped Pete on the shoulder. He flinched, turned round, and peered at her.

'Hello again.'

He blinked.

'Charlie, from the other day. Di's friend. I know I'm in my scruff, but I don't look that bad.'

He smiled without warmth at her stained trousers and old sweatshirt.

'You're different.'

Charlie, who most of the time disregarded what she looked like, was suddenly aware of how ancient she must seem, with her straggly hair and soft belly that had never been flat since having Casey. Still, and she drew herself up to her full height, her legs were muscled from walking, and she knew she had good skin. Probably everyone over 30 looked the same to him anyway. Home from work she'd bundled her notebook into her bag and thrown on the first thing to hand. She sniffed herself. The sweatshirt wasn't exactly clean. He, on the other hand, was dressed as if he was in a staff meeting, in a shirt topped by a V-neck jumper.

'So you're involved in the community garden proposal? I thought you weren't much of a gardener?'

'I'm not really. Lara dragged me along.'

He sipped at his coffee, eyeing the door. He seemed excruciatingly shy, with old acne fissures flaring up in the harsh light.

'Does she drag you along to everything?'

Panic flooded his eyes, and then he saw she was teasing, and relaxed his shoulders.

'She's quite a force of nature,' Charlie added.

'Aye, so she is.'

He sounded more Irish now.

Ask questions, she told herself. *That's how you find out things.*

'Been here long, then, Pete?' She heard herself echoing his way of speaking.

'What do you mean?'

'Lived here long?'

'I'm in my second year.'

'So you're studying law, Pete?'

Get their name in at every opportunity, and the interviewee will relax. She'd read that somewhere. Instead, the forced intimacy seemed to annoy him. It would her.

'Do you mind me calling you Pete? That's what Lara called you.'

'My family call me Peter,' he said, which didn't answer the question. He curled his toes up and down, and locked and unlocked his fingers. She could hear the cracking.

'What type of law are you studying?'

Pity was evident on his face.

'It's a general law degree. Last year we did criminal, and contract. Then it's tort, land, constitutional and administrative,

161

EU, equity and trusts. Plus, some optionals. I'm doing criminal procedures, and then Intellectual Property, and I might do medical law, or human rights.'

'Sounds exciting.'

'There's a shedload of reading.'

'I bet. What would you like to specialise in?'

'Not sure yet. Maybe Land Law. Or Intellectual Property. That's going to become a big thing.'

'I'm sure you're right.' She had no idea what it was.

There was silence between them, and then she laughed. 'Well, your knowledge could prove handy if we end up in dispute over the allotment.'

His face coloured.

'I'm not qualified; I can't really give advice. Liability and all that.'

'Oh. But you'll be raking in the money eventually.'

It wasn't a question.

Something like guilt passed over his face. Again, no answer. Charlie filled the silence.

'My grandparents came from the North. Came over for work during the depression. It's beautiful over there.'

'Aye, you said you had relatives. Some of it's beautiful, so it is.'

Charlie was waiting for more, but he wasn't biting.

'Your parents must be very proud of you.'

He shrugged his shoulders.

'No, really, it takes a lot to buckle down to a course. I'm hoping my daughter will study at university. History, maybe. Of course, some people don't get the chance.'

Sadness or fear, it was hard to tell, but a flicker passed over his face.

The age he was, thought Charlie, he would have seen things during the Troubles, and his family would have told him stories. Everyone she knew in the North knew someone who'd been affected.

They were agreeing that yes, the community garden could be great if it was managed properly, when Lara bounced over, and caught the tail end of their conversation.

'Of course, it won't make up for the council trying to sell off the allotment. That's another battle. We've got to fight that, and not let them palm us off with another allotment, while somebody rakes in more money than they need, building houses that no local could ever afford.'

Charlie nodded. When the funeral was over, she'd have to rouse Frank, get him to join in the protests. How would he cope without the allotment? He'd already picked out a rose bush for Darren.

'You seem pretty involved in all this. There are lots of good ideas.'

Lara nodded.

Charlie cleared her throat. Keep the conversation going, get them talking, say anything.

'Sorry for being nosy, but I can't help being curious. There can't be many students who have allotments. I meant to ask you last time. How come you've got a plot, Lara? Don't you have to be on the waiting list for ages?'

Keep them talking. You had to exploit every opportunity. You never knew when you might find something out. *The allotment, that's what Lara liked talking about.*

Lara laughed.

'A girl at my uni studying biology asked did we want to work it while she went off to London to do an MA. She got the lease from her grandad. Wanted us to keep it ticking over. She said as long as we look after it we could have next summer as well. Plant some salads and vegetables. Pete here's been helping me dig and weed. I haven't told her the council are trying to sell off the site. She wouldn't be too pleased. He'd tended it for ages. I can't wait to get going properly in the spring.'

'That's great,' Charlie said. Stella was right. It was good to see students making themselves part of the area instead of passing through.

And right on cue, Stella floated up, all smiles, pleased with the meeting.

'I see you've met some of the students. You wanted to ask me a few things. Come through to the back?'

Her voice rose in an upward inflection, like Lara and Pete's voices.

'How's your friend?' Lara called out, as Charlie marched briskly after Stella in an effort to keep up.

'Well, you know…'

'My mum always says that's one sorrow you can never really get over.'

'Your mum sounds like a wise woman.'

Lara smiled.

'She is, I love her. Well, nice to see you again, we better go, we've both got assignments due. This is all very exciting about the community garden. Good to have something positive to look forward to, after all the…' She tailed off.

'I know, it is. Oh, and the funeral's tomorrow.'

'I hope it goes well. Sorry, you know what I mean. As well as it can.'

'Come along.'

'Are you sure? Isn't it private?'

'No, Di said to tell anyone who helped out that they are welcome. And we're not having a priest or a vicar. I'm organising the service.' It was the first time she'd said this out loud. Now it was real.

Lara smiled.

'That's so cool. A friend of my parents whose daughter died of leukaemia, she had her sister do the ceremony, and it was lovely. Much more personal.'

'Hope so. You know the crem?' It's up near the dual

carriageway. Here, I'll give you the address. Not far. It's easy to spot. The bus stops right outside'

She scribbled on a piece of paper.

'11 o'clock. We've got a double slot. Forty minutes.'

'Are you sure it will be OK for us to come?'

'Absolutely. Di would appreciate a large turnout.'

'Well, we didn't really know him but we'd like to pay our respects, wouldn't we, Pete?'

'Aye, of course we'll come.'

'OK, see you then. Thanks.'

They trooped off, the girl bouncy and lively, and the boy reserved and careful in his movements. An odd couple.

Two more hours and she was on shift.

The conversation with Stella yielded an attendance list showing the regulars at meetings before the summer. Lara was one of the regulars. Stella thought it was the same group who had a kick-about in the park, and she gave Charlie the name of one of the organisers.

'I get the feeling it was kind of unofficial,' said Stella. 'Not sure it was organised through the university. Still, they would have run some checks,' she added, picking up on Charlie's thoughts.

'And you need student involvement. I'm really pleased at their participation in this. Students get a bad name, but these are a really good lot.'

Charlie now had a list of names to follow up. Those, and Darren's girlfriend, were the next port of call.

First home, and then to Di's. She'd promised to pop in before work.

At home there was no Casey, but a note: 'Pizza. Di's.'

Casey didn't mince words. She phoned as Charlie was packing her work bag.

'Di says she knows you're busy, Mum, and you've done an awful lot for her. What flavour pizza do you want? I'm having

165

pepperoni and cheese. And Mum?'

'Yes, darling?'

'I've already helped her sort and iron her clothes for tomorrow, so you don't have to do anything. You can just relax.'

'Thanks, darling.'

'We went to see Darren, Mum. It was awful.'

'I know, love, I know. Tell me about it when I arrive.'

As she walked the short distance to Di's, Charlie forced back tears. It brought you up short seeing somebody you knew dead. Early that morning, Chapel of Rest. He didn't look like Darren anymore. You never got over the stillness. As soon as you walked in, your stomach went, and you cried. And then kind Richard, who had put a vase of fresh chrysanthemums at Darren's head, brought her a coffee with sugar in, and a posh biscuit and touched her arm.

'Stay as long as you like.' She put her hand on Darren's cold hand, and squeezed his cold shoulder, and smoothed out a non-existent crease on his Newcastle shirt. And talked to him, telling him that she knew he'd been trying to improve his life, and do better for his mum, and that it wasn't fair, that he didn't have the chance now. And she kissed him on his cold forehead and said goodbye.

'I'll look after your mum, and James,' she whispered, and everything fell away, all the anger at Di, all the disappointment. Pretty basic. Be kind.

And Di was trying to be kind back. The offer of pizza was surprising, and Charlie was grateful. At home there was little to eat.

She thought of all the things still to do. The order of service leaflets were ready to distribute on seats, flowers were getting delivered in the morning, food had been ordered for the function room of the pub, James had given the music to Richard, someone was bringing CDs to the pub, and she had gone over her speech. What could you say about a 15-year-old boy? Everything lay ahead. They would all drink too much; they might even start dancing. She strode the short distance to Di's house, preparing herself for Casey's upset. Darren's was the first dead body Casey had seen. Poor kid.

Pizza with her daughter, and Di and James. Break bread. That's all they could do. Casey would stay at Di's tonight, Charlie would go over the funeral stuff one last time in work when the men were asleep, and tomorrow they'd get through this together.

She pressed Di's bell.

18

TUESDAY 22 OCTOBER

IN CRIME FILMS, the murderer always turns up at the funeral. Charlie, scanning the gathering, was on alert.

The crematorium was new built, surrounded by a long drive, and spacious greenery. Modern, energy efficient, all cold clean lines, vaguely nautical looking, plain. Soothing, like a Shaker house. None of that Gothic over the top pierced hearts and hands, crowns of thorns, this building was functional. As Charlie stood at the front near the lectern the afternoon sun slanted through the abstract stained glass windows, sending lozenges of light dancing. There was a faint smell of furniture wax and the occasional scent of flowers. Two burly men dressed in black tailcoats, and John and James carried in the coffin, directed by Richard to a dais next to the lectern. They lowered it down, and took their places in the congregation.

The coffin was draped in Newcastle colours. Around the side were photos of Darren going from being a baby to a 15-year-old, with his family, friends, alone, and a repeated border of a recent drawing by James of Darren. The effect was cheerful and festive, but it caught you by the throat. Under the closed lid, Darren had on his number 9 shirt.

The front pews were full of Darren's relatives, with his mother's all on one side and his dad's on the other, like in a wedding. Except for John, who took a seat next to Di and put his arm around her, holding her up.

Frank's words surfaced: 'There's no harm in John. He's just not a very good criminal. So unlucky.' His 'bad luck' ran to holding things, minding things, not being able to say no to people.

Di had left him in the end because he was always getting caught holding the goods. Whoever he was working for always mysteriously disappeared, and John, with misguided loyalty, never ever said anything. It was no kind of life. Good job Di didn't rely on him anymore, as he'd probably end up back in jail soon.

Charlie stood with her hands on the lectern, waiting for the music to finish. The Fugees, *Ready or Not*. It seemed totally inappropriate, and she was glad they didn't have the video, but Di had said it was one of Darren's favourites. It was that or gangster rap. She tried to calm her breathing, and loosened her grip on the lectern.

A coffin always sobers you, she thought, no matter how pretty the flowers are surrounding it, and they were pretty: chrysanthemums, calla lilies and freesias, set off by greenery. The coffin so still and flat, Darren lying in it.

Hyper-alert, she scanned the rows, suspicious, looking for clues. The smallest thing could be significant. Everyone was still a suspect. John, for a start. He had a grievance against Di for keeping him apart from his son. He'd wanted Darren to live with him: 'A son needs his dad,' he often claimed, but then he'd end up in jail again, and Darren himself had decided to stay with Di. Not being James's father, he'd never shown Di's first son much interest. All they'd heard from James's dad was a crackly phone call off the rigs. Hopeless dads really, both of them.

Something else. John had a temper when he'd been drinking: he was a loud and aggressive drunk. Hard to believe now, with him white-faced and moist-eyed, arm round Di. Could Darren have pushed him over the edge? Could John have hurt his son? Charlie shelved the question.

The congregation shuffled in. Charlie's eyes swept the first rows, and settled on Di. Could she have hurt Darren? Charlie dismissed it. Not because a mother couldn't kill their child. Of course they could. But if Di had killed Darren she would have whacked him at home. You wouldn't get her walking through mud in the park. You wouldn't get her walking. She might not have been the greatest of mothers, but then who was? Besides, Di couldn't keep anything secret. She would have confessed. And the police must have checked out her movements. On the other hand, could her concern be an elaborate charade to cover up guilt? No, she didn't think so; Di wasn't that good an actor. But stranger things had happened. Keep the idea on the table, Charlie thought.

Frank, hunched over next to John, was the one person who loved the lad unconditionally, the only one who could always see the good in him. But the fishing they'd enjoyed together seemed to have been a while back, and Darren had strayed recently. Frank hadn't been very forthcoming when she'd questioned him. Maybe he wasn't telling her everything. The argument, had it gone further? Had Frank's patience worn thin? She'd have to push him.

Just behind was Darren's girlfriend, Mercy or Melody or something. A slip of a thing, dressed in a pale summer dress as flimsy as a cobweb, with the thinnest of jackets, as if she was going out for a summer meal. She had the jerky movements of someone on medication. They hadn't been a couple long. James had said she was also very good at art, producing dark and jagged collages, and was planning to go off to art college. From the way she looked now, she wouldn't be able to get out of bed for a few weeks. But still, she'd been close to Darren, and needed questioning. Charlie hadn't yet arranged to see her. Must do that, she told herself.

Charlie sifted through assorted relatives and friends but could make excuses for all of them.

She caught Richard's eye, and he mouthed, 'One.' One

minute.

As well as family and friends spread along the seats, students sat in a subdued group at the back of the crematorium. She made out Lara, who waved, and Pete, but didn't recognise any of the others. Good of them to come. They all looked the same, with the good bone structure and straight teeth of well-looked-after kids. She still needed to question them. It would be a trip to the football organiser. Charlie wiggled her fingers back at Lara.

Some relatives gasped at the words in the song. But the students were unfazed. She impressed their faces on her mind. She'd tie in the details from Stella's list and make sure she spoke to them all.

The last entrants, an elderly couple on sticks, made their slow way to their seats, the usher closed the doors and after a few coughs, silence descended save for the sound of a mechanical digger in the road outside. Charlie cleared her throat.

'We are here today to say goodbye to Darren John Pearson. Darren was 15, and we were all saddened by the circumstances of his untimely death. But friends and family are going to take it in turns to speak now, remembering Darren in his life.'

She breathed slower as she stood aside, ushering the first speaker forward. One of his friends. At least, unlike the priest at Sean's funeral, she had got Darren's full name and age right.

As she expected, most people were really bad at speaking, and resorted to tears and 'I loved him' and 'Stay strong, bruv.' 'Always in our hearts' said one particularly dippy relative, who had hardly ever been near Darren, and had banned him from her house after he robbed her purse. Gastric Band Suzy went on about what a 'beautiful person' Darren was. Patently untrue. What was it about death that made everyone come over all sentimental? Couldn't they be honest? Darren's head teacher spoke of Darren being a 'real character', who was 'overcoming his challenges', on his 'learning journey'. In between the speakers James had slotted music, some with thumping beats she vaguely recognised, interspersed with Di's choices: *Abide with Me* and *Swing Low, Sweet Chariot*.

Then it was Charlie's turn to speak.

'Darren John Pearson. 1981-1996. Fifteen. What is there to say about a 15-year-old?' Charlie began. 'Everything is future. Darren was born in the same hospital as my Casey.' In the second row, Casey bowed her head. 'And he announced his entry with a loud yell. And he kept on yelling and making his mark,' she said, launching into anecdotes about his childhood, most of which featured escape, moving on to fishing trips with his grandad. 'He loved his granda,' she continued. Frank sat up straight, proud. 'Darren could be a little sod,' she added. There were gasps. 'He was awkward, rude, impatient, careless, could be a bully.'

People sat with their mouths open, puzzled. Some shifted in their seats.

'Stubborn, lazy, silly, selfish…'

Whispers hissed round the crematorium. John fidgeted on the edge of his seat, looking as if he was going to jump up and hit her. Frank had stiffened, and Di turned from John to Frank and back in confusion.

James stepped forward, and smiling, continued, 'He was also cheeky, funny, lively, honest, energetic, loyal, kind and hard-working when he wanted to be. And he loved his mum.' James acknowledged Di. 'And he loved his girlfriend.' He nodded at Melody. 'And he probably even loved me. He was my brother. I know we loved him.'

A collective sigh went round the room.

'We miss him.' James's voice cracked.

'And as we sit here today remembering Darren,' Charlie continued, 'we remember that he was 15. We don't know what Darren would have gone on to do. He thought he had his life ahead of him. And he was trying to change his life, get back on track. And now his brother James is going to show us some images of Darren, as we remember him and say goodbye.'

Behind them on the wall, to the sound of *Amazing Grace*, James projected photo after photo of Darren: Darren as a baby, Darren as a toddler, Darren with his tracksuit on, Darren at the sex museum in Copenhagen, Darren in his football kit on the way to the match, Darren with James and his mum at The Hoppings Town Moor fair the previous year.

Boxes of tissues were being passed along rows by the time the photos were finished. When James followed with short videos showing Darren playing football, Darren talking to his grandad and Darren running round and round the back yard, most people were crying.

As the videos finished Charlie waited for the sniffles to die down. Automatically, she put her hands together: 'We're now going to have a moment of quiet. Use it for your own memory of Darren, or for a prayer, or reflection. And after that, we will say goodbye to Darren, as his earthly body leaves us and we hold his spirit in our hearts.'

Charlie closed her eyes and saw Darren as a three-year-old, riding his first bike, drunk with the excitement of propelling himself on wheels.

And then they all stood, and filed past the coffin, placing a hand on it, feeling the warmth of the wood, smiling at the photos, and James's artwork.

When The Saints Go Marching In accompanied them out. Di's choice. And somehow, it buoyed them up on this most miserable of days.

Next came the back room of the usually dreary Blackstock Arms, which after the crematorium felt snug and alive. They started on sandwiches and crisps and tea, and moved on to the bar. People erupted into song, and some even got up to dance, remembered themselves, and sat down. A few drinks later they were up again, and stayed up, flinging their arms and legs around.

They drank steadily, anaesthetising themselves. Di went round the tables, thanking people for coming.

James, who seemed tipsy, put his arms round Charlie. 'You've been great, Auntie Charlie, great. I'm mortal.'

She squeezed his shoulder. Poor lad, let him relax for once.

'You'll look after Casey, won't you?'

'Of course I will,' she reassured him.

'I mean, really look after her, especially now?'

Casey was dancing round with a school friend as if she had forgotten the occasion. What did he mean? Casey was cut up over Darren of course, but so were they all. Such a lovely boy, James, always so sensitive.

'I will, and you look after yourself, James. Your mum and you need a break.'

'Oh, we're getting one. Didn't my mum tell you? We're off to Spain on Thursday.'

'Yeah?'

'She must have told you?'

'I'm sure she did, it's not gone in, there's been so much going on,' Charlie lied. She felt cold in her stomach, and furious.

'She would have told you, Auntie Charlie, after all you've done for us. We're going to stay with granda Eric and grandma Alice. They were really upset they couldn't be here to say goodbye to Darren. They tried to come, they even booked the flights, but granda's not been too well, and his doctor said it was best if he didn't travel. We thought we'd have a little thing out there for them. Are you OK?'

'Fine. Just going to check on the food. I hope you have a good break.'

At the bar Charlie drained a glass of wine, and ordered another. What a cow Di was, not even telling her. She had the chance last night after pizza. Charlie was well into her second glass when Casey appeared.

'Hiya, Case. OK?'

'Fine. You did well, Mum. It must have been hard. You haven't lost it.'

'Thanks. No. Are you really all right? James was worried about you.'

'James.' She looked across at him fondly. 'He's palatic. I'm fine. What about you? You're downing that a bit quick, aren't you?'

Boot on the other, Charlie thought, her head swimming. Casey was sipping vodka.

'Listen, Case, you'd tell your old mum if there was anything wrong, wouldn't you?'

'Course I would, mum, course I would.'

'Didn't you want to talk to me about something?'

'It can wait. This isn't the time.'

'Sure?'

Casey put her arms round Charlie. 'Yes, I'm sure, Mum, I'm sure.'

Charlie breathed in her daughter's warmth. Casey was too warm. Maybe she was coming down with something. Charlie should concentrate on Casey. Casey was her family. Forget all this idea about being a detective.

The barman scrutinised his watch, and another bartender whizzed round picking up glasses. Di swayed round the floor, holding on to James. The sandwiches had curled up; the floor was wet with beer and a couple of broken glasses swept into a corner. People laughed and joked, as if it was an ordinary party.

Casey untangled herself.

'But I did want to ask you something, Mum?'

'What, darling?'

'Why haven't I got a dad?'

For a second Casey looked like the smiley little girl she once was, thrown up in the air by her daddy. But then her expression changed to her habitual slightly pissed off look. She arched her back, and gulped down her drink. Why this sudden obsession with dads?

'You know what happened, darling. We talked over that the other night.'

'No, I don't, not really. I don't know why. I mean, that was ten year ago. Why have you not got together with anyone else? What's wrong with you? You could have given me another dad, could you not?'

'Listen, Casey, let's get you home, and we'll talk more tomorrow.' Almost from a distance, Charlie noticed how Casey's voice was getting more Newcastle. She'd always had a soft North East lilt. Now, with the drink she supposed, Casey sounded broader. Yet she didn't seem drunk. Charlie, on the other hand, felt her head pounding. She'd have some hangover in the morning.

'Will we? Aren't you at work tomorrow? Or at your friend Di's?'

'Well, yes, of course I'm at work, and maybe I'll call round to Di's.'

'Oh, no you won't,' Casey shot back, a knowing grin on her face. 'She's off to Spain. Didn't she tell you?'

'James,' said Charlie feebly.

'So James had to tell you? She couldn't even be bothered to tell you herself? After all the running round you've been doing?'

'She probably forgot.'

'Forgot? She could have told you last night when we were eating pizza. Yesterday I was beginning to feel sorry for her. When we went to see Darren, Mum, it was awful. He was so still and white, and his fingers had swollen up, it was horrible. And then she bought us pizza and I thought she was getting better, appreciating what she had, being nicer to people. But James told me later they were off to Spain, and I knew she hadn't told you. Why didn't she tell you?'

Charlie shrugged. 'I don't know. She needs a break.'

'You need a break as well. We all need a break.'

Casey was shouting, but everybody was caught up in their own conversations and nobody had clocked them, except James. He squinted over with concern.

Yes, I wouldn't mind swanning off to Malaga, Charlie thought. Why hadn't Di told her? She should stop all this nonsense about finding Darren's killer. She was no detective. Let the police get on with it. She didn't have to help Di anymore. But even as she thought this, she knew she would go on. It wasn't even about Di. She was doing this for Darren, and for herself. She needed to be good at something, finish something. All these years of stop-start jobs, all that study she'd started and never finished, all those skills she'd tried to learn and only got so far with. She was going to carry this through. She was going to find out who killed Darren.

'See, it hurts, Mum, doesn't it, when people around you don't tell you things? I wanted to tell you things, Mum, but you're always at Di's. If you're not at work you're at Di's. I never see you.' And then Casey was all soft wetness and sobbing in Charlie's arms. And that's how she was all the way home.

Charlie fell into bed that night shattered. She dreamt of walking behind Darren. He kept turning round and beckoning her to follow him, but she couldn't catch up.

19

WEDNESDAY 23 OCTOBER

SO MUCH FOR resolutions. Charlie only vaguely remembered making an arrangement with Melody at the funeral, but Melody's phone call asking her to come half an hour later than planned gave her time to take a shower and wake up. So it was getting on for lunchtime by the time she arrived at Melody's ground floor flat, a bus ride and a walk away. They were now sitting in Melody's living room. She'd left Casey, who claimed she didn't have any classes, in bed.

'How are you?'

'OK, I suppose.'

Melody had a gentle North East accent, more Middlesbrough than Newcastle.

'You did well at the funeral, you did.'

'Thanks.'

'I couldn'a stood up and talked like that, like. Where did you learn to do that?'

'Dunno. My mother always said I had a big gob on me.'

Melody laughed, and then covered her mouth. Her front teeth were discoloured. 'I daresn't laugh, you know what I mean.'

'Or you'll cry.'

'Aye. Nowt's real. I'm just in bits.'

'I know.'

'What it is, right, is that sometimes I forget and I think me and Darren are going mooching round the town, and then I remember. Or I'm doing something ordinary, and then it hits me again, like.'

'I know.'

'I miss him, you know. I really do. Before, I was happy as.'

'We all do.' It was true. She missed the cheek of him, his liveliness.

'How is that poor lass who got attacked?'

'Think she's recovering OK. They've charged someone, you know?'

'Aye, I heard. Dunno what's happening round here. It used to be cushty. I never worried about nothing. Now…' She threw out her hands.

'I'm sorry; I know it's a hard time, just after the funeral and all. You don't mind me asking you a few questions?'

'No, fire away. I like to talk about him. I don't want people to forget about our Darren. Away now, where's my manners? Tea or coffee?'

'A tea would be lovely.'

'Make yersel' comfy, give us a minute.'

And it'll give me a chance to look around, Charlie thought.

The place was neat, with bright cushions piled up on the two-seater sofa and two armchairs, and a big TV, and photos on the side cabinet of two girls who looked like Melody, and an older couple, her parents she presumed. There was another photo of Melody with her arm round Darren, the pair of them laughing. This took up centre stage above the gas fire.

But the walls in the flat were thin and badly insulated and the window frames rattled, and even though the fire was on full, Charlie kept her coat on. She knew the bathroom would be freezing, and the living room would be the only remotely warm room in the house, so that when you leapt from the bath you'd have to gather the towel around you and warm yourself in front of the fire. The flat was at the end of a cul de sac and took the full force of the wind. You could hear a baby crying in the flat above, footsteps, and a woman shouting. On the main road she'd passed a scabby looking supermarket, an Indian takeaway and a video shop.

Melody came back in with hot strong tea and a plate of digestives. They dunked and sipped.

'You might be wondering why I'm asking questions, when the police are already investigating?'

'But they might miss something, mightn't they? My mam allus said the police don't know everything, they make mistakes. She loves that *Silent Witness*.'

Charlie smiled. Everyone did. She'd heard a little girl on the bus on the way here telling her mother she wanted to be a forensic scientist when she grew up.

'Had you been with Darren long?'

'Proppa going out, not that long. But we'd known each other for ever, ever since primary school in Chilly Road. My family moved here from the Boro.' Melody laughed. 'I'd always liked him, but you know, you go round with the lasses, until everyone starts pairing off.'

'So when did you get together?'

'About a year ago. We got talking at a school disco and he says did I wanna go out, so I says aye, and then we started.'

'What did you used to do?'

Melody giggled. 'You know, the usual. Hang about. Go into town. Go to Whitley Bay ice rink. Go the pictures.'

'Did Darren like the pictures?'

'Course. Who doesn't? I love the pictures mesel.'

'Did Darren go much?'

'We used to go about once a fortnight, depending on what was on.'

'Newcastle?'

'Course.'

'Did Darren ever go to any other pictures?'

'Dunno. Oh, aye, yeah. Told me he went to Durham once to some little cinema, Robins or something. Said he saw some

French film. Couldn't understand a word. I used to take the piss, says he could hardly speak English, never mind French.'

She laughed, and covered her mouth.

'Did he say who he went with?'

'One of his mates. Never asked. He was always doing mad things. Try anything, he would.'

'Did Darren seem in any way different in the last few months?'

Melody seemed surprised at the question, but grew thoughtful, and chewed the end of her nail. 'Funny you should ask that. The police asked us that as well. I just says nae, cos it was too soon after and my head was like mush. But I've been thinking about it an all.'

'And?'

'Aye, I think he had changed, I think he was trying out his wings, you know.'

'What do you mean?'

'Doing different things, like? Like he asked me did I want to go to an art gallery exhibition in Newcastle. Called something daft like *Serious Games*. Says it was all about interactive media, whatever that means. He would never have asked that before.'

'And did you?'

'No, I couldn't, I was helping my auntie get ready for her wedding, she likes me doing her nails, says I'm artistic.'

Charlie smiled.

'I would have gone though. Even though I've decided I'm not going to art college. Tattoos, that's what I'm gonna train in.'

'Good you know what you want to do.'

'Tattoos are gonna be big you know. Most people think they're common. My granda had one from working on the ships. When I'm 18 I'm gonna get one of Darren. And there's a tattoo parlour in Newcastle that says as soon as I've finished my education I can go back and sign up for an apprenticeship. They've seen my drawings, but they say I have to build up my portfolio.' She had become animated, and seemed younger, alive. Youth. How you got over things. Then suddenly it was like the air was being expelled from her lungs, and she sat back and collapsed.

'Is that right? That's all really good. Coming back to Darren. Did he go to the exhibition?'

'Aye, I think so. He might have done. If not that one, another one sometime round then.'

And then Melody went quiet, lost in her own thoughts.

She brought more tea, and showed Charlie some of her paintings, including one of Darren, with wild eyes and hair. And then shyly she showed her a drawing of a design for a tattoo of a chain with the initials DP and MC intertwined.

'Lovely,' said Charlie.

They chatted generally, but Charlie knew that Melody had given as much as she could. The poor girl looked exhausted, as if she hadn't slept properly for weeks. She promised to get in touch if she thought of anything else, and Charlie left her looking through photo albums.

On the bus Charlie examined her notes.

Interest in film?

Interest in art?'

All kids changed. All kids tried to be very different from their parents. But still, the Darren that was emerging was definitely a different Darren to the one they'd all known. The question was – who or what had caused him to change? Who had he been hanging round with? Someone he didn't feel able to tell his family and mates about? Every answer brought another question. But that prickle of excitement was back. She wouldn't stop now. She had to keep on. That teacher who'd yelled at her once that she never finished anything, she would show them.

She called in at a greengrocer on Shields Road on the way home. Mushrooms. Mushrooms on toast, and scrambled eggs.

She'd wake Casey and they could have time together before work tonight. That would set them up. They needed their strength. Forget doing it for Di. She was doing this for herself.

20

FRIDAY 1 NOVEMBER

CHARLIE GAVE DI'S place a quick once over, fluffing up cushions in the living room, and airing rooms. She bought milk, a couple of frozen pizzas, teabags and a few bananas, and placed a bunch of freesias on the small kitchen table. Di and James rarely ate in the kitchen anyway, but usually perched food on their knees in the living room. Enough. The place looked better than hers, where a layer of dust made her sneeze, and fluff balls had taken up permanent residence on the stairs and under radiators. She couldn't remember the last time she'd deep cleaned her own house. Or washed her clothes properly. Every day she hand-washed a bra and top, after three days swapped her trousers for an identical pair until the working week was out, and hoped no one would notice that she wore the same clothes all the time. Nah, Martin was a slob.

The taxi idled outside, a door slammed and trollies rattled to the door. She switched on the heating and kettle and filled the percolator with coffee grounds. Arranged a plate of shortbread. The sound of keys, the front door banged, and then someone hot-footed it upstairs. James, probably desperate for the toilet.

'Fuckin' whore,' he shouted down the stairs, and slammed a door.

She wasn't sure who he was referring to. It didn't sound like James.

Di breezed into the house dressed in a colourful long skirt and a sleeveless top much too skimpy for a November morning. She kissed Charlie on both cheeks, something she had never done before. The top didn't do much for her complexion, being bright orange. Her skin was peeling pink.

'Bloody hell, it's freezing in here. Get the bloody heating on.'

'It is on.'

Di ignored her and turned the dial up to 30.

'I was thinking of your bills.'

'Oh, sod the bills. Life's too short. Get the kettle on, pet.'

Charlie felt like the hired help.

'How was your holi…?'

She started as a skinny olive-skinned man stepped out from behind Di. Two of him could have fitted into Di.

'This is Pablo.'

He flashed a smile, put his hand out to shake hers, thought better of it, and kissed her on both cheeks. He was dressed in jeans, boots, a puffa jacket, and a beany hat. Di and Pablo looked like they had been on different holidays.

'He's gonna be staying here for a while.'

'Oh. That's nice,' she added. Who was he? 'Drink? Coffee? Cup of tea?'

She chatted with Di while Pablo smiled and nodded. Yes, Di's parents were OK, they were so cut up about Darren, and really sorry they couldn't get over for the funeral, hard for her dad to travel after the operation. Yes, the weather was wonderful, plenty warm in the day, although you needed a cardigan at night, no rain, but you could still swim in the sea. She'd had a good time, but she was glad to be home. Di kept staring at Pablo as if she wanted to eat him. He leaned towards her, and held her hand and gazed into her eyes. After a while Charlie got the message that she was in the way.

'Don't you want to know how I've been getting on?'

Di looked blank.

'Investigating?'

Di cut her off. 'Let's forget about it for a while, eh, pet? I'm only just back from holiday. I'd like to stay relaxed.' And she glanced at Pablo, who gave her an OK sign.

Charlie left them to a brimming ashtray, the fire on full, Pablo's hand on Di's bum, heavy metal booming out of James's room. A thin blue haze rose up towards the living room ceiling, like in an old film. The place was already its usual tip, with scattered crumbs and an accumulation of cups. She doubted Di and Pablo would spend much time in the living room.

'I'll just say goodbye to James.'

Di waved her hand in the air. Pablo had put on some fast, vaguely Latin sounding beat and they'd locked eyes again, wriggling their hips and waving their hands. Pablo had more co-ordination than Di. It was the first time she'd seen Di dance. It was not a pretty sight.

When Charlie knocked at James's door, there was an indecipherable mumble.

She interpreted this as, 'What do you want?'

'To see how you are. How was Spain? Are you OK?'

He opened the door, rubbing red eyes. There were streaks of black on his face.

'Spain was OK. Not Mum.'

'What was wrong?'

'She was a cow.'

'Don't call your mother a cow, James, especially after all that's happened.' *Even if she is*, she thought.

'But she was. First night there she didn't even speak to Grandma and Granda, and I don't think Granda's very well, not after his operation, and it was good of them to let us stay, they haven't got that much room, and Granda has to get up in the night, something about his…'

'All right, I know, so what happened?'

'She took me out with her, like, and she was in the bar

drinking tequilas, flirting with everyone an' all. I left and she stayed up till all hours. Came crashing in, woke up Granda, I was sharing with him, and he couldn't get back to sleep. Selfish cow.'

'Well, she needed a break; it's been hard for her lately.'

'It's been hard for us all. He was my brother, like.'

That 'was' touched her. He didn't say 'is' anymore.

'I know, love, I know.'

She put her hand on his shoulder through the gap. He was so young. He pulled the door back wider and stood in the doorway.

'Then she brings back this Pablo guy to meet us. Pablo lives in some village outside the resort. He's got eight brothers and sisters for fuck's sake. Course he says aye when she asks does he want to come back to England with her. He's canny. Is she stupid?'

'She's not thinking straight. It'll blow over.'

Grief sex. Charlie had never heard the phrase until after Sean died. But she remembered that time, when you were all over the place, and you could have shagged anything that moved, just to be alive. Part of her, Charlie had to admit, was jealous. To have somebody look at you like that, care for you, that would be something. Only lovers cared for you that much. Di hadn't even asked anything about her or Casey. But then that was grief: no room left over for anyone else.

'Will you be OK?'

'Yeah, Auntie Charlie, I'll be OK. I need to get my head down. I want to go back to school. I didn't really want to go on holiday; I didn't feel like a holiday. I wanted to see Granda and Grandma, you know, but I didn't feel like… not without Darren, you know? '

'I know, darling, I know.'

'I want to do well at school this year. Stop messing about, you know, study, finish my A levels, get away from Newcastle.'

'And you will. Things will get better.' It slipped out automatically. Would they? His expression was sceptical. How? Just because the worst had happened didn't mean there couldn't be more of it.

'Anyway, I'm off, got to catch Casey, she said she was going out. I hardly ever see her nowadays.'

'How is Casey?' he asked cautiously, not meeting her eyes.

'What do you mean? She seems fine. The usual. A bit tired. Probably all the coursework.'

'Talk to Casey. She needs you.'

'You wouldn't think so; from the way she goes on.'

Did James know something? Casey had always confided in him.

'It's just her way,' he said, turning his face so that she couldn't see his expression. Suddenly his body movements seemed leaden, so much older. He shouldn't have had to go through this so young. It wasn't fair.

'Send her my love. And tell her to look after herself.'

'Of course I will. But you're getting me worried now. She's not thinking of jacking in school, is she?'

'Talk to her.'

'The anorexia's not coming back, is it? I couldn't go through that again.'

James snorted.

'No. She's fine about eating now. That was that one time when she was 13, and all the girls were egging each other on. She says she'll never get like that again.'

'What is it then? She should stay on at school. She shouldn't make the mistakes I made. I always wanted to go to university, I had plans. I wanted to do physics. Be an astronaut.'

James snorted.

'And she's so clever.'

Charlie trailed off, and zipped up her coat.

'I know,' said James.

Something bubbled at the back of her mind. Something didn't add up. She'd have to tread softly with Casey; she never liked being told what to do.

Like mother, like daughter.

'Bye. See you soon. On second thoughts, why don't you come round to our house, see Casey? If you want to escape from the lovebirds, mind. Stay a couple of days. We'd love to have you. Besides, I wanted to ask you a few things.'

'Thanks, Auntie Charlie. I might do. I tried to lie down in my room. Have a siesta. Can't sleep anyway,' he said. 'With all the noise. I need to sort out my portfolio.'

'Bring it round. You can do it there,' she told him. 'I mean now. Come now.'

'OK, I will, but Auntie Charlie?'

'Yes, love?'

Charlie was impatient now, wanting to get home.

'I wondered if…'

'What?'

It came out curter than she meant it to, but he didn't seem to notice.

'I've got this thing through.'

'What thing?'

'This thing that me and Darren applied for.'

'What are you talking about, James?'

'The Great North Run, the application. Me and Darren, we got a place.'

'That's great.'

'But Darren's not here, Charlie, and I don't want to do it on my own. My mam said you used to run.'

'I'm sure one of your mates would do it with you.'

He shook his head, and thrust a piece of paper at her.

'Would you do it with me, Charlie would you run with me? For Darren. We could collect for charity.'

And that's how she found herself agreeing to enter The

Great North Run with James, and committing herself to training a few times a week. Didn't they say that running was good for thinking? All the way back with James she kept smiling, as she held her jacket closer, ready to face Casey.

Casey greeted James affectionately. She made them all beans on toast, and then said she had an essay to finish for after half term, but that she'd be down a bit later.

'Come up after you've finished with Miss Marple,' she grinned.

James grinned back. Away from his own house, and his mother, he seemed more relaxed. Leggy, he sprawled on her sofa. Boys were so in your face; they took up so much space.

'What is it you wanted to ask, Auntie Charlie?'

His eyes were serious. One day this lad would make a fine partner to someone, and a fine father.

'You know I've agreed to do you a favour going in for the run?'

'Yes.' He was wary.

'Don't worry; I'm not going to let you down. It's just I need to ask you a few more questions.'

'Oh.' His shoulders released. 'I was wondering what was going on, whether you'd found out anything more. I know my mam doesn't seem that interested, she's so taken with that Pablo. I feel a bit sorry for him, I do an' all. I know my mam's only using him, she'll get shot of him eventually.'

'Well, maybe she just needs someone being nice to her?'

As soon as she said it, Charlie knew she was talking about herself. James didn't seem to notice.

'The police haven't told us anything. In Spain I heard grandma saying to Mum that there was no point you poking round anymore. "Darren's dead, pet," grandma said. "And nothing's going to bring him back." She's right, isn't she, Charlie? He'll still be dead; it's not going to make any difference whether we find out what happened. Besides, the police are working on it. After that attack on that girl, they got interested again.'

'They did. But they've got someone for that attack now. And they haven't said there's a connection. I know they're doing their job, I'm sure they're very good at what they do.'

'But they're not us, are they, Auntie Charlie? And they didn't know Darren.'

'True.'

'He was my little brother.' James gave a heart-wrenching sob.

Charlie let him cry, without attempting to comfort him. After a few minutes she said quietly, but with conviction, 'All we can do now is help find whoever did it, make sure they don't do it again. Can you bear to answer a few more questions?'

James looked up with tear-stained eyes. 'Why are you carrying on, anyway? No one would blame you if you gave up. My mum doesn't appreciate what you've done, and she doesn't treat you very well. She didn't even tell you we were going to Spain.'

'I was the same when Sean died. You're all over the place. You lash out. You don't know what you're saying.'

He stared at her in surprise.

'And your mum was good with me. She let me rant on. That's what you do when you know people, you let them rant on. That's what I'm doing now. So, are you ready for those questions?'

For answer he took out a small sketchbook and shaded in a man's face. It was a life-like drawing.

'Who's that?'

'No one in particular,' he answered. Drawing seemed to calm him. His breathing was steadier, his body loose.

'It's good.'

'Photography's more my thing. Darren was much better at

art, you know; he would have been good. He was improving every day, as if he could see more, you know. Mum's got all his drawings; she keeps them in her room.'

Charlie made a note to ask to see them. Maybe Darren had drawn the person who attacked him.

She began her questions. Yes, Darren had changed lately, said 'he had plans, wanted to improve himself.' That he wanted to get himself fit. They got on to the kick-abouts with the students. James was getting restless.

'Can I go up and see Casey now? You've already asked me about this.'

'But was there any student in particular he got to know?'

'Nah, he wouldn't have had anything to say. He said most of them were a bit too posh for him.'

'Most?'

'There was one guy, mind, Darren got friendly with him. An older student, think he's left now.'

Charlie felt a prickle. Why had nobody mentioned this person? Who was he? Did the police know about him?

'Aye, he said this guy was giving him advice on how to buckle down to study. Some kind of mentor. Said he knew what it was like; he was the first of his family to go to university. I remember Darren saying he was an inspiration. Said most students were posh bastards but that guy was alright. Said you didn't have to be posh to be a student, you just had to work.'

'Do you know what happened to him?'

'I know he was going abroad for a few months, that's what he said. Working in a bar somewhere. He might be back now.'

'Thanks, that's really helpful. Just one last thing. What did he look like?'

'A big man. Tall, you know, but bulky as well. Dark hair, curly, quite long. Kind of intense-looking.'

The same description that Pete had given. She needed to

get hold of this man.

Then Casey bounced in, admired James's drawings, and rifled through his sketchbook.

'I thought you were coming up to see me. Wow! Are these your drawings? They're really good. And your photos, you're really coming on.'

James smiled. 'These are just preliminary sketches. But aye, my tutor was pleased.'

Oh, please let him have a life full of joy, Charlie suddenly thought. *Don't let Darren's death blight his whole life.*

Question time had ended. Charlie shut her notebook.

'Are you thinking of keeping it up, the photography?'

'I told you, Auntie Charlie. Yeah. I'm applying to art college for a Foundation year first. And then we'll see.'

'That's good. Can I see some more of your photos?'

Casey was hopping up and down, fired up on something.

'Yeah, I was just sorting them out. My tutor wants to see my portfolio tomorrow.'

He had a shy proud smile on his face as he showed them his work. Buildings, people, landscapes.

'These are good. Have you got any of Darren?'

'Of course.'

'Show me.'

He picked one up and handed it to Charlie.

'I thought I could do a little exhibition, you know. Mam says I should try the library. Our art teacher had an exhibition in a launderette.'

Casey giggled. 'Cool.'

Charlie laughed, and fingered the photo of Darren. His face was fuller than she remembered, and more open.

She skimmed through others, and stopped on a group photo taken at a football practice. Charlie peered closely. The figures at the back were a little blurred. Hard to make out. But the stance was familiar.

'The ones he had the kick-about with? Is that Pete?'

James peered at the photo. 'Might be, or might not.'

'Pete said he didn't really play football with them. Said he only went the once,' she said more to herself than anyone else.

'Well, maybe that was the once. Or maybe he made a mistake. What does it matter?'

'And who's that tall guy at the back? Looks a bit older than the rest of them?'

'Oh, that's the guy I was talking about, the one that Darren got friendly with.'

Charlie examined him. Tall, curly hair, intense-looking.

'You think he might be back from his travels?'

'Might be. Said he was coming back November time, after the season. Why?'

Casey picked up the photo and stared. 'I know him. He works in Woolworths in Clayton Square. I saw him the other day when I went for some pick 'n' mix.'

'Really?' The prickle of excitement started again. She could hardly keep it out of her voice. A break at last. She impressed the guy's image on her mind.

'You could call in. What do you want to speak to him for anyway?'

'I will. Only want to check up on a few things.'

'Anyway.' James stretched his lanky body on the sofa. 'I said I was only talking to you if you promised to do the Great North Run.'

'And I said I would. What about you, Case, do you fancy going in for it as well?'

'Why?' said Casey, hard-faced. 'Are you implying something?'

'No.' Not quite true. Casey was looking a little porky. Did she get enough exercise? And she was always eating.

'There's no places left,' said James quickly. 'They're all gone, it's dead popular. I'll send the form in then. And it doesn't run itself. We've got to start training.'

Charlie got the feeling that she was being manipulated. What were these two up to? But she put suspicion aside, said that of course they would start training, and told them she'd leave them while she made them all lunch.

As she went into the kitchen, she heard Casey say, 'Thanks', followed by, 'Is she really going to do it?' and then they were laughing. She wondered what Casey was saying thanks for, and promptly forgot about it as she went through her diary to figure out the earliest chance she'd have to call in at Woolworths. At last she might be getting somewhere solid. The sooner she questioned this guy the more chance they'd have of going back to some kind of normality. Ordinary life was what she desperately craved, normality. No more shocks or surprises.

21

SATURDAY 2 NOVEMBER

AFTERWARDS CHARLIE THOUGHT what a stupid thing to do, to meet a stranger to ask him questions about the murder of your friend's son. But when she'd called in at Woolworths and explained, the guy, Chris his name was, was perfectly friendly and happy to meet her in his lunch hour to answer any questions. He got the mistaken impression that she was a journalist writing a piece about community involvement by students, and she never put him straight.

They met in the Barnes Wallis, a pub full of old men spitting and playing pool, and watching TV. There was a photograph of sodden fields, and geese, big skies, and flatness: the East of England, further south, a different land.

His voice was North East, but he had a touch of something else – French, or Spanish intonation – she couldn't put her finger on it.

He was tall, stocky, with dark curly hair, dark eyes.

'How long have you been away?'

'A few months. Went down to where my mother's family came from – the border of France and Spain, Basque country. Thought I'd give it a go, see if I could make a living, like.'

'And did it work out?'

He laughed. He had a pleasant, open face. 'Obviously not, otherwise I wouldn't be working back in Woolies.'

'Sorry.'

'Not your fault. I'll get something better eventually. Fantasy, wasn't it? My dad was always going on about how lovely the place was, how welcoming the people were. I don't know whether it was the place or my mum that he loved more. But he was so in love with my mum.'

'Was?'

'She died in April, just before my finals. She'd been ill for ages. And then he lasted long enough to see me graduate, died shortly after.'

'Tough on you, I'm sorry. Losing both parents in such a short time.'

'Thanks. It's almost like they were hanging on, you know, until I was about through. I went over there for my mum really. I promised her I'd give it a go. Besides, I was all over the place. I just needed to get away.'

'So what was it like then?'

'Pretty enough, and the food was good. And the people were friendly. The language was hard, although I'd picked up a bit from my mum. But it was full of old people. A bit like here really.' They glanced round. Most people over 70, and some seemed as though they shouldn't still be alive, with pale, wrinkled skin and knobbly veined hands.

'The young ones had all left for London or Barcelona, where the work was. I stayed as long as I could – got work in a bar. But I missed this, you know.'

They were down a side street in the centre of Newcastle. Opposite was a greasy café offering all-day breakfasts: fried eggs and bacon and big mugs of tea. An elderly woman rocked backwards and forwards at a table. In the pub, the one younger man cleared his throat, and coughed a phlegmy smoker's cough. Charlie got a sudden feeling that he was about to burst into operatic song. The voice of the barmaid went up and down. *Aye Jago, nae Jago.*

They were both eating stringy tasteless toasted cheese sandwiches.

'Sorry, I know you're on your lunch hour. I'll get to the

point. I might have misled you slightly. I'm not writing an article about community involvement.'

'You're not?' The lad still seemed completely guileless. But then, psychopaths were good actors. 'Why did you want to talk to me then?'

'Did you read about what happened in Heaton Park a few weeks ago?'

'I've only been back a couple of weeks. Took the first job I could get.'

'Did you hear about the murder?'

'I heard there was one. Didn't really take much notice. Heard a young lad was killed.'

'Well I'm a friend of his mother.'

'I'm sorry. Poor woman.'

''Yes. And I'm sorry to have to tell you that you knew the young lad who was killed.'

'Did I? Who?'

'You remember as students you used to have a kick-around with the local kids?'

'Aye.' His brows knitted. 'Was it one of the lads?'

She nodded.

'Do you remember any of those kids?'

'Aye, a few. Their school made the arrangement with the uni. Some of us became mentors.'

'Mentors?'

'You know, inspiring kids who might not have thought of going on to university. From "non-traditional" backgrounds, as they say.' His face had drained of colour, his eyes grown darker.

'Do you remember Darren?'

His mouth opened and closed, but no words came out. 'Darren?' he whispered at last, and then looked away when she nodded. His shoulders heaved. She let him be as he collected himself. Then he spoke, visibly trying to calm himself. 'What

198

happened?'

And so she explained it all, and told him of Di's request, and he listened gravely. Then he said what a good kid Darren was: 'Funny, quick, you know, really bright. He was well capable, you know. Much more capable than some of these twats who have everything handed to them.'

There was anger in his voice. Good, Charlie thought, you could use anger. And then, apologising, saying she had to do this, she asked him questions about how often he'd met Darren, and whether it had ever been alone.

'Always in public,' he confirmed. 'I know where you are going with this. We had to be checked out before we could be mentors. I'll give you the name of the person at the uni who organised it all. I did it because I thought it would look good on my CV. But I liked Darren, he was alright, I felt like we were getting somewhere. I had people who helped me get to uni – I wouldn't have got there otherwise. I had one teacher who really believed in me, and a youth worker who encouraged me – I wanted to give something back. I assume the police haven't picked up anyone for it?'

She explained about the early arrest and the lack of progress since.

'So they've got nowhere? They'll not pull out all the stops. Not for someone like Darren. They'll see what he was, not what he could have been. He was a canny lad, Darren. I can hardly believe it. Poor lad, he was so full of life, and he had so much going for him. Don't know what the world is coming to.'

He sounded older than his years. Charlie had forgotten how bad the sandwich was, and took another bite. She nearly gagged, and washed down the lump of fat with synthetic orange juice that stung the back of her throat.

'So you're helping out your friend?' His voice was stronger now, determined.

'That's right.'

'And you don't know where to start?'

Was it that obvious?

'So how can I help? I'd like to, for Darren's sake. He didn't deserve to end up like that. What can I do? Don't know how much use I'd be. I only work in Woolworths.'

He had kind eyes, myopic and blinking. There was a sense of calm about this guy which was very soothing. You could see why Darren would have been inspired by him. He would have been a kind of father figure, someone to look up to. Father. Casey had never had a father who encouraged her into adulthood. A wave of tiredness hit Charlie, and sadness so deep it was like she could never get to the end of it. All those years of mourning, all those years of not reaching out. What a waste.

And then it hit her. This guy was offering help.

'I realise, mind, that if you do want me to help, you've got to check me out first. You've got to put everyone under suspicion. Including me. Any more questions? Fire away. And I'll certainly go to the police, tell them everything I know.'

So she took the number of the university contact, and questioned him, grilling him about his friendship with Darren, and what they used to talk about.

'Why didn't you declare yourself to the police before?'

'I've only just got back, and I wasn't here in September. I will go now though. I can fill them in on background, let them know what Darren was like, make them see him as a person.'

'And the police will ask you, but did you notice any change in Darren?'

Chris stroked his chin, as if he was used to having a beard.

'Come to think of it, there was something different about him just before I left. I thought he was angry at me cos I was going off, but he said not, just that he was getting into different things. I was worried about heavy drugs, but there was no evidence of that. I don't know what it was. We used to get on well. I think he saw me as an older brother. I know he had an older brother an' all, but you know, someone already out in the world. Darren was interested in the fact that nobody from my family had ever been to university, that I was the first. "Do you sit round all day reading books and thinking?" he asked.'

Chris laughed.

'I told him probably more drinking than thinking, but yeah, I loved my time at uni, it was like I was alive for the first time, I could feel my brain expanding. I tried to tell him that.'

He spread his hands out, and it was as if the café, the road, the people, all the solid things had become fuzzy and insubstantial.

'Give me your phone number, Chris, and I'll phone you in a couple of days when you've checked in with the police and I've contacted the uni, and I'll give you mine.'

'Champion,' he said, like someone much older. 'Anything for Darren. Let me know if you need any other information.'

And that's how she got herself a helper.

22

SUNDAY 3 NOVEMBER

'READY?' JAMES JERKED his thumb towards Di's front door.

Charlie nodded. 'I don't want to hold you back.'

'You won't,' he said with assurance, his voice deepening. He was becoming a man. 'I'll just keep looping back. My basketball coach says the important thing is to train regularly. And stretch. That way you don't end up with injuries.'

'Bye, Casey,' Charlie shouted up the stairs. Last time she looked, Casey was still in bed, but now she appeared at the top of the stairs, rubbing her eyes. She was always so sleepy nowadays. What was wrong with her?

'Where are you off to? Thought maybe we could watch a video together later. Seeing as how it's your free day.'

'I'm going for a walk and a little run with James.'

'Are you really going to enter the race, Mum? I didn't think you would. Since when have you been interested in running.'

'I've got to make a bit of effort. And I did used to run.'

Casey looked flabbergasted. 'You should be careful. You haven't run for years, have you? Are you sure you'll be able to do it?'

No, was the answer.

'OK, then, go on your little run. I'll be fine. I'll do my homework first and then I might have another snooze. I could sleep forever.'

'It wouldn't hurt you to join us. Maybe wake you up.' As soon as Charlie said it, she regretted it. She bit her lip to stop herself from saying any more. Casey was so sensitive nowadays, ready to fly off the handle at the remotest sniff of criticism. She certainly could do with a run. She was looking fatter in the face, a bit tubby. She used to be such a skinny wee thing.

Casey pulled a face. 'I'm going back to bed. Enjoy your run.'

'Come on, Auntie Charlie, you're trying to get out of it.' James encouraged her out the door. 'The lass is tired, leave her be.'

And then they were outside. They stretched near a wall. She followed James, and it felt good to surrender, have someone else in charge. That was the thing about being a single parent, you got so used to doing everything yourself: cooking, shopping, the lot. If you didn't do it, nobody else would. If you ran out of milk at midnight you were the one who had to walk to the all-night garage in your nighty with your coat over it, leaving your daughter asleep, hoping no one would steal in and murder her, past groups of lads with nothing better to do than sit on the wall munching crisps and drinking cans: 'Howay there, hinny, in your nighty?'

It was a surprisingly mild afternoon for the time of year, with soft light, no rain in the air, that lazy Sunday feeling. Not often she had a whole Sunday off. May as well enjoy this last bit of good weather.

'Good weather for it,' James said. He trod up and down on his toes and the balls of his feet, stretching out. 'OK?'

'Yes, sure.' She copied what he was doing, lost her balance and had to hold on to the wall.

He laughed, turned to hamstring stretches and lunges and squats and then they relaxed their arms and hands and heads. She felt tight muscles warming up and lengthening and imagined herself running over the Tyne Bridge with thousands of others. In the pictures they didn't all look slim or young or beautiful. There were all kinds: runners dressed as Mickey Mouse, the man who always carried a fridge, and the goths and punks and cancer care people and the NHS workers against the cuts.

'Right, I think we're ready.'

Her stomach lurched. Now? She didn't think they were actually going to run. It was like when she learnt how to drive. She thought the first lesson would be theoretical, a gentle introduction. But no, the instructor had her stopping and starting in the first hour.

'Don't worry; we'll walk the first lap. Across the top of the park, and then round.'

She let her breath out. 'Are you sure?'

'No need to be so nervous.'

But what if she fell flat on her face? What if she broke her leg? Or hurt her knees. What if…?

'Walk fast now, to get our heart rates up.'

So they did. She enjoyed the rhythm of her legs moving, her feet on the ground, her breath coming steady. At the end of the first lap she was out of breath.

James, an attentive coach, told her to 'Breathe. Deep breaths, breathe.'

Sunday mid-afternoon. People walked their dogs, and accompanied kids to the swings. Various sized children on bikes and scooters and roller blades careered down hills. Roller blades put Richard, the funeral director, in mind, and she smiled. Shafts of weak sunlight through bare trees, freshness almost like spring in the air. Deceptive. The short day would close over and soon shed its warmth. Not long before shadows lengthened and the afternoon darkened.

'Now we're going to walk a minute, jog a minute, walk a minute, jog a minute. Just go at whatever pace is good for you.'

So they did, walking and jogging, if you could call it that, she'd seen elderly women with walking frames going faster than she was moving, but her feet left the ground at least.

And this took her by surprise, like flying, when a plane

accelerates and then suddenly you are up, earthbound no more, and you can't go back, you have to keep climbing.

The first two laps were bearable. It was as if her body knew what to do, muscle memory locking in. James chivvied her along, looping forward, running on the spot, and circling back. On the third round she felt her knees knock, her thighs burn, there was not enough breath in her body. She forced her feet down, legs becoming heavy.

'Breathe,' James shouted. 'Breathe.'

Damn all those times sitting around eating cakes, damn. The sweat began to pour off her, her breath was rasping. James, taking his duties seriously, kept glancing over.

'Alright?'

'I'm not going to drop dead on you if that's what you think. I used to be a runner, you know.'

'You can tell. You're getting back into it.'

And she was. They jogged the next lap, and as they tackled the incline near the children's swings, she got into her stride, loping and leaning forward. Coming down the other side was the worst, feeling the jolt to her knees, her thighs constricting. This was near where Darren was found. James must have realised that. Was it his subconscious, making him circle round the last place his brother drew breath? Did he want to lay down new memories? Plaster over the sadness? There was no police tape, no sign that anything had ever happened here. Darren was gone without trace, as if he had never existed.

To her surprise they were already round the other side of the park.

'Half a lap more?' James asked. 'Then we'll walk.'

She nodded, following him, more slowly this time, breathing through the stitch in her side. He stuck to his word, and they walked the last half lap, and stood by the wall, cooling down and stretching. As her breath slowed, cramp buckled her thighs and feet.

'Stretch it out,' James advised, catching the expression on her face. 'Keep walking round to cool down. I'm just off on a couple of laps.'

And he bounded off, pushing against the air, making it look so easy. Beautiful. Soon he ran past, and was off again and back. Twice more he shot through, and then finally walked to a stop, and methodically went through his stretches, grinning.

'I owe you that drink,' Charlie said. 'Thanks.'

The trembling in her thighs had slowed. The deal was that she would run with him, they'd train together, and he'd help out with the community garden. He'd done more than enough already, shifting bricks and rubbish for the community group.

'You'll ache tomorrow,' James warned her. He grinned again. 'Mine's a water and a hot chocolate. And a cookie.'

She hadn't seen him smile so much since Darren died.

For half an hour, content, they sat in the park café with young families and couples with panting dogs that lapped water out of bowls. Crows cawed above the skylights. Then the sky clouded over until there was only a single patch of blue in the sky. James slurped at hot chocolate, and gobbled a cookie, she drank a latte. They both gulped down water.

Soon the rains would be back again, soon they would retreat indoors. But for now, through the windows they enjoyed the last of the weak sun on their faces. It grew chilly and they pulled their sweatshirts back around them.

'You did OK,' James said. 'Not bad for an old woman.'

Cheeky sod. She punched his arm. So long since they'd had a laugh.

'Seriously though, I think you'll be OK. I'll work out a proper training schedule, make a chart. You'll be doing distances in no time.'

She smiled, grateful to him. But this was for him as well. A project. Lads liked projects, numbers, naming things, counting things. He was probably still measuring out the time since

Darren died, counting the weeks. After Sean died, she counted the hours; later the days, weeks, eventually months. Months became years, and sometimes she lost track, once telling people it was nine years. When she checked, it was only eight. It was as if Sean had died again. With Darren, the time was still measured in weeks.

This was how you got through things; this was how you lived, counting.

'Seven weeks since Darren died,' James said, picking up on her thoughts.

'Darren would have been proud of you organising this. He looked up to his big brother.'

'We'll do it for Darren. It's all I can do for him now. Maybe if I'd listened to him more.'

'It's not your fault.'

'I know that. We'd worked out a training schedule, you know. He was going to take this seriously; he wanted to sort himself out. This was part of it. He knew he'd messed up at school.'

And now he won't get the chance was the thought between them.

'I know, love.'

James had emptied a small packet of brown sugar onto a saucer, and was stirring it round with a teaspoon.

'I loved my brother, you know.'

'I know you did, pet.' It slipped out of her. James laughed.

'Careful there, you're turning Geordie.'

THEY HAD NEARLY finished their drinks when he pointed at a couple running past.

Lara and Pete. Charlie waved, and shouted, but they were gone, Pete having difficulty keeping up with Lara, who moved with the leggy ease of a natural athlete.

'It'd be funny if they're going in for the Great North Run as well.'

'Thousands are.'

She pulled her sweatshirt closer to her, chilled.

'Thousands,' repeated James, his face red and shiny.

The crows were making a hell of a racket and flying backwards and forwards as they circled to roost. Seagulls were massing on the bowling green, dive-bombing and squealing. Dark clouds over the trees.

'Come on, let's go, it's about to rain.' James took control.

Sure enough, the skies opened. Charlie arrived home soaked but exhilarated, ready for the shower, but filled with new energy. She turned the shower on full and rushed into her bedroom for clean clothes. She was about to step into the shower, looking forward to the hot water soothing her aching legs and tired body, when she tuned into a new sound: Casey crying. She threw her T-shirt back on. Casey on the bed, a towel speckled with blood between her legs. She took in the scene at once, got on the phone, and held her daughter, soothing her, stroking her hair, calming her. Not the time to ask her why she hadn't told her.

The ambulance came quickly.

As Casey was lifted onto a stretcher, Charlie noticed, as if in a dream, that there was a dead rat laid on a torn-off sheet of the local paper outside the front door. The ambulance people side-stepped it without a word. It occurred to her, as if from a long way away, that the rat couldn't have got there by itself. But then she dismissed it out of her mind, and concentrated on her daughter, rubbing her between her shoulder blades, something she'd loved as a child, stroking her hair, telling her that everything would be all right, not knowing if that was true. How could she not have noticed her daughter's condition? All the signs had been pointing in that direction. Poor Casey. And she had obviously been trying to say, in her own way. How unaware could you be of your own child's state? What a crap mother she was, totally unobservant, wrapped up in her own concerns, and Di's. She needed to look after Casey. Casey needed her. She held her daughter to her. Then the ambulance came, and calm voices and swiftly moving hands and feet took over, ushering them in.

23

SUNDAY 3 NOVEMBER

THE NURSE BROUGHT them tea on a tray.

'There you go.'

'That's kind of you.'

'Would you like a biscuit? Afraid there's only Rich Tea.'

She produced a sorry packet, and Casey, back sitting on a chair by the bed, took a biscuit and dunked it. She looked so incredibly young, her skin clear and blemish-free. It didn't help that she had on a school T-shirt that she'd worn for bed. Everything had happened in such a rush there hadn't been time to pick up anything else. She'd been examined and had an ultrasound, and nurses had come in and checked the bleeding, and now they were waiting for the doctor.

On the wall was a sign: *What to do after someone dies*. Tactful. There were also adverts for playgroups and breastfeeding support groups and the Still Birth Association and second-hand baby clothes and baby equipment. Charlie's eyes fell on an advert for a cot.

The doctor looked about ten, with narrow-rimmed glasses, a spotty face and an angular, boyish frame. How could this boy be in charge, know anything?

But he was talking as if he knew his stuff, saying that spotting was very common and that the scan had showed that everything was in order: 'Baby developing nicely, on the right centile for near the end of the first trimester. Week 13.'

Thirteen weeks already. Christ. Charlie jumped. Thirteen weeks, and she hadn't noticed anything.

'Blood pressure fine, no indications of anything out of the ordinary. Any questions?'

Casey cried softly. Charlie patted her shoulder absent-mindedly and listened carefully as he told them what to look out for, and said to come in again if they had any worries, any at all.

'The important thing now…' he said, lowering his head – Suddenly he looked 20 years older. There were great dark bags under his eyes; his skin was pale and unhealthy. These junior doctors, they worked 60-hour shifts and lived on chocolate and crisps. No wonder they partied hard. If you were surrounded by illness and suffering all day you'd party hard – '… is to have as much rest as possible. Go home and curl up in bed, look after yourself.' There was an expression of longing on his face.

They took a taxi home and Charlie stopped off at the supermarket for fruit and pastries, which they ate with hot chocolate and juice, and then flopped on Charlie's bed watching *The Simpsons*, until Casey fell asleep.

Later, because they needed to get out, she took Casey for a coffee at the Hellenic Coffee House, the only place open on Sundays. It never closed. If you went past late at night there would be two or three customers in, the same as on the odd occasion she'd had to catch a very early train. Casey had a decaff. The coffee wasn't Hellenic, but powdery and weak, about as far from Hellenic as you could get. They drank it with white sliced toast, and there was an overriding smell of grease. It was the type of place where hot drinks arrived with sugar already in them.

Charlie kept going over the news. Casey pregnant. How could she have missed the clues? Casey vomiting, saying it was cream cheese and prawns; the way she was always starving, and tired; the glow she had. Her crankiness. How warm she was. How she smelt different. Charlie cursed. And there she had been thinking Casey might be anorexic. Bloody work and bloody Di taking all her attention. Obvious really. The tampons in the big box in the bathroom hadn't gone down in months. The bathroom bins weren't as full. Thirteen weeks. If Casey wanted to sort it, they'd have to move quick.

Charlie welled up. She was angry at herself, and angry at Casey. Who was the father? Stupid stupid girl. She, Charlie, had a job and a promise she had to fulfil. Casey had school. There was no time in their lives for a baby. Babies took up all of your time. She damped down her emotions. Cool rational thought, that's what Casey needed now. She was only 15, for Christ's sake. She didn't need to ruin her whole bloody life. An abortion was still a simple operation at this stage.

And yet there was a small fizz of excitement at the thought of new life. This baby wanted to be here. She would become a grandmother. Plenty of people her age had been grandmothers for years. If she hadn't lost the first baby she would probably be a grandmother by now. She well remembered the blood, the sense of sadness, of failure. How she would have given anything for that baby to survive. And she knew, as she watched her daughter staring at a baby in a pushchair, what Casey's decision would be. Because she'd nearly lost it, she would want to keep it. The smell of a new baby, the soft give of them, the malleability, the way they folded into you, trusting and open. Charlie pushed away the thoughts. Casey was much too young. Charlie would have to play Devil's Advocate. Just because Casey nearly lost it didn't mean she had to keep it. There was plenty of time for children later. She'd have to be hard with Casey. But Casey's decision, Casey's life.

Then somehow without speaking about the subject they were back home drinking weak tea out of china cups, the cups the only thing that her mother had given her when she moved from her old house to a smaller flat, after Charlie left home.

'You've had them cups for ages, haven't you, Mum?' Safer

talking about cups, safer keeping the conversation practical.

'I have. I took them with me from flat to flat.'

From the psychos she shared with to the landlords who asked for extras, to this small house she moved into with Sean.

'We've been OK, Case, haven't we?'

They'd been happy enough; Charlie had taken on a succession of jobs, anything to keep them. Cleaning for learning disabled adults was better than working in a supermarket, and then she became a dinner lady. Now she was at the hostel she'd given that up. But still, she missed the kids, with their funny ways and the things they said and the cards they brought in.

'Do you remember when you had that job, cleaning for Sam?'

Sam had Down's Syndrome, and lived with her boyfriend, Syd. Sam had loved the power of doling out Charlie's payment for cleaning, carefully peeling off notes from her wallet, or pointing out a speck of dust under the cooker that Charlie had missed.

Charlie laughed. They'd get through. With this job at the hostel, they were doing better. She could take on more shifts. Even do a part-time college course, improve her job prospects. Scribing for students all that time ago had given her a taste for study, but that could wait a year or two more. Or maybe there'd be classes with a crèche, and she could take the baby off Casey's hands while Casey did her GCSEs. Two hours a week to start. Anything. A language, sign language or something. Signing would be good. But she was getting ahead of herself. Nothing was definite yet.

'Remember Harry left me a few hundred quid. I've got that put away. It can be for uni. Or a holiday. Or anything else.' *A crib, and stuff for the baby.*

Casey nodded.

'Harry was good to you, wasn't he, Mum? Leaving you that.'

Thank you, Harry, Charlie mouthed. Harry, her gay friend who'd died the previous year, had turned back to religion in his final months. Lung cancer. Sod's law, as he'd given up smoking years before. The funeral was conducted by a serious, tight-faced Anglican, dark and subdued, completely unlike him. The money would be a godsend now.

Automatically she started calculating the cost of nappies and babygros, what she could give up to help Casey. They had a yard, they could use real nappies the first summer, dry them in the open air, the sun. *What sun?* A sudden memory of Sean enthusiastically hanging out a line full of clean nappies hit her. He'd loved to watch them flapping and writhing, bleached white by the sun. Then he'd gather them in and fold them neatly and put them on the shelf by the cot. Cheaper than disposables, he said. It wasn't really if you factored in the detergent and the softener and the cost of the nappies. But the pleasure he took in hanging them out, and gathering them in: the only man she knew who found nappies sensuous. By the time he died Casey was walking and talking and long past nappies. There were still a few lying round somewhere. She'd search them out.

Stop that. Tell her how hard it is. It's not just going gooey-eyed over the baby all clean and changed and sweet-smelling in their pushchair. It's feeding them in the middle of the night, when you can hardly hold your eyes open, but daren't sleep in case you squash them. It's a winter's day in a strange town where you know no one and everything's shut that doesn't cost money. It's colic and fevers and trips to A&E.

Casey was still a child, scarcely able to look after herself. How could she look after a baby?

Casey steered the conversation back to her grandmother. 'Your mother was a bit of a lady, wasn't she, Mum?'

Charlie laughed. Even though her mother had lived in a council flat all her life, proud of not caving in when people started buying theirs, she had acted like royalty, decorating her windows with flounces and flurries, and when her eyes started going, wearing her sunglasses to the shops with a scarf tied Princess Grace-style. She always said she was happy paying rent; she didn't want the responsibility of repairs. 'I just phone up and eventually a nice man comes out and fixes things.'

Charlie sighed. She could do with a nice man fixing things.

'You're so unlike her, you know, Mum. I wish I'd known her better.'

'Me too,' thought Charlie. All those years of stupid arguments, and at the end, none of it really mattered. Her mother had been a character. She should have paid more attention to her, instead of picking fights and criticising.

'Do you remember?' said Casey, and then they were talking about her mother's eccentricities; her 'delicacies', as she called them; the 'nice' things she collected, useless things like fish knives and cake stands, cheese wires, champagne glasses. The afternoon teas she made, with sandwiches with the crusts cut off, small slices of cake, scones.

'You're the complete opposite.'

It was true. A knife, a plate, a fork, a cup – Charlie used the same one all day, rinsing them through. Whenever Casey was away she lived like a nun, dressed in layers of clothes, turning off the heating, and living on soup. Charlie couldn't get excited over food. She got hungry, she ate. The day after day of cooking on little money had deadened her interest. Sad really. Her mother on the other hand, no matter how broke she was, would always arrange the food so that it looked good – a sprig of parsley, a slice of lemon, an artfully prepared tomato.

'Just because I'm having a baby doesn't mean my life stops.'

Charlie's heart leapt. Casey had that stubborn look Charlie recognised. She'd got it from her. Oh, her lovely girl. *Tell her how hard it is.*

'It's a big responsibility, you know. You're only young. And what about the father?'

Casey ignored the last question.

'I know, that's what's good,' said Casey blithely. 'I'll have lots of energy. All these women who have babies when they're 38, no wonder they're knackered. It's just when I saw the blood, Mum, I made a pact with myself. If this baby survives, I promised myself, I'm going to be the best mother ever. Before, I was going to have an abortion. I'd made an appointment. I was figuring out when to tell you.'

'It's 24/7.' *Come down hard.*

'But you'd help, wouldn't you, Mum?'

'I've got work.' *I've got a life. I want to do things.*

'Of course I'd help.'

Charlie waited, hardly daring to breathe.

'I've been looking at unis that have good childcare,' said Casey.

Charlie sat up.

'I figure I'll be better off in a city rather than out in the middle of nowhere. There'd be transport. And babysitters,' she added.

She must have caught a look of disbelief on Charlie's face.

'I still want to go to university,' she said. 'I still want to have a life.'

Charlie raised her eyebrows. 'Course you do, darling, course you do. It's just it might not be so easy. You might have to adapt your plans. Or put off things for a little while.'

'That's what you did, Mum, wasn't it?' said Casey gently. 'And look what happened.'

She'd only ever given Casey the barest outline. Leaving school half-way through her A levels, pregnant. And then losing the baby. Too late to go back to school and no thought of anything different. Lots of her friends already promised places at college and uni. Starting work in a succession of insecure, badly paid jobs where she never seemed to get paid for holidays. Wanting to get back into study, and then after Casey was born somehow it never being quite the right time, with them always needing cash. And then Sean dying. Survival.

'My history teacher says I'm heading for an A star in my GCSEs, and I want to do my A levels, get my exams. I'm still ambitious.'

'Oh darling.' Charlie didn't dare speak. She didn't want to tell her how hard it would be; she didn't want to put a dent in that wonderful confident young personality. Why shouldn't she aim high?

'He says if I keep on working the way I'm doing...'
Charlie waited.

'He says eventually I could apply to some really good unis. Maybe even Cambridge.'

'I'll put the kettle on again,' Charlie said, getting up.
'I still want to know who the father is. They should take responsibility as well.' She wanted to cry.

'It's complicated. He will, eventually. And if I breastfeed, even if the baby comes early, I can still do the exams. I just need someone to hold the baby. I'm sure we could work something out. I haven't lost my mind.'

Charlie kissed her girl, so full of plans.

In the kitchen while she waited for the tea to brew, she allowed the tears to fall, the tears that she had never allowed her 17-year-old pregnant self. She'd known of other girls pregnant during that time. Sandra Wills, 15, whose parents shoved her off to relatives in Norfolk. Returned a year later, pale and thin, with a new hard face. Did her exams and her mum pushed the pram around, said it was her menopausal baby. Sandra gave up art, took up physics and chemistry. Wits said she should have studied biology first, but she ignored them. The art teacher left, and Sandra Wills went off to Durham and never looked back. Her mother jumped off the top of an office block years later. Poor woman.

Charlie poured milk into cups. When Christine Scully became pregnant in the fourth form, her mother took her out of school and the family moved soon after. No thought of her returning to education. Once, back home, Charlie saw a woman who reminded her of Christine, but this woman looked years older than Christine would have been and had two children in a pushchair, one in a sling, and two older kids. Her hair was stringy and her face had that droopy middle-aged look, her skin sallow and lined. She was smoking. She'd been a shy luminous girl who was very anti-smoking when everyone was trying it to look cool. Later, Charlie discovered it was her.

She snapped to, pouring the tea into cups. Casey wouldn't end up like Christine Scully, old before her time. And Charlie wouldn't pretend the baby was hers, and throw herself off an office block. It was going to be hard. But the flicker of excitement was taking root and growing.

Then the phone rang. Chris, informing her that he'd checked in with the police. 'I'll show you the evidence,' he offered. 'Did you speak to the uni guy?'

'Not yet. I will. Had a lot on.'

'Well, do so, but if you think you can trust me, I've talked to some of Darren's mates and arranged for us to go and see them. Working Men's Club.' He named a date. 'Ring me when you figure out what time's best for you. They'll be there for about three hours. And we also need to talk to the other students. Probably best if you did that, some of them know me.'

Charlie felt a wave of tiredness. 'I will. Thanks for doing all that – I'll get back to you soon. Hang on, how did you get my number? I didn't give it to you.'

'Hope you don't mind, I looked you up in the book. Phone me. Bye.'

Of course. So much to do.

When Charlie woke in the middle of the night she went in and covered Casey, always a messy sleeper. She felt a new resolve. If this baby could survive, she could figure out who killed Darren. She had a helper now. They needed to get a move on. Casey would call on her more as the pregnancy went on. Nothing was going to be easy. She took out her notebook and a new rollerball pen, put the side light on. Drew a line down the centre of her notebook. **Suspects. Motives. Opportunity.**

She began to fill in the list. She needed one of those big white boards on the wall that they had in detective stories on TV.

Three o'clock in the morning found her in the living room, pinning lining paper to a cork board. She could keep the cork board behind the table. She dug out index cards, wrote each suspect's name on it, with details about them, their alibi, and questions.

In big letters, she wrote: **Victim** Darren Pearson Aged 15. She dug out a picture of Darren, grinning in his tracksuit, and pinned that up.

Suspects.

It was a long list.

Arrows spidered the paper. So many connections between people. But she was missing something, she knew. There was something lurking at the back of her mind, she couldn't put her finger on it.

When Casey stirred upstairs at seven Charlie was still at it. She hid the board quickly behind the table. She had a lot to do. There was no definite suspect. Yeah, she hated Michael, and she suspected him of something. But she had nothing on him really. Anything against him was circumstantial. Just because he was a creep didn't mean he was a murderer. She'd have to plan how she was going to find out more about him. And did she even trust Chris? An older guy who starts up a friendship with a younger man? He seemed nice enough, but what was that about? She needed to check him out with the university.

She lay on the sofa and closed her eyes. She woke to the TV on loud, Casey snuggling in to her, an afternoon film. She made them snacks and they slobbed, content.

24

TUESDAY 5 NOVEMBER

CHARLIE WENT RUNNING again on Monday with James, and despite the aching ankles and legs, slept better and woke up optimistic.

'All those endorphins,' Di laughed. They were in the hallway of her house at three in the afternoon, Charlie having knocked for James. 'Sex does it for you as well.'

Charlie had been on an eight till two, but Martin had told her to leave early, there wasn't much to do. 'Enjoy yourself, go to a bonfire,' he said.

All over the city, bangs and flashes had started up, even though it was still light. Charlie had nothing planned. Casey was going to a mate's bonfire party with a friend. Charlie never really liked municipal displays, with the oohs and aahs as everyone marvelled on cue at the fireworks, and the bad jokes of the local compere they always roped in. She preferred the anarchy of when she was growing up, with kids dragging mattresses and anything remotely combustible to the nearest bit of waste ground. She liked that sense of danger, that anything could happen.

They were laughing at Di's remark, and she was just about to ask Di whether she had anything planned, when Charlie realised there was a man behind Di. For a minute, she thought Di had got herself another man, and felt a momentary stab of jealousy. She pulled at her running shorts self-consciously. But Di still had Pablo. This guy was a stranger. She shifted from one leg to another. Nobody usually saw her legs, and she was aware of not having shaved them for months. There didn't seem much point in the winter, as they were often running in the dark. She hunched her shoulders. The sports bra made her nipples stand out and before she zipped her hoody back up she got the feeling that the man had caught a glimpse.

'G'day. Hi, I'm Steve.'

He held his hand out. Automatically she returned his handshake. Strong firm grip, short, neat nails. Casual trousers and T-shirt, a kind of worn, rumpled look about him.

'Charlie.'

'Oh, James has told me all about you.'

He flashed her a smile. He was tanned. Most people tanned in November were bright orange, courtesy of vertical tanning machines, or fake tan. His looked golden and natural, and his voice had a touch of Down Under. She blushed, and lowered her face to hide it. She was a sucker for Aussies, ever since her first holiday abroad in Corfu with a bunch of schoolmates. Aged 16, they latched on to a big casual group of Australians, and a gang of them watched sunsets on the beach, Charlie and her friends white and skinny, the Australians bronzed and confident in their bodies. It was the first time, with the feel of the warm water, and the heat of the sun, that she'd thought of her body as something you could revel in.

'Glad to have met you at last. Thought James had made you up.' His eyes scanned her in a frank way. Somehow it wasn't creepy.

'I'm James's new support worker.'

Support worker? News to her. The surprise must have registered on her face because he quietly responded: 'To help him cope with everything that's happened.'

She suddenly had an urge to talk to this man. He had that type of face. You wanted to open up to him. She wanted to tell him about how she'd been a student support worker, how interesting she'd found it, all the things she learnt, particles of physics and history and chemistry and politics and English. Nobody was ever interested in hearing about that job. They thought you took notes and made tea and pushed wheelchairs, but it was a whole lot more. She wanted to talk to him about 'Support' and what it meant, she wanted to tell him the picture she had of hands holding you up, carrying you.

'Oh. Good luck,' she said. It sounded wrong, but he smiled anyway.

Di had retreated through to the kitchen, and James bounded down the stairs. God, the young had so much energy.

'Oh, sorry Charlie, I can't go running today, I forgot to tell you, I had this meeting arranged with Steve, and then I've got basketball practice later.'

A sports bag lay at his feet.

'Oh.'

She'd been looking forward to the run, clearing her head and emptying out the smell of the hostel.

'Oh, well.'

'Tomorrow, Aunt Charlie. Will you be OK? You should still do some stretches. My coach says that at your age, you need to keep up training, otherwise it takes longer to recover.'

'Hey, less of the "At your age." I'm not in a wheelchair yet. But I will do a few stretches, maybe go for a walk. Tomorrow's OK. Same time? I'll have a coffee with your mum. She in the kitchen?'

She was already halfway there, turning her face away from Steve, in case he caught her confusion. She wanted to get away from this man. He was gorgeous.

Steve gave a friendly, amused wave, and then he and James, heads bent, trotted off to the living room and closed the door.

Di was immersed in the usual smog. She held up a jar of instant coffee, spooned some in a cup, and filled it. The cup was not particularly clean. The coffee was disgusting.

'Where's Pablo?'

'Buggered off down to London, he's got some mates there. Knew it wouldn't last. He was a nice lad, though. Did me good. Cleared me out, you know. Took my mind off things. Biscuit?' Di sounded particularly Yorkshire today. It was like she was putting it on.

The shortbread biscuits were stale.

'What are you doing here? Haven't seen you for a while.'

'I came round to go running with James. I told you.'

Di had the attention span of a gnat.

'Surprised you're keeping that up. I wasn't sure. He wasn't either. Said he left a message on your answer machine, but you didn't get back to him.'

Charlie said nothing. She rarely checked messages. She worked on the basis that if someone really wanted her, they'd try again until they caught her.

Di spread herself out over two kitchen stools, putting her feet up. She looked puffed up and pasty again, as if she was back on the white bread and cigarettes diet. The kitchen was in its usual state of disarray, with everything a little grimy. Charlie didn't know why she bothered to clean. She might have known that Di couldn't keep it up. She'd always been a slob. Strange that, when her mother was obsessively clean and tidy. Before she moved to Spain, Alice used to boast that her kitchen floor was clean enough to eat off. Problem was, you never did feel like eating in her house. First there were the coasters. Then the plates, then the napkins. And she cleared up every crumb after you, almost before you'd finished eating, removing all traces. It made you lose your appetite.

'He's all right, though isn't he?'

'Who?'

'Don't pretend you haven't noticed. Steve. He's gorgeous, isn't he?'

'Where'd he come from?'

'Some charity, they work with teenagers bereaved by

violence. You know I had so many people phoning me up the last few weeks I didn't know whether I was coming or going. But this lot asked did I want any support with James. Must have been a bad day, or I liked the sound of the guy's voice, but I said yes. James doesn't talk much about Darren, you know. Sometimes I don't know what to do with him, he's always hanging round here, getting on my nerves. He's looking out for me, poor lad, but he doesn't realise it's annoying. It's a good idea, don't you think – get someone in he can talk to, someone who will actually listen?'

'Yeah, it's a good idea.'

'I do try and listen to him, I really do, but it's like I can only concentrate for a short time. Anyway, enough of all that. When was the last time you got off with anyone?'

Charlie began to count on her fingers. 'Months? Years?'

And then they were giggling like teenagers, bending over, holding their stomachs. When Charlie straightened up, Steve was standing in the doorway. How much had he heard? He was gorgeous. His legs were hairy and muscular, you could see the outline of his muscles through his T-shirt, and his hands were big and capable. His face was lined in the harsh kitchen light. All that sun, it had an effect, all that surf. Somehow it made him more appealing. Charlie yawned, suddenly very tired. She put her hand to her mouth, and caught Steve's glance.

'See you, mate,' he shouted to James. 'See you next Thursday.'

He turned to Di. 'I think he's doing OK, James. He's a good lad; you hang onto him, there, Di?' There was silence, and a momentary flash of pain on Di's face. 'Sorry. I've got a big mouth on me sometimes.'

'No offence,' said Di, with an almost coquettish expression.

'I'll just shoot through. I left the motor at the office. I'll see myself out. It seemed like a great day for walking, but I'll catch the bus back. Next left and then second right?'

'Charlie here's going that way. She can show you.'

'OK. Sure it's no trouble?'

'Fine,' said Charlie, pushing herself off the kitchen stool. She glared at Di, but Di only smiled.

'Thanks, that's good of you.'

Charlie ignored the smile on Di's face. But Steve saw the kick she aimed at Di's shin. And grinned.

'Sorry, my foot slipped.'

And then she was grinning as well. They were all grinning.

After that it was simple, no thinking involved. They chatted all the way to his bus-stop. He was easy to talk to. He had a wife and kids in Sunderland. They were separated, although he had the kids regularly. He'd just been back to Oz; his dad wasn't too well. He made her laugh, with his tales about his travels and his misunderstanding of the local accent. Puppy-like and youthful in spite of the grey hairs, he seemed good-natured and enthusiastic.

'You know the bridge in Newcastle is a prototype for Sydney Harbour Bridge? No wonder I feel so at home.'

As his bus arrived he asked did she fancy a drink that night, so later they had a drink, in a wine bar up the road from her. The night crackled and banged around them, there was the smell of gunpowder in the air. And for the first time since Darren's murder, she relaxed, and forgot her worries about Casey and the pregnancy, and the fact that she was supposed to phone Chris back and arrange a time to see Darren's mates, all that went out of her head, as she gave in to the beginning of something, and took her eye off the ball.

25

MONDAY 11 NOVEMBER

LUNCHTIME, AND CHARLIE, half-asleep, was wandering round the local shops in rather a daze when she bumped into Nia Hughes, who she'd known at secondary school back home. And a daze was the only way to describe the state she'd found herself in over the past week. Meeting Steve had blindsided her, caused her brain to go fuzzy, made her forget things, lose concentration on the investigation. Not that much had happened yet. But it would, that was obvious. He was so different to Sean, but similar somehow. Comfortable in his own skin. No agenda. Dismissing her mottled legs and the extra layer of fat she self-consciously pulled at round her belly: 'Nobody's perfect,' he said, laughing, and pulling her close. Charlie was still on a high. They'd met a couple of times in the last week, kissed and hugged, and he'd held and stroked her hand, which felt curiously intimate. At the same time, they talked and laughed about everyday things. It felt easy.

'Oh, I haven't seen you for ages. Why didn't you call me? I left my number with Di.'

Charlie shrugged. Nia was a pain, that was why. She pecked Charlie on both cheeks, as if they were proper friends.

'Fancy a coffee?' said Nia. She'd been annoying at school and was annoying now, but some connection fired in Charlie's brain. Nia worked in the police station. She might be able to access files, find out something about the police investigation. So Charlie agreed. Now she was waiting in the queue, she was reconsidering. Nia Hughes had always been up herself. It was just by chance that they'd ended up in the same neck of the woods, as Charlie wouldn't have actively sought her out.

They were in the Hellenic, with its pictures of Mount Olympus, and the smell of fried eggs. Nia had her concerned face on.

'Di said I should see you. That you were doing some investigating.' She made it sound slightly seedy. Big mouth Di. 'Poor Di, I feel so sorry for her. I can't imagine what she's going through.'

No, you can't, thought Charlie. *For a start, you haven't got the imagination, and secondly, you're not interested in anyone else.*

Nia's voice was syrupy with concern. She was a bad actor.

'You're trying to find out who killed Darren? Shouldn't you leave that to the experts, the detectives? They know what they're doing, and they've got the resources. Have you got any qualifications?'

She sounded out every syllable, her Welsh accent more noticeable. Maybe she'd decided that Welsh was sexy, or maybe Charlie had just forgotten how broad she was.

'Seven O levels and a couple of A levels.' Charlie couldn't resist.

Nia drew in breath, and then laughed: 'You always were a joker.'

Charlie put on her sympathetic face. 'I know the force is really under stress. They don't have enough… She couldn't bring herself to say 'manpower'. Probably women did most of the work. 'Staff,' she ended the sentence.

'I know,' said Nia, 'It's terrible, there are murders that haven't even been solved, and…' She realised what she was saying, and stopped. 'They're all so tired, poor loves. None of their marriages last.'

Her expression was innocent. Charlie wouldn't have put it past her to have had a hand in messing up a few marriages.

Nia portrayed herself as a femme fatale. She'd told Charlie once that her name meant 'Bright radiance.' She was a plain, rather dumpy woman with an unusual name, but men were fooled by makeup and perfume and a simpering manner. Most men were idiots. Not all men. Steve wasn't an idiot. She had a warm glow in her belly when she thought of him. They'd only seen each other twice and she was still breathless with the newness of it all, how easy and natural it felt. She could be herself with him. So she felt unusually tolerant towards Nia, dull Nia who could only mouth others' opinions.

'They *are* very short of staff,' Nia agreed, as if she was personally responsible for the police force. 'They don't really have the staff they need to keep on this case.' She put her hand over her mouth, as if she'd said too much. And then she carried on, as if it didn't matter anymore. 'I'm telling you this in confidence, of course.'

'Of course.' Charlie widened her eyes in innocence.

'But between you and me, I've heard certain detectives say that they've not been pulling out all the stops on this one. That if it was a pretty girl there would have been more of an outcry and more resources employed.'

Charlie kept her face blank. 'Another coffee?' she asked pleasantly.

Charlie watched the proprietor, a wizened old woman, spoon powder from a giant catering-size tin of coffee with no recognisable name. The coffee here tasted like shit, but it was hot.

'Thanks. And I wouldn't mind a teacake,' Nia called over.

Charlie ordered two, and the woman slowly toasted them one at a time, and then lathered on cheap margarine with her blue-veined, arthritic hands. Why didn't she put them both in together? Charlie gave Nia the one buttered first, the margarine congealed and cold.

Once she'd finished her teacake, which she ate delicately

after cutting it into pieces, and picking out and eating all the currants, Nia spoke more freely. She was obviously impressed with herself and her pivotal role in the police station.

'Yes, everything comes through me; it's a very responsible job. I have to type and file, and follow up reports.'

Charlie didn't ask her anything; she knew it would mean listening to Nia drone on for at least ten minutes. 'I'm sure your job is very important.'

Nia's eyes flickered. Had she twigged that Charlie was mocking her?

Charlie diverted her. 'Di's my friend, and she's going spare. We just wondered whether the police had any more leads.'

Nia looked horrified. 'You do know the Official Secrets Act covers us civilians?'

'Oh, I know how responsible your job is, Nia.' *You pompous self-obsessed bore.* 'I wouldn't ask you to tell me anything you didn't feel comfortable about.' The lie tripped out easily. 'I'm not asking you for any actual information; I know you haven't got access anyway.' She waited.

'I have actually,' said Nia. 'Everything comes through me.' She blushed. 'Maybe not everything exactly. But since I've worked there I've taken a professional interest in the cases that come through. And I read a lot of crime stories.'

'Always wondered about that. Do the police read crime?'

Put the punter at ease. Make your body language relaxed. Talk crap. Listen.

And then Nia was off, babbling on about different detectives. She kept mentioning one in particular. Charlie wondered if she was shagging him. Nia's own husband was a mild-mannered short-sighted man from Darlington, practically blind, proud of his wife and his dumpy children.

'So what has Detective Bonner said about Darren's case, Nia?' Nia might like hearing both their names in the same sentence.

"To be honest Ni," he said. He calls me Ni. "I think we're grinding to a halt on this. We're scaling down, getting nowhere."'

'Scaling down? They've hardly started. It's only been a few weeks.'

'I know, terrible, isn't it? But that's what Detective Bonner said. It's all these drugs gangs – they've got their hands full, like.'

Just as she thought. Zilch. After another coffee and another teacake Nia promised to let her know if there were any developments. 'Only as a favour, like, seeing as you're asking, thinking of Di, and I couldn't really give you any confidential information.' She emphasised the *confidential*. 'I would like very much to keep my job. I like my job, and the other people at work.'

I bet you do.

'Of course,' Charlie said sweetly. 'Thank you so much. I'll give you a ring next week. Check if anything's come up. Or if there is anything I could do with a bit of help with.' Charlie knew she was being a cow. She didn't care.

'You do that, Charlie. I'd like to help in any way I can. For Di,' she added, as if her motives could be misunderstood.

Nia kissed her cheeks again. There was a faint smell of orange coming off her, like that 1970s scent Aqua Manda. Nia had confirmed that the police were getting nowhere. Charlie had carte blanche to carry on. The orangey scent hung in the air.

26

WEDNESDAY 13 NOVEMBER

IT WAS DIFFERENT in schools nowadays. When Casey came home she was buzzing with news. The air still smelt of fireworks. Outside, there was still the occasional sharp crack of bangers, and the fizz of a late firework, even though Bonfire Night was ages ago now.

'The school's going to be really good about it, Mum,' Casey said. 'Of course I've only spoken to the nurse, it's all confidential with her, and nobody else would be allowed to discuss anything unless you're there. I gave her permission to tell the head, and she says make sure we're at the open evening tonight. Says it'll be a waste of my education to leave. They'll appoint a liaison worker, and I'll have to see them every week. They've got loads of leaflets about nurseries and breastfeeding and stuff, and she says I'll get an automatic place in the nursery up the road, and I could nip back at lunchtimes, to feed the baby, you know. You are coming, aren't you?'

She'd run out of breath, and suddenly looked overwhelmed. 'I want to use my brain, Mum. I want to get myself sorted.'

Charlie nodded.

'Lucky, Mum, that the baby's due during the May half-term.'

'Babies don't always come when they're supposed to, you know.'

'This one will. So will we go up the open evening together? The teachers want to talk to you.'

And so they walked up together. Casey hadn't attended an

open evening for years. She'd always told Charlie that pupils weren't allowed. The school was packed with pupils and their parents. Casey chatted to her teachers while Charlie sought out the head. She passed through a hall and along a corridor lined with a plethora of young men. All tall, most with spots, short hair and long. She stared after them. *Which one was the father? When would Casey tell her?* It wasn't the time to ask her now. She always avoided answering the question when Charlie brought it up, muttering about it being 'complicated'. How complicated could it be? The guy had had his fun; he should take responsibility.

The head was younger than she expected, and clothed in a smart suit, looked like a business executive.

'Has Casey thought about afterwards?'

He didn't use the P word. Charlie told him of their plans.

'Well, the baby's due during the May half-term. If it comes early I can help out, and there's the Mother and Baby Unit. She'll have the summer to get adjusted, and from September she's getting a place in the nursery nearby. She'll be able to go to the nursery at lunchtimes.'

He looked blank.

'To feed the baby.' Obvious he hadn't liaised with the liaison officer. You had to spell things out. He was a strange-looking man, with a small head and blue eyes too close together.

'Oh, I see, I see,' he said, as if by repeating it twice, it would make it true. Charlie had the weirdest feeling that he was pretending to be a head teacher. 'I just like to keep in touch with what is going on with my pupils.'

Give the poor man a chance. It wasn't his fault Casey was pregnant.

'And how is Casey feeling about her exams? Given the circumstances.'

She wanted to grab him by his suit jacket and say, 'She's still the same Casey, she's still got a brain, she's pregnant, not lobotomised,' but she didn't. She decided to be charitable. Stressful being a head, Steve had said. 'Try and see it from their point of view.' So she talked on about the need for support for Casey.

'But don't forget she's young and energetic. She's got that going for her.' It wasn't all doom and gloom.

When he glanced at his watch, she started for the door. He stood up as well. 'This is a first for us, you must realise. We're feeling our way.'

Charlie kept her gaze on him. Steve was right. Maybe they were trying their best.

'And she's a spirited young woman, your Casey. I'd hate to see that squashed. We're supporting her as much as we can. I have a team in place.'

Of course he had. Female teachers who took care of details. Charlie squashed her bitterness. That wasn't fair. Things had moved on since she was at school.

'Thanks.'

Charlie shook his hand, a mixture of feelings overwhelming her. Casey was lucky that he hadn't thrown her out. It was not back in the 1960s. Casey was not Christine Scully.

At home, there was a phone call from work, the young worker putting Eddie straight on. Eddie was incoherent, panicked. Something about a cat, and how he couldn't get hold of Martin, and he knew that she wasn't on shift yet, but…

'Tell me what happened, Eddie,' she said. 'Breathe.'

Turned out the cat, which Eddie had loved, was dead, and someone had nailed it to the fence outside the hostel.

'I'll get my coat,' Charlie said, running out of the house, leaving Casey with a halo of light around her, like a Madonna in a Renaissance painting.

'I wanted to ask you what it's like, Mum,' Casey shouted after her.

'And I want you to tell me who the father is,' Charlie thought. It could wait. No point pushing her, or she would clam up again. Be patient, bide her time, Casey would tell her when she was ready. Did the father even know yet? As long as it wasn't that bastard Michael. She shuddered. It couldn't be. James? They were quite close. But that would be weird. Someone else in school?

Casey's young face beseeched her.

'Does it hurt, Mum? Really hurt?'

She put her hand on Casey's arm.

'We'll talk tomorrow. We will.'

A quick kiss and she was on her way. The image of the cat nailed to a fence kept surfacing. Then the rat on newspaper outside her door. The broken window, the brick. Somebody out there didn't like them, that was for sure.

27

THURSDAY 14 NOVEMBER

SHE'D FINALLY MANAGED to calm Eddie own by performing a funeral for the cat. They'd put it in a cardboard box, along with its bell and its scratchy toy, and Eddie wrote an awful poem in which the word 'love 'appeared six times in 12 lines, and then they'd solemnly buried Brutus in the small patch of soil near the greenhouse, and Eddie had put up a cross.

So when Charlie walked into the Working Men's Club bar area with Chris at around half five, what with meeting Steve, and the drama over the cat, she didn't exactly feel emotionally stable. Silence descended, like when a stranger walks into a bar in a Western. Older men appraised her, decided she was no threat, and went back to their pints.

She spotted Darren's friends easily enough. Older than Darren, but not old enough to be drinking in here. Clustered round the pool table, one about to take a shot, they gazed at her impassively.

'Howay, lads.' It didn't sound right coming from her. Apart from an 'Areet, lads', Chris stayed quiet at her side.

'This your toy boy?' one lad ventured, and they spluttered. One met her eyes. He was dark-haired and brown-eyed, slim and wiry, good-looking with regular features and olive skin. 'Who are you, like?'

'Charlie.'

'What kind of a name is that? Are you a lesbo?'

'I'm a friend of Darren's mother, she asked me to poke

around a bit.'

Bad choice of words. This provoked a few smirks and titters among the group. Charlie ignored it. *Treat them like adults. They nearly are.* Chris caught her eye. 'Ask you a few questions, like?' Unconsciously she had made her voice more North Eastern. She hoped they didn't think she was taking the piss. 'Di said to contact Greggo.'

'Aye, that's me. I'm Greggo.' He surprised her by putting his hand out. They shook. 'And who's this? '

'Chris – don't know if any of you remember him? He used to play football in the kick-about up in the park with the other students when Darren played. Did none of you go up there?'

There was a chorus of 'Nahs', but one lad appraised Chris: 'Are you a student? You don't look like a student.'

'Used to be. I work in Woolies.'

'Aye, I remember you. Areet?'

'Get the lass a drink, lads,' said Greggo, as if they'd passed a test. 'And the lad. Where's your manners? Tea, coffee, or something stronger?'

'Tea would be fine,' Charlie said primly. 'Just milk.'

'Same for me,' said Chris. She doubted the barman would serve them alcohol in front of her.

Once their drink had been brought over, the group sat in a huddle. A quiet authority came off Greggo. He was obviously the ring leader.

'Not at college or school, lads?'

'Training day,' they said in unison, and laughed.

'It's just that if there's anything about Darren you could tell me – anything that would give us any more to go on – that would be really useful. His mam's desperate to find out what happened.'

There was a sympathetic murmur amongst the lads. But one short-haired, pockmarked lad thrust his face forward. 'Howay, man, woman, why are you nebbin' into all this?

Thought that was the job of the pollis.'

'Darren was areet an' all,' said another lad. 'Mint.' This lad was morose-looking, picking at an imaginary piece of thread on his tracksuit. 'Away and get the bastard that did this.'

'Yeah, the police don't gi a fuck,' answered another.

'What makes you say that?'

'They only searched an all when the family pushed them, is that reet?'

'It's true, man.'

They all nodded.

'Did youse lads go on the search?'

'Aye. Course. Anything for our marra.'

She sipped the strong tea from a big mug which said Newcastle 5, Manchester United 0. Glanced at Chris. He carried on sipping his drink. He'd hardly said anything so far, but he made her feel safer. It was like having a minder

'Did Darren change lately?'

'Aye, his socks,' answered another lad, quick as anything, and then they all started laughing, as if they had suddenly been given permission to lighten up.

'Divvent be taking the piss of the lass,' said Greggo. There was another chorus of 'Ayes, areet then,' and then they started exchanging anecdotes about Darren's exploits, and she sat listening to the rise and fall of their voices, their joshing and ribbing of each other. They stopped and started, got excited, and then grew subdued again, guilty at being alive while Darren wasn't.

One started asking questions of Chris. 'Is it true you lived abroad? What's it like? My grandma's from Italy. I'd like to go there. Newcastle's a dump.'

The others shouted him down.

Someone else had heard Darren talk about the mentoring. 'He said you didn't have to be a posh bastard to go to uni. How did you do it? Were your family loaded, like?' Then Chris was telling them his story, and they sat round, entranced.

When there was a lull, Charlie dug around in her pocket and produced the cinema ticket she'd found in Darren's hoody. She'd forgotten to give it to the police. She'd have to hand it over. It was evidence. Lucky she'd found it before she put her clothes in the wash.

'Any of you lads go the pictures with him to see this?'

'Did it have explosions in, or guns?' one of the lads asked.

Greggo took a quick look at the title. Shook his head. 'It's in French. Can't speak French.'

'Neither could Darren. Only Geordie,' and then they were off again, laughing.

'Prefer car chases myself,' Greggo said quietly.

'Did youse ever go the pictures together?'

'Aye, sometimes.' The morose one. 'Sometimes, on Saturdays, doon the toon. Belta. Bag of popcorn, pop.'

'What about Darren? Did he keep going with you all?'

'Mostly, but those last few weeks he kept saying he was busy, like, that he had plans.'

'Did he say what plans?'

'Nae, man, he wasn'a a bairn. Yi canat keep tabs on him.'

Greggo picked up a pool cue and rubbed his fingers along it. They were getting bored now and itching to get back to their game. And annoyed at her stirring up their guilt. They should have noticed something that could have saved their mate.

'The lads are getting restless,' said Greggo.

She wrote down her number, and asked him to contact her if there was anything else he thought of. He said he would and she and Chris took their leave. They were a funny, lively bunch of lads. In spite of their messing round, she knew that most of them were at school or college or working and were devastated about Darren. One thing was sure; if he hadn't even told his mates what he was doing, what had Darren been up to?

'What do you think, Chris?'

'Nice bunch. You can tell they were fond of Darren.'

'Where to from here?'

'Woolies for me. I'm on shift. Store room. Packing. I'll have a think, and phone you. We'll get somewhere, don't worry. We knew it would take ages. You need to chase up the other students, remember. And worth checking in with your police mate.'

'You're right,' said Charlie. 'I'll get back on the case properly. I've been…' *What? Distracted?* 'You go to work. Think about the contact with Darren. I know you said you thought something was going on. Were there any incidents that made you think something was wrong? Or anything that rang alarm bells? It doesn't matter how daft it feels, or how small. You saw Darren during that time, and that was maybe when he met his killer. Sometimes it's the smallest things. So phone me if you think of anything. But I'll follow up the other things we mentioned.'

Charlie suddenly felt clear and in control. They had to keep at it.

Chris broke into her thoughts. 'The thing is,' said Chris. 'We know that Darren was meeting someone he didn't want his mates to find out about. The question is, who?'

28

BACK AT THE hostel, Eddie had put up a shrine to the cat in the hall, with a blurred picture of Brutus, his poem, and an old cat collar. Some of the men sniggered as they went past, but nobody hassled Eddie. They had all been fond of the cat, and the place felt more empty and abandoned without it around. But something else took over. Another attack. A girl, found behind a house a few streets away.

In the office, they watched the news on Martin's small portable TV. The detective speaking looked tired and haunted, as well he might. Bloody and battered, as the news reports said, but alive.

'This young girl has been through a terrible ordeal,' said the detective. 'The victim of a savage sexual attack. Police are investigating links to any previous attacks but at this stage our priority is to find the perpetrator before they act again. Her family have requested privacy. The victim was able to give us a good description of her attacker, which will be issued shortly.' He looked directly at the camera. 'I appeal to the perpetrator of this crime to give yourself up. You will be caught. And I appeal to everyone. If anyone you know has been acting suspiciously, please contact us. You will not be wasting our time.'

There were questions from reporters about whether this attack was connected to the previous one, and Darren's murder.

'We are looking at all lines of enquiry,' said the policeman.

Then the camera panned to a small gathering of women near where the girl was found. The women, a mixed group of younger and older, held placards: 'Safe streets for women,' 'Let women walk in peace.' 'Reclaim the streets.' Charlie peered closer. Somebody that looked vaguely like Casey was in the group. But Casey was at school. She didn't get a good look anyway, as Martin flicked the off button, and dunked his chocolate biscuit in tea. 'Scary,' he said. 'It's not safe round here nowadays.'

'I thought they had someone for the last one,' said Charlie.

'They did, but he's out on bail.'

'He'll be the first one they check.'

'Of course. Bastards.' It was a general comment in the direction of the residents behind them. 'I wouldn't be surprised if one of our lot had something to do with it.'

'You can't say that. '

'Can't I? Look at them.'

The picture gallery on the wall showed a collection of men with missing teeth, narrow foreheads and suspicious glares. They wouldn't be your first choice to let in your house.

'The only remotely normal-looking one is Michael,' added Martin. 'And he's the biggest psychopath of all. Where was he when the attack was supposed to have taken place?'

'At work.'

'The police will be checking harder this time. This is getting beyond a joke. If I was a woman I'd be scared to walk the streets.'

'Tell me about it.'

'Do you think they'll bother much?'

'What do you mean?'

'Haven't you seen? You know. Already there's been something on the news saying the girl attacked wasn't exactly an angel, had run off a few times and fallen out with her family. As if the poor girl had brought it on herself.'

'What's that got to do with it?'

'Exactly. Somebody's daughter and all that. I bet if it was Michael Howard's kid they'd be trawling the streets for whoever did it.'

'And they seem to have forgotten about Darren,' added Charlie.

True. Nothing was happening. Chris had gone quiet, and the only thing she'd heard from Nia was a garbled phone call saying that a big case was 'going down'. She'd obviously been watching too many crime stories on TV.

Martin said nothing.

NEW POLICE TURNED up that afternoon, polite but stern, checking everybody's movements, making phone calls, taking copies of the rotas. They left, saying their colleagues would be back.

As Charlie started home that evening, she saw a figure in a hoody dart down the alley. The figure looked familiar. On second glance, they'd gone. She was spooked, and wondered if she'd imagined it.

At home, she drifted off on the sofa, so that when the phone rang she was disorientated and groggy, and what Martin was saying didn't make sense.

'Windows broken round the back. Don't know how they got in. The alarm must have gone off, but nobody local heard anything.'

When Charlie got to the centre, first warning Casey to stay at Emma's that night, she saw scrawled on the wall outside: 'No paedophiles here. Paedos and rapists out. Lock 'em up.'

The graffiti chilled her. Someone who could spell, she noted. Worried for Casey, she phoned to check she'd arrived at Emma's.

Nowhere felt safe. A nervous, jittery atmosphere had descended. Charlie knew that the more things happened, the more their centre would get blamed.

Charlie phoned up an out of hours emergency cleaning team who asked for double when they heard the address. 'Danger money,' they said, laughing. Charlie stayed at work until it was done.

'Get a taxi,' Martin urged, but a taxi would cost a few quid. Why shouldn't she walk? It was gone midnight when she left, the streets empty and peaceful. Steve had offered to meet her, and stay at hers. He was back for one night from a residential training course, and then off to Sunderland the next day to look after his kids. They'd hardly seen each other. The promised sex hadn't happened yet. Every time it was about to, something intervened. Charlie wondered if it would all fizzle out. She regretted turning down his offer to meet her. But she didn't want to start that, being scared to walk the streets on her own.

'You don't know who's out there,' was Martin's parting shot.

But she did. Men outside were just like the ones in the hostel. Some men hated women, some men attacked women, resented them, wanted to keep them in their place. Some men didn't.

She kept glancing over her shoulder, more nervous than she cared to admit, and in the shadows, once or twice, she got the feeling that someone was watching. She wouldn't want Casey walking alone in the dark. So why did she take chances? Time to get the bike back out, she resolved. You felt safer on wheels. She made the rest of her way home along the main road; the steady stream of lights from late night taxis a comfort. Pubs had long turned out, and there were no stragglers. Somewhere up near the park, where Darren was found, she heard the flutter of birds and the chattering of magpies. It sounded strange in the dark. *One for sorrow, two for joy.*

Her nostrils held the scent of the heavy duty chemicals

the cleaning team had used. She breathed in cold air and took in the outlines of trees, but in her mind she still saw ghostly shadows of words on the wall: paedophiles, rapists. It was true. Orchard House was a festering sore, full of paedophiles and rapists and arsonists and thieves and violent men. What was she doing working there? The dirt and smut of the place seeped into you, and you never got clean. Too late to phone Steve now, and he'd gone for a few days. Eejit. Wearily, she made her way home. And was delighted to find Steve waiting for her on the step. They crept in like teenagers, and lost themselves in each other's bodies.

29

TUESDAY 19 NOVEMBER

'YOU'RE LOOKING FITTER.'

She turned to see Michael running his eyes up and down her. Morning in the hostel, grey light coming through the shuttered windows. Men coming in with smoothed down wet hair, putting toast in the toaster, frying eggs, eating cereal.

'Careful who you're talking to, I'm in charge here.'

Whenever she was near him, her skin prickled. This latest attack had unnerved her. That day in the park they'd rowed, and then what happened? A poor girl got assaulted. Were the two things connected? Even if the police found nothing to link Michael to it, she didn't believe he wasn't involved in some way. With his past, he couldn't just change overnight. He despised women, manipulated them, and thought he was better than them. But did he despise them enough to attack them? Steve had made her wonder that. Said one type of offender rarely became another type. She thought of him all the time. The word that came to mind was 'delicious'. She could eat him. They wouldn't be seeing much of each other as his life was so complicated at the minute, taking his turn to look after his kids, sorting out things with his wife and keeping in touch with his Aussie relatives. But the time they had together was easy, and joyful. The only sex so far was that snatched at her house the previous week.

She shuddered. The physical effect Michael had on her made her want to run away. Had his mother felt the same way about him? What a terrible thing that would be, for a child, to know that not even your parents liked you. She didn't know that much about him. Only what was in his file, and gossip. He'd gone to a 'good' school in Reading, whatever that meant, had started on his A levels. Biology, English Literature and Physics. And then he'd begun his 'other' career, and now he was here.

'Just saying, I saw you running in the park with some young lad. Is he your toy boy?'

'Mind your own business.' What was Michael doing in the park? Was he spying on her? He couldn't have been the figure in the hoody, he was in the hostel. But he could be working with others. He was clever like that, she wouldn't put it past him getting others to spy on her, annoy her. He had a technique of making others feel important.

'So he is then. You're a dark horse. Didn't know you had it in you.'

His eyes appraised her, roaming from the top of her head to her feet, lingering on her breasts and below her belly button. Charlie blushed. Bastard. She felt like he could see through her and knew what had happened with Steve. You looked different after sex.

'If you must know, he's training me.'

'Training you for what?'

'The Great North Run.'

There, she'd said it, it was real, just like it was real that Darren was dead, that he was never coming back, and that they were running for him.

'Good for you.' And in spite of the patronising tone in his voice, it was as if she grew taller. When did she ever get praised?

'I mean it. Just saying, you're looking better.'

She smiled. And stopped. She didn't want to smile, not at him, didn't want to give him the satisfaction.

'You probably better start cutting down on the crap

though.'

She looked at their respective plates. He had kiwi fruit, banana and grapes neatly arranged, a low fat yoghurt, and crispbread with peanut butter. She had a bowl of sugary cereal and a can of lemonade. He had a point.

'Healthy mind, healthy body,' he smiled, and bit into the crispbread.

Bastard.

Charlie couldn't help but glance in the mirror on the way to the kitchen. It was too soon for the running to have made a difference yet. But there was something different about her. Attitude. Or the way she held herself. She stood taller, elongating her spine and lengthening her neck, balancing her head higher. Her skin was still good, and her hair thick. *Be proud*. Sean had always said that. And tears welled up, because Sean wasn't here to see her, and ask how she was getting on, and never would be. What is the sound of one hand clapping? An old physics teacher of hers would come out with this one regularly. But Steve was alive. She hoped it would work out with him. They were still tentative with each other, circling round.

But she couldn't shake her suspicion of Michael. Couldn't they question him more? Had he seen anything? She fingered the card the older policeman had given her. And then returned it to her pocket, and went back to Michael.

'Did you really see Darren with someone that day?'

'Said so.'

'So why not tell the police? It could be important.'

Michael looked at her. He wasn't going to say anything.

So she phoned the policeman. He listened quietly as she poured out her suspicions: 'I know I haven't really got anything to go on, but he did say he'd seen something. How am I going to get more out of him?'

'You know you can't accuse someone without hard

evidence.'

'I know, but…'

The man's tone was reassuring. 'Tell you what, pet, I'll go along to his workplace again, see if we can get him in again as a material witness and all that. Did you say it was a temporary worker who'd filled in the rota? We'll locate them. No problem. You can't say fairer than that, can you?

When she looked up, Eddie was in the doorway, a serious look on his face. In his hands he held a soaking wet banger.

'I put it under the tap,' he said. 'It nearly went off.'

And then she was on the phone to the police again, reporting an escalation in a series of attacks on their hostel. She spelt out the broken window, the dead rat outside her house, the graffiti, the dead cat, and now this banger. 'It'll be a fire next time,' she said. This time she got an efficient young woman who said officers would be round immediately.

30

TUESDAY 26 NOVEMBER

THEIR RUNS THE next week were postponed several times due to it pouring with rain, so it was a while before she was at Di's again. Charlie could hardly believe the person who opened the door. Tanned, with her hair done, and immaculate makeup and nails, Di was wearing a kaftan that suited her, made her boobs look smaller, and shrank her waist, and high heels that lengthened her legs.

She twirled at the front door.

'Do you like it? Suzy gave me a makeover. Free,' she added.

'Yeah, it's great,' said Charlie.

And she meant it. Di looked a million times better, in a kind of celebrity style way.

'I'm going to watch my diet, eat a bit healthier. Herb tea?'

'Ordinary for me.'

'Oh, I think I'll join you. Those bloody herbs are making me run the toilet all the time.'

Charlie laughed. Hard to think of Di and herb tea in the same sentence. Di boiled the kettle, and dunked their teabags. Something else was different. The air was clear.

Di saw her looking.

'And I'm cutting out the fags,' she added. 'See, I'm all patched up.'

She showed her arm.

'How are you feeling?'

'Better, I think, I mean I had to get myself together for James's sake, and besides, Suzy said there might be TV appearances.'

'What do you mean, TV appearances?'

A shadow passed over Di's face. *Just because she's acting mad,* thought Charlie, *don't forget she's lost her son.*

'It's just, as Suzy says, there's interest. There's a director keen on doing a programme about parents who have lost children. One of them reality things. And what about you? You've got a glow on you.'

Charlie blushed. Di always found everything out.

'How are you getting on with lover boy, eh? I saw the way you two were eyeing each other up. Come on, tell.'

'Nothing to tell. We've had a few drinks.'

'And?'

'And mind your own business,' Charlie laughed. 'Taking it slow. He's been off on another training course, and now he has to go and look after his children all week.'

'Do you like him, though?'

Charlie took her time answering.

'I do. I really do.'

'Good for you,' said Di.

'You could do with some happiness. Sean wouldn't have wanted you to stay miserable.'

'Who said I was miserable?'

Di laughed.

'Well, all I can say is that you don't look miserable now. Anyway, what about the other news? When were you going to tell me?'

'You know?'

'I wangled it out of James. He can never keep anything from me. Apparently Casey told him ages ago.'

'I figured that.'

'Is she OK?'

'Think so. She seems fine. We had a bit of a scare a few weeks ago, but she's OK now.'

'What about you?'

'It's all a bit sudden. A lot to take in. It'll be hard, but…'

'But lovely,' said Di firmly, 'the best news this year.'

And then they got back to talking about Darren.

'The police have only contacted me a couple of times,' said Di. 'And now they've arrested someone for that second attack, suppose their focus is on that. Did you see it was somebody dead respectable? Some businessman from out of town? 2.4 kids and all that? Said he thought the girl was a prostitute from the way she was dressed. When she said she'd report him, he went for her. Can you believe it? His poor wife. But it means the police have lost interest in Darren. They're probably so chuffed at picking up someone for the two attacks, the heat's off. The public reassured, and all that.'

And suddenly, behind the makeup, the scaffolding of Di's face disintegrated, and in the hard clear light streaming through the kitchen she looked old. That's what grief did to you, bashed you in the guts so that you dissolved, your skeleton hardly able to hold you up. This was the moment when Di would usually reach for her cigarettes, and maybe a glass of vodka or a can of extra strength lager. She patted her pocket as if she'd lost something, then plucked a tangerine from the mound piled up in the fruit bowl. Up until now it had contained bills, old pens, paper clips, odd receipts and pairs of broken sunglasses.

Charlie leaned against a kitchen cabinet. Everything was gleaming. Someone had been busy.

Di clocked her glance.

'I paid someone to clean it. This woman from an agency. Polish, she was. Really nice. Didn't cost much. I couldn't face it. Every morning coming down to the dust and dirt. I wanted to stick my head under the bedclothes. It was Suzy who said use the Spruce agency, that they were good.'

She lifted one of Darren's football trophies from the

sideboard.

'See?'

'Best overall player,' Charlie read.

'No dust.'

'Amazing.'

And it was good to see everything without a film of dirt.

'But what about your poke around? Getting anywhere?'

'I've been in touch with the police a couple of times with some things.'

'What things?'

'I don't want to get your hopes up.'

'So?'

'Haven't heard anything. I think the detective in charge is off sick. But they might have something going on behind the scenes. I've got a contact.'

'Doubt there's anything going on. Otherwise they would have told me.'

'They've said nothing?'

'Zilch. Everyone seems to have forgotten about Darren.'

'We haven't. I've been busy on this; I have been digging. And I've had someone giving me a hand. But I'm not an expert at this, remember.'

'But you're so good at this type of thing, Charlie. You know what to ask. And you stick at it. Something in you. You don't give up.'

'I hope not. I keep thinking I'm close to finding out something important. And then it goes. But I thought you didn't want me to go on.'

'What gave you that idea? Of course I do. It was just, with the holiday, I wanted to relax, forget about it all for a while.'

'Understandable.'

Di flicked her gleaming hair back. It didn't move.

'I do think the police might have missed something.'

'Like what?'

'I dunno. Someone Darren met, someone he became friendly with, anything.'

'Can't think of anyone.'

'Did he ever go anywhere after school? Besides football?'

'Only to that film club.'

'What film club? Nobody mentioned that.'

'I don't know. Something to do with the university, I think. Talk to James again. Or ask Melody.'

'I will. Where was it?'

'I don't know. Somewhere up near that student pub next to the betting shop. I don't know. The police asked me all this. I presume they checked it all out.'

'Who did he go with?'

'Mates.'

'What mates?'

'I don't know; I didn't keep a list of them.'

'We should find out who they were and go through them.'

'OK, I'll have a think. But it couldn't have been any of his mates, could it?'

Charlie thought, 'It could have been anyone,' but asked, 'Was there anything else he did?'

'I don't know. He was a 15-year-old boy. I didn't keep tabs on him. You should ask James; he knows more what Darren was up to.'

If you had kept tabs on him he might be alive now. For a minute she hated her friend, hated her trumped up, polished appearance, her being alive when Darren was ash and bone. And then it passed.

'I'm not saying that, I know, it's just...'

'It's not going to bring him back, is it? I know I asked you to help, but it's not really going to make any difference, is it? I'm tired, Charlie, I'm so tired. I just want to lie down and sleep and not wake up and... I thought I was OK, I thought going to Spain had perked me up, but it's all worse than ever. Maybe you should leave it, Charlie. Maybe you should concentrate on Casey – she'll need you more now. And see how it works out with Steve. Be normal. I've got to pay attention to James. He's all I've got now. Maybe we'll never know.'

And then Di cried and mascara streaked her face.

'Anyway, here's James. Go for your run. Leave me and stop asking questions. Ask your questions elsewhere. Go.'

And so Charlie ran, and she did ask James more questions. And even though she hit more brick walls, Di suggesting she leave the investigation made her more determined. Steve liking her had given her more confidence. A warm feeling bubbled up. She tasted the sweetness. She was going to keep at this until the truth came out.

31

WEDNESDAY 5 FEBRUARY 1997

IT WAS A phone call from Chris that seemed to wake Charlie from a long winter. Mid-morning, Casey at school, Charlie fairly well rested after a few hours sleep. The days were lengthening, but the pavements were slippy with ice and you needed the heating on all the time. Neither Charlie nor Casey could wake up in the morning. Casey had overslept a couple of times. Charlie felt like she'd been sleepwalking all winter.

Chris was talking rapidly, sounding excited. He had moved to Nottingham during the Christmas holidays, but was still on the case. He'd gone with her to interview the other students, when Charlie was too tired to trust herself to ask the right questions. That never brought anything up anything new, but at least made them feel they were covering all bases.

Now he had news for her.

'Slow down, slow down. What is it?'

'There was something niggling me. You know when you get the feeling that you've missed something.'

'Yeah.' She certainly did.

'Well, on my day off I came up to Newcastle and went to see the guy who used to organise the kick-around at the university. I know him, he's a nice guy. We got chatting, and he said it was a crying shame about Darren, he was a good lad.'

Was this going somewhere? she wondered.

There was silence at both ends. Chris always took his time, he couldn't be hurried.

'Anyway, I asked him about the checking they do when

they sign people up for mentoring, and the kick-around. See if there were any discrepancies, you know. I remembered they wrote to my head teacher about me. So I asked him, did he remember anything that had worried him?'

'Go on.'

'Well, all he'd say at first was that we were all checked up on to see if we'd murdered anyone. Sorry, I didn't mean it like that.'

'It's OK.' Charlie was thinking rapidly now. She hadn't really considered it before, but it made sense that the mentors should be checked. The students playing football seemed much more casual, but she supposed the university had to do something. Otherwise anyone could join in a kick-around with the kids.

'Well, you know that Pete?'

'Yes.' The back of her neck prickled.

'Apparently, from the register this guy took, he did attend a few times.'

'He told us he only went once.'

'I know. And I know that it was always crowded, but I'm sure I saw him more than once. And the practice is that if anyone goes more than once they have to register and fill in a form.'

'OK.'

'Well, the guy wouldn't let me look at the forms.'

'Of course not.'

'Said his job would be on the line if he did. Everything is supposed to be confidential.'

'Right?'

'But he said something had been bothering him about that. Said it took ages to get Pete's form back, he had to keep hassling him.'

'I'm like that myself with forms.'

Why was she playing Devil's Advocate? She knew this was leading somewhere.

'Well, he couldn't show me the forms. But then he went out the room and left Pete's on the table.'

'And what?'

'That's just it. Nothing. A lot of it was blank. The bare minimum. There were gaps.'

'What do you mean – gaps?'

'Well, he went to school in a little village called Porthalbert. Hard-line Protestant, I think.'

'He told me as much himself.'

'Then he started secondary school in Newtonards.'

'So?'

'But then there's a blank of two years, before he's back in the same secondary school again.'

'And?'

'When the guy hassled him about filling in the blanks, he just said he went away to school.'

'Well he might have done. His parents might have saved up, sent him to private school.'

'So why didn't he put that on? He'd probably be proud of it.'

'Did the guy ever find out where he went?' Already she was calculating. Everyone knew that a gap in an adult's CV could mean prison. But Pete had been too young.

'Anyway, something stuck in the guy's mind. He said he overheard Pete once mentioning a place where he'd been to school – Millisle.'

'Well, there you go. It's probably some two-bit private school, his parents stuck him in there for a couple of years and then gave it up.' Charlie felt a crushing sense of disappointment. She'd really thought Chris had had something.

'Well, I just think it's worth following up,' he said stubbornly.

She couldn't stand the thought of disappointing him, so promised she would, and then they got onto other things, and he told her about his job in the record shop. 'Much better than Woolies,' he said, and they were training him up to be a manager.

They said goodbye amicably, and she told him she'd be in touch soon. Then Charlie got herself ready and took herself round to Di's.

Di took one look at her and declared that Charlie could do with a holiday.

'It'll perk you up. I wouldn't have survived without going off to Spain again over Christmas. Take Casey out of school for a week, go off somewhere.'

'But what about…' Charlie tailed off. What about Casey's education? She needed to do as much as possible before the baby was born. And what about Darren's killer? The investigation had failed so far; everything had ground to a halt. First the build-up to Christmas, and then Di away for two weeks, and with Charlie doing extra shifts and management having the brilliant idea of a carol service by the men, and all that entailed. And then it was January and both she and Casey had the flu, then cold after cold. It never stopped, there was always something standing in the way.

She only now felt she could lift her head. All her work gone to nothing. Charlie was disappointed with herself. She would follow up Chris's idea, but couldn't see anything coming of it. Not a bad idea, a holiday. She'd have to go to the head and plead special circumstances. In the past the school wouldn't have cared if Casey had stayed off. Kids disappeared for weeks and no one said anything. But there was a new Education Act, they'd had a note about it, and this new head was a stickler for the rules, he would follow it to the letter. But they could take homework, and it would only be a couple of days Casey would actually be off school, if they went in half-term. Besides, Casey was doing well, she'd be fine. And soon they wouldn't be able to get away very easily. He'd accept that.

'You need a rest,' insisted Di. 'After all the help you've given me. Christmas was hard. I've hardly seen you since.'

An understatement. No one had felt like celebrating, but they'd all ended up in Di's house having a turkey together and watching the *Only Fools and Horses* Christmas special when Del Boy and Rodney become millionaires, before James and Di flew off to Malaga on Boxing Day. Di said she couldn't face those first Christmas holidays at home.

'Go see your manager. Casey looks knackered as well.'

Charlie was surprised at Di even being aware of someone else. She'd changed.

It was true, Charlie was exhausted. She kept falling asleep at work, and Martin had sent her home once, saying she was no use to herself or anyone else. So Charlie asked to see the Head of Division in Newcastle. Half-term was coming up, and if they had a little time on top of that week they'd be able to recharge their batteries. The head of Casey's school gave in. Which just left work.

The following day, Thursday, she was off to see him. Head office was on the Quayside, a new office block, all clean lines and artificial looking flowers which turn out to be real, and a great view of the river. At night, she knew, hordes of men dressed in fright wigs, gorilla outfits or bondage gear under plastic macs, or occasionally Bo Peep complete with a shepherd's crook and sheep, wandered about swigging beer, and lasses in not more than a bra tottered their way along the cobbles. In the morning there would be vomit in the street, cleaned up quickly if they were lucky, as if the night hadn't happened.

This morning Charlie picked her way along cobbles, narrowly missing a patch of vomit. There was a large footprint in it. She wore heels and a suit with a skirt just above the knee. She kept pulling it down. Steve had said he liked her legs. She was getting used to him being around, enjoying his touch. He'd met Casey by now, and she liked him because he treated her like an adult. But back in Sydney his dad had a relapse, and Steve was taking leave soon to go help his brother.

She cursed the heels. God knows why she'd worn them. Her back ached. She tucked her bum in and tried to elongate her spine, but she was unsteady. She'd never mastered the art of heels. Same with makeup, which she had on now. No one would notice. Over 40 you were invisible, genderless to some men. She smiled as she picked her way along the cobbles, remembering the boyfriend who kept asking why her eyelashes were so short. His previous girlfriend had always worn false eyelashes and he genuinely thought all women did. She told him she was allergic to the glue. He didn't last long. If only men knew the lengths women went to.

The main office was all glass and windows. The Head of Division was in his thirties, a polite young men at ease with her. She wondered how you got to be Head of Division.

'Thanks for coming,' he said, shaking her hand. 'I'm glad you're here. I wanted to have a little chat anyway.'

Little chat? The most ominous words in the English language, besides 'bus replacement service'. He was going to sack her. There was a fly stuck behind the blind, buzzing. She watched it for a while. An older woman put her head round the door and offered tea.

Charlie sipped from the china cup. It felt good to drink out of proper, clean cups with a saucer. She feasted her eyes on the tea, as if for the last time. Earl Grey. She hardly ever bothered with anything other than bog standard. But this was smoky and lovely.

'Stunning, isn't it, the river?'

Charlie agreed.

'I could stare at the water all day. It's always changing. In a few years this whole area will be lively again, not just at night.'

'Will it?' There was hardly anyone about. It was a sunny but cold day.

He changed tack.

'Everything all right at home?'

'Fine.'

Why was he asking her that?

There was a discreet plate of small chocolate biscuits. *If I had your job*, she thought, *I would be eating chocolate biscuits all the time.* She'd be the size of a house; her figure would bloom and expand.

'Nasty business you've had up there. Good that they've caught the guys who attacked the girls. Two separate perps, I heard.'

She smiled at the word coming out of his mouth.

'Sorry, I like cop shows. But you know what I mean. No word yet on what happened to your friend's son?'

She shook her head.

'I wanted to talk to you about how things were at the centre. Any more trouble? Local management don't tell me much. Think if they keep me in the dark it's less worrying. But I'd rather know, otherwise I don't know how to help. Lead me through it all then, if you don't mind. Have there been more attacks?'

'No, it tailed off during the winter. It's been quiet since the graffiti.'

'Very upsetting though.'

'Yes, very upsetting,' she agreed. An understatement. More than bloody upsetting. The bricks, the rat, the cat, the graffiti, the banger. But in this fancy office, with the glass that separated them from the outside world, and the muted sounds, upsetting was about as far as it went.

'Drink up. Some more tea?'

She accepted, and they sat in silence for a minute. Only after she put her cup down did he say, 'So, how can we help you?'

Charlie liked the 'we', although there was no one else around. She tried to lower her shoulders, stuck somewhere up near her head, and take in the man. Pale faintly lined skin, blue, not unkind eyes. He probably had a couple of kids and a wife who worked as hard as him.

'I need a rest.'

His eyes met hers, and for the first time she saw the tiredness there. The lines round his eyes and mouth were deeper than was evident at first glance.

'Don't we all?'

Then she remembered that he had a Down's Syndrome child, in and out of hospital for heart operations. Once, his young, glamorous wife came to meet him at a work event, and beneath the perfect grooming and the good looks you could see the tiredness and bags around her eyes. There'd been obvious affection between them. Charlie liked him for that.

There was a picture at his desk of a child pushing a plastic walker. Behind him, his wife, slim and beautiful. He caught Charlie's scrutiny, and she blushed, as if she was intruding.

And because she was embarrassed Charlie talked, and told him everything that had happened. About Darren, and her suspicions of people, about the attacks on the centre, about Casey. He was easy to talk to. He listened. She liked him.

'You do know there was a complaint against you? From a Michael Faseby.'

She'd thought as much, wondered why nothing had happened.

'But your colleague supported you.'

'Michael…' she began, but he put his hand up.

'I'll stop you there, pet. Don't tell me anything. Your colleague spoke up for you. None of the other men said anything. It was dealt with. You're obviously under strain.'

Tell me about it, she thought. She unknotted her shoulders. Sometimes tiredness went so deep you just wanted to sleep and sleep. Charlie wondered whether it was like this when you died, if death was just being very tired, when you didn't want to make any more effort and you just wanted to sleep.

She could see why he was good at his job. He had that quality of listening which most people didn't have. He actually took in what you were saying. His body language mirrored hers, he nodded at all the right points, he touched her arm, and he handed over tissues. He did all the things a good counsellor should do and then he said nothing, just sat back, and was silent. The silence grew, and Charlie wondered if he was a Quaker. A lot of them had that stillness. Then the silence filled the room and they went past embarrassment. She became aware of every inhalation and exhalation. It was like doing meditation. Nothing mattered except this moment.

His face cracked into a smile.

'Quite a year,' he said. 'So what do you need?'

And that's how he signed her off for one week: *Special Circumstances Leave*.

'Goes without question. You've been a loyal member of staff, always competent and often much more than that. The way you saved that lad when you hadn't been in the job long took great presence of mind. We're lucky to have you.'

He ordered more tea and a hearty sandwich for them both, and they talked about their children, and how they were always a worry, but you would never do without them. Without directly referring to his son, he said that every situation taught you something, 'and the biggest thing you can teach your kids is how to imagine themselves in someone else's shoes. Worth more than all the GCSEs put together,' he said.

Charlie agreed. After half an hour, the receptionist popped her head round the door to remind him of his next appointment.

'Thank you, Marie,' he said, and smiled, and the easy camaraderie between them made Charlie's heart leap and gladden. Some people could treat other people right, it was possible.

He stood up and shook her hand.

She was still so surprised at being treated like a human being she wanted to kiss him. She'd never been cut any slack before. By anyone. The feeling was strange and wondrous.

'Enjoy your holiday,' he said. 'Good luck.'

Charlie floated back home. Darren's murder seemed far away. She'd recharge, and think. Sometimes things could be easy. She ran the last part, eager to tell Casey of their holiday. They'd start packing right away. Forget all about everything else. Relax.

32

11-18 FEBRUARY

WHICH IS WHY they found themselves the following week in West Cork, examining postcards of various very hairy men with flowing beards: 'The wild men of West Cork.'

She couldn't imagine how all that hair would help them get a wife, which is what they said they were looking for.

The hostel, and Darren's murder, and the attacks on the girls, seemed far away and unreal. One day she and Casey climbed the Stairway to the Sky: one hundred and ninety-nine steps. Some were slippy, overgrown with lichen. At the top they looked out over the harbour. Swans glided on silky water. There was a small maze and tended gardens. Raspberry canes, and early seeds already sprouting, she didn't know what. The air was mild and still, save for the cawing of rooks.

Another day they went inside the minor stately home, and wandered round. It had only opened for half-term week, and seemed unprepared for visitors. Everything was in a state of faded grandeur – the paintings were displayed in a dim light, some of the banisters needed a coat of paint, the wooden floors had splinters in them, and the windows didn't fit properly. But on the top floor, where the owners had made no attempt to tidy up for visitors, and had paintings and tapestries stored willy-nilly, banged up against each other, she looked out over the bay, and in the view over the harbour, the town looked luminous, as if it had been painted in silver, piercing the shell she'd built up, to make her cry. She missed Steve. He'd been in Australia for so long, she didn't know if he ever would come back. His father rallied and relapsed, rallied and relapsed. Selfishly, she wished he would hurry up about it.

And then they packed into the lounge below, and drank tea served in chipped china with home-made scones, and listened to a recital.

They were staying further up the road, at an over-decorated place with a tepid outdoor swimming pool slimy with algae that Charlie plunged into twice, and Casey refused to go near, saying she would probably catch something. The air outside was cold enough for your breath to show. The water was warmer, but as soon as you lifted your head you were chilled.

'You're not in Russia,' Casey cried. 'Winter swimming? You're mad.'

But it was strange and exhilarating to swim with no one else around. Near the pool was a chilly summer house with deck chairs and a smell of chemicals. A man with sticky out straw-like hair, who Charlie had thought at first to be the gardener, but who actually turned out to be the owner, welcomed them with a strangled Anglo-Irish accent.

He chortled at her swimming: 'I haven't prepared the pool properly yet. I usually wait until Easter.' Then he agreed that if there had been anything living in the pool it would be dead with the cold. 'Aye, you'll be grand,' he said, chuckling to himself.

In the room there were teabags and a hair dryer, and in the bathroom a big old fashioned bath with claw feet. Every surface was covered in a doily or a flounce.

For breakfast, they were served toast and eggs and cereal, all from great silver platters and ornate toast racks, and they drank from old faded glasses and ate off pretty, chipped vintage plates.

They didn't do much that week, but agreed that was what holidays were for. Casey, a chameleon, acquired a rosy glow, and an Irish tinge to her voice. She always adapted to what was around her. The local people had a relaxed, practised charm about them; the pace of life was slow. The pair of them slept long, ate well, and walked in the fresh air. At night Charlie enjoyed a Guinness or two in the pubs which, even at this time of year, were crowded with French and German visitors and locals, but never felt hurried.

One day they took tea in an empty tea room in the middle of the afternoon, eating scones and butter and jam, and drinking from a massive teapot that could have done six people. Another day they ate a vegetarian meal in a self-conscious place trying to rise above being a bog-standard café. When Casey asked for tea, 'What sort?' a spotty young man responded, reeling off a list as long as your arm.

Casey reddened, flustered. 'Normal.'

The man laughed, as if she had said something funny.

'Black,' Charlie said.

'No, what sort?'

You felt daft looking at all their selection. Fairtrade this, Fairtrade that. Charlie didn't want all the choice. She wanted to order tea and for them to put it in front of her, hot and refreshing, without a debate. It hurt her brain to have so many choices. It was the type of place where the portions were massive, but Charlie couldn't have said what she was eating. It didn't taste much of anything except Marmite, and took her back to the seventies, when veggie food tasted like this. It looked delicious, and sounded healthy, but tasted like shite.

Better was the fish and chip shop, where they had a sit-down tea. The batter was fresh and crisp, the chips deliciously hot and vinegary, and the man running it, with the kindest face in the world, had a courtesy that made Charlie want to cry.

'Is that hot enough for you? Can I get you anything else? You're not in a draught, are you?' he would say, as he waited on them with care and attention. And she thought again that true courtesy is what makes a person feel better. Nothing to do with manners, and how you hold your fork, but how you make the other person comfortable, at home.

They also turned into regulars at The Rapallo, run by a man from Milan and his boisterous kids and smiley-eyed wife, who presented the scrambled eggs on toast as if they were caviar.

In a hotel on the harbour, the barman brought her Guinness with a perfect head. Everyone else was on shorts or cider. An old woman was saying how the young ones wouldn't have to be away off to America or England any more as there was money in Ireland now.

'We have the new buildings, now so, they're grand,' she added. 'But the money from Europe it'll be drying up eventually so.' She spoke fast, and Charlie had to strain to catch everything.

'Surely not?' someone asked, and like Charlie, they looked around at all the new offices and houses, and the people who were taller now, with better teeth.

'Ireland's changed. We're on the up,' one man said. But still the old woman shook her head.

Half-way through the week they decided on a flying visit to the relatives up North.

'They'd never forgive me if I brought you over here and we didn't call in,' Charlie told her daughter.

It was hardly 'calling in' but entailed two trains and a bus to end up in the village on the Ards peninsula where her mother's relatives lived. After squashing their visitors into bunkbeds left behind by children who'd departed for university in England, never to return, the ageing couple, cousins of her mother, were kindly hosts, and although they didn't drink themselves, got Charlie in a bottle of wine. Nobody mentioned Casey's bump, prominent but well-hidden under voluminous layers of clothes.

One evening they went to the pub, and even before they

sat down, drinks appeared in front of them. Charlie bought a round back, and then they left, before it went on all night. She'd forgotten that you couldn't just have the one in the village pubs. You either drank or you didn't. Which was why many people didn't.

They spent days walking by the lough, and staring out at islands of green and brown, ate heartily, tasty local potatoes and fish. Went searching for dolphins but never found any. The final day they took it easy, eating early, lazily watching *Changing Rooms*. Charlie was rifling through the local paper, reading a sad story of a woman who had committed suicide, leaving teenagers and a husband. Her aunt glanced over.

'Sad business that, sad business.'

'Do you know the woman?'

'No, but the woman who runs the teashop, her husband's folk are members of that church.' Protestant. The village mentioned was Porthalbert, a hard-line Loyalist village. Something pinged in Charlie's slow, relaxed brain. Porthalbert. Where Pete was from. It came back to her instantly. She'd travelled through it a few times on the slower coastal bus on the way to her aunt's house: King Billy graffiti, and No Surrender signs, and red white and blue paving stones. The harshness of the accent coupled with the grey breeze block bungalows, especially in the winter, made for a closed and wary atmosphere. The people were polite and not unfriendly, would talk about the weather and the wind. But conversations never got any further.

'What happened?'

Her aunt wrung her hands, reluctant to talk.

'Paddy says we shouldn't speak about such things.'

'Paddy's not here.'

'True. It's nice to have a woman around to talk to. Paddy never wants to talk about anything.'

Paddy was out at a meeting about restoring the village hall, which had fallen into disrepair. Casey, worn out by all the fresh air, was fast asleep upstairs.

'And it's old news, so it is, no point raking it up.'

'Tell me. I'm interested.'

Just like when she was a child and persuading her aunt to read her a bedtime story, eventually Charlie wore her down, and the aunt haltingly told her about the woman, a Catholic in a mixed marriage, whose youngest son had been 'interfered with'.

'She never got over it, poor woman, but the worst thing was, nobody really believed them. They said the son was attention-seeking, because he kept getting angry at teachers and was eventually expelled.'

'Poor woman.'

'Aye, surely. The poor wee woman, she blamed herself, so she did. And she'd been fine and healthy, but after that she was always under the doctor. Or so Eileen in the teashop says,' she added lamely, as if to distance herself.

'How awful.'

'Aye, it was, and as I say, the worst thing was nobody believed them, and they got no help with the son when he was getting out of hand. It was only when it happened to another family, a much better-off one that had connections and wouldn't take no for an answer, that something was done.'

'What?'

'Well, that family made sure the young man was taken to court. If he'd done it twice, there was no knowing what he might grow up to do, they said. And there were rumours about another wee lad, but I don't know what came of that, so I don't. Because he was underage, the young fella who did it couldn't be charged as an adult. They put him away for a while, place called Lisnevin. Used to call it a training school. Juvenile Justice Centre. Supposed to have been an awful place. Said it was like a prison. Sure it was over an old prison. 18 months, I think he got.'

'Lisnevin. Where's that?'

'Away up near Millisle. Sure, it's his parents I feel sorry for.'

Her aunt's words echoed from far away. Millisle. That was the place where Pete had said he'd been to school but which didn't appear anywhere in his records.

'It was his parents I feel sorry for; they had to live in the same village. Imagine the shame of knowing what your child had done. Euch, why are we talking about these horrible things? I'll say a prayer for that poor woman, God rest her soul.'

Charlie focused back on her aunt. She couldn't do anything about it all now. But when she got back…

'And her poor wee boys and her husband. I hope the church goes easy on her, God bless her soul. It's a mortal sin, but sure you know that, even though you've been brought up a heathen in England.'

'Isn't there some get-out clause?'

Her aunt grinned, exposing brown teeth. She still had lovely skin and good cheekbones. She must have been beautiful once. As if on automatic, she recited: '"Fear, force, ignorance, habit, passion, and psychological problems can impede the exercise of the will so that a person may not be fully responsible or even responsible at all for an action." But enough of these maudlin things – you, young lady, away yourself to bed, you need your sleep, so you do.'

Next morning as they were leaving, her aunt pressed £100 into Casey's hands. 'For the wain,' she said.

33

WEDNESDAY 19 FEBRUARY

NEXT THING THEY were in Manchester Airport, after twelve at night. Rain battered against roofs. With no train until five, they took an all-night coach to Newcastle. Charlie drifted off. Red and white and blue paving stones. Mortal sins. Informed intellect. The phrases littered her dreams.

She had a few hours sleep and was woken by the phone. Martin. Impatient.

'I phoned you at that number you gave me. Why didn't you answer the phone? Where have you been?'

'Travelling. You know where I've been. On holiday. What's happened?'

And that's how she learnt of the fire. It was only a small fire, now reduced to a pile of ashes and a scorched post at the entrance.

'You've called me back for this? I'd just had a good holiday. I was relaxed. It could have waited a couple of hours. I'm on shift tonight. I was going to sleep some more.'

Martin said nothing, but took her into the office, silently made coffee and handed her a cup.

'And yes, I had a very nice holiday, thanks. How have you been?'

'Sorry, I should have asked, it's just everything's been kicking off here, and Michael got injured. Good job we didn't have a full house, with Dave back in jail, and Carl and Nick transferred down South.'

She was glad those two had gone, but sorry for Dave.

'It could have been a lot worse. Scary.'

'What do you mean… and Michael got injured?' Not that she cared about him; he could rot in hell for all she cared.

'He's in hospital. Minor burns to his face. It was a petrol bomb in a milk bottle. I wonder if it was meant for him.'

'Why would someone throw a petrol bomb? And I thought our address wasn't advertised.'

'You know as well as I do that everyone round here knows who lives in this place. Or if someone else wants to find out, they easily can. You know that. Besides, this came out just before you left. Maybe this is something to do with it. Probably helped stir up things again. They'd gone quiet on us for a few months. You were in too much of a rush, so you didn't see it.'

He shoved a copy of the local rag towards her.

Residents complain about dangerous criminals living locally, she read. Below the headline was a blurred photo of the centre. There was also a series of interviews with local people, mainly a couple of 'spokespersons' claiming the area had 'deteriorated' and how they were 'scared to walk the streets'. One man said he was organising a petition, and collecting signatures and letters from people who were opposed to the centre. He said he belonged to an Evangelical Church. The same church as the man who'd carried out the attack on the second girl, it turned out.

Martin was looking thoughtful.

'So they'll be prime suspects, then? But they've got what they wanted, haven't they?'

'Aye, getting us out, of course. All that good work with the community festival has gone to pot,' he said. 'We're on our way out.'

'What do you mean?'

'The men are frightened. The ODCs like Eddie are scared to go to work. He says people in the supermarket have been staring at him, asking if he had anything to do with the attacks.'

'What did the police say?'

'They came and took photographs of the fire scene, and they're supposed to be coming back, but they say they're short-handed, I wouldn't hold my breath. Saving this lot from frying is probably not a priority.'

'If it's evangelicals, they'll probably confess… and be all righteous about what they've done. Anyway, there must be fingerprints somewhere?'

'Yes, the police dusted for them, but it was a bit half-hearted. These guys are the lowest of the low as far as they're concerned. I get the feeling they couldn't care less if Orchard House went up in flames. I'm almost beginning to feel sorry for some of the men myself. Especially guys like Eddie.'

Eddie. Of course. Who had more reason than most to have it in for Michael… 'Are you sure he's got nothing to do with the fire?'

'Didn't you think I thought of that straight away? And the police. They did forensic tests of course. He's got a perfect alibi for the night in question. He was at his stepmother's, helping her decorate.'

'But he might have got somebody else to do it. I thought he hated his stepmother.'

'According to him, they're quite pally now she no longer drinks.'

'Do you believe him?'

Martin looked doubtful for a minute.

'Has she backed him up?'

'The police checked her out.'

'So what do we do now?'

'Tidy up. Carry on, I suppose.'

The place looked desolate, like no one lived there. Most of the men were at work. In the kitchen the remains of food and pots and pans were scattered over the floor. And the smells.

She had forgotten the smells. Socks and deodorant and sweat and stale cooking and cigarettes. She breathed in deep and a wave of burnt air hit her.

'I'll start tidying. Didn't the police offer any protection?'

'Didn't you see that guy outside when you came in?'

'I thought he was a dosser.'

Martin smiled, showing those even white teeth. 'I'll give you a hand first, it's a big job. This lot's not going anywhere.'

'But seriously, what are we going to do?' asked Charlie as she wiped cupboards dry from the water sprayed on it, and put plates away.

'Carry on, as I said,' said Martin. 'Fail. What was it that Beckett said? Fail better.'

Martin surprised her sometimes. It made her smile, which took away from the dismal surroundings and the cold.

They cleared and cleaned, and threw things into black plastic bags and wellied into the floor. This used up some of her energy and aggression. By the time they stopped, exhausted, the place looked almost habitable. And then they did a room inspection, passing the electrician's scrawls on the open circuit board: 'Danger. Do not touch. Rewiring. AC DC.'

When the men, including Eddie, came back, they were subdued. He didn't even ask about her holiday and wouldn't meet her eyes. Could Eddie have done this? Was he capable of it? All the peace and relaxation of the holiday had disappeared, and she felt her shoulders knot up again.

They agreed that as there was no electricity in the kitchen and only one working kettle in the office, for tonight, management would approve pizzas out of petty cash for everyone.

She stumbled home after a couple of hours, pulling her coat around her, and fell into bed. Casey was snoring in the other room. Only as she was falling asleep did an image of red, white and blue pavements come into her mind. 'The poor wee woman blamed herself… the boy was put away. Lisnevin. Millisle. Youth Justice Centre.

34

TUESDAY 18 MARCH

AND THEN EVERYTHING went out the window again. It took two weeks for the hostel to be fully habitable. Every spare minute was spent arranging furniture and throwing out stuff. And then Casey was overcome with a nesting instinct, and insisted they get their place ready early. They had nappies in piles, wipes, clothes in drawers, and a mobile set up above a baby's cot, a night light, all in the spare room that would now be the baby's room. Or a dumping room, more like. Charlie didn't have the heart to tell Casey that the baby probably wouldn't sleep in a cot for ages. She herself had had illusions before she became a mother. She'd thought she'd be able to do things while the baby slept. In reality, when Casey was young Charlie kept breastfeeding her because she liked lying in bed reading books. It was the only time she got to rest.

Let Casey be deluded. She'd learn. When the room was ready to her satisfaction, Charlie thought that she'd get back to investigating. The police announced that a member of a Christian evangelical group had been collecting signatures and whipping up opinion against the hostel. But there was no connection to the fire. 'Some rogue group,' claimed her friendly policeman. 'No one really wants your place here. It could be anyone.'

Two o'clock in the morning and Charlie felt she'd been asleep for five minutes, although they'd gone to bed at ten. Casey, increasingly uncomfortable, had for a while been waking up in the night for the toilet, unable to relax, her belly so big now. The midwives had decided that Casey was further on than they'd first thought. The last midwife visit had been the day before.

'Baby's dropped. Getting in position. Not long now.'

'But it's not due yet,' said Casey, put out. 'I've got coursework I've got to finish.'

This midwife was young, educated, and quite posh. But she had a warm manner and listened carefully to Casey, and didn't treat her like a stupid young girl. 'Babies come when they're ready. She smiled. 'How are you sleeping?'

Casey rolled her eyes and the midwife sympathised, saying, 'It won't be long now, and at least then you'll be able to lie on your back or stomach.' Charlie had drifted off and mumbled agreement as they talked positions, and the midwife went through the checklist of what was needed.

'Bag packed? Snack? Telephone numbers? Nighty? Toiletries? Nursing bra?'

That was then.

This was now.

'Mum, it hurts.' Casey was standing on the bedroom floor, a wet patch beneath her. Her face flinched with pain as a contraction hit her.

Charlie phoned the midwives and they arranged an ambulance. She walked Casey round while they waited.

'Breathe,' she said, massaging Casey's back and head.

The ambulance came quickly, and they were whizzed off, Casey put in a wheelchair and onto a bed while the staff examined her, apologising all the while, and everything slowed down.

'Four centimetres dilated.'

Charlie nipped out to the toilet, and dawdled back, looking out of the corridor window. If you craned your neck you could see the river. Down by the quayside diggers were dismantling old warehouses, ripping up pavements, extending roads.

Cranes, haulage trucks, men in hard hats and hi-vis jackets. Charlie fancied she could see all the ghosts of the people who'd worked in the warehouses, or on the river. People were digging up history, concreting over layers of people's lives, making new. All that sweat, all that noise, gone. Up river, down river. The big fat old river carrying them, holding them. Everything came back to water.

'Mum!'

A loud, desperate cry. Then she was back in the room, standing behind Casey, as, grunting, her daughter walked or hobbled, at times bending double with birth pangs. Charlie fed her ice pops and a banana, wiped off sweat, and moistened her lips with a sponge.

'It hurts, it hurts…'

'You're doing really well there,' said the Irish midwife. She had a pale exhausted face and smelt of mint.

'The contractions are speeding up, but it'll be a wee while yet. Stay on your feet as long as you're able. Gravity helps, sure. I'll be back in a minute; I have another lady about to pop.'

And then Casey was shifting round, assuming different positions on the bed, trying to get comfortable, contractions closer and closer together. Charlie led her to the toilet, helped her shower, walked around more, and held onto her. Casey was fading, going off into her own world. Then she vomited, and rallied, and swore at Charlie: 'Fuck off. Leave me alone! I don't want a bloody baby anyway. Why are you here? Don't touch me.' The shouts brought the midwife back. She kept her voice calm and guided Casey back on to her side, with her top knee bent, all the time soothing her. Time slowed. They were in a boat on the sea. There was nothing but the rhythm of the contractions.

Then Casey was upright on the bed, and pushing, the midwife willing her on. Charlie stood in front of her daughter, stroking her head, giving her a sponge to suck on, wiping her face.

'I can see the head,' the midwife said.

'It stings… it stings!' Casey cried.

'Pant,' the midwife ordered.

And in the mirror the midwife held up, Charlie saw dark hair, and thick creamy vernix, smudges of blood, pink skin, the ripples of a spine. And then she held her daughter's shoulders and Casey gave an almighty push and the midwife cupped her hands ready, green cloth waiting to land this baby, receive this child. The head eased out and the curled-over body and squashed limbs unsuckered and lengthened out and with a loud cry this space-creature, her grandchild, plopped and dived into alien air. Instantly Charlie's body tingled, as the baby fixed his eye on his mother. He had her.

After what Casey claimed was 'the best tea and toast in the world', they looked at him in wonder while behind them bare-skeletoned buildings spoke of something new as people scuttled round and lights came on and the sun came up over the Tyne and the baby snuffled at Casey's breast. And the fire and the attacks and Darren's murder were all whirling round at the back of Charlie's mind. So tired. Everything new. His fingernails, his toes, the whorl of his hair.

A kick of excitement in her stomach. She was a grandmother. She touched the head of the baby and watched Casey cradling him, holding him, examining every part of his body. And then she got her notebook out while Casey drifted off, and the hospital settled into routine. She looked over her notes, her mind clear at last. Time was short. She had to find Darren's killer. She had to make things safe for this new arrival.

She examined her earlier lists.

Michael?

A stranger?

Eddie?

Pete?

Red and white and blue pavements swam into view.

'It's his parents I feel sorry for. Imagine living with that, with what your child had done.' Lisnevin, Millisle. She had to go to a library. She needed to look up that court case. She started up. Pete. She had to find out more about him.

35

TUESDAY 18 MARCH

THE VISITORS STARTED straight away. When Di arrived, in spite of the herb tea and low-fat everything she said she was on, she smelt faintly of booze. Charlie was feeling charitable. Could be mouthwash, some of that really strong stuff did have alcohol in it, and sometimes people using it had been breathalysed. It wasn't. When Casey handed over the baby, Di cried. Charlie and Casey left her to have a cuddle alone.

'Come on, let's get a brew.' At the door Charlie had an urge to snatch the baby back from Di. She'd lost her son. Would she harm their baby? Di's face told her no. After a while she joined them in the kitchen, cradling him in her arms.

She thrust him at Casey. 'He's beautiful.' Tears wet her eyes as she deposited a Babygro and a Boots voucher. 'Well done,' she shouted behind her. 'He's perfect. I love his tiny fingernails. And his toes.'

James arrived later, and he grew quiet as he examined the baby, exclaiming over his skin, eyes and hair.

After a few hours, Casey was allowed home. Charlie couldn't wait to get out of the hospital: the smell, the bareness of the wards, the big windows, which induced vertigo as you gazed over the city. She wanted to be back in their own house, amongst their own things, their own smells: the Moses basket, the baby's blankets, his small vests and babygros and booties piled up, ready and waiting. They bundled into a taxi and Casey held him tightly while Charlie carried everything else. They'd accumulated an incredible amount of stuff already –

nappies and clothes and breast pads and wipes and a changing mat and a sling.

Frank was waiting on the step when they got home.

'Thought you might need a hand, pet.' He carried bags upstairs, turned the heating on, brought them tea and a pint of water and a doorstop cheese sandwich for Casey, who declared herself 'starving', unpacked a quiche, put it in the oven on a low heat, handed them a wrapped-up parcel, saying it was 'something for the baby' and headed for the door.

'Here, before you go, have a hold at least,' said Casey.

'Are you sure, lass?'

He held the baby tenderly, tears coming into his eyes.

'Champion. Best news ever. He's a proper bonnie laddie.'

Shyly he gave him back.

'I'll let youse get some sleep. You could open the present later. And divvent forget the quiche is in the oven. Twenty-five minutes. Keep your strength up, lass. I've put home-made coleslaw in the fridge. My own cabbage, like.'

Casey of course opened the present as soon as he'd gone, while they stuffed their mouths with crumbly pastry and strong cheese. It was a Newcastle United top, number 9. And the smallest pair of football boots in the world.

The day passed in a happy haze, with a continuous stream of visitors, but by the evening Charlie was tired and restless. Most people were sensitive, stayed a short time, had a drink and left. By evening they'd accumulated a few bottles of cava, and one of real champagne, courtesy of Suzy. They toasted the baby, and Casey had a sip. She seemed to have a new lease of life. High on her achievement, with her rosy cheeks, you'd never have thought she'd just given birth.

In the afternoon Martin turned up with a collection of cuddly toys. His wife was petite where he was large, and quiet where he was loud. She laughed at his jokes, and stared with frank envy at the baby. Martin had let slip once that they would have liked children, 'but it wasn't to be' and that they were being considered for adoption.

Eight o'clock, Charlie cooked oven chips and fish fingers, the most she could manage, and was washing up, ready to turn in, when the doorbell rang. Ignore it, she decided. A long day, and who knew what the night would be like? The midwife had visited twice, and helped get the baby on the breast. He'd latched on well, but Casey was still anxious, and unsure that she was doing it right, and her breasts were sore. Charlie had tried to reassure her, and kept feeding and watering her, but the poor girl was exhausted.

'Are you sure he's getting enough?' Casey kept asking the same pale-faced Irish midwife as before, who answered calmly that 'Baby' was getting all that he needed. 'Just check his nappies and make sure that he's bright-eyed and alert, and you'll be fine.'

Yet even in the few hours since birth, Casey had grown surer, more confident. She'd look up with an expression of delight: 'Have you seen his little hands, Mum? And the length of his lashes? And how lovely his eyes are?'

Charlie remembered that stage. While the milk was coming on, you were all over the place – ecstatically happy one minute, weeping the next. And starving. She could still taste the large fruitcake a friend had brought after Casey's birth. She'd eaten it all, slice after slice, savouring the Brazil nuts and dried fruit.

THE BELL RANG again.

'Let's leave it,' Charlie shouted. She went up the stairs towards Casey's room. 'The midwife said rest when you can,' Charlie warned. 'He might sleep for a little while now. You could get your head down. It's only the first night and you don't know what it'll be like. We don't have to answer it.'

But Casey met her half-way down the stairs, and laughed.

'I want to show him off, Mum. I want everyone to see him.'

She went to the front door, light on her feet. Charlie guarded the baby, asleep in his Moses basket, face occasionally twitching as if he was dreaming, his skin smooth and pink with heat spots the midwife had assured Casey were nothing. Charlie closed her eyes. She could only help out for a couple of days. She'd used up all her holiday. Soon enough Casey would have to manage on her own. Maybe one of her friends could stay over. The school had said they would send work home until she was up to collecting it. God knows how she'd keep up.

When Casey headed the small group heading back into the bedroom, she looked impossibly young and pretty, with red cheeks. Behind her were Lara and Pete. Lara apologised profusely, saying she knew it was late, but she'd had work, and she'd just wanted to pop in and say congratulations, she loved babies, she had loads of cousins, and she'd met Pete as he was coming out of the law library, and she hoped they didn't mind him tagging along.

'I'm babbling, aren't I?' she said, and Charlie nodded, tensing up at the sight of Pete. To disguise this she handed them rapidly cooling tea from the half-filled teapot. She couldn't be bothered to make more – her legs were trembling with tiredness, and there was a pounding pain in her head from the cava. Pete wasn't getting near her grandchild.

Casey, beaming, passed Lara the baby, and then Lara went quiet as she examined him, from the curl of his perfect fingers to the stretch of his back.

'Gorgeous,' was all she said, welling up. She was crying when she handed him back. Casey offered him to Pete to hold. Charlie was ready to spring, snatch him back, but fortunately Pete waved them away, shrinking from the baby: 'I'm not so good with babies.' And then the baby started crying anyway and Casey pulled up her nighty. Charlie caught Pete's eyes bulging at the sight of Casey's enormous breasts, but her daughter, unaware, latched the baby on and sat back against the pillows, swigging water.

'We'll leave you in peace,' said Lara. 'Once again, well done!'

They deposited a bundle of presents and cards.

'I'll look at them later,' promised Casey, her eyelids drooping. 'Thanks for coming.'

Charlie waved them off, locked the door and turned lights out. No more phone calls, no more visitors, they agreed. Charlie went to her own room, but the next few hours were a blur of feeding, crying, and changing and then the whole cycle started again. It was nearly two before Charlie left Casey and the baby deeply asleep. Charlie pottered about downstairs, wired. No point trying to sleep yet, she needed to relax and calm down. She arranged cards over the fireplace. Most were classic blue for a boy baby cards with football boots and cars and dogs. Charlie found that vaguely depressing, that he was seen as a boy first, a baby later. A few were yellow. Lara's was blue and loud and full of exclamation marks. Pete's was different. A Degas painting of dancers rehearsing. She read the back: *'La classe de danse' vrs 1873-76 Edgar Degas 1834-1917 Huile sur toile, 0.85x0.75 MO.'*

Something about the card bothered her. She had seen one exactly like it. Where? Past exhaustion, she finally dragged herself to bed. She had to go the library, look up that court case. Just as she drifted off to sleep, she remembered where she'd seen that card before. Darren's room. Her night was full of anxious dreams. A river, a baby, a bridge.

36

TUESDAY 15 APRIL

THEY SAT IN the baby clinic together, staring at posters of bonny toddlers and beatific mothers, and waited for the nurse to bring Daniel back. Charlie had her notebook out. She was doodling: 'Michael. Eddie. Pete.' Lately Di had been glaring at her. Not once had she said, 'You were supposed to do something.' But that's what she was thinking. Now that Daniel was born and they were getting used to having him around, surely, Di was implying, Charlie could be back on the case.

A month before, Charlie had decided to follow up on the Irish connection, go to the library, look up the case her aunt had mentioned to her. But the days fell away with the baby and work. She needed to make time. She had almost convinced herself that those postcards, common as they were, didn't mean anything. Convinced herself that it was just a coincidence that her aunt and Pete had both mentioned Millisle. She had stopped herself from phoning the friendly policeman again. What would she say? 'I heard about a case in Ireland. It might be the same person.' She needed to look up a local newspaper, and law reports. O'Reilly had already told her she needed evidence. As the next best thing to the police, she had asked Nia to help look up whether juvenile records carried over into adulthood. But Nia, with all her talk about being at the centre of the action, seemed incapable of independent thought, and had been rather vague and non-committal when she came back with her so-called research. Vague and non-committal summed up her character really. Nia was an eejit.

She'd have to try her again, spell it out. There was something not right about Pete. But then there was something shifty about Michael as well. Since the fire the small pink scar on his face made him look more human somehow, more vulnerable. He wasn't perfect anymore. Even Charlie felt sorry for him now, and he exploited it, getting his way even more, asking people to pass him things.

'It's your face, not your bloody hands,' Eddie had snapped, but Charlie had done his bidding, even making him a cup of tea. Sometimes he seemed almost human. 'Whoa, stop there,' she told herself. Getting soft in her old age.

She'd thought she was good at this detective stuff, but all she'd done so far was bark up the wrong tree. She should leave it to the professionals. But the police seemed to have forgotten about Darren. Catching his killer wasn't a priority anymore. Now that the two men were awaiting trial for the attacks on the girls the pressure on them to get results had dropped, and the atmosphere everywhere was less tense. People were saying Darren's murder was a one-off, a stranger passing through, one of those things that you never got to the bottom of. People were beginning to forget about him. Every day there was more news, every day his death moved further away.

And the days were falling away with the new baby, in an endless trough of exhaustion. What with all this new health and safety training at work and her shifts, and with the baby waking up at night all the time and worries about the hostel closing, and their jobs being transferred to Gateshead, and Di reverting to being a bitch again, selfish and self-obsessed, and that cow of a friend Suzy hanging round, it was all too much. Neither she nor Casey had had enough sleep for weeks. Charlie knew her face was pallid, and lines had deepened round her eyes. Sometimes her hands shook, she was so tired. She didn't know how much more she could take. If Steve was here she might feel better, but he was in Australia on extended, indefinite leave, his father's illness terminal. It was harder in a way having had him around for a while. All those years on her own and she became used to it. Now she missed him with an ache: his touch, and the feeling of having someone on your side. Now it was back to doing everything on her own.

She was figuring out how to broach the idea of Casey getting her own place. Now she was 16, Casey could apply for a Housing Association flat. But as soon as Charlie started thinking it through, it all seemed impossible. How could Casey go to school and look after a baby by herself? They'd sent a home tutor round, but that dried up. Casey had a place in the mother and baby unit for May, but that was weeks away. She was trying to keep up with schoolwork; the school had said she could go back full-time in September, when she had a place in a nursery, and Casey had even said she might try attending before that. Charlie couldn't see it.

''I'll get a childminder,' Casey had stated confidently that week. 'And Emma's bringing me work home.'

Charlie didn't have the heart to ask her where the money for a childminder would come from. Things weren't working out her living there with the baby. OK, Daniel was lovely, Charlie loved him fiercely, whenever she saw him she wanted to eat him up, bury her face in his compact little body, his baby smell. But a baby took up space and time and money. Everything was chaos. You put something down and you couldn't find it again. The floor was full of nappies, dirty baby-clothes, a sling; the washing machine was always on; the food disappeared as soon as it arrived, with Casey always hungry; and they constantly ran out of teabags. The girl had said the day before she was going to sign up for driving lessons as soon as she was old enough.

'You can apply for a licence at 16 and three quarters. I've got less than seven months. We never had a car growing up, and it's too awkward on the bus. Most of my friends' families have cars. How come we don't? Can I have lessons for my birthday?'

Charlie didn't bother answering. Did she know how much cars cost to run? In the wrong again, parenting skills deficient. And how was Casey ever going to pay for lessons? Charlie felt old. Life was speeding up too quickly. She wanted her own life. Would Steve return? And if he did, would he reconcile with his wife? Was what they had just a pleasant interlude in a long dry spell?

When Charlie's notebook fell on the floor, Casey shot her a puzzled glance. Charlie stuffed it back in her bag. Casey hated not having her full attention.

'Mum, I'm just going to see what's happening with Daniel. The nurse has been quite a long time. It doesn't take that long to weigh him.'

'I'll come with you.'

Charlie dragged herself up. There was a nagging feeling in her stomach, a sense of encroaching darkness. The same feeling she'd had the week Sean died. Where had that come from? They were in the bright and cheery baby clinic, surrounded by friendly and competent midwives and nurses. Casey had taken to motherhood, being a relaxed and benignly attentive parent, much less neurotic than Charlie had been at her age. Daniel was doing well, putting on weight and filling his nappies regularly, rewarding them with smiles, and clear eyes. Breast-feeding was going fine, apart from the occasional cracked nipple.

Charlie parked the thought of asking Casey to move out. How could she? She was only 16; she needed all the help she could get. Charlie would have to keep supporting her through to her A levels. And after, probably. Important that, the girl needed qualifications, she didn't want her to go down the same route she had. The school had been good. Casey was lucky.

'What's your baby's name?'

The reception nurse scanned a list.

'There's no record of a Daniel here. I'll check with my colleague. Be back in a minute. Maybe Nurse has taken her in to see Doctor. What was the nurse's name?'

The nagging feeling grew in Charlie's stomach.

'She didn't say.'

'What did she look like?'

'Brown straight hair, pale, thin.' This from Casey, chewing her nail now, like she used to.

Momentary puzzlement stole over the nurse's features, then she collected herself, and became crisp and efficient.

'Did she have a uniform on?'

'Of course.'

'Could you see her name tag?'

Casey screwed up her eyes. She shook her head, and then moaned, 'What's happened?'

Next thing security men ran along the corridors, alarms went off, red lights flashed, doors locked down, and several police officers appeared. Mothers clutched their babies to them in panic.

'There's no need to be concerned,' said a midwife, reassuring each mother. But women held their babies closer, knowing there was.

The nurses were kind to the pair of them, sat them in a private room and brought hot sweet tea and posh oatmeal and chocolate chip cookies which fell in their tea and stained their hands brown. Charlie had a terrible headache; Casey kept her head in her hands. When phoned, Di came straight along and ferried them in drinks, and sat and stroked Casey's hair.

Charlie's imagination ran riot. It was something to do with Darren's death. The person who killed Darren knew she was getting close, and had pounced where she was most vulnerable. They would kill Daniel as well, and it would be her fault that she'd put Casey and him in danger. Charlie sat up rigid in the chair. She should phone that nice policeman and tell him. He would listen, not make her feel stupid. He'd said to phone. The thoughts went round and round in her head as she breathed stale hospital air, heard the clanks and whooshes of a busy ward, the sound of footsteps, doors closing, the cry of babies, the low murmur of voices, nurses talking through cases with colleagues as they changed shifts, the tired tread of those leaving.

They heard Daniel from the other end of the ward before they saw him, and Casey ran to him, her breasts visibly leaking through her top. When the young policeman, swaddling him in a baby blanket, handed him over, Daniel cried, smelling his mother, and she sat and kissed him all over and held him tight and put him on the breast. It had only been two hours. When he'd fed and the doctors lay him in a cot to check him over, Casey hovered, fierce as a lioness, defying anyone to hurt him, and cradled him back into her arms as soon as they'd given the all clear. Nothing wrong with him, they declared.

The police let them go home, and the evening paper carried a headline: 'Snatch baby grieving mother.'

'I just wanted to hold him,' the abductor was reported to have said. The photo showed someone with a thin frame being bundled into a police car, head covered by a blanket. An anonymous member of the woman's family confirmed that the woman had given birth to a stillborn child several months ago. 'She would never have harmed the baby,' they claimed. 'She loved babies. She will be very sorry for any distress she has caused the baby's family.'

Charlie phoned in sick to work. She did feel sick. Sick with worry and what might have happened. All her fault, all her fault. That night at home Charlie sat up, imprinting the image of Casey and Daniel into her brain. The streetlamp was throwing a stringy light over them and it was as if they were sprinkled with gold. She was blessed. Di didn't have that any more, Di didn't have her child. What had the Head Office guy said? 'Be able to put yourself in someone else's shoes.' What if Daniel had died? She would not be able to bear it. For the first time she allowed herself to feel the weight of Di's loss. Before, she'd understood with her head. Now she felt it in her body, and cried, the tension of months overflowing.

Be careful what you wish for, she reminded herself. This time would not come again. She would not ask Casey to move out. Casey would stay for as long as she needed. They'd muddle through, and she would cherish her grandson, as Sean would have done. *He would have made a wonderful grandfather.*

Then she got out her notebook and through her tears looked over the scrawled notes. Still work to do. No point going to the police yet. She needed some hard information. Besides, she wanted to show she was good at this game. Time to get some help. She'd ask Donny in work the best way to approach it, and pick up where she left off all those weeks before.

37

WEDNESDAY 16 APRIL

CHARLIE HADN'T BEEN in a library for ages, except for the little one down the road, and she had read all the books there. Over time, through funding cut after funding cut, the library had stopped buying books, and more and more DVDs had appeared, free newspapers and recently, computers. It called itself a Learning Zone now rather than a library, and there was little to read, and people sat talking and drinking coffee and everything was done by machine. Librarians no longer stamped your books, but you scanned them in yourself. There were fewer staff, and their service desk had contracted, so that now it was hardly big enough to balance a book on. Charlie fed her own reading habit by buying second-hand crime books from a stall in the market, and selling them on when she'd read them. It was like chewing bubble-gum. She could never remember which books she'd finished, and in her mind all the plots ran one into another.

But this library was different. Donny from the hostel, busy studying for an Open University law degree, had told her to try the university library, after she'd explained what she wanted to do. He said if you asked nicely, they could give you a temporary day pass, no problem.

'For longer, it's more complicated, but for a day pass, they're fine. You just have to convince them you need to use it, that you can't get the information in your local library. Are you any good with law books? Do you know how to look things up?' And he'd shown her some of his. They looked unbelievably dense. How was she going to get anything out of them? It would take her ages to read them all.

'You don't have to read everything. I'm learning that about the law. You need to learn where to search. Use the index, scan the headings, and find case precedents.' That morning in work he'd given her a crash course, so that she felt reasonably competent.

He didn't even ask her why she was doing this, for which she was grateful. Self-motivated himself, he probably thought it was a project. The thing about Donny was that he was more interested in knowledge for its own sake than he was in its practical application. She didn't know if he had any chance of ever practising law when he finally qualified. There were solicitors who had murder convictions, solicitors who had been jailed for fraud, like he had, and all kinds of other offences. But he ploughed on with his law books. Meanwhile he was helping to hold up the allotment redevelopment plans by mounting a legal challenge. The building firm that had planned executive homes on the site had gone bust, and the local paper had come out in support of the campaign to save the allotments, digging into their archives to do a history of the site. Donny had put in hours poring over the legislation. A local firm of solicitors who had given advice were so impressed by Donny they'd recommended him for a job that had come up with an advice agency they often worked with. That was heartening, and Charlie felt a small bubble of satisfaction.

This library was quiet, with lots of space, and new books, as well as ancient tomes that the librarians brought up from stacks, and displays and notices about how to research.

Charlie took a seat and dumped her bags. The seats were leather, worn in the middle, the desks were wooden. She opened the law book the librarian had brought her, and breathed in.

Something about the smell of this place was familiar. Then she remembered. For a short period at school they'd had an arrangement with the local university library, which had allowed them all temporary cards, to 'give them a taste of higher education'. After a session in the library she'd wandered off to a café and sat among all the students with their good teeth and gangly limbs, loudly and confidently spreading over several seats and tables, taking up space, as if they were entitled to it.

In another library session, they were allowed to wander amongst the stacks, and she found herself in the Canadian literature section, and later in the Australian. She was entranced, devouring novels and short stories, skipping from the Australian tropics, with stories set in houses on stilts, dodging redback spiders and snakes, to the frozen North, looking out for moose and avoiding bears. Alternately sweating and freezing, at night she dreamt of mangoes, and fur boots. For a while those places were more real to her than her surroundings, so that when she came out of the library, and encountered mild local weather, neither cold nor hot, and a grey murky sky, it took time to adjust.

She focused back on the words in the law book. Jurisdiction. Statute of limitations. But she couldn't resist checking out the students around her. On second glance, the students didn't all have perfect skin or teeth. Many were spotty, and some were disabled: one in a wheelchair; one who peered hard at the books kept close to her face; one fiddled with his hearing aid. And there were occasional older people, either staff or mature students.

The building was light and airy, the assistants helpful. They had directed her to the law section, helped her get the books, said to come back if she needed anything else. Of course, she was the age of the students' mothers. Or she could have been a professor. But it wasn't that. The world had changed. Young people were more democratic.

She read through the law reports.

Section two, sub section a) ... the carrying over of juvenile records...

Questions in the House of Commons...

BY THE TIME she left the library, with a short break for a coffee that made her heart race, she felt she'd taken an important step forward.

Pete could have a record, and no one would know. He could have done terrible things as a child, and no trace would have followed him here. Police authorities had no obligation to alert other forces.

Things were falling into place. But still, she needed evidence. She didn't really have much to go on yet except her instincts. She would phone the police. And she needed a photo to show Di.

As luck would have it, Casey had one.

'Just got these printed,' she said, spreading them out on the kitchen table at home, Daniel asleep in the buggy.

'It's taken me weeks.'

'That's a good one, isn't it?' she asked, picking up one of herself with Lara and Pete the night they visited, arms round each other, Casey holding Daniel.

Charlie agreed, and quietly, when Casey wasn't looking, she borrowed the photo. She was back on the case.

When she phoned her policeman friend O'Reilly and explained, he was a bit non-committal: 'Well, that's very interesting,' he said. 'It's a long shot though. Tell you what, I'll get Nia to do a bit of research.'

Charlie explained that she'd already asked her for help, but she'd come up with nothing.

'Local papers,' he said. 'The British Library keep a copy of every paper ever published. The case must have been reported in the courts, even if his identity wasn't disclosed. We'll get the dates, see if they fit. Bring him in. I'll get Nia allocated to it straight away. The British Library have a reading room at Boston Spa. She can access everything there on microfiche. We'll send her on a day out. I'll keep you posted. Give her something to do. I'll OK it.'

She didn't know if he even had the authority. But that was that. She'd done her bit. Time to sit back and let the police get on with their job. She wouldn't let Casey or Daniel out of her sight until O'Reilly got back to her. Her suspicions might be wrong, but she was taking no chances. Pete was getting nowhere near her family while she tried to be patient, and waited…

38

FRIDAY 18 APRIL

CHARLIE COULDN'T SETTLE, itching to hear back from Nia. The weather had warmed up, and Casey begged all week to go the seaside: 'I never get out the house, and Daniel needs his first taste of salt air.'

To shut her up, and because getting away from Newcastle and having some fresh air seemed like a good idea, Charlie agreed. To have the Saturday off, she had to work two double shifts. She was just finishing her second double on the Friday, ready to leave at six, when Michael came into the kitchen.

'I'm making tea. Do you want some?' As soon as the words came out of her mouth, she regretted them. Making tea for him for the second time, as if he was a normal human being. The first time was on his arrival, before she knew what he was like.

He stared at her, and the new scar on his right cheek seemed to quiver: 'Prefer my own. I like it made a certain way.'

'How are you doing?' Again, the words came out of Charlie's mouth almost of their own accord. She was trying not to stare at his scar. Not very nice to be scarred, no matter what a bastard he was. Never mind, she'd be at Whitley Bay the next day. They'd eat ice creams, relax, let Daniel wiggle his toes in the sand. Di and James had said they would come as well. A fine weekend was promised. It would be good to blow the cobwebs away.

But then there was the smell of Michael too close to her. The kitchen was empty save for them. All the men were in their own rooms or the common room, and Martin was in the office. Didn't Michael understand about personal space?

'You're looking fitter now. I could almost take a fancy to you. Mind you, I haven't had sex since…'

Charlie stepped back, suddenly scared. Michael was capable of anything. The sounds of the others seemed so far away. She could smell his minty breath.

'I did see Darren with someone, you know.'

In spite of herself she was curious.

'That time I was on the bus, and late for work. There was a traffic jam, we were stuck. I saw him.'

Charlie gathered herself. Michael was full of shit. Just because he had a scar on his face now didn't make him less full of shit. He liked to manipulate people, he liked to make out he was important.

'SO WHAT? THAT was a week before he died. The police know he went off to Brighton. It doesn't mean anything. '

'It does. I'd seen the guy with him before.'

In spite of herself she was interested, and inched forward, although all of her body was screaming *Move away.* Maybe Michael did know something? Maybe he would phone the police? Maybe not. Michael played games.

'Scared, are you?'

'No.' She tried to make herself bigger. There was no panic button. If she screamed, the walls were solid. Who would hear her? Martin often wore headphones.

'Who was it you saw him with?'

'That would be telling.'

'Who?' She didn't mean to shout, but she did.

'Why? Are you going to hit me again? Go on. Try.' He was too close to her again. There was that animal smell… She turned away. But Michael was straight back in her face.

'You don't really know what I did to those girls, do you?

They said I never touched them. They might not remember.'

And suddenly, as her slow brain registered that she was in danger and that she should run, he took her by the throat and held her against the wall. She spluttered and coughed, and tried to remember the moves she'd learnt in a self-defence class she'd been sent on a few years ago. The titles of the sessions were clear in her memory: Where to kick, How to escape a choke hold. But it was as if there wasn't enough oxygen for her to think.

'That Pete, there's a lot more to him than you think. It's always the quiet ones you have to watch.'

She wanted to tell him that she'd already worked it out, that he had to tell the police, back her up, but her chest was tight and she couldn't speak. He rubbed himself up against her. She held her body rigid, and tensed, to use her weight to push him off. Then something shiny flashed past, there was a crash of metal on the floor, and Michael fell backwards. Eddie, balanced on the balls of his feet, knees flexed, glared down at Michael on the floor. His eyelids fluttered and a red weal from the tray pulsed on his forehead.

'You OK, Charlie? Always knew that martial arts class would come in handy one day,' said Eddie with that ingenuous smile of his.

Casey was hysterical when Charlie phoned home to tell her.

'So we can't go to Whitley Bay tomorrow?'

'No, something I've got to do first.'

O'Reilly came straight away after Charlie called his direct line. By this time Michael was subdued and sitting in the office.

'Whatever next? Can't you stay out of trouble? It seems to follow you around,' the policeman chided her.

Charlie smiled shakily.

'What happened with Nia? Did she get anything?'

'She said she'd leave you a message. Don't you ever listen to

302

your answering machine? Speak to her when you get home. She phoned me – says she's got a photo to show you. You might be on the right track. But we'd better deal with this first.'

Eddie hovered in the background when the police arrived, chest puffed out proudly.

'Now then, me laddo,' said O'Reilly, smiling at him. 'What have you been up to?'

'He attacked Charlie. One of the lads at work showed me this Thai boxing thing… or mebbies it was Chinese. Worked a treat anyway.'

'Good lad. Come down with us, we can take a statement at the station. I'll take yours later, Charlie. Go home now, be with your family… and speak to Nia. She's due back tonight. Michael Faseby will be back inside by then. Where he belongs.'

And that was it. Michael was gone from her life.

39

SATURDAY 19 APRIL

THE ANSWERING MACHINE light was flashing, but when Charlie picked up, the message was indistinct and unclear, as if coming from underwater. She made out 'afternoon'. Nia was due to bring her findings round. They'd spoken briefly the night before. Yes, there was a photograph, Nia said. Yes, she'd found out something. Charlie had by then convinced herself she was completely wrong, and it was just coincidence Pete had mentioned Millisle. Probably the cases in Ireland had involved someone else entirely. It was a stranger passing through who had killed Darren, and they'd never find out the truth.

She was antsy, and tired of waiting. She needed something to do. So she decided to go to the meeting about the community garden before she started a late shift. If Nia hadn't come round by then she'd confront Pete herself tomorrow. Stuff waiting for the boys in blue.

She was about to leave when Nia arrived at the door, breathless. She insisted on having a cup of tea, and took her time laying out photocopies of local papers on Charlie's kitchen table. The first was a short report in the *Down Recorder* saying a minor had been found guilty of offences against three other minors, and sentenced to 18 months in youth custody. No names were given, and the judge warned the press of the need to preserve anonymity in cases of this sort. The second article was a blurry photograph of a formally dressed couple, the man in a stiff-looking suit and tie, the woman in a knee-length skirt and boxy jacket. There was an interview with the couple, a Mr and Mrs O'Driscoll, parents of one of the victims. It seemed they had waived their right to anonymity and chosen to speak out, warning other parents to watch out for a hidden threat to their children's safety. 'We never in a million years thought our child was at risk,' the father was quoted as saying, 'not from such a grand young fella.'

Charlie sighed heavily. 'So?' she said impatiently. 'This doesn't prove anything. Yes, the dates add up but we're still no nearer knowing if it was Pete who did this or not.' She was annoyed with Nia, who always messed up. She talked the talk, made out she was important, yet she was just rubbish, an airhead. She had the usual smug smile on her cow-eyed face. But her voice was gentle, and very Welsh suddenly.

'Charlie, bach, look behind the couple. There's someone else in the photo. It's a long shot, I know, but it's obviously someone else connected to the case. If you could do some more snooping, make that connection...'

And Charlie looked. The boy's parents had braced themselves for the photograph. They stood unsmiling, shoulders brushing in mutual support. And in the background, captured in the gap between the two sombre faces, was a woman: dark-haired and with a heart-shaped face. Charlie caught her breath. A woman she recognised from the photograph glimpsed in Pete's room... His mother. Yes!

In a daze she thanked Nia, said she'd phone O'Reilly, and that she was going out.

'You're welcome,' said Nia, looking a bit hurt.

'I owe you a drink,' Charlie said, and her friend's face brightened.

AT THE COMMUNITY garden, the green compost they'd put in to improve the soil had sprouted and grown tall and now they were digging it in. The spring bulbs planted in containers around the site had bloomed and faded, and now the tulips were out, in bright yellows and reds. The ground was warming up, becoming fertile, days were getting longer. There were plans for setting out flower and vegetable beds. It was too late for seeds, but they were going to put in plantlets and bedding plants.

Equipment had been donated, and someone with a van was going to collect horse shit from the police stables.

'Rather you than me, mate,' said one guy, a Londoner originally it seemed.'Wouldn't fancy getting in the van after that pickup.'

The guy in charge of the manure had no sense of smell. Fortunately.

The local garden centre had donated 20 baskets, and trays of bedding plants to fill them, and people put up their hands to volunteer to fill them. Charlie helped out, potting up baskets. It was pleasant, mindless work, and she was glad to do it while she thought through her next steps. Phone O'Reilly, get the local police to check with the Northern Ireland force, confirm Pete's identity. How long would that take? What if a detective was off sick again? Could she wait that long?

As if being carried along on a wave, she waited while they divided into groups to talk about the shed, flowers, and vegetables. It was like being back at school. The potato people didn't speak to the flower people, the 'children in flats need gardens' group didn't speak to the 'older people want a bit of peace' group. Of course, they weren't called that, but they might as well have been.

Charlie joined Frank in the shed group. He had already asked her if she was OK, and she'd reassured him, although he looked doubtful and kept glancing up at her. He'd become enthusiastic about the garden, and had also got himself on the committee to save the allotments.

'Why don't we try solar power?' he said suddenly. 'I've been reading about Spain using solar panels to provide hot water and energy. We could put solar panels on the shed.'

'The shed's not even south-facing,' someone pointed out.

'Light-capturing tubes,' murmured a long thin insubstantial tube of a guy.

'Could you please explain, Mr Thompkins? What exactly does this entail?' asked Stella, alighting on their group.

And the guy explained in a lugubrious tone about how even if the surface of a roof didn't face south, you could attach a tube that would capture light, from around the corner, or from the ground.

'Like a submarine?' asked someone.

'Like a submarine,' he agreed. 'Of course, all this is ahead of its time.' And then he went on to tell them about a 'tracker', which could follow the sun around and do the same function.

'So the shed and the garden could get electricity from solar panels?' asked Charlie, to make sure. She wasn't that interested in solar panels, but her brain felt slow and sluggish. She knew she should act, make a move. There was no point waiting.

'That's right. It'll cost a bit more. But worth it. In the future it'll pay its way. Everyone will be doing it. You mark my words.'

'How much more?' an older gardener asked, not letting this go, and Mr Thompkins, stroking his beard with one hand, did a back of the envelope calculation, and read out a figure.

In the end they voted for an ordinary shed, after agreeing that Newcastle wasn't Andalucía. Mr Thompkins went back to stroking his beard, and when she looked again, he was gone.

The meeting drifted to a close. There was not much more to say. With any luck, they agreed, the garden would be up and running properly by the summer. In the back of her mind Charlie knew it would be a place to sit and watch Daniel while he played, a place for him to let off steam when they couldn't face the walk to the nearest playground, a place for Casey to meet other parents.

Charlie had made her mind up. She'd phone O'Reilly first, then she'd confront Pete. Or maybe she'd confront Pete, and then tell O'Reilly, who'd only say to wait. She was about to leave when Lara rushed in, red-faced, and grabbed hold of her arm.

'I thought you might be here.'

'You OK?'

'I've got something to show you. Come outside.'

They sat on the bench outside the hall. It was a fine clear evening, spring well on its way. Town was already full of girls in short dresses, with no tights, and lads in shirtsleeves. The days had lengthened. Soon they would put a blanket down for Daniel and they could eat outside.

Lara opened a large leather bag with trembling hands and handed over a Newcastle scarf.

'What are you giving me this for? I don't go to the match.'

'It was in Pete's room. I said I was putting on a wash and asked did he want anything thrown in. He told me to look in his room.'

Charlie dropped the scarf. A tingle ran up her arm.

'Maybe he wanted me to find it? Maybe he's tired of carrying this around with him. Maybe...' Lara began crying.

Thousands of people had Newcastle scarves, Charlie told herself. She even had one herself, left behind by a former boyfriend of Casey, an ardent fan.

'Don't you see... don't you see what this means? Pete supports Exeter. He's never supported Newcastle in his life.'

Slowly, with distaste, Charlie picked up the scarf. It wasn't a run of the mill, mass-produced acrylic one. This was hand-knitted, lumpy with irregular stitches, a strand of wool clumsily tied off at the back. Di's knitting. Charlie shoved the scarf in her bag.

Lara's eyes were red and frightened-looking. 'I'll leave it to

308

you,' she said, her lips trembling.

They both stood up.

'We'll go to the police together,' said Charlie, decisive suddenly. It would be madness to confront Pete, she couldn't put Lara in danger. Let the police deal with it. 'They have to question him. We can't.'

'No,' said Lara, but they kept standing, leaning into each other, fearful of what was to come.

And then, almost as in a dream, they found themselves on the way to the police station.

'I should phone Di,' Charlie said.

'No, not yet. Wait. There might be an innocent explanation. We might be wrong.'

Charlie said nothing. They both knew they weren't.

Lara, in just a T-shirt, was shivering. The fresh day had turned nippy.

'Look at you. You're freezing. Go home and get your coat or jumper, I'll meet you outside the station.'

Lara made to run off.

'Hang on a minute though, where's Pete?'

'He's got a lecture, and then a seminar. He won't be back until much later.'

'I'll wait at the entrance for you. Be careful.'

Lara held up her hand in acknowledgement and bounded off.

Ten minutes later and Charlie cut through a passageway between houses on her way to the main road. She felt rather than heard someone come up behind her. Automatically she moved out of the way. Everyone used these shortcuts; nobody wanted to walk the long way round. She was focused on what she'd tell the police. They'd have to take her concerns seriously now, be forced to stop dragging their feet and investigate properly. The footsteps behind her continued, rhythm matching hers. Halfway down the alley she turned round: Pete, pale and scared-looking.

He pushed past her and blocked her way, so that she had to stop. He'd been crying. She saw again what a good-looking boy he could be if the expression on his face altered. There were houses either side of the passageway, she reminded herself. Even if most people were at work, kids would be coming home from school soon, parents walked younger kids down this alley, and teenagers jostled their way home along here.

Keep him talking. Buy time. Use his name.

'Are you OK, Pete?'

'What do you think, sure?'

'What do you mean? Anything wrong? Something you want to talk about?'

She'd walk past him and on to the police station. The police would arrest him, and find out what had happened, and Di would have her answers. He was only a boy, a frightened boy.

'My seminar was cancelled and I came back early. I saw Lara. She can't hide anything from me.'

'She loves you.'

'Suppose she does, poor wee girl. I don't love her. I'm not capable of loving anyone.'

'That's not true, Pete.' Use his name often.

'That's what the psychologist said all that time ago in that awful place. Lisnevin. Dissociative thinking. Unable to understand others' point of view. "A worrying lack of empathy with the feelings of others." Eejit! Do you know, they actually had smoking breaks built into the timetable? They practically encouraged us to take it up. I did in the end, just to blend in.'

She wasn't interested in his sob story. What time was it? Charlie didn't dare glance away at her watch. Surely the schools would be out soon. Someone would be bound to turn up. Lara was an intelligent girl; she'd phone the police if Charlie didn't meet her as arranged. Unless Pete had hurt her... No. The police would come and find them. He wasn't a bad lad; something had probably tipped him over the edge. Keep him talking.

'What would you know anyway?' Pete asked, picking up on her distraction, wanting her to focus on him.

'You wouldn't know what it's like to be locked away. To go to lessons with brainless eejits, and that's just the teachers, sure. I was better than all of them. Having to report for smoking breaks. Everyone did. I had to go cold turkey when I left that place.'

Everything had gone very quiet, and the temperature had dropped, like it does just before it snows. Sometimes it snowed this late in the year. If it snowed no one would hear them, his footprints would be obliterated, he'd get away. There were no sounds from houses each side. If she screamed, would someone look out of the window, come to help? *Casey*, she thought. *Daniel. Di.*

'They never loved me.'

'Who?'

'My parents. He wasn't my dad, you know, he just married her. My mother's a whore.'

'I'm sure she's not. Lots of people have step-parents.'

'Not where I come from. And when we were growing up everything was fine and upstanding, my mother bending over backwards to be respectable. Tea on the table at five on a Sunday, after hellfire and damnation in the church in the morning. But I could see through her. Do you know what an Ulster Sunday was like? Like death. Everything closed, even the swings. And then *he* found out my mother had been going to a hotel, and drinking…'

Charlie said nothing. She was sizing up the distance to the end of the alley. Her training meant she could run. If she screamed now, surely someone would hear?

'He didn't touch her. He just got the local vicar to have a word, and she was away to the doctor. Ended up on tablets.

She was like a zombie. The mother I'd had wasn't there anymore.'

Blame it on the mother. The usual story. Charlie didn't know how much was true, but she didn't care. She needed to get away.

She shifted her weight slightly forward, so that he automatically stepped back. The closer to the end of the alley, the more chance she had of making it.

'So what happened, Pete?'

'I didn't hurt those boys. We were just messing around.'

He didn't seem to care what he told her. Not a good sign, she knew.

'Did it get out of hand? Weren't you older than them?'

'Not much older, and that youngest one, he was a filthy wee creature… he wanted it more than me. The others… the one from a nice family, it was innocent really. Giving him comfort in a cold world. Better with me than some old Holy Joe groping them on the sly. I was doing them a favour, getting it over with.' Charlie breathed hard, and edged forward. He seemed to cotton on to what she was doing, and stood still. She slowed her breath and spread her arms by the side of her body, widening her chest and making herself bigger. She was a warrior.

She didn't want to get any closer to him. How long had they been there? Where was Lara? Where were the police? She thought of Daniel's bright little face. This bastard wasn't going to finish her off. She wanted to see her grandchild grow up. Daniel needed her. Casey needed her. Charlie stood up to her full height, planted her feet, and centred herself. Her neck long, she spoke deliberately. *Keep him talking.* Get the truth out of him. If that was possible.

'What happened with Darren?'

He looked at her for a long minute, and then shrugged his shoulders, as if to say, 'What the hell?'

And then he finished his story.

'Darren was all right, so he was. I liked Darren. I got to know him last year. Got talking after a kick-around. I just happened to mention I had a ticket to a wee film, and asked did he want to come along?'

'And did he?'

'He did, aye. He was going to bring his dopey girlfriend. She hung off his arm like Araldite. Last minute she had a cold and decided to stay in. That was lucky.'

Lucky for her, thought Charlie.

'So what did you do?'

'We went to the film. Some kind of Eastern European one, from before the fall of the Berlin Wall. We couldn't understand it of course, but there were subtitles, and they made us laugh, it was so badly translated. Darren was clever, you know; he could figure things out for himself.'

'Nobody said he wasn't.'

'So we started meeting regularly – a film, or the art gallery. He got interested in art history, said he might go to college and do A levels eventually. I encouraged him.'

'I bet you did.'

'Why not? That fat cow of a mother of his, she didn't want him to make anything of himself, she just wanted him to get a job in a call centre. He would have died in a call centre.'

Somewhere far away birds chirruped, cars started up. No one was coming. *Keep him talking, keep him talking.*

'So then what?'

Pete tapped his feet impatiently and threw up his arms.

'We'd arranged to meet when he first got back from Brighton. There was a new exhibition on at the Laing, and I was after wanting to tell him about it. I thought we could go along later in the week. I met him up near the playground in the wood. It was raining and there was no one else about. But when I arrived he laughed at me. Said some of the kids had called me a queer, and said I'd been grooming him. "Have you been grooming me?" he asked, and he was laughing in that way he did. "Because I've been grooming you as well. I'm not really that interested in art, or in all those crap films you keep taking me to. I just like getting out of the house, like, and I like all the drinks and meals you've been buying me," he said. It was as if he'd punched me in the stomach.'

'I thought he liked me,' he continued. 'I thought Darren liked me. It all would have been OK if he'd stayed quiet. But Darren… you knew Darren, that wee boy couldn't stay quiet. He was always the one for the last word. Instead of stopping talking, so, and walking away, he carried on and on, so he did, said that he was bored with all these outings, and that didn't I know I was a sad weirdo anyway, and probably a poof, and why was I hanging round with a younger lad, didn't I have any other friends? And he threatened to tell his mum, and report me. And he knew about the work experience I'd been doing with the firm trying to buy up the allotment. I hadn't told Lara. She would have stopped speaking to me.'

So Pete did have some feelings. That was something. Charlie edged away.

'And I couldn't let him tell people about us, could I? They would have found out about the other things back home, and thrown me off my course, and I'd have not made it as a lawyer, and that wouldn't have been right, would it? I would have made a really good lawyer, so I would.'

The 'would have' chilled Charlie, but she forced herself to stay calm. Breathe.

Pete had his head in his hands.

'I saw red. I didn't know what I was doing.'

He was lying, telling her what he wanted her to hear. Yes, he'd have made a good lawyer. She knew that he was about to tell her the truth. Which meant he wouldn't let her go. She'd never get to tell Di what she'd found out, she'd never get to see Daniel again. *Keep him talking, keep him talking.*

His eyes looked far away and almost child-like as he spoke. *He wants to explain himself, he needs to confess.* He'd probably been a lovely boy once until the wiring in his brain went wrong, until a switch flipped and the neural pathways took a wrong turn.

'I thought I had put my past behind me, I was starting again, so I was, but if Darren was going to report me, it would all be dragged up. All that work, all that study, for nothing. I would have been a good lawyer.'

She had to get away. He might have a knife, or more.

They were the only two people in the world.

'Go on. What happened, Pete?'

'So I pushed him. That's all, I pushed him. And he fell on a big stone and then there was blood and I shook him and shook him and his eyes rolled back in his head and then he was quiet.'

She was contemplating this, thinking how it could have been an accident, accidents happened, when she realised Pete had a rock in his hand.

'Which is why I have to do this to you now. I don't want to, sure. But you're the one who worked it out, not Lara, and she won't tell on me about the scarf. I can't lose everything. I've been getting eighty per cent in my law exams.'

With that, he stepped forward and Charlie took a step to the side. She wasn't going to wait for a blow to the head. She wasn't going down without a fight. Even if he got her, it was difficult to kill with one blow. Darren had had an especially thin skull, Di had told her. But Charlie didn't have an especially thin skull. She had a thick skull. She'd fall down, let him think she was really hurt, and then jump up and kick him and run and run. She planted her feet, and watched for his next move. Pete staggered forward, losing his balance.

The policeman behind him was dressed in a black flak jacket. There were others standing back, blocking the mouth of the alley.

'Now, then, son,' said the PC as he wrestled Pete to the floor. 'Give it up, bonny lad. It's over.'

Lara was standing at the end of the alley, with Casey behind her, and they rushed forward, hugging Charlie to them as Pete was bundled into a blue van.

40

TUESDAY 29 APRIL

PETE'S PARENTS WERE the last people Charlie wanted to see, but they were over, seeing him in Durham, and Lara asked her to call in.

'I'll cook something,' she added, sniffing.

'Don't bother,' Charlie was about to say. She'd seen the remains of Lara's vegan surprise in her kitchen, but Lara insisted. Charlie admired her guts.

'And did you know Pete was working for that firm, the ones that were trying to buy up the allotment?'

There was a new bitterness in Lara's tone. She didn't wait for an answer, which saved Charlie having to admit she did.

'There'll be no one else here anyway. My housemates have suddenly decided they need to go to their parents, so I'm in the house by myself most of the time. I could do with the company.'

Poor girl. Her faith in people shattered.

Casey was angry when she found out.

'What are you going round there for? Why do you want to meet his parents? Di better not find out. She'd go mad.'

'I know. Make sure you don't tell her. They've done nothing wrong.'

'His mother gave birth to him, didn't she?'

That's right, blame the mother for everything.

When Charlie got to the house, incongruously carrying a bottle of red wine, as if they were celebrating something, Lara held the door open.

'It's only his mum. His dad decided he had to go back. But his mum is hoping for another chance to see Pete. Come and meet her. She's staying a few days until she can get a cheap flight.'

She ushered Charlie in, before Charlie had time to ask anything. How much of what Pete had said in the alley about his parents was fantasy?

'Christine, Charlie.'

'Pleased to meet you,' said a tiny, hunched over woman, as she held out her hand, fiercely sucking smoke into her lungs.

Automatically, Charlie shook her hand. The woman before her had aged 20 years since the photo in Pete's room had been taken. Her hair was now white, and she moved hesitantly, like someone much older. Christine accepted a large glass of red wine, and glugged it down. The table was pretty, with tulips and a tablecloth, the house very quiet.

Lara carried a casserole dish through to the table. 'Shall we eat?'

They talked of Christine's flight over, the weather, fishing up the coast where she lived, the price of potatoes and milk, how beautiful the countryside was this time of year. The casserole was surprisingly tasty, and they tucked into a big salad and a yoghurt chocolate pudding.

Afterwards they sat in the living room. The wine had loosened Christine's tongue. She accepted another roll-up from Lara, and giggled like a schoolgirl: 'I'll be getting to like these. I'll have to keep it from my husband. He wouldn't be too pleased.'

How odd the things people fixated on. *Your son has been arrested for* murder. *Your life will never be the same again. Do you think your husband will care about a few roll-ups?*

They sat in silence, but as the evening wore on, Christine spoke. They let her, Charlie filing away the story, working out an edited version she'd give Di. It would all come out in the trial. If it got that far.

Yes, he'd been a quiet and solitary boy. 'But no harm in him, you know. The way some of those wee boys would pull the wings off butterflies and tie tin cans to cats' tails, he was never like that.' *Not like Michael, or some of the other men in the hostel,* Charlie thought.

'So what did he like to do?'

Charlie found it hard even using the name now. It felt contaminated, and every other Pete she met in future would remind her of him. But Christine was smiling.

'Peter always had his head in a book. Reading. Bible stories he started off with. Always asking questions. How big was the whale? Did Jonah really go inside the body of the whale? What did he eat? And David and Goliath. How big was Goliath? He was always a wee bit obsessive, liked arranging things. Used to alphabetise his books, and he'd never go to sleep unless the curtains were arranged just so. Sometimes I had to draw them several times before they were right, according to his standards. One of the teachers suggested he had that OCD.'

She laughed fondly.

'And then he started getting bullied, and all that business started, so it did.'

'What business, Christine?'

Christine's voice came out weak and little-girlish, as if minimising what had happened.

'There was a wee lad; they said Peter interfered with him.'

'Did he?'

Christine nodded.

'He told me as much himself, but said the lad had led him on. But how could he have if Peter was so much older? Because we were respected members of the church and everything, and that wee lad came from a rough family from the estate, they believed Peter. He swore he hadn't really done anything. And I believed him at first. You believe your own child, do you not? It was only afterwards, as I was thinking it over.'

An old fashioned wind-up alarm clock on the side ticked loudly. A tap dripped. A light pattering of rain fell on the roof. They were in a boat tossing on the sea. No future, no past.

'But that wasn't the end of it, was it, Christine?'

Christine didn't look at them, and recited in a monotone. 'Two more young lads, and this time from the church, and their families were well known and well liked, and they found one of the lads' jumpers in Peter's room. The RUC said some people keep things as a kind of trophy. That was the one that went to court. Peter had to plead guilty and they put him on supervision. He was in one of those training centres for a while, up near Newtonards. It's been on the news, not a nice place. And a hard place to get to on public transport. Then they let him out because of his age, and the school agreed to take him on again. They thought it was all over, so they did.'

Charlie and Lara refilled their glasses and gulped. The wine tasted like blood.

'He had a caseworker, and the caseworker reassured us, said sometimes children grew out of these things. He said Peter was a clever lad and we should concentrate on the positive and encourage him to apply to university in England. A fresh start and all that. When he got a place here studying law and he was so excited, we thought it had all ended, we thought he'd be OK. And when he mentioned his good friend Lara we thought he'd settled down at last.'

She shot a fond glance at Lara. Lara squeezed her hand.

'And did you hear about what happened to Darren?'

'No, but at Christmas Peter was very quiet. I knew something was wrong. And he used to be such a beautiful boy.'

Tears fell down her face as she carried on speaking, but Charlie had tuned out. She'd heard enough. There was a jam jar of flowering narcissi with creamy flowers on a shelf and a sickly sweet scent permeated the air. The scent of death. She let Christine talk on. Never again would anyone let her talk about Peter like this. From now on Peter would be Pete who killed that young boy, Pete the paedo, Pete the murderer. But for that night they let her talk of Peter, the boy he'd been before all this. Were the seeds already in him from young? Was he always hard wired to do something like this?

And then, after two glasses of wine, it came to her. She didn't believe that anymore, she couldn't, not with Daniel and Casey to fight for. Human error, bad luck, circumstance, there was nothing mysterious about what had happened. And the men in the hostel, it was part of that. She couldn't give up on them all. Donny was doing his law degree, and Graham was going to start a business. Even Michael, with his bubbly scar, would come out one day after serving his time, and have to do something, get more work in a restaurant maybe. And Eddie, who she was sure wasn't totally innocent; Eddie lit sparks to feel warmth in his life. There was nothing black and white. Nobody was totally good or totally bad. Everyone was capable of redemption.

Her whole body ached. She wanted warmth, human warmth; she wanted Steve to return from Australia and to fold into him. Sean was dead, he would want her to be happy, he would be proud of the small things she was doing to make everything better: 'You're bloody good at all this detective stuff,' he'd say, 'Now get organised, and do it properly.' Darren was dead. He'd be laughing, and saying, 'Enjoy yourself, Auntie Charlie.'

The dead are teaching us something, she thought. Cherish these moments, these flowers, these drinks, these ordinary yet extraordinary things, these children. There was nothing more achingly miserable than what Pete had done, snuffing out the light of a life.

Lara had her arm round Christine, and they were both

crying, so Charlie slipped out and walked home in the long light evening. Let them mourn.

Behind her, she knew, Lara would snap to, become practical, and clean up, make coffee, and the pair would put on faces to meet the world, and carry on.

41

SUNDAY 14 SEPTEMBER

THE MORNING OF the race it was cold and Charlie turned over in bed and thought, 'No.' Then she got up and dutifully downed her protein shake and banana and toast. The pasta from the night before sat heavily on her stomach. She did her stretches and walked around the house, imprinting images in her mind, looking at everything, as if she might never see it again. What if she had a heart attack and didn't come back?

Then Casey was up with Daniel and they got the bus to town, and she handed over her packed and repacked sports bag to Casey, who said she'd meet her at South Shields. Steve had phoned from Australia. His father had died a week ago, they'd had the funeral, he was coming back. He'd be there.

And then she lined up with James at the start of the race with hundreds of other runners. Di was at the start as well, shouting 'Good luck' and 'See you soon' and embarrassing James by kissing him sloppily on the cheek. Everything had happened so quickly. From agreeing to go in for the race to the little runs with James, to the longer training sessions and the build up to distances, to this. She wasn't ready. She'd never be ready. And then they were off, and soon they were heading over the Tyne Bridge, the great mass and noise of them. Breathe, foot down, breathe, foot down.

There was a man in a Mickey Mouse outfit, and women dressed as Minnie, and a guy in a Superman outfit, and one with a ball and chain, and somebody pushing a piano, just like she thought there'd be. It wasn't a plastic piano, but a proper full-size piano, on wheels. And there were girls dressed as Barbie look-a-likes, and lads in Viking wigs and pigtails and flouncy dresses, and a man in a top hat. Dolls in prams and the man with a fridge. The whole fantastic pile of them, taking the first hill, and then down and along and parallel to the Tyne as they pounded past. Come on, come on. Grabbing bottles of water, throwing it over themselves, chucking the bottles at the side of the road. Come on, come on.

Somewhere round five miles she knew she couldn't go on. She went on.

Her knees hurt, she had a stitch, and her legs were tight and ungiving. And James, bless him, not even out of breath, put his hand on her shoulder and they ran together, breathing in sync, matching their pace, and she ran through the pain.

Afterwards, when Di asked her how she'd done it, she couldn't honestly figure it out. Everything ached. Your legs, your ankles, your knees, your lungs, your teeth, your arms. But you put one foot in front of another and followed the person in front of you, and after five miles, came six miles, then seven, then eight, then ten, buoyed up by the crowds, and then they were rounding the last bit towards South Shields, and seeing the sea cheered her, and gave her a new lease of life, her breath coming short and fast now, an ache in her legs which she knew would take a week to get over, cramp in her thighs and calves, knees grating. James, only a little red in the face, trod on the spot with his long legs, waiting for her, and cheered her on.

'You're doing great, you're doing great. Come on, now, come on. Nearly there.'

People were blowing trumpets and letting off balloons and streamers: 'Come on, well done, well done. Nearly there.'

She concentrated on each breath. In, out, in, out, in out. Each fall of her foot. Heel down, ball of foot, toe. Her knees locked and her thighs were thunder. She saw the events of the year as a series of images: Di crying, and smoking on the sofa;

Darren lying in his Newcastle kit, the first glimpse of Steve; digging the ground at the allotment; Daniel's birth; Daniel in the policeman's arms; Eddie smiling over his records; the pile of ashes after the hostel fire; Donny holding his law certificates; Christine crying and smoking at Lara's. And now this race.

Something was pushing her on through the last bit. She drifted off. Once, before Casey was born, she and Sean had toyed with the idea of going on a pilgrimage to the shrine at Santiago de Compostela. Neither of them was religious, but something about the idea appealed: carrying everything on your back, staying in *refugios*. She still had the official booklet, stamped with the shell of St James. In the most desolate parts of the walk, high in the mountains, it was said that many had a sense of someone by their side, willing them on. The religious claimed St James; others said oxygen deprivation.

She'd fallen pregnant with Casey and the pilgrimage had never happened. But now, with her breath coming fast, and her body trembling and her top soaked with sweat, she thought, 'This is my pilgrimage.' Now she felt Sean beside her, willing her on, she saw Darren laughing, willing her on. Almost a year since Darren's death.

'I carry your heart with me (i carry it in my heart)' said one placard, and she mouthed along with it, remembering the English literature professor, the ee cummings expert with muscle disease that she'd scribed for, how, bent over, unable to make eye contact anymore, he delivered his lectures with passion and feeling to a group of 18-year-olds who looked past his body and saw the man. She carried their hearts. That's what you did. You carried their hearts in your heart.

And her hearts would be waiting at the finish line. Casey and Daniel and Di and James, and Steve. And there'd be a shy sun-tanned young man, the father of Daniel.

'A good lad,' Di had said, and she believed her. Time for

explanations later.

'Come on, Charlie, come on, Charlie.'

When her legs buckled and she stumbled, James put his hand on her arm and pulled her up.

'You OK?'

He'd taken off his T-shirt, and tied it round him. Underneath, on his singlet, was a photo of a smiling Darren. 'Come on, lean on me.'

So she did, and together they crossed the finishing line, hand in hand, James spurring her on.

MOTH

BENJAMIN MYERS

TURNING
BLUE

NOTHING STAYS HIDDEN FOREVER

TURNING BLUE
BENJAMIN MYERS
ISBN: 978 1 911356 00 4

A tour de force of plotting and atmosphere,
Turning Blue is a terrifying, gripping tale of
hidden lives, and hidden deaths.